THE WOMAN IN
THE SUN HAT

Daniel Damiano

fandango
4
Art House

"Daniel Damiano has written an extraordinary novel. *The Woman in the Sun Hat* takes us on a journey from start to finish that not only invites us into the world of the protagonist Peggy Bubone, but helps us to inhabit that world with her in all its sometimes uncomfortable, emotionally challenging, earthy, and ultimately invigorating glory. At times so deeply moving in its depiction of Peggy's life that continuing to read felt like a personal excavation. This is a novel that begins far away from where it ends and yet somehow brings together the strands of a woman's life in a way that is both breathtakingly beautiful and heart-wrenchingly painful."

-J. Wolff, Notes from the City

"Daniel Damiano's stirring first novel not only creates a gripping tale of family disaster and deception, but he also takes on many myths of modern life. - *The Woman in the Sun Hat* is a novel imprinted by a distinguished voice and led by a heroine memorable for both the ordinariness and the super strength of her resolve."

- Sunday's Mail

To Ma and Gram

Special Thanks

I wish to sincerely thank my friends and loved ones who lent their support and provided valuable feedback; Judy Alvarez, Lee Anderson, Ellen Barry, Maryann Bertollo, Andrew Davies, Dick Manness, Jack McCleland, Natalie Monarrez and Jannie Wolff.

1

She then started typing:

Chapter 1 – *Mrs. Prager died earlier this week. I never thought she would play much of a significant role in my life, other than the woman who sold me 7-Up and Bubble Yum as a kid. Yet somehow, when I returned to Kelp Stream, she would end up being the only presence that made me feel at all like I was missed. I never really felt like I was returning home in any sort of storybook, Wizard of Oz-like way. It was more as if I were sucked into my past like a merciless vacuum and amidst the kaleidoscope memories that I had preferred to forget was this kind woman who simply remembered me as a nice girl. She knew nothing of my adult life. Only what I chose to tell her or lie about, as we reacquainted. She told me her husband died a few years earlier. She had kids, grandkids. Now she was dead. As I write this, I'm still wondering why I can't seem to get over it. It feels like all the good that there was in this oppressive town has died with her, and left me alone with the yellowed photo of Sylvia Plath on my childhood ceiling; her eyes still there looking down at my twin bed like an eccentric aunt. Even she must be saying "Why haven't you killed yourself, like I did?"*

I had everything once. That is to say that I thought I did. Now it all feels like a ruse intended to lead me back here, at least for a time. Perhaps to see Mrs. Prager before she left the earth.

Or, perhaps, to see my mother before she does.

About 3 months prior, Peggy was speaking before her 1st period Literature class at Cold River High School; the most elite high school in central Long Island, and one that was not easy to be on staff at, especially for someone like her, who had been exclusively a housewife and mother for much of the last decade and a half. Nevertheless, she felt she earned her way in, having an impressive Princeton education and having taught literature and creative writing previously before becoming pregnant with Nicky and, two years later, with Luna. And the timing was right, if even overdue in Peggy's eyes. It was also a booming financial period for them due to the enormous success of Mike's dermatology practice – to the extent that a local periodical once referred to him as "One Man You *Want* Under Your Skin". Plus the kids were a bit older now, which allowed for a bit more parental flexibility. Above all, she was quite simply itching to pick up where she left off. She had accumulated vague story ideas for novels over the years, but it seemed that as soon as there was a prime moment to sit down and type "Chapter 1", a peanut butter handprint on a cabinet would appear or a knee scrape or any in a myriad of adolescent distractions courtesy of either Nicky or Luna, leaving her creative momentum to soon fade into chicken marinade preparations for an evening's dinner party.

But while writing beyond a grocery list would prove challenging, teaching was something that she was always eager to return to and knew that once she got over the initial butterflies of speaking before a class for the first time in years, she would seize it with abandon.

For her, literature was a warm afghan in which she could drape herself, and she took great joy in sharing her personal feelings on material with others, conveying what moved her about a particular work – what it made her feel, any catharsis she may have gleaned. Sylvia Plath's *The Bell Jar* was one of those books, which she had to assert to make a part of her curriculum. Back when she was in high school, this novel had a sort of engagingly dark reputation that preceded itself, not unlike Salinger's *The Catcher in the Rye*. Of course, this largely came from the obvious parallels between Esther Greenwood, the protagonist of *The Bell Jar*, with Plath herself. *"Why such a choice?"* she would be asked by school administration, which, for a self-proclaimed progressive school, was somewhat surprising. There was a consensus that it was too bleak, too dark, too depressing, even too "existential"; all of which were accurate enough for a book about a young woman's nervous breakdown. However, in Peggy's mind, they were neglecting the fact that the best of art was not easy to take and should prove challenging – like the paintings of Rene Magritte or Francis Bacon, the poetry of Plath or Anne Sexton, the photography of Diane Arbus, and so on.

Such cultural acuity belied everything that Peggy came from, especially in the small working-class, boondock town of her youth, where *Interview with a Vampire* would equate to fine literature – provided anyone knew it was a book before the movie.

In the end, administration yielded to Peggy's preferences and allowed Plath to be included, trusting the results she would render from the wealthy if jaded students she would be teaching and, potentially, influencing.

A student read the last line:

The eyes and the faces all turned themselves toward me, and guiding myself by them, as by a magical thread, I stepped into the room.

Peggy would take a satiated moment, as this was their first completed book of the semester, before gradually going around the room and inviting the students' assessments as to what the book was about. *"Depression", "Death", "Madness"* were the rote responses, while others gave more rambling explanations. Peggy would not disagree with any of what was said, but was certainly hoping for more profound feedback.

The spoiled and advantaged made up no small part of her classes, though she also felt that there were at least a few who had the potential to make their own significant contributions to the world, outside of the ridiculously affluent environs they may have been born into. In particular, there was Tricia Wentworth; certainly not the prettiest or the most popular in a room that consisted of all but herself and a mop, whom Peggy felt had great promise based on previous papers she'd written. However, she was almost catatonically shy about speaking in class, to the point where Peggy feared this could be an impediment for her later in life.

She had seen a lot of herself in Tricia. Though, as a girl, Peggy was more attractive in the traditional sense, she didn't seem to know it back then and had a relative shyness when it came to speaking publicly, which she eventually grew out of by her last year of high school. She did not foresee this level of extroversion in Tricia, necessarily, but had on more than one occasion kept Tricia a bit later, if just to gently convey that she knew Tricia was smart and that others could be inspired by her, as opposed to degrading her for her intellect.

Peggy posed another question to possibly generate a more stimulating discussion, "What would you say contributed to Esther feeling the way she did? Do you feel she was just sick?"

Some blind gazes, followed by some inaudible murmurings pushed out like a slow wave...

"I think she was," exclaimed Mark, another one of Peggy's kind-of-hopefuls. "She... It seemed like she just felt... numb. Like life wasn't really that interesting for her."

"And you think being numb to life is a sickness?" Peggy asked, with a half-smile.

"Well,..." Mark stammered a bit, and tried to think a bit more on it before, "I mean, she...yeah, I think if you just, like, don't know how to really function, there's something wrong. Right?"

"But is having a disconnect from life a justification for

what Esther experiences? Shock therapy? I mean, we can't fathom it now because we don't really use such methods anymore, but back in the 1960s, this was still deemed a very serious form of treatment. Do you think what she felt or what she was experiencing warranted that?"

She wanted to move on from Mark, and looked at Tricia, somehow believing that she would have an interesting observation about this, but noticed a shifting in her eyes for fear of attention being drawn to her pale un-rouged skin and straight dirty blonde hair, before the ever-dutiful and knowingly-glamorous Susan Floss chimed in, "I think it's barbaric. I agree, she was disturbed, but there should've been something else offered to her."

"Like what? Medication?" Peggy asked.

"Right."

"So you think Esther was ill and this wasn't something she could've worked out herself somehow?"

"I..." Susan buckled, then thought, "Well,... not really."

Peggy took a beat, attempting to mask her feeling that this was a rash analysis, especially from a born *richie* who couldn't have less identifiability with the character of Esther Greenwood. Susan was beautiful, and Peggy never saw her alone in the hallways or at lunch, and was certain that at least three boys carried her books and that she was allowed parties every Saturday, and was probably never admonished by her parents. She heard through the grapevine-of-varying-accuracy that her father owned a professional hockey team, was on the board of the National Rifle Association and had residences in at least 3 states. Even if some of this was speculative, Peggy would prefer that the last response not be from Susan Floss,... but the bell ring would make this a certainty.

Peggy stopped Tricia discreetly as the other students hurriedly filed out, "Hey, I'd like you to have a nice answer to that question tomorrow, okay? You think you can give me something?"

Tricia was likely more comfortable with Peggy than

any teacher she had ever had, and even still had a hard time looking her in the eyes, intimidated by her seeming confidence and natural beauty.

"How about it, kiddo?" she continued with a reassuring smile. "No pressure, but think about it. Hey, I get nervous up here too, but if I don't say something, we'll all just be staring at each other." Tricia appeasingly nodded and tried to smile, almost leading Peggy to think that the poor thing might give herself the plague just to avoid having to fulfill such a request, ...as she ambled off into the hallway.

Regardless, this was another good day, the kind that Peggy would savor, especially when she could challenge a student whom she saw aspects of herself in – whom she believed in. The only thing more invigorating were the possibilities of tomorrow.

For now, however, there was a joy in the unknown.

Two miles away, Mike was performing a skin screening on Ed Herskel, a pallid but sharp-tongued former Brooklynite in his 60s, "So how was West Palm this year?" Mike asked, as he perused Mr. Herskel's bicep.

"Same every time we go. The wife drinks the sun like a martini, and I almost get heatstroke," he half-joked.

"I hear ya'," Mike laughed.

"If we were down there year round I'd be in my grave before my time, I'm tellin' ya', doc."

"Hey, I know. It's not for everybody. My folks're there now."

"They like it?" Mr. Herskel asked, with skepticism.

"They do, actually. I mean, they're from Jersey, so it was an adjustment, but they rest better there, they say."

"Well, good for them," nodded Herskel.

"They're actually flying in to see us tonight."

"Oh, that's nice. Any special occasion or jus' t'see ya'?"

"Well, they always wana' see their grandkids, that's for sure. But actually we flew them up for my birthday," as Mike began to lock in on a particular mole.

"You still celebrate?"

"I know, I'm too old, right?"

"Nah, you're not.   Ya' jus' don't see men make as big a deal about birthdays, especially the older we get. I think I stopped at 10," Herskel gave a playful elbow to Mike, who couldn't help but laugh.

"I know, I know. I feel the same way, but my wife said it's a milestone this year."

"So ya' flew 'em up on your nickel? What a good son."

"Yeah, well..." Mike modestly smiled, while eyeing a mole more closely.

In truth, it was Mike's proposal, not Peggy's, to have his parents up for his birthday festivities. Not only was he turning 40, a milestone indeed, but it would also be a celebration of his success – the first chance his parents would have of seeing the new house, the even more lavish neighborhood, the sunken pool in the back, the fountain and backyard garden (in which they grew everything from eggplant to zucchini) and, accompanied by their close friends of similar stature in the community, a prime opportunity for his parents to experience the pinnacle of everything their son had worked for.

"Hm, I'm not crazy about this fella," Mike said, with his perfect balance of humor and doctorly concern, turning a particular mole into a pesky animated character.

"What? Whata' y'mean?" Mr. Herskel asked, with mild concern.

"It's just a little dark for my taste, and it's coming up a bit," as he inspected the mole more closely.

"Coming up a bit?"

"You putting on protection when you go out, Mr. Herskel?"

"Yeah, always."

"Not just in Florida. You gotta' do it here too, okay?"

with gingerly admonishment.

"I do. My wife comes after me with that stuff like she's basting me for Thanksgiving, f'Godsakes," with a slight touch of panic in Herskel's voice.

"Okay, well, that's what I wana' hear. The sun is what it is, but we gotta' do what we can on the other end. Especially with the UV rays, so..."

"So what are you thinking it is?"

"Well, I think it's worth looking at further, which isn't the end of the world. Better to err on the side of caution, right?" Mike smiled, as he continued to scope the thighs of Mr. Herskel, who was a tad more rigid now, but at least he believed he was in good hands.

An hour later, Mike sat behind his desk to discuss the results of a biopsy performed on Claire Resnick; not only a patient but a friend to Mike and bestie to Peggy ever since they met at the Cold River Country Club several years prior.

"Well, I don't want you to worry, because this is rectifiable..." in his ever-comforting baritone...

"Oh, shit, Mike..."

"Claire, it's fine. Listen to me."

"Okay. Alright," as Claire took another in a series of deep breaths.

Mike continued, "So the sample that we extracted from the two moles on your back indicated clearly that we should remove them."

"*Should* or *need to*?" she asked.

"Well, both. *Should* because it's basal cell carcinoma, which means it is a cancer, though it hasn't spread and is in no way fatal, at this stage," he assured her.

After another breath, "Okay, that's...that's good then, yes?" with tepid relief.

"Yes, it's very good, Claire. Okay?" he assured, with a smile.

"Okay, good."

"It's so good, you'll be kickin' our asses in doubles again before you know it, okay?" Mike smiled widely.

"Since when did *that* ever happen?" as Claire wiped a relieved tear...

"Hey, miracles can happen!" he needled with a grin, "But, listen t'me, we do have to nip it in the bud before there's any possibility of its metastasizing, and this is exactly the right time to address this, okay?"

"Okay," she nodded.

"So let's make an appointment to do this. Monique has my book, but I know I have a couple of slots next week and I'd like to get this done sooner than later, okay?"

"My God, I'm so thankful for you, Mike," she said with her customarily dramatic appreciation.

"Stop it, okay?" as he waved her off with comedic modesty.

"No, Mike, please, this is...y'know, this isn't easy. I mean, you work hard your whole life, we have kids that haven't even... It's just...the thought of..."

"I know. I know. But it's all good. It's gonna' be all good, okay?" he assured.

"With you, I know it'll be," her voice now cracking a bit.

"Hey, hey, hey, stop making me blush. Go see Monique, okay? We'll set ya' up."

With that, Mike and Claire hugged. It was obviously more than patient/doctor at that moment. For Claire, she was entrusting a friend with her health. Her future. Like many women in the community of Cold River, Claire had lesser career ambitions than she did aspirations for her children. She wanted to be alive for the graduations, the weddings, the births of grandchildren,...even the deaths of elders – or at least her still living mother.

While she struggled with certain personal issues known more to Peggy than to Mike, the moment of her diagnosis suddenly lent brevity to her life that she hadn't before considered. She had always had an admiration for Mike, given his profession and ever-present confidence which seemed adaptable to any situation, but in this moment, he was more than a distinguished doctor with an endless knack for crude pimple jokes - he was her knight in shining armor.

Peggy came home with Nicky and Luna in hyperactive tow. Since Nicky attended the same school that Peggy taught at, this was fairly easy since they then would just drive half a mile to pick up Luna at Cold River Middle School before heading home. While it worked out conveniently for Peggy, Nicky was always loath to make public that his mom was a teacher at his school, often sneaking through the cafeteria exit to the teachers parking lot with his coat over his head like he was being taken into custody.

Nicky was rarely vocal in his feelings to his parents at this stage, but was clearly of the mind that his assimilation into any of the adolescent clans would be greatly compromised with the knowledge that he was the son of a teacher, particularly as a freshman. However, he managed a few friends - mainly the boys he knew in junior high who had a not unusual nerdy obsession with technology; the latest diversions that often resulted in people driving their cars off bridges due to the sheer obsession. Nicky was smart and had potential, even exhibiting a gift for graphic design which was somewhat encouraging, but Peggy also had a concern which was very much a plight of modern parenting; were the diversionary video games that they gave him as a pacifier earlier on disrupting his attention span, his ability to appreciate books, art and nature? Much of this seemed to be getting lost on him already, at the ripe old age of 13, but she still had hope. Luna had more of an unabashed closeness to her mother and, having her druthers, would be fine to only be taught by her. Though only 11, she seemed to show a talent for writing, particularly poems, song lyrics and some short stories. Most were a little precious, but slack could be cut given her youth and her emphatic girlishness. One of her more inspired works to-date was a children's book she wrote at 9 called *The Hyena Ballerina*, aptly centering on a hyena who becomes exiled from her pack when she makes the pivotal decision to join a local ballet company, while swearing off killing or eating animals in favor of a dancer's diet of plants and shrubbery. She also possessed a real appreciation for nature, chastising anyone for swatting so much as a fly in her presence, though yielding to innocent childlike hypocrisies when it came to waterbugs – a rare finding in Cold River but, without question, *those* needed to be killed.

This was a very important night, and Peggy made sure the kids were as aware of it as humanly possible; their father was turning 40 – their grandparents were coming up from Florida for this – and many of their closest Long Island friends and neighbors were to be in attendance.

It was as if this was the world premier of a movie they had worked years to mount, which was now about to get its first official screening for everyone who mattered to them.

For Peggy, she was prideful of Mike's achievements in his now 40 years. While she was thrilled to have her own career again and a greater sense of self outside of being a mother and wife, she could only look at Mike with love and admiration for what he had given her. They had two kids, a beautiful new house just a mile from a beautiful if slightly smaller house they moved from over the summer. They had a nice and respectable circle of friends, had seen much of the country, several countries in Europe, as well as Australia, Jamaica, with new destinations planned. Bliss was this.

This evening was to represent the current apex of their achievements, which she felt at least more a part of now that she was bringing in her own income, though it paled significantly to Mike's, like the size difference between a T-Rex and a Chihuahua. In one of Mike's more condescending jabs, he even once said that Peggy's salary would be the "pocket change" of the household – as if to be clear that, while he supported her going back to work, he was the breadwinner.   It was one of those moments that she would remember stinging a bit, if only gently. For even in their arguments, Mike had the ability to cleverly decide when a spat should cease – not with anger, but with his best doctor's bedside baritone which would lull so many of his pimpled patients over the years into sedation better than any anesthetic.

Further, while Peggy perhaps could fail on her own due to a still shaky self-confidence, she could at least take comfort in knowing that Mike would be her net. Therefore, all would always be well.

Clink! – went one glass after another, over the zombie-eyed jazz trio stationed in front of the fireplace and playing predictable age-themed music throughout the night. At this point, they were in the midst of "Young at Heart", which was as on-the-nose as one could get for an adult birthday cele-bration. This followed tritefully bouncy renditions of Neil Young's "Old Man", the Beatles' "Birthday" and Stevie Won-der's "Happy Birthday", among others.

Conversations permeated throughout the grand living room, after a succulent salmon feast catered by Peggy and Mike's favorite local restaurant – *Le Sec*. Nicky and Luna and the children of various friends of Mike and Peggy played in the game room, which contained a sizeable plasma screen filled with large bopping Pokemon-like characters pursuing various types of brightly colored candied objects.

All the while, Mike's parents, Vic & Elaine, the oldest of the 50 or so in attendance, would be approached by various friends of Mike's and asked endless variations on the same – *"Aren't you proud?"*, as if Mike had put twenties in everyone's pockets to say it. But it was always clear that Mike was re-soundingly the favorite son; his younger brother, Vic Junior, who had become sort of an unspoken disaster of myth, a virtual vagabond with a drug-dealing history, had long been out of touch with the family, with the exception of the occasional bi-annual letter from somewhere asking for money.

Peggy talked to her friends Judy and Gwen, fellow wives and mothers of Cold River, with the usual topics ranging from local gossip (an unbridled specialty for Judy and Gwen) to their kids; both the ones they had pride in and the ones who were becoming concerns, as well as how they hardly saw their 6-figure salaried husbands anymore and, ultimately, a somewhat backhanded *"So how's the teaching?"*

Peggy appreciated the fact that they would even remember, especially after Gwen's particularly long tangent on anal warts and hot flashes, though it always seemed that Peggy would get two minutes into a particular story about her connection with a student or a clever response he or she gave, before a glaze would gradually appear over their eyes like a descending curtain.

She also had grown afraid of coming off as boastful, which she was trying to be more cognizant of. After all, Judy and Gwen worked – had what one would call careers, and yet they hardly ever managed to speak of them. Judy had her own cyber-based cupcake business, which she'd bring up on the rare occasion when she had a sizable event, which was becoming less frequent, no doubt due to the unspoken fact that Judy was to baking what a bear was to accounting. And yet, bless her heart, she managed to bring 100 of her "special minis" with her this evening – the red velvet that Peggy would be obliged to try tasted like something akin to cream-laden woodchips, which she'd need to chase with her handy glass of Pinot in order to avoid choking.

Gwen was in real estate and was actually responsible for Mike and Peggy getting their current home, and certainly made a nice nickel for herself in doing so, though the whole act of "selling" seemed to be growing tiresome for her. Her husband and golf partner to Mike, Bill, was a trader, and even Gwen would confess that their dinner conversations had dwindled down to all but an emoticon, as if their own success attributed to an ultimate lack of chemistry, akin to oil and sand – *perhaps the ingredients to Judy's cupcakes.*

Deep down, Peggy did feel that what she was doing and had the potential to do was more cathartic, and perhaps Judy and Gwen picked up on this. It wasn't writing, but it was connecting with minds that she could help mold. While it was harder to stand in front of Nicky and command a similar attention now that he was ensconced in the cyber obstacles that befell most of his generation, there was something about speaking to 20 faces at a time and garnering their interest that made her life infinitely more desirable. She even noticed that it added greater dimension to her relationship with Mike, who sensed this change in her and seemed to be pleased by a vibrancy in Peggy that had begun to wane as the children were getting older. They were even having more regular sex, which Peggy also felt she had on most of her female friends, though she often played along with her fellow wife/mothers who used their sexual dormancy for comedic mileage.

Eventually Peggy and Claire would catch sight of each other. After the obligatory exchange of kisses with Judy and Gwen, Claire would promptly whisk Peggy away, clutching her arm in a vice grip as they glided towards the kitchen – "Did he tell you?" she whispered into Peggy's ear, with the dramatic tone of Norma Desmond from *Sunset Boulevard.*

"Tell me what?"

"He's going to need to operate on me."

"Mike? No he didn't tell me. Are you serious?"

"Of course, patient/doctor confidentiality, I guess. Yeah, next week. It's a good thing he mentioned it at the club otherwise I wouldn't've paid it any mind. Bless that man!"

Peggy was taken aback, only because she didn't recall that Mike had made a comment about the infamous mole on Claire's left arm when they were all having lunch last month, and yet it made sense. He made such observations before to friends on casual occasions and, sure enough, his concerns always seemed to be founded.   She even once recalled him expressing concern of a particular blemish to a mohel (pronounced moil) at the bris of Claire and Ray's eldest son Albert, whom Peggy and Mike were godparents to. Mike would later conclude that the mohel had early-stage melanoma, which he was able to subsequently remove. That happy ending aside, it also spawned the irresistible phrase "the mole on the mohel" which, at the time, became an infectious giggle-infused chant among the entire Bubone household akin to Dr. Seuss. An 8 year-old Luna would even be inspired to create her own little song, which she got in the habit of chanting whenever she was nervous about something:

> *The mole on the mohel*
> *Was as big as a boil*
> *And wouldn't go away*
> *The mole on the mohel*
> *Would fall into the soil*
> *Now the mohel is okay*

Peggy conveyed her warm confidence to Claire that Mike would successfully remove any trace of benign cancer, as he had done countless times before. While Claire claimed that she had already felt this somewhat, even if she had a bit of a flair for the dramatic, she undoubtedly needed Peggy's assurance. They liked each other quite a bit, which was fitting since they were now best friends, even if their conversation topics did not extend much beyond those with Judy and Gwen. It was even somewhat ironic that Claire came from a far more cultured background than Peggy and yet seemed to have comparatively little interest in culture, whereas Peggy would often enjoy field trips to the city to see theatre with Mike or taking the kids to the Guggenheim or the Whitney museum on a given weekend.

And yet, it was always assumed that this was more-or-less the background that Peggy came from; refined parents with eclectic taste and genuine artistic savvy. A myth not-so-much inferred by Peggy as assumed by her circle who, fortunately for her, were often too self-involved to ever probe deeply into her past.

While there was an obvious difference between Peggy and Claire as far as upbringing, there was also something germane that may have ultimately been their subconscious bonding point.

The most basic truth was that Peggy was raised, *if one could call it that*, by her mother to whom she had now been estranged for 17 years in a low-to-middle income household in the bleak town of Kelp Stream, New Jersey, while her father vanished early in Peg's life, as if a wind that was barely heard. Claire, in contrast, came from affluence; raised in Manhattan by an investor father and somewhat-known actress mother.

What Peggy most identified with in Claire was the over-zealous desire of wanting to be the opposite of what she knew as a child regarding how she was raised. For Claire, she would give so much of herself to her two children as if to overcompensate for what she felt bereft of from her emotionally absent parents. She doted. She wanted to be there to the extent that her omnipresence was in danger of having the opposite of the desired effect.

While Peggy's focus extended beyond motherhood, the years of not working allowed her to at least attempt to be instrumental in the growth and development of Nicky and Luna, while also battling a fear of possessing any of her own mother's less desirable tendencies. She knew they were there, but success, affluence and their strong reputation as a family had by and large done well to keep these obsessions at bay.

Meanwhile, Mike was holding court, as per usual for such gatherings – tonight being no different. He was surrounded by friends old and newer, from college and those he met in more recent years – some also current patients. All successful to varying degrees, and some with varied degrees;

bankers, brokers, lawyers, some in different aspects of the medical industry, all chomping on Cubans and dripping White Russians in a circle around Mike.

Jack was a good friend of Mike's, whom he met in college and would later attend the same dermatology school with. In many ways, it was as if they were given the same map and stepped into the same set of laid footprints, even if Mike was a size 12 to Jack's 11-wide.

Ray, Claire's husband and friend to Mike, was among the boisterous group, and had just prompted the two veteran dermatologists to regale the oddest shaped birthmarks they had ever seen on a patient, which was soon riffed on by Mike and Jack to *Abbott and Costello-like* proportions:

"I had a guy who had a birthmark of Joseph Stalin hugging Art Garfunkel on his back that I swore was a tattoo," laughed Mike. "But I told him that I only needed to remove half, okay? The guy says, *'Please tell me you're taking away the Stalin'*. I said, *'Sorry, my friend, it's the Garfunkel!'*" as boisterous laughter followed. "Jack?", as Mike invited him to best his story.

"Alright, I had a woman who had a penis-shaped mole right under her navel," Jack exclaimed. "I said, *'if you're not gettin' any from your husband, at least you got that.'*"

Guffaws predictably abounded...

"You didn't say that!" yelled Ray.

"I did. She's still a patient too," Jack laughed pridefully, as their dermatological one-upsmanship continued...

And while others would conclude that Mike's success simply came from being well-respected in his profession, Jack was also the only one who could make the observation that, even for a dermatologist, Mike was doing exceptionally well. He even began to jest to Mike how two guys with the same talents and similar personalities, with practices on either end of the same town, could be incurring such different results; as if the majority of potentially cancerous moles were confined to the east side of Cold River.

Peggy miraculously managed to hear the phone ringing in the kitchen amidst the cacophony of laughter and boisterous conversation, underscored by the band's strident rendition of the Grateful Dead's "Touch of Grey". On her way there, she seemed to be stopped, kissed, embraced by many who she hadn't managed to spend as much time with up until then, eventually untangling herself from their affections before picking up the phone:

"Hello. Bubone residence!" still laughing from something said on the way.

She heard nothing,...but sensed a familiar hesitancy on the other end.

"Hello?" she repeated.

She thought she heard the same inhalation of a cigarette, and then...a dial tone.

She would normally not pay much mind to a simple hang up, except that this was about the sixth time it had happened in the last couple of weeks. So despite the festive distractions, she suddenly couldn't help but start considering the possibilities:

That same hesitance. That cigarette sucking sound.
Could it be my mother?

"WHERE'S MY GORGEOUS WIFE!" yelled Mike grandly and tipsily, as if he had been summoning her from Mount Aetna, now accompanied by many thunderously calling Peggy's name, which thrust her out of her momentarily pensive state and back into the role of celebrated hostess.

She returned, "Oh, God, is he gonna' soliloquize now?"

Guffaws abounded...

"Don't be such a friggin' Lit teacher. Get up here, you!" he bellowed, standing atop their granite coffee table, amidst half-empty champagne flutes and plates of shrimp puffs.

Laughter and applause ensued, as Peggy traipsed through a newly made path from the kitchen with exaggerated elegance, her arms bent and positioned as if impersonating Bette Davis milking her Oscar strut.

"Coming, dahling!" as she made her way to the table, alongside Mike.

As Mike was about to speak, Peggy noticed that the kids were not around, "Wait a second, where are the kids?" she asked.

"They're in the game room. Let 'em be," he replied with a warm slur.

"No, no, no, they can put down the joysticks for 5 minutes for this."

"I may talk longer," he chimed.

"Then they can take a nap, but they have to be out here," she insisted.

Continued guffaws from everyone, which ascended and sustained, as if an audience watching a vintage night club act.

"Someone get the kids out of the fucking game room!" she exclaimed jokingly.

"You're gonna' curse too?" Mike said through laughter.

"Sorry, everyone! Please excuse my Pinot-infused tongue!"

"Yeah, the wine brings out Peg's inner New Jersey!" he followed.

More guffaws, as the half dozen kids who occupied the game room were brought out, looking like they were about to be led to a sausage grinder, with only Luna's enthusiasm a stark contrast to Nicky's and every other child's expression of adult-imposed dread.

Mike and Peggy looked out at the many smiling faces which had comprised those dearest to them. If a moment could be bottled and relived, this would certainly be one of them; Peggy and Mike, arm and arm, lovingly gazing into each other's eyes as applause and glass clinking gradually ebbed.

Mike began again, slowly, savoring this;

"Alright, so…in case some of you don't know, I'm 40 today."

Laughter at the obvious...

He continued, "And in being 40, I can't help but take some stock. Truly, it means the world to have the most important people in my life in one room tonight. I mean, you really know you have special people in your lives when there's over 50 of them in your house and no one's managed to clog the toilets."

More guffaws...

"Not yet!" yelled Larry, a friend and lawyer.

"Right, the night's still young," Mike agreed, as he continued. "Anyway, I guess you can't hit this age without being somewhat reflective, right? You think, wow, it's all gone by so fast. I had a wonderful upbringing courtesy of my great parents, Vic and Elaine Bubone, who are here tonight..."

Applause ascended, as a tear streamed down Elaine's face, as an equally proud Vic kissed her temple, with his dear granddaughter Luna now clutched in his lap.

Mike continued, "Then along came this beautiful Lit major I met in college, who made my life so much richer and who's been my rock, my inspiration, my...my..."

"...wife?" Peggy ably filled in the blank...

"My sentence finisher!" he followed, as the laughter continued...

"I love you, darlin'," he said, looking into her eyes. The joyful envy in the room was as rich as molasses on cheesecake in that moment, as they pecked.

"Alright, alright, continue," she said, with pleased embarrassment.

"Okay, okay, fine," Mike turned out again. "Then one-by-one, our gorgeous and talented children, Nicky and Luna, came into the world – " to which Peggy interrupted, "Thank God it was one-by-one!" as more laughter ensued....

Mike continued, "Yes, thank God, or I never woulda' heard the end of it. In any event, these two came into our lives, and they've kept us on our toes in such a variety of beautiful and sometimes annoying and frustrating ways."

More laughter meshed with endeared sighs...

"And, of course,...our friends here tonight. You're not just here because we wanted you to be here but because we *needed* you here...and we couldn't imagine our lives without you, as friends, as neighbors, as family to us all. We love ya'."

Mike raised his glass, as did most everyone else, as "Happy Birthday" began being energetically crooned, soon accompanied rather wonkily by the band. Throughout, Peggy and Mike remained standing on their coffee table, "You happy?" she knowingly asked, not just as a wife but as the chief and tireless organizer of the evening's festivities. "Whata' *you* think?" he rhetorically replied, smiling with relaxed joy.

They then kissed, as if the stroke of midnight on New Year's Eve, with Peggy oblivious to the fact that her heel was now immersed in pâté. And in that moment, she recalled the first time their lips had touched; where she was then, where she was now. Any momentary gaffes that took place over the course of their relationship, including her brief stage of drinking a bit more than she normally did, were overwhelmingly submerged by this moment. Sixteen years of marriage went by and what was a turning point at the beginning of their courtship seemed a dream now. But it was real.

And, on top of everything else, no one clogged the toilets.

2

The next day, Peggy was re-opening the discussion with her final period class about the themes of *The Bell Jar*, which would ultimately dovetail into an essay assignment in which students would further expand on their thoughts and any parallels to their own experiences, however remote.

The cliffhanger question before yesterday's bell was if Esther Greenwood was "sick" and, if so, was there a way out of it other than death or the brutal shock therapy she would undergo.

Once again, amidst a few astute observations were the usual variety of rambling assessments, some more mono-syllabic or ill-conceived, as Peggy made it a point to circulate this question thoroughly throughout the class – remembering what it was like to feel lost in the sauce of a classroom, as she recalled several of the apathetic teachers of her youth simply calling on the same blonde do-gooder students, content to sacrifice class absorption for expeditiousness. But she had greater aspirations for herself and for her students, wanting everyone to raise their game, if at all possible. This was not just a class – this was, at least she felt, a philosophy that could have relevance to their lives down the road, or at least inspire deeper thought, which may have ultimately been beyond most of them,…especially the kids who were virtually incapable of sentences beyond a phrase due to the clenched silver spoons in their mouths.

Just as there appeared to be a lull in the momentum of

responses, Tricia raised her hand as if nervously punching the sky. It seemed as though she was feeling out what the rest of the room had to say before concluding the right time to make her nerve-racked entrance. She spoke methodically but with a degree of self-awareness regarding her fellow classmates,... taking a breath while sensing their eyes upon her:

"I think...I think Esther was misunderstood because... no one else that she knew had her feelings. Her sense of... disconnection. And that...that made her feel like an outcast. Like she *was* sick. Because she wasn't like everybody else. I think that's what the book is about, more than anything. At least for me. It was about conformity. If she just went along with how everyone behaved, her mother wouldn't've felt that there was something wrong. There was a bravery in her...just being who she was, even if she was confused or lost or wasn't in touch with her feelings."

"You thought she was brave?" chimed Susan Floss, with an audacity that suddenly added a rare tension to the room.

"I do."

"How was she brave by being...being...?"

"*Sick*? I mean, if...if you think that she was and just...just want to write her off as that, then you can't see it. But if you see that she was just misunderstood, or just needed...help... And not just medical help, but help of meeting someone else who...who understood where she was coming from or...what she was confused by. I mean, it just doesn't make... It's sad to think that she was just sick and she was fated to die young because...she was "sick". What's the point of a life like that? To shock her into being normal? *They* were sick to think that that would help."

There was an unusual stillness in the room after Tricia spoke, with some seeming genuinely impressed, while a few of the usual brats waited for someone more courageous to initiate laughter. But to Peggy,...this was a breakthrough. For Peggy, this moment seemed to transcend past prideful moments in her life; when *she* first received encouragement from a teacher, Mr. Gadds, who acknowledged an exceptional oral essay she had presented on *The Grapes of Wrath* in her sophomore high school English class, or when she got a scholarship to Princeton and seemingly shed the skin of all that she was born into. Even more than maternal pride; seeing Nicky and Luna first speaking, walking or taking their first independent toilet poops.

This was a student of hers whom she seemed to get through to; whose understanding of a work she admired was perfectly captured for all to hear.

It had never made more sense to Peggy than in that moment, and she was never happier.

And then,...there was a knock on the classroom door.

Peggy would open the door at a moment of great satisfaction. While she was occasionally interrupted for the request of a student, it was Jocelyn, the principal, who was at the door this time, which was already unusual.

She had a rare serious look on her face, which quickly erased the beaming smile on Peggy's as Jocelyn softly asked her to come out into the hallway and close the door behind her. Jocelyn's grave expression suddenly gave Peggy cause to think that maybe something had happened to Nicky or Luna. Soon her mind began racing; *an accident, kidnapping, oh my God...,* as Jocelyn took a breath before speaking:

"Peggy, I got a call about your husband."

"About my...? Oh, my God, is he okay?"

"His lawyer called. He's been arrested."

Inexplicably, Peggy appeared to go deaf. Jocelyn's lips were moving but she could only hear a disturbingly high-pitched whistle-like sound that would normally occur if one was too close to a gunshot – and this was a cannon. But there was no mistake; Mike had been taken into custody.

Jocelyn had no further details, as she led Peggy down the hallway to her office, where she soon sat down next to Jocelyn's phone, next to which was a post-it note reading *"Call Larry Grubman"* along with his number, before Jocelyn left to give her privacy.

Larry was a friend to both Mike and Peggy, in addition to being a lawyer who Mike had consulted with on a few menial issues in the past. He was at their house the previous night to partake in one of the most joyous celebrations of their lives and now would be the bearer of unfathomable news; "Insurance fraud," he said.

The ringing increased in Peggy's ears to the extent that she thought a pack of dogs might soon bust through Jocelyn's office door.

"Larry, explain this to me. I don't... What is this?" she stammered in a hushed tone.

"I know. It's a little insane. He's fine, though. Don't worry -"

"But I'm...where should I go? Where is he?" as panic started to settle in.

"Peg, it'll be fine. I'm sure it's an error."

"Insurance fraud?!"

"They don't have anything. I'm sure it's a mistake."

"Well, Larry, what do we do in the meantime? He's still in jail, right?"

"Yes, and so we have to wait until the judge sets bail, which they won't be able to until Monday."

"What?! Why?!"

"It's because it's afternoon on a Friday and the judge is a lazy prick. It'll be fine," he assured.

"Where is he? I need to see him, Larry," a desperate quiver now in her voice...

"You can't, Peg."

"What do you mean I can't, Larry? He's my husband -!"

"Peggy, they will not let you see him now. He's in custody. We just gotta' tough it through the weekend and we'll bail him out on Monday.".

"And what're we supposed to do until then?" she asked.

"It'll be fine. Just remain calm and don't talk to the press, if they contact you. All you can do is just be prepared for the unexpected right now, okay?"

"Unexpected? What? What can be more unexpected than *this*?"

What was more unexpected was when Peggy arrived at Mike's office with Nicky and Luna to find federal agents seizing items. Monique, Mike's dutiful if genuinely flabbergasted receptionist, was already outside and not allowed admittance into the office. As soon as she spotted Peggy, she ran to her as if she was fleeing from an inferno, clearly so beside herself that there were practically two of her:

"Oh, my God, Peggy, I can't believe this..." she cried.

Peggy could barely get out "I tried to call but I couldn't get – "

"They're taking everything!" Monique bellowed.

'What?"

"Everything – the computers, the phones, all the patient files..."

"Oh my God..."

"They just barged in with a seizure warrant," Monique explained in a panic. "He was in the middle of a biopsy when they practically kicked down the door, Peggy. Oh, my God..."

More accurately, 57 year old Audrey Kovalt's bare ass was about to be lanced when agents barged in; nearly giving her a heart attack and the agents an inadvertent mooning.

While Peggy knew Mike had already been taken in by now, she thought this would be the one place to get some sort of an understanding as to what happened and, in so doing, could better assess what mistake could have been made by the authorities.

Monique continued, "I'm supposed to go down for questioning with them. This is all beyond belief..."

"What did they tell you?"

"Just that they were taking him in for fraud. I can't believe it. I mean, it can't be true."

"It's not true, Monique. This has gotta' be a mistake," Peggy assured, more so for her own need to believe it than for Monique's. Yet, as stressed as Peggy was, she was somehow relieved to be distracted by a hysterical Monique, whom she managed to calm down somewhat, as they watched agents parade virtually Mike's entire office into a van. The kids remained in the backseat of Peggy's car, knowing nothing as per her design, though sensing something was off by the speed of her driving and how little she spoke on the way.

While Nicky was fittingly distracted from the proceedings by his ever-present game-gadget screen clutched in his grip, Luna managed to crane her neck to see the cars surrounding her father's office, as she attempted to come out:

"Luna, stay in the car, okay? Everything's fine."

"Mommy, what's happening?"

"They're just doing some…work on your dad's office, that's all. Play a video game, honey."

"I don't wana' play a game. What's going on?"

"Nothing. Read your book, honey," as Peggy approached the car in an attempt to block Luna's view.

"I don't have a book!"

"Then take the one in my briefcase. We'll be home soon. Just stay in the car, honey!"

Luna tepidly went back into the car, watched Nicky intensely fixated on his game where candied objects were avoiding other types of candied objects, then reached into Peggy's purse and pulled out Sylvia Plath's *The Bell Jar*.

Peggy could only conceive of giving them diversions at the moment, especially as she saw little option. She couldn't begin to make sense of this for herself yet, let alone attempt to explain it to them. She could only affirm that this was an egregious faux pas which would soon be rectified, and one that would serve as prized material for the next dinner party.

Hours later, Peggy sat with the kids at dinner, in a virtual haze. Unable to concentrate on anything, and having exhausted all of her questions to the extent that she was now hoarse, she barely managed to over-nuke some left-over salmon from the previous night's party, which Nicky and Luna picked at as if it were a laboratory frog.

She hadn't explained what had happened and, at this point, resigned to simply say little and give them no access to TV or anything cyber-related, as she chewed endlessly on the elasticized green beans. Her mind was fatigued from trying to wrap her head around what had suddenly whisked her husband away in an instant. *Insurance fraud? What does that mean? How could he have possibly been accused of such a thing?*

Peggy continued to muse over the possible sources of such an accusation. Could it have had anything to do with Mike's former partner, whom he had a sort of acrimonious parting with several years ago? If so, why would this be happening now? Perhaps a patient with an axe to grind? And Monique certainly was as in the dark as Peggy, even though she was responsible for submitting much of the paperwork, the insurance reportage, etc. *It must've been a patient who accused Mike wrongfully.* After all, it appeared to Peggy that, at least in the U.S., the innocent-until-proven-guilty theory often was out of balance with so many who had been falsely accused and, in contrast, needed to be proven innocent.

What was worse was that the phones, both the landline and her cell, were now ringing in a continuous stream, making the house sound like a game show for hours – the voicemail boxes of both now full with much of last night's guest list hearing or having heard a rumor, or through local news reportage, that Mike was arrested; *"Is it true?" "Are you ok?"* Peggy had, at first, wished Mike's parents didn't leave that morning for Florida, as she could have used the support,...but then just as quickly thought twice, realizing the stress that they would undoubtedly add to this situation. The best case scenario was that they would find out nothing until this was all resolved.

"Will Daddy be home tonight?" asked Luna, repelled by her rubberized salmon, yet sensing that something was askew.

Peggy had not said much to this point, other than that Mike's office was being redecorated and that there were...*complications*.

"Daddy's away for the weekend, honey. He'll be back on Monday."

"Is it because of the office?" Luna asked.

Peggy was losing track of her own fabrication, "What do you mean?"

"Is he at the office with the moving men?" Luna followed.

"The moving...? Oh. No, honey. He had... There's a conference in the city this weekend, so he's going to be there."

This wasn't the worst lie, as Mike had often gone to conferences out of town and would often be away on weekends or two-day patches.

There were always innovations in the world of dermatology; advancements in equipment, things it was important that he be abreast of in order to remain competitive and up to code.

Peggy even wondered if this was the result of a colleague who was simply jealous of Mike's success. Could it even have been Jack, Mike's near twin from across town who had jokingly mused aloud about the disparity in their incomes, despite their identical professions and practices?

"Why aren't you answering the phone?" asked Luna.

"Because it's not important. I'll get back to them later."

"Who is it? It sounds important."

"It's fine, honey. I've spoken to a lot of people today and I just need to rest my voice."

"It could be daddy."

"It's not!" Peggy snapped, then softening with regret. "It's not your daddy, honey. He's sleeping now. He's had a long day."

She then turned to Nicky, in his own world, looking at the game screen on his lap,

"Nicky, eat your dinner, okay? You can give that game a

break now."

He ignored her, while increasing his focus...

"Nicky, did you hear mommy?" chimed in Luna.

"Shut up, Luna. You're not my mother," he snapped.

"You're right, *I* am. Don't talk that way to your sister, and Luna, I don't need your help. Nicky, shut the game off now," as if her desire to keep Nicky in the dark on this issue could not trump her impatience at how much time he was giving to these stupid games.

Nicky turned it off, sat and sulked for the moment, before reluctantly picking at his food.

"I know it's not the nicest dinner we've had of late, but it's been a long day. Just eat what you can and then go to bed, okay?"

"Go to bed? It's not even 8, and tomorrow's Saturday," Nicky protested.

"I want you to go to your room and not watch any TV then, okay?"

'Why not?" he asked, his curiosity seeming to have peaked only because of privileges that were being inexplicably revoked.

Admittedly, Peggy's plan was a tenuous one, at best. She soon realized that in this day and age it would be hard to withhold information from a newborn baby, let alone from a 13 and 11 year-old for longer than an evening. She refused to have the TV on, assuming that something may have been broadcast, which probably led to the avalanche of calls. At the same time, she had confiscated Nicky and Luna's phones, which were mainly intended for safety anyway, but what else could she really do to have them avoid hearing something from an outside source other than lock them in the attic while slipping food under the door? With the way things were going, Peggy would try it and, within minutes, have Child Protective Services at the door.

If nothing else, she realized that there would be no better way for them to hear such news, however fleeting it was, than from their mother.

Peggy spit a much-gnawed green bean into her napkin, "Nicky, Luna, stop eating for a minute," she said softly, as if to lubricate a jagged rock.

"You just told me to eat," Nicky whined.

"Yes, alright, and now I'm telling you to stop. This is important."

Nicky and Luna stopped, looked at each other for a second, momentarily on the same page of uncertainty.

"So...I didn't want to tell you too much here, because this is a situation that will be all better by Monday. But, until then, if you happen to hear things about your father, just..." she looked at Nicky and Luna, clearly unclear as to her intent. "In other words, something's happened that was very...unexpected. Your father is currently... Your father has been incorrectly accused of something that he didn't do."

"What didn't he do?" asked Nicky.

Peggy was hesitant, struggling to edit what she said in her head before the words gravitated to her tongue and caused undue panic in the kids.

"He is accused...of doing something that is illegal regarding his work, which he did not do. But there's a misunderstanding right now, and so you may hear things."

"Hear that he did do these things?" asked Luna.

Peggy paused, barely able to look Luna in the eyes now, but committing with all her maternal muscle, "Yes, that's right."

"That he killed someone?" asked Nicky.

"Nicky, that's insane!" she exclaimed, with stunned indignation. "No, he didn't kill anyone. What the hell are you watching?"

"I'm not saying he did it, I'm just asking if that's what he's accused of?" he warily defended.

"No, for Godsakes! Not at all. It has to do with...with paperwork," she feebly defended.

"Paperwork?" followed Luna.

"It's complicated. I don't even understand it myself, but it's perfectly rectifiable. It's a mistake. People make mistakes, even police. They've just made a mistake regarding your father, which is why...why he's not here"

"I thought you said he was at a conference," Nicky probed.

Peggy took a beat, questioning how deeply she should pursue this explanation, but trusting that telling Nicky and Luna as much as possible before anyone else did was best:

"He's...he's currently in police custody."

"What does that mean?" Luna's voice now slightly trembling...

"He's in jail?!"

"Nicky, he's not..." Peggy thought to lie, because the mere question coming out of her still impressionable son's mouth in the presence of her even more impressionable daughter was simply too much to bear. However, she could only concur, after a pause pregnant enough to deliver triplets; "Yes, he's...for the moment, temporarily, he is currently in the custody of the authorities, but he'll be home on Monday."

After an odd silence, as if this was the first time something Peggy said permeated the filterless Nicky and Luna at the most precocious stage of their lives, Nicky asked, "Is he definitely gonna' be home on Monday?"

"Yes, definitely," she said, confidently.

"Because the problem will be solved, right?" asked Luna.

"Um...well, it won't be solved, necessarily, but he'll be home."

"You mean they're just gonna' let him go even though they think he still did...whatever they think he did?" Nicky's inquisitiveness now becoming more annoying than his usual disinterest.

Peggy now felt like a neophyte attorney before two woefully inexperienced judges. Knowing pretty much only what Larry divulged to her, while not getting much additional information from any of the agents at the office, "Well, what happens is that they need to set bail, which is how much it will cost to get your father back home. So we'll pay the bail and...then he'll be home."

"Wait, is that like a bribe?" asked Nicky, showing his own understandable legal ignorance.

"No, it's...just how the system works. Look, all you need to know is that your father will be home and this will all be fine. I've already called the precinct and they said your father is doing well, so just know that he's fine. We're fine. And this is simply a mistake. So if you hear anything from anyone, don't respond. Just ignore them."

"Hear from who?" asked Luna.

"Anyone. Anyone who brings this up, okay?" Peggy answered. "And this weekend, I don't want you going anywhere. No playing with anyone. Just...let's stay home together, you can do homework, play games and read books, whatever, but no internet, no texting, no...no anything else until I say so, okay?"

"Oh, man..." whined Nicky, whose friend Lane had invited him over for a birthday party on Saturday.

"Nicky, I need you to be a grown-up here, even if you're not there yet, okay? This is serious. It's a small sacrifice for one weekend. Just call and tell Lane you don't feel well," with a piercing urgency he had not heard from his mother in a while, if ever.

He resisted belaboring the issue, as Luna remained quiet, with a tear in her eye. Peggy could not act as if it wasn't there, and could no longer resist showing tears herself, ...but she would not break. She was strong, at least for now, and knew this was a momentary storm they could wade through and there was no better way to do so then staying home together.

"Come on, let's finish eating, okay?" her voice nearly cracking.

Nicky picked at his salmon, both unusually pensive and

still disappointed that his Saturday was now compromised.

Luna tried to hold her fork, but her sadness clearly imposed on her appetite.

Peggy softly summoned her to come over, as Luna rushed to her lap. She cried a little into her mother's neck, embracing her tightly, before Peggy gave Luna her fork…

"Let's share mine, okay?" she said with a forced smile.

She and Luna shared the same plate, amidst sniffles and a few tears that inadvertently basted the salmon. They all said little else for the rest of the evening.

3

After the kids were asleep, Peggy called the precinct where Mike was being held for about the 4th time since the afternoon. While she could obviously not speak to him, she at least wanted to know that he was ok, if he'd eaten, and that he wasn't being treated like Brad Davis was in *Midnight Express*. Whatever officer picked up gave her lip service to the effect that he was fine and advised her to stop calling, which did little to comfort her or diminish the utter surrealism of the day. She could not fathom sleeping, and opted to listen to all of the messages that had been recorded from earlier in the day through the evening until the mailbox maxed out on both her cell and landline. There were calls from Gwen, Judy, Jack, other friends, Cinda, who was a colleague of Peggy's at school, *a journalist from Newsday wanting a fucking quote...* In the middle somewhere was Vic, Mike's dad, obliviously letting them know that they got in okay and that they would have stayed longer, were it not for Vic's needing to return for surgery on his knee. After swallowing all of these messages like tacks, she felt she needed to decide a course of action to get through the weekend and do what she could to quell the potential fire of misconception that now seemed to permeate much of their social circle.

The upside was that all of their friends who called appeared to only want to know if it were true and, if so, what they could do to help, never seeming to believe that Mike was actually guilty of anything. Nevertheless, Peggy was loath to engage with anyone beyond simply saying that this was clearly a mistake and all would be resolved by next week. However, she also had a need to be pro-active in some way, so she invited the Queen Bees of the gossip circle, Gwen and Judy, over for lunch on Saturday. Not only would it help to vent about how genuinely ridiculous this was but also it would somehow obligate them both to not take dramatic license with anyone else. It was important to Peggy that it be made clear that Mike was innocent, both for their standing in the community and her own sense of integrity.

After all, she did not come all the way from the dilapidated town of her youth, where middling aspirations were as common as the potholed roads, only to be embarrassed among central Long Island's elite.

She also wanted to invite Claire Resnick, who was also friends with Gwen and Judy, though more distantly (and perhaps cautiously). However, oddly enough, Claire was not among the callers and, since she was even a current patient of Mike's, Peggy did not want to complicate matters by informing her of something she and her husband Ray may have been unaware of.

Fortunately, family contact was easier to avoid than friends. Mike's parents were already back in Florida with no instantaneous access to local news. Any aunts or uncles of his were likely to not have heard anything, since they lived in other areas of the country, and Vic Jr. was well out of the picture anyway, *if not dead*. Peggy had no attachment to her birth family. With an absent father, no known living aunts or uncles, and no siblings, what little there was consisted solely of her mother, who presumably didn't even know where Peggy was living now, as it'd been years since their last and most colorful correspondence.

Therefore, Peggy convinced herself that she was taking as much control as humanly possible over a situation that could quickly bubble over like hot magma. With the arrangements to have two of her close friends over tomorrow, having the kids at home, and her constant calls to the precinct and to Larry, it all seemed that every proper wheel was in motion for a soon-to-be resolution to a bizarre bureaucratic blunder.

Still, it was easier for Peggy to consider boxing a hippopotamus than sleeping this evening and so, at 2:45am, she decided to finally break down and see what had been written about Mike's arrest online. She braced herself upon entering Mike's name, before a few local articles popped up; "Esteemed Cold River Dermatologist Arrested" was the general headline. The information contained in all the brief articles was the same; Mike had been taken in by authorities under suspicion of submitting *allegedly* false diagnoses to insurance companies, so as to be compensated for performing *allegedly* unnecessary surgery.

These details were not revealed by Larry, who in all likelihood did not want Peggy to inundate herself with the allegations, in the hopes that they would ultimately be disproved anyway. Nevertheless, to read this in print was like a punch in the gut to her. Not that it was true, but that it was her husband's name being dragged through the mud; the father of their two children.

She even felt a regret about Mike's party, as it appeared to draw more attention from their immediate circle. She felt now that, while there was much love in the house that night, there was also likely to have been some envy and, perhaps, the envious now had a degree of satisfaction in this humbling incident, however unfounded.

"You look terrible. Have a cupcake," exclaimed Judy, referring to the six enormous iced manifestations on the backyard patio table.

Gwen and Judy arrived at noon to see Peggy who, admittedly, was worse for wear after having slept a good 20 minutes, at best. With their mimosas clasped in hand that Gwen took it upon herself to make, and the kids occupied inside, Gwen and Judy probed Peggy for anything that she knew which could have led to Mike's arrest. She admittedly knew very little about Mike's day-to-day operations, other than that he amassed many patients, was trusted, respected and could have only made any sort of insurance gaffe in error. Other than that, she could only say what she had been told by Larry and the authorities, only now the enormity of this was exacerbated by her assuming that much of Long Island somehow knew of Mike's arrest and the allegations which prompted it.

"It's a mistake and they'll find out soon enough. It's all a mistake," she repeated like a mantra, as she sipped her mimosa, trying to remain as composed as possible – and trying not to chug.

She certainly had her own motives for inviting Judy and Gwen over. Yes, supportive company, a sounding board of sorts, as she had certainly been for them at less severe times, but she also needed to assert how absurd this was and, further, to gauge through them what others in their circle might have already perceived; *Did anyone think that Mike was a criminal? Could anyone have seen this coming? Was there ever a belief that we never really belonged?*

Peggy would not verbalize such Nixon-like paranoia except to ask if they had spoken to others about this, to which Judy and Gwen claimed only their spouses. And yet they assured her that they knew this must be a mistake. Gwen had even cited a story of a family she sold a house to some years ago. The husband had been accused of misappropriation of funds at several high-end nursing homes that he owned out of town. He was arrested for taking the rent checks from families and depositing them in a personal account, amounting to millions. He was subsequently sentenced to several years in prison. In the meantime, his wife and kids couldn't afford the house, had to move to a small town somewhere where they ended up renting. The wife was disgraced, after having been a Vice President of a successful marketing firm, and ended up becoming an administrative assistant for a plumbing company or some such thing. Then, one day, the kids came home and found the mother hanging from a pipe in their bathroom. The two daughters then made a suicide pact so that they wouldn't have to live with their grandparents or in foster care. A few months later, the husband was released when authorities admitted he had been falsely charged, and they ended up arresting his partner, whom authorities ultimately concluded had set him up. However, his entire family was now dead.

"Anyway," Gwen concluded brightly, "the point is that he was innocent."

Peggy looked at Gwen,...hardly comforted by this.

The rest of Saturday bled into Sunday like oozing tar. Peggy was on a semblance of auto-pilot, knowing she had to be in some type of motion throughout the house so as not to further concern the kids, but at a loss of how to distract her mind before Monday would arrive and give her reason for optimism. For now, she appeared frozen in time, while somehow managing to check in with the kids to make sure they weren't thinking of their father in Turkish prison-like despair.

They had all of their meals together, and Peggy made it a point to steer the conversations to anything but the present limbo. Throughout she would receive more calls from friends, associates... She selected which calls she'd return, some intentionally at later times so as to be able to more safely leave a reassuring message. The conversations she would have were selective and kept brief, with Peggy, now on next to no rest, only able to offer slight variations on the same optimistic phrases; *"All is fine"*, *"It's a misunderstanding"*, *"It'll be cleared up on Monday"* and *"It's all good"*, as Mike always said. Of the notable exchanges, she spoke with her principal, Jocelyn, who, at this point, was only concerned about Peggy's well-being and was genuinely surprised that she had expected to return to class as early as Tuesday. Of everyone she spoke to, Peggy put the most effort in hamming up her optimism in speaking with Jocelyn, for it was too important for her to not be deemed stable in a position she had cherished.

She spoke to Jack, Mike's friend and friendly crosstown dermatological rival, though she felt funny about doing so at length, especially since Jack continued to ask questions that were beyond Peggy's knowledge. His relentless probing for details only served to increase her suspicion that perhaps he had something to do with this.

The only person who knew about what was happening and who Peggy felt comfortable in speaking about this to in detail was Larry, which was apt since, as Mike had been a savior to many patients, Larry needed to be theirs. She spoke to him two or three more times, as if to get new information, though there was clearly none for him divulge. Larry had of course seen Mike, and said that he looked fine, though he complained about his uncomfortable jail cell cot. However, as savvy a lawyer as Larry was, it was clear that he could not see this coming any more than Peggy, nor would he have ever assumed Mike was capable of anything unsavory. As a friend for many years, he shared the same optimism as Peggy in Mike's innocence and, as his lawyer, was obligated to feel even more that this was an offensive miscarriage of justice.

"Peggy, don't make yourself nuts, okay? Get yourself some sleep. Rest your brain and, on Monday, I'll pick you up and we'll go down together like I told ya'. Stop playing detective," he said with a chuckle.

"What if the bail's too high? What happens if we can't afford it?" she desperately asked.

"It depends on the judge. It might smart a bit, but you guys have it. And when he's exonerated, you get it back anyway, okay? It'll be fine," with his usual assurance, which was just barely enough to get Peggy off the phone.

She also made several more calls to the precinct, much

to the outward chagrin of various police officers.

Still no call from Claire.

At this point, Peggy had a dilemma. She wondered how Claire could not know. As preoccupied as she was with her recent diagnosis of benign skin cancer, was Claire, ever the drama queen, suddenly possessed with such sensitivity that she, somehow, felt it best in such an extreme circumstance to let Peggy call *her* if she needed her? Did she just not want to impose?

That simply didn't make sense to Peggy,...or maybe it was just her paranoia kicking in.

In any case, it was just too much for her to call Claire first, not knowing if there was already a feeling that was growing roots; that Claire believed that Mike was guilty and that she had possibly been among his falsely diagnosed victims. In that moment, she regretted to hope that Claire, her best friend, did in fact have cancer, just to prove Mike's legitimacy. As if that single diagnosis would be enough to exonerate him.

Sunday night, Peggy went to bed, closed her eyes slowly and, to her surprise, even managed a dream. It was a new one, to be sure. A dream that Carl Jung likely would have had a field day dissecting given the stew of subconscious turmoil within her, combined with her unbridled eagerness for the sun to rise:

A fierce wind circulated around her on, what appeared to be, a beach without an ocean. In the distance were various silhouettes that she gravitated to. Her dog that she had as a young girl, Wojo, came up to her and barked a kiss. She went to touch him but he ran into the coming tide of silhouettes and oceanic murmuring. Toasts were being made, and there was laughter coming from somewhere. The wind built and faded in an instant. She wanted to reach Wojo, but it appeared that he was now far away. She saw what looked like Mike in the distance, at his most celebratory; raising a glass and grandly reciting inaudible lines from something. Those who surrounded Mike who appeared to be his usual hangers-on ul-

timately appeared to be afflicted in some way; ashen and emaciated. Peggy couldn't tell if these were people they knew or characters from a book come to life. Mike continued speaking unintelligible sentences, as Tricia, Peggy's personal favorite student, was transcribing his inaudible speech into a stenography machine that was strangely discarding pieces of salmon. Peggy circled around looking for a safe familiarity, but was continually roped into the lack of cohesion. She appeared to move in a circular fashion, twirling, only to occasionally catch a glimpse of another familiar face; Claire was saying something under Mike's inept utterances. Judy was sitting at a table piled high with her own dreadful cupcakes that managed to look even more ill-formed than usual, with the icing crudely scotch-taped on to the base. Larry tried to approach Peggy but was sucked back into the ocean of silhouettes and oceanic murmuring. The sound built in sync with the pace of Peggy's spinning like an out-of-control ballerina... Mike continued to speak without coherency and began to be shouted over by a scintillating male voice she had never heard before – "Order! ORDER! I SAID ORDER, GODDAMNIT!!!!!!!" – the volume persisted as did Peggy's spastic twirling, while, in the distance, cries from children that rose like a developing earthquake.... A jolting knock on an unseen door which eventually appeared to be a gavel being thunderously slammed onto a timpani-like drum – "Order! ORDER! I SAID ORDER, GODDAMNIT!!!!!..."

She awoke, gasping a silent scream, sweat saturating the sheets, her breath heavy...

She looked at her clock to see it was only 3:55 AM.

With tears in her eyes, she picked up the phone and auto-dialed the precinct. A different officer would pick up, to whom Peggy could only reply, "Please tell me that my husband is okay..."

4

$250,000 later, Mike was finally home with Peggy. Larry drove them back, stayed for some time to speak with Mike privately regarding a plan of action for the pending trial, and now, with the kids still at school, it was finally just Peggy and Mike alone. They sat close to each other at the dining table with lukewarm coffee before them. Mike was visibly exhausted, his back on the verge of sciatica from 3 nights of sleeping in a jail cell. After the bail proceedings, the culmination of this whirlwind was him speaking with Larry for almost three hours, rendering him physically and emotionally sapped. However, despite Peggy's equal lack of rest, this was her first chance to be solely with Mike. And as much as she sympathized with his fatigue, she felt as if they might not have many private moments like this for a while and, therefore, needed to take the opportunity to have the basics answered from Mike himself. While she started off questioning him gingerly, it soon spilled over into an avalanche of inquiries, as if seeking an explosively definitive answer underscored by Hollywoodized vindication music. There needed to be something that would solidify Mike's innocence and truly render the burden of proof on his accusers, whoever the hell they actually were. She still was unsure. *A disgruntled patient? His former partner somehow sabotaging him after so many years? Could it have been something that Jack had manifested in some way?*

"Honey, can't I just sit here with my coffee and we'll talk

after I take a nap?" he said testily.

"Mike, I'm just trying to make sense of all this for myself, okay?".

"There *is* no sense to this, okay? That's what's so insane about this. It's an accusation, and it's wrong," as he begrudgingly sipped.

"But who's accusing you?"

"Didn't Larry tell you this?"

"Told me what? He explained the charges and told me they're unfounded. That's what I know," she said with restrained frustration.

"And that's all that's important to know," he tersely replied. "It's all bullshit, Peg. This stuff happens in the medical profession all the time. I just didn't think I'd have to experience it, but I am. But it'll be okay, alright? You get too big, too successful, people wana' bring you down. All they gotta' do is say something and then I'm the one that gets his name in the papers. I'm the one who gets to sleep on a metal table for 3 nights staring at a Goddamn concrete wall."

He appeared to be on the verge of letting his exhaustion get the better of him, but managed to restrain himself, seeming to understand Peggy's right to have a more thorough understanding of what was happening. Her name was his name, after all. It was Nicky's name. It was Luna's name. He understood that even the verdict of his innocence could not so quickly absolve him and wash away the blemishes that come with such accusations, though he certainly wanted to believe it and was determined to.

He took a breath, smiled weakly at Peggy, gently took her hand from the table…

"Honey,…I love you, and I would never do anything to jeopardize this family. I'm not perfect, honey, but just…" he paused, gathering himself. "I worked too damn hard and studied too damn long. And I'll… I promise, I'll tell you more when I've gotten some zees on a real mattress, okay? But I don't want you to worry. This is a mistake and it'll be rectified. Okay?"

He kissed her on the forehead, then went upstairs to take a long overdue nap, while Peggy sat and thought to herself – ***Does*** *this happen all the time in the medical profession? Who would want to be a doctor of any kind if this was likely to happen? Wouldn't it be easier to be an accountant or work in a bank?* Nevertheless, Peggy desperately wanted to believe him, and even hoped that in his getting some rest and gathering a semblance of his usual and formidable strength that they would be able to sit down with a glass of wine and discuss the further details of this. And in so doing, she would at once be as close to satisfied and confident in a positive outcome as she could be.

But this could not come fast enough.

Peggy went to school the next day, for the first time begrudgingly. Void of the usual sense of pride she carried with her like her pocketbook as she walked down the corridors, now it was all she could do to go through the motions in each class, attempting thoughtful discussions with her students which she eventually found herself losing track of by 4th period.

She had yet to have the opportunity of a proper discussion with Mike about what was happening, which certainly aided in her distraction. Instead, Mike slept soundly most of the previous afternoon into the evening, waking up for a brief intermission to gnaw on some now quite gamey salmon and see the kids, who certainly gave their father extra attention. Luna, in particular, would latch on to Mike, appearing to have the same curiosities as her mother, though only having the capacity to hug Mike so hard that it almost exacerbated his back issues. However, Mike could only wince with pleasure at the touch of his beloved Luna, to the point that tears began to form in his eyes. Nicky also seemed to lose his usual sense of apathy with everything that wasn't digital, as if realizing for the first time that life can be surprising in the least desirable of ways. Amorphous. Sensible only in its nonsense. However, Peggy's 13 year-old son having such a sage outlook was unlikely. More fittingly, the kids simply were trying to make sense of the wrench thrown into a tire that had, up until now, run quite smoothly. And while Mike led the kids to believe that the worst was over with his ever-present if mildly fatigued Italian-American bravado, Peggy had no choice but to know better, for there was still going to be a trial due to Mike's Not Guilty plea. This meant that a defense team would be coming after him like an unrelenting swarm of barracudas in an attempt at bringing down a big fish.

Such an oceanic metaphor further reminded Peggy to finally get rid of the leftover salmon, but it also reinforced her need to have a thorough conversation with Mike after dinner, when the kids were asleep.

In the meantime, she managed to eke through the day, saying little regarding what was happening. And while most of her colleagues that she usually exchanged no more than pleasantries with didn't know Peggy well enough to say anything outright, she did seem to receive a fair amount of *Holding up okays?*, which certainly suggested that they were aware of something.

Jocelyn called Peggy in on one of her off periods to simply "check in". Once again, little was said directly, but it was clear that Jocelyn wanted to get a general appraisal of how she was doing, to which Peggy summoned all the positivity she could muster and dispel any myth of wrongdoing. For the moment, this appeared to satisfy Jocelyn, though Peggy also sensed in her an unspoken expectancy for when the other shoe would drop. For now though, Jocelyn could only have two perspectives to go by; what she may have read in the local news and what the wife of the accused was telling her, who also happened to have grown into one of the more popular teachers on staff.

Shortly after, Peggy and Cinda, her closest colleague,

had lunch together, as they sometimes did. On this day, however, Peggy would have certainly preferred to be alone, but felt it wise to keep up appearances and try to sidestep the obvious as best she could. It appeared at first that Cinda, not unlike Jocelyn, simply wanted to know how she was coping, was she getting rest and such, though at least Cinda's inquiry did not come with a sense of judgement about how Peggy would be continually productive in class should this issue become more drawn out, both legally and publicly.

While Peggy knew less personally about Cinda than she did her more socially-based friends, particularly Claire, Gwen and Judy, she felt that she actually had more of a soulful connection to Cinda purely based on their mutual love of literature and the arts. For one, Cinda taught a germane subject, English and Creative Writing. They were also both wannabe writers and voracious readers since childhood, often agreeing on the overrated status of one so-called "classic" while bemoaning the undeserved disregard for a more obscure one. Sometimes they even had pleasant yet stimulating disagreements over a work, be it by a novelist, a poet, a playwright or a painter, which created an aspect of joy in Peggy that she hadn't had since college with her close friend and roommate Tina, whom she even shared a foray into lesbian experimentation.

Given the basis of their relationship, Peggy certainly was not in fear of anything in the presence of Cinda, let alone a sudden outburst of lesbianism. Actually, Cinda may have been the safest one to be in the company of during this time, outside of Larry and her own family. And Cinda was already somewhat soft-spoken anyway and would never be one to initiate such a discussion with anyone else, especially based purely on speculation.

Then, just as Peggy took the first bite into her chicken salad sandwich, Cinda revealed something;

"My husband was a patient," she said.

Peggy was frozen for the moment, a splotch of mayonnaise in the corner of her agape mouth, as Cinda continued,

"He told me after he read about it online, then I put two and two together," Cinda deduced, never having met Mike herself. "It was about 3 years ago. He hasn't been back. It's funny, he has a history of melanoma in his family and so I was urging him to go back for another screening, but he's always been one to put that stuff off. But he remembered liking Michael. Said he never laughed so much in a doctor's office."

Peggy was actually somewhat eased by the positive experience Cinda's husband had conveyed, and the fact that it had been a few years since he had been treated by Mike lent further credibility to how good he was with his patients. How this was all such a farce.

She swallowed and wiped the mayonnaise from her mouth, "So, I guess, everything checked out okay when he went?"

"Actually, Peggy," she replied, "it's the funniest thing. He needed to have part of a mole removed."

Peggy gulped, as Cinda continued...

"He'd had it since childhood, and even I thought it was something that should be looked at. Then again, I'm a bit of a hypochondriac," she noted with a chuckle. Peggy weakly smiled, as Cinda continued, "When he told me that it was going to have to be removed, I assumed it was the whole thing, ...but it was only the Garfunkel."

Peggy took a moment, assuming she misheard, "The what?"

Cinda snickered at the memory, as she described it, "It was the weirdest looking thing, Peggy. You'd think it was some sort of Rorshach image, but when you got up close, it looked like Joseph Stalin hugging Art Garfunkel."

It was all Peggy could do to not spit the mouthful of coffee she had across the room, instead opting to gulp it down the wrong pipe and momentarily gag, which Cinda attributed to her simply finding the vignette amusing. Little did Cinda know that this was one of Mike's famous stories related to his work, one he had told on countless occasions, at dinners with friends, at dermatology conferences, even as recently as his 40th Birthday celebration all of days ago. Suddenly the nameless origin of the most famous mole in Mike's heretofore distinguished dermatological career had a face - the husband of Peggy's closest colleague; a kindred spirit whom she had known barely three months.

While Cinda never alluded that she or her husband thought any differently as to the accuracy of Mike's initial diagnosis, it unsettled Peggy. Now there seemed to be very few people who she knew that didn't have a connection to Mike's career, creating a now unbearable urgency to know more.

At the end of the school day, Peggy drove home with the kids, as per usual. Nicky and Luna went into the house where Mike had spent the majority of his day self-sequestered, unshaven and clad in his satin bathrobe like Hugh Hefner, while Peggy remained in the car and took a moment to summon the awkward courage to call Claire, whom she had still not heard from since Mike's arrest. Further, Mike had not mentioned talking with her as a patient, nor speaking with Ray, Claire's husband and his good friend. Nevertheless, she now felt compelled to take her own initiative in at least contacting Claire in an attempt to alleviate the discomfort which seemed to be rising like a sordid soufflé.

After she slowly dialed, it was of some relief that the call went to Claire's voicemail, which allowed her to leave a somewhat pre-scripted message, with a tenuous balance of concern and joviality:

"Hey, Claire – hope you're okay, honey. Haven't heard from you, so I just wanted to check in and see if you were okay. We've had a somewhat eventful few days (she lightly chuckled), *if you haven't heard, but all's good. All's just fine, so... Anyway, please give me a call when you can. Love to Ray and the kids."*

She clicked off, took a breath and, if nothing else, felt the proper seed had been planted, assuming it would only be a matter of time before Claire would respond.

Later that night, the kids went to sleep, as Peggy sat across the table from Mike. She was even more anxious than the previous day, with another cup of lukewarm coffee before her. However, she sensed that Mike, even having caught up on some proper sleep, did not have any more desire to engage in this discussion.

In fairness, it was also not a day without its own stress for him. He had to meet with Larry earlier in the day, which was taking its toll, though he had little choice. But that wasn't even the worst of it. By far, the worst for him was having to call his parents, Vic and Elaine, and inform them of the recent events. As expected, they hadn't heard anything as yet, so they were literally hearing news that their "favorite son" was going to trial for the first time from Mike himself, which of course brought upon a significant degree of apoplexy.

It also did not need to be stated that this was beyond painful and embarrassing for him.

Vic and Elaine were concerned, scared, panicked and indignant all at once, but they never assumed that Mike was culpable in any way. They quickly concluded that a currently unnamed jealous party was out to destroy him. Of course, his father and mother (on both phones in their townhouse) came at Mike from both ends with their own barrage of questions like a paternal tribunal, but Mike resisted going into the details with them, claiming exhaustion and mental fatigue, while only asserting that he was innocent, had a good lawyer and that all would be resolved soon enough.

Peggy knew that calling his parents with such news took just about everything Mike had, since he had worked all of his adult life for their unbridled pride in what he would achieve. And while their pride was unwavering, it did not make it any less devastating for him to relay the accusations, especially since he sensed that others close to him may be growing skeptical. This feeling was magnified when Peggy had discovered that he had not heard from Ray, Claire's husband, which was strange indeed, considering the time the four of them had shared together, not to mention Peggy and Mike being godparents to their son Albert. Peggy then asked if he had contacted Claire, since not only was she a patient but was due to have a biopsy later that week. Of course, this could no longer happen due to the momentary suspension of Mike's medical license, but it was nevertheless surprising when Mike revealed that he was leaving such responsibility to Monique, his receptionist.

"Why do you have her calling Claire?" she asked.

"What do you mean? Claire's a patient and Monique's my receptionist," as if surprised by the inanity of her inquiry.

"Mike, Claire's a friend," she noted.

"Yeah, and she's also a patient," before sipping his coffee.

"Okay, but why are you delegating this to Monique. Are you paying her?"

"Yes, of course, I'm paying her. She works for me," as if it was business as usual.

It turns out that even though Mike could not practice legally and had all of his medical files confiscated by the authorities, he was apparently paying Monique "off the books" to call patients whose contact information he still had by leaving voicemails at late hours so as to avoid interaction. This would be followed up by letters that she would send out on his letterhead claiming that, *"Due to soon-to-be rectified circumstances beyond current control",* his office would be temporarily closed but would resume full operation soon. In Mike's mind, this was the best way to placate his patients who had pending appointments for screenings and surgeries, and hopefully avoid their concerns during this unexpected sabbatical.

Of course, this revelation that Monique was still being

paid by Mike when their bank account took a considerable hit for $250,000 bail, not to mention that Mike could not work, was troubling for Peggy. For even if they still had ample savings in two accounts that Mike had, the fact was that their only current income was from Peggy's "pocket change" as a teacher, as Mike once referred to it.

What others were perceiving was the elephant in the room along with the other large animals, which started to make the Bubone house seem like a waiting pier for Noah's Ark. But for now, it only mattered to her that she be more in the know, to which Mike finally appeased. However, it came down to a very brief description, as if on the unspoken condition that Peggy would not inundate him with follow-up questions:

"They're trying to say that I was making inaccurate diagnoses. That I was performing operations on some people who didn't need them and then taking the money from the insurance companies," Mike slurped his coffee, swallowed. "It probably was only one or two *unproven* complaints from I-don't-know-who, and I think they just want to exaggerate the number to justify shutting me down so they can act like they're being proactive instead of sittin' on their ass, like they normally do."

She absorbed this with a certain relief that she was hearing this from the only voice that really mattered to her, but also with some befuddlement.

"*Who's* saying this?" she asked.

"The Health Commission," he replied, tersely.

"*They're* complaining?" she followed, trying to grasp this.

"No, they're saying that there's complaints," as he sipped.

"From who? How many complaints, Mike?"

"Peg, I just told you."

"No, you didn't. You didn't tell me who or how many, honey -"

"Yes, I did," his testiness growing.

"Mike, you said it was probably only one or two actual complaints, but they claim that it was more - "

"No, that's not what I said. That's not what I said at all."

"Fine, what did you say then?"

"I said that there were *probably* one or two 'unproven' complaints, but they just want to say it's more."

"So...*are* there more complaints?"

"There were *not* more complaints, honey. They're just *claiming* that there were likely more cases where there was a misdiagnosis. And they haven't revealed who, okay?" as he swigged his coffee. Peggy was now a bit lost in his description which, in turn, forced her to get up, take a few musing steps around the table,...before sitting down closer to him:

"How many are they claiming?" now in a methodically hushed tone.

"Who?"

"What do you mean who, Mike? The ones with the power to arrest you. The...the Health Commission, the police, the FBI, anybody who's put us in this position... What are they – ?"

"Peggy, you wanted to know what was happening and I've told you," he said firmly, as he clutched his *#1 Dad* mug like a chalice. "There's a trial coming up and I'll have to go into all this then, and I've already had enough grilling from Larry, so I don't need this right now."

"What don't you need? I'm your wife, Mike!"

"I know who you are!" Mike raised his voice, before becoming cognizant enough of the kids sleeping upstairs to soften his tone. "I know who you are, honey, and it's because of who you are, *my wife*, that I am trying to not inundate you with all the bullshit minutiae of what's happening here. All you need to know is that your husband is what he's always been. I'm a damn good doctor, Peg. My patients think very highly of me."

"Honey, I know they – "

"I am respected in the community, and it's all being questioned now because some others have an agenda, and I don't know who they are, okay? It's bullshit, Peg. They don't have anything on me except bogus accusations and now the burden of proof is on me," Mike banged the table as he got up to place his coffee cup in the sink, while Peggy sat with this. Realizing, in fact, that he was right that, in the eyes of American society, the burden of proof *is* on the innocent, for it was quite possible that, even if Mike were to be absolved in court and have his license re-activated, there might still be a stigma that would be hard to remove – accusations being a potential verdict in themselves.

"You can't blame me for asking questions, Mike. I just need to know this for my own sanity," she quietly defended.

"And I'm answering your questions. I answered it in all the detail that you need. I'm innocent. Listen to Larry. What does Larry say?"

"Larry's not you. He has to believe in your innocence to defend you, but all that matters to me is what I'm hearing from you."

"Fine, then forget Larry. Listen to what I'm saying and stop asking the same Goddamn questions, Peg."

"The only question I'm asking that you haven't answered is how many counts of fraud are against you," now unwavering, as Mike began to walk in a hostile circle in the kitchen like a bull being taunted by a red dish towel...

"I told you..." under an angered whisper.

"You didn't tell me how many – !"

"MANY!!!"

This word emanated from Mike like projectile vomiting and reverberated throughout the house like a cavernous echo, which recalled their trip to the Grand Canyon last summer. It was a word that went to bed with her that night, entered her dreams, woke up with her, made her breakfast and burnt her toast. It almost called in sick for her, but she somehow realized it would not do her any good to stay home, especially now that Mike was there.

It was a big house but, right now, it may as well have been a matchbox.

He never came to bed that night. He sat in his office, possibly typing an e-mail to Larry, possibly watching some diverting *Saturday Night Live* skits on YouTube that would momentarily take his mind off of all this, while puffing on one of his oak tree-sized cigars.

What was only clear was that they didn't seem to be of much help to each other at the moment.

5

——

The next few weeks saw Peggy in a sort of perpetually hypnotic state. She led classes efficiently enough to not draw undue attention, found excuses to avoid lunches with Cinda, managed brief phone conversations with Judy, Gwen and a few other more distant friends, and even spoke little to Mike at home outside of issues with the kids. Aside from that, she managed to function well enough, but it was becoming more of an effort to be on auto-pilot. Stress fueled her dreams, often resulting in Dali-esque surrealism without the melting clocks, leading to her waking up in the middle of the night and walking through their lavish garden, embracing the artistry of the perfectly red tomatoes and green cucumbers ready for picking before the weather would get too cold, recalling a fond memory from her childhood which stuck out now like a golden sunflower on a heaping mass of debris:

Ms. Dulcy, a gaunt and hook-backed old neighbor of her and her mother's, who no one ever dare spoke to, kept a garden in the back of her dank and dilapidated house which, for much of Peggy's youth, looked on the verge of being condemned and was rumored to have been haunted. Those rumors aside, she had a fairly nice if modest vegetable garden she was said to have started after her never-seen husband died mysteriously; his death no doubt aiding in the rumors of her house being besieged by poltergeists. Nevertheless, it inspired Peggy to start her own garden in the backyard at the age Luna was at now. Once a few days had gone by, young Peggy would seize any opportunity to check on the production with her pooch

Wojo, usually prompted when her mother would go on one of her many colorfully drunken rants; she recalled the first sign of growth, the first tomato that had formed, as if her first child, well before she ever thought of having any of her own. And like that first child, with her pride came a fear that there could possibly be some deformity – perhaps it would have grotesque gaping holes or weird lacerations on its skin. But this one was perfect. And in its perfection, she would realize that she had an ability that belied anything she had witnessed in her mother, who equated gardening with ruining an already neglected lawn.

The fact that Peggy, at 11, despite the turmoil that could have so easily engulfed her in its undertow, found it within herself to give life to vegetables that hadn't existed before became emblematic of hope beyond the seemingly endless overcast skies of Kelp Stream, New Jersey.

Now Peggy, at 39, caressed a plum tomato in her current garden, as the sun rose on a new morning. She thought of how far she had come, where things were at now, how things would change if the worst-case scenario came true. Suddenly a tomato would no longer be just a tomato, but a symbol of how things can be created and just as quickly destroyed by circumstances beyond her control.

She still believed Mike's innocence, but it was more tenuous now. The fact that he could not look at her, was loath to speak in much detail, that he was trying to keep the best face on for Nicky and Luna's sake but seemed to act towards Peggy as if she were an impediment to his daily well-being, created a distance between them as his trial date approached. Given their mutually erratic sleeping habits, they were barely in the same bed now, let alone having any sort of intimacy. This sort of distance was comparable to a period of a couple of years starting when Nicky and Luna were around 10 and 8, respectively, in which sex grew to become something that people only did on cable, when Peggy began to exhibit a wariness of existing solely as a mother and wife, but was emotionally ill-equipped to come up with a solution – especially since Mike appeared to be content with her role. She looked back on this period as sort of lost years for her, especially as she failed to generate any writing in her downtime. Instead, she began drinking a bit more, enough to supplant her creative inspiration; *Hemingway without the talent,* she internally jested.

It got close to being dangerous, until one weekend, when Mike was at a convention in Ohio, when the kids were asleep, Peggy looked in her bathroom mirror already with a stem glass in hand at 9:30am on a Saturday, and seemed to look through her own skin to her soul, managing to scare herself straight. She could only equate it to a sort of self-imposed exorcism, which even included vomiting in the sink, as though refusing to digest the evil spirits. Her mother drank, which may have been the ultimate catalyst to this sudden awakening.

That was as bad as it ever got, which was bad enough for her,...and yet it appeared that no one was ever the wiser as to her struggles – unlike now. Now their collective turmoil was on exhibit. Now all the vacations, celebrations, adulations and inspired fornications were a distant memory. Now their lives amounted to a bridge between those glorious events and a jury's verdict.

Still, she could live with the momentary strain between them if only she had certainty with regards to Mike's innocence and, with such assurance, could disregard any outside perceptions; all the elephants, aardvarks, rhinos and other mammoth creatures in the room would easily vacate if she simply felt confident that her loyalty to her husband was not blind.

But for now, the word "Many" was still with her,...echoing.

It seemed that it was both eons and a nanosecond between Mike's arrest and his trial date. Larry deduced that the turnaround time was so quick because the state was anxious to make an example of medical practitioners who were alleged to have committed such crimes. Regardless, the trial was a weekend away. Peggy drove home with the kids on Friday, knowing that on Monday it would begin and might soon end, for better or for worse, not long after. She ate very little during this last week (possibly a broccoli stem and a plum), slept even less, spoke even less than that to everyone outside of her students and the kids. The weekend was not going to be made any easier; Mike's parents, Vic and Elaine, would fly up on Saturday, stay with them and, of course, they would all be there with Mike in court on Monday. But it was stressful in that Peggy, who was already straining to keep a best face on for the kids' sake, would basically have to don nothing short of a Kabuki mask in the presence of Vic and Elaine. It wasn't so much to disguise her worry, but that the weeks leading up to this had created a void between Mike and Peggy that she was uncomfortable in having on display.

Since they hadn't ventured out as a family for much of these weeks, it was easier to contain the dysfunction within the house, but Vic and Elaine would expect Peggy to be Carol Brady or some such domestic equivalent – as undyingly supportive as they.

An unexpected inspiration took over as Peggy was nearing their local gourmet market, *Dispiace's*. With unbridled compulsion, she corralled the kids inside and deployed them each to meet her back with specific items, while Peggy grabbed some Cabernet, some fine cheese, organic breadcrumbs and other culinary accoutrements for that night and the weekend. She realized that, in less desirable times, she often would find something within herself to bring her out of a potentially emotional chasm; this time she would will the family into making the next 3 days into as much of a vacation as they could have within the safe confines of their lavish home. Tonight, she would make Mike's favorite dinner - eggplant parmigiana with a side of spaghetti squash. She would cook everything from scratch, as she liked to do when she had the time and energy. Since she had gone back to teaching, she would go to such lengths less frequently. But on this night, Peggy would throw herself into preparations with utterly reckless abandon. She would orchestrate Luna and Nicky as sous chefs for undemanding chopping and mincing, as Chris Martin crooned "Everything's Not Lost" from Mike's favorite Coldplay CD. All the while, Mike looked on with admiration at the sudden ebullience, sneaking in for a piece of mozzarella, dancing ineptly with Luna in his arms as he held Nicky by his waist, sipping wine, followed by a kiss on Peggy's cheek – the first one in a while; *How good his lips felt*, she thought, reminded that he was her husband; not an unshaven stranger squatting in their home, shrouded in cigar smoke.

Tonight, she felt she knew him again.

The unspoken goal on this night was to not discuss anything beyond this day. Peggy wanted the family to simply enjoy their dinner – only this meal, only the four of them together. Only positive discussions were to cross the table.

Later, they would watch a DVD together, the animated *Ratatouille*, which was Luna's favorite, as they all noshed on popcorn. Peggy and Mike seemed to simply enjoy the enjoyment, as it appeared Nicky did as well, while Luna was once again re-inspired to badger Peggy and Mike for a pet rat, as if they were all as endearing and comically adept as the lead character of Remy in the film. They had lost Lucas, their golden retriever, to cancer about a year and a half ago, and Peggy and Mike had been back and forth on getting a new pet anyway, especially for the kids. Another dog was a possibility, maybe even a cat or hamsters, but now it was like deciding to have a 3rd kid – the timing just could not have been worse.

After the movie, the kids went to bed. Mike and Peggy went to the backyard, looked at the crisp evening sky, and eventually started to make out like teenagers in the back of a movie theatre. To each of them, this was so unexpected that they probably felt like strangers to each other, which only appeared to increase the sexual intensity. They made love that night, for the first time in some time, and not quietly either. *God knows if the kids heard and, if so, what they thought* – but their potential trauma would be a small sacrifice. Peggy needed to feel as she was feeling this evening, submerging everything else so far beneath the surface that she had hoped it would eventually pop up in China and become another family's problem.

On Saturday afternoon the family picked up Vic and Elaine at the airport, both looking thinner than the last time they were up, all of weeks ago. It was clear that the impending trial had affected their appetites and their sleep; Elaine more so than Vic. Yet the intensity of their hugs were as merciless as ever. They gripped on to Mike so hard that a vertebrae nearly popped, forcing Peggy to take the wheel back home, as he was still recovering from his exacerbated back issues from his weekend jail stay, further enhanced by the unexpectedly voracious sex the previous night. The day would have all the potential to be every bit the contrast to last night's festivities, for no sooner did the car doors close and the seat belts buckle than did Vic and Elaine start with the questions, which they more or less answered themselves:

"They don't have anything to go on, right?" asked Vic.

"Of course, they have nothing. He's innocent. Like Mike said, it's a conspiracy," chimed Elaine.

"I jus' don't understand why they went after you. You gotta' small practice. You're not some...some mass conglomerate, f'Godsakes," Vic continued.

"Exactly, they should go after THOSE bastards. They're all out for the dolla'!" exclaimed Elaine.

The back and forth continued for what-seemed-like miles, with Mike barely able to interject the occasional "Ma" or "Dad" in order to feebly try and steer them off topic. Peggy was usually not one to intercede when it came to Mike and his parents, but it was getting to a point where she would have little choice, especially in the presence of the kids, even with their headsets on;

"I was watchin' that show the other night, with the scams and everything. *American…* What is it, *American Skuz?*"

"*Sleaze*, Vic," Elaine corrected.

"Right, right," Vic continued. "They had this guy who ran some nursing homes up here. They said he was scammin' residents, takin' their money for his personal use, all that. Guy was arrested, went to jail. While he's in jail, his poor wife hangs herself, both his daughters kill themselves. After all that, he didn't even do it. It was his partner. Guy gets outa' prison n' his whole family's dead."

"Why the hell are you bringin' that up for, Vic? This is stressful enough," Elaine wisely asserted.

"I'm jus' sayin' they made a mistake; *he was innocent.* That's my point, f'Godsakes," Vic defended.

Peggy nearly drove off the road at Vic's retelling this story, which she had heard just weeks ago from Gwen, who had sold a house to the very family. And as was the case then, there was little consolation that could be gleaned from a falsely accused man whose entire family committed suicide.

"Look, let's discuss this later, okay? You just got in…" inserted Mike, to which Peggy would feebly add, "Yeah, and we're trying not to discuss this stuff in front of the kids, okay?"

"The kids? What, they're in their own world back there, with the headsets'n the whatnot. They don't know what we're talking about, Peggy…" insisted Elaine, as she continued, "What is Larry telling you? He can get you exonerated, right? He's a good lawyer. Of course, he's an excellent lawyer," Elaine continued, with her knack for blending questions with her own answers, as if nothing she would hear could be greater proof of Mike's innocence than her own rationalization.

"He'll get justice for him. They have nothing. Mikey

said it himself – there's allegations of complaints with no real complaints," proclaimed Vic.

Peggy was struck by this, understanding more of what Mike said coming out of Vic's mouth than she could comprehend from Mike himself.

But there were complaints, Peggy thought. *Someone complained. Someone started this, right?*

She was still vague as to the details, mainly because she stopped probing Mike for answers to avoid further arguments. She also felt odd about inquiring with Larry separately, even though she was Mike's spouse. There was also a part of her that was simply afraid to know too much. Nevertheless, her own internal questions and observations, dormant for a few pleasurable hours, were now resurged within her brain like an unstoppable train, as she narrowly avoided hitting the occasional mailbox:

If there was any merit to this, wouldn't Larry recommend this not go to trial? Isn't it more expensive to go to trial, after all? Larry must believe in Mike's innocence, right? He has to believe that any witnesses that come forward'll be exposed as sheep in wolves clothing. Thank God Larry wasn't a patient or else that would likely compromise his ability to represent Mike. Right?

The stream of thoughts and questions continued, momentarily drowning out the cacophony of Vic and Elaine. Later, Larry would come over to discuss more things with Mike in his home office, in preparation, and Peggy would insist that he stay for dinner, as if Larry were a necklace of garlic that was keeping the vampires at bay. Again, Peggy summoned all the positive energy she could muster into leading Nicky and Luna through dinner preparations for another lavish feast, which they seemed to be effectively swept along with. While Luna would always be naturally willing to help her mother, Nicky appeared to go along more by the herculean force of his mother's convictions. In the meantime, Mike would be in the living room under the protective shroud of Larry, Vic and Elaine. Occasionally he would pop in the kitchen for a piece of cheese and kisses all around. However, the fleeting moments when Mike and Peggy would catch each other's eyes with the memory of the previous evening would be consistently interrupted by Elaine's ubiquitous entrances, which would be followed by her animated chopping of whatever vegetable appeared on the butcher block, while spouting on about Mike's innocence. This quickly turned Peggy's fun-filled food preparations with the kids into an abrasively monotonous public access cable show – hosted by a belligerent old woman.

Peggy seized any opportunity to steer the conversation back to the kids and to her job, which worked in fits – the latter subject made less of an impression on Elaine, except for the fact that she knew it was the only household income at the moment. Her opinion that Peggy made so little even prompted several offers of money loans, which were continually and politely refused by herself and even more emphatically by the pride-fueled Mike, who was steadfast in his belief that this would pass; the trial would be short, his innocence proclaimed, and his license reinstated, with the only gaffe being that he may lose some patients.

Eventually, purely as a device to muzzle Elaine and Vic, Peggy had Luna and Nicky show recent school projects to their grandparents, as Peggy continued prepping for dinner. Nicky brought out his notebook computer and displayed a slideshow of some graphic designs he came up with, with his usual lack of enthusiasm. The exaggerated sounds of the adults being impressed by his work echoing from the living room was now like the soothing sounds of the sea to Peggy's ears. Having the kids display their talents to their doting grandparents was the greatest diversion she could have come up with, as she inspected the mushroom chicken in the oven.

Then the phone rang:

"Hello?"

There was that silence again. That cigarette sucking sound...

"Hello?!"

More silence, another inhalation...

"Listen, who the hell is this...?!" demanded Peg, in a hush, before the caller hung up, as per usual.

Mike came into the kitchen just as Peggy said this, noticing the distress on her face.

"What happened?" he asked.

"They're calling again, Mike. I don't know who this is. Who the hell is this?!" she said with great unease, as Mike put his arm around her, "You really think it could be your mother?" he asked, innocently.

"Maybe, I don't know, Mike. I mean, who else could this be? Who else is this screwed up?! My God, she's scaring the hell outa' me," her Jersey girl slipping out, as it often did when she was not quite herself - or too much of herself.

"OH, MY GOD! NICKY!" screamed Elaine from the living room, which incurred a similar one from Peggy, even though she didn't know quite what she was screaming at; it just seemed to make sense to join in.

Mike and Peggy ran into the living room to find Vic and Elaine shaken by the image that Nicky had displayed to them - of all things, the famous 1968 photo of a North Vietcong member being shot in the head at point blank range by a South Vietnamese Chief of Police. Nicky had basically colorized the photo, adding copious amounts of blood and brain matter emanating from the head of the victim. If there was artistic merit in making one of the most shocking images in the history of 20th century photojournalism even more shocking, then Nicky was Picasso. However, it was not a moment of pride for them as parents.

"Nicky, what the hell is this?" Mike exclaimed.

"It's jus' something I put together. I didn't mean to show it," as Nicky picked up his computer to bring it out of the room...

"Don't tell me you showed this in school," followed Peggy.

"No, it's my own project," Nicky weakly defended.

"Project? Project for what? What made you do this?!" Peggy demanded, her fear from seconds ago replaced with indignance, as Larry, Vic and Elaine watched on awkwardly...

"I just thought it was a cool picture and I wanted to play around with it..." now with an increasing lack of artistic integrity...

But Peggy's anger coupled with the phone hang up and everything else that she was attempting to camouflage finally spewed out like a geyser – "You shouldn't even be looking at this! *This* is what you do? Play those Goddamn games and look up photos of guys getting their heads blown off?! And you show this to your grandparents and to Larry like you're proud of it?! Now everyone thinks you're gonna' be a Goddamn serial killer, and who are they gonna' blame for *that*?!!!"

There was silence.

Mike appeared to be as surprised as everyone else with how this prompted such ire in Peggy, especially since if there was anyone who would have artistic appreciation for Nicky's attempt, it would be her. But there was something about the image's unequivocal violence that seemed to expose something for her that she was appalled to have revealed, resulting in a display that was more emotional than anything she ever exhibited in the company of her in-laws, let alone anyone outside of the family.

Nicky ran up to his room, as Mike touched her arm gently, "It's okay. You don't need to go off on him like that. What's wrong?"

"You're asking me what's wrong?" she asked rhetorically. "Have you lived in this house, Mike? Do you know what's happening here?"

There was another awkward silence,...before Larry chimed in with his usual dose of lawyerly levity, "Hey, no worries, guys. Ya' got some talented kids there. All's well, okay?"

At a certain point, when it became apparent that the tension was not thinning out, Larry discreetly went out back to get some air, as Vic and Elaine remained on the couch like a woefully disappointed audience.

"Peggy, it's alright. I was just...a little shocked, that's all," Elaine added, now more so by Peggy's display.

Peggy was at a loss of how to respond, since it appeared that a merely unfortunate occurrence morphed into something larger as a result of her reaction. Was going off on Nicky in front of everyone a crossed line that suddenly made her a bad mother? *Did this suddenly take precedence over the fact that Mike has been accused of insurance fraud – "many" counts?!*

She went into the kitchen, hostilely opened the oven and could no longer determine how much longer the chicken had to cook, and now feared inflicting salmonella on everyone. Everything became distorted in this moment. The control she tried desperately to have over a bad situation was now exposed, possibly even usurped by her burst of excess. A sudden paranoia developed as she lamely attempted to caramelize the sliced carrots; doubts that Vic and Elaine may have had about her character being confirmed by this moment, potential trauma to Nicky and Luna... Leading to another unstoppable train of internal questions:

Why have I not heard from Claire? Who is calling and hanging up? Are Judy and Gwen spreading rumors about us? Is it really my mother fucking with me? Is Mike really innocent? Is she trying to reach out or just rub my nose in this shit? Who did I make love to last night – and will I ever have that again? These carrots are liquefying! Is Mike really innocent? What if he goes to prison? Elaine and Vic are unbearable – no wonder Vic Junior's on drugs! Is Nicky becoming disturbed as a result of this or just a normal 13 year old boy? Mike has to be a victim, right? Otherwise, what is all this? These carrots are gonna' be too soggy! What about Thanksgiving? Christmas? These carrots are ruined! What does it all mean?

Why the fuck is this happening to us?!!!

6

Dinner conversation very much remained on the surface. It was apparent that, at least in the presence of Peggy and the kids, the topic of Mike's case was being avoided. Instead, Vic talked about his new cast-iron knee while Elaine complained about their flight, never failing to recall the *"old days"* where you could get a Salisbury steak in economy class without having to take out a loan, to which Larry would drone on about the economics of the airlines, the endless lawsuits pending due to crashes and bombings – *to think that such a topic would actually be preferred.* Mike regressed into exhaustion, thankful for Larry's presence, if only to keep the bullshit floating in lieu of silence or the occasional, *"Pass the carrot puree."*

Nicky sulked through dinner, the residual effect of Peggy's admonishment, which she would plan to speak with him about before the weekend was out. For now, she was more than a bit exhausted herself. Luna was more disappointed in that the issue with Nicky upstaged the poem she had wanted to read:

"Mommy, can I read my poem to grandma and grandpa before they go to bed?"

"Well, I think they may be a little tired from flying and all. Why not read it tomorrow, honey?"

"We'd love to hear it," said Vic and Elaine, in usual sync as to their adoration of their precious girl, while ignoring Peggy's suggestion.

"I think tomorrow might be better," noted Mike, which stuck out since these were pretty much the only words he would utter.

"Why not tonight? Nicky got to show that man getting killed," Luna sassed, clearly not grasping that the intent was to not make Nicky feel worse.

"Luna, we're not saying don't read it, we're saying read it tomorrow, okay?" Peggy asserted. "Your grandparents came all the way from Florida today and I think they've had enough entertainment for an evening."

"Florida's not that far away, and it's not that late for them –" Luna's persistence was in rare form, prompting Mike to drop his fork on his plate, "Luna!" He needn't say a thing more, as Luna went back to her plate, her face matching Nicky's as she subtly poked at a lonely mushroom. Peggy was relieved that Mike would actually seize the parental authority in that moment, for two such admonishments by her in front of her in-laws in one night certainly would not lessen her own neurosis, and the unsettlement he knew she was feeling. At the same time, she was also unsure just what prompted his reaction to Luna, whom he never reprimanded, even during her most unruly phases. *Was he upset at Luna's obstinance? Is he upset at me for being upset? Is he feeling the pressure of things and can no longer mask his stress? Does he have doubts about justice being won?*

Maybe he simply wants this all to end soon so that things can be normal again.

In any event, after the last pieces of marble coffee cake were finished, Larry went home, the kids went up to bed and, soon after, Vic limped up to one of the guest rooms with his practically bionic knee, alongside Elaine's animated assistance, to retire for the evening.

Mike and Peggy filled up the dishwasher, then went upstairs where, after a kiss on the cheek, he would have a glass of brandy and another oak-tree cigar in his office, while Peggy saw nothing left to do but go to bed, hoping her subconscious would not roust her in the middle of the night with images of Mike getting his brains blown out by a strange Vietnamese man.

Nicky wouldn't come down for breakfast in the morning, which only kept the incident of Peggy's display in the air. Still, she made eggs and toast for everyone else and there was some discussion on what everyone could do to keep busy while Mike met with Larry and his assistant in Larry's office for some final prepping before Monday. Loath to even fathom being trapped in the house with Vic and Elaine for too long, Peggy proposed driving them and the kids to *Harbor by the Bay* for lunch, where they could watch the boats. After Mike left for Larry's office, Peggy went upstairs to talk with Nicky, as everyone else got changed for the day.

Nicky refused to let Peggy in, at first, before finally opening the door. His room was dark, except for the light emanating from his notebook computer. He lay on his bed and stared stone-faced at the screen, as Peggy sat at the foot.

"You wana' look at me for a second?" she asked, though Nicky acted like he didn't hear.

"Nick, c'mon. Close your computer and listen to me for a second, okay? It'll be painless, I promise."

After a moment, Nicky begrudgingly did so.

"I didn't mean to embarrass you like that in front of everybody, okay? It just caught me by surprise. I heard your grandmother yell, and I was already... It was just not the best time for me to be...surprised like that, and I overreacted. And I'm sorry, okay?" Nicky remained still, staring off. She knew it didn't take much for him at this stage to clam up, but she couldn't go into tomorrow knowing that Nicky was not speaking to her while his father stood trial.

"Nicky, don't hold a grudge, okay? I told you I didn't react well, and the polite thing to do is acknowledge what I've said."

He remained staring off, further challenging Peggy's patience. She wondered if she should throw his computer across the room or simply wait for him to soften.

Silence continued, as Peggy looked at Nicky, who still refused to look at her...

"Nicky,...tomorrow is a very important day for your father," she said softly but firmly. "We need to be there for him as a family. We can't be mad at each other now. We have to all be strong together. Your dad needs us. *I* need us. We all need each other, so try and remember that."

He remained still and appeared to sit with this a moment, before whispering, "Is dad going to jail?"

She did not see this coming. Since the weekend that Mike was arrested, she had avoided addressing this situation directly with the kids, and yet it had never stopped. It was always happening over these many weeks, it's just that everyone seemed to respect Mike's desire to sweep it under the rug until the rug was so lumpy that they were losing their footing. But there was some satisfaction to Nicky's question in that he was aware of what was happening more so than Peggy was giving him credit for. Yes, he could be anti-social and, at times, possess the attention span of a flea, but she was nevertheless moved by his concern.

"No, he's not," she replied, with forced confidence.

"Did he do anything wrong?"

"I don't think so, honey," she answered, carefully. "Your dad's... He's worked very hard to give us so much. I don't think he would ever do the things that they're saying but...sometimes it's hard to prove away what others may accuse you of. It's just how things are in the world. So...we just have to hope that others think the same way we do."

"I don't know what to think, mom," he replied, sounding almost like a man in his uncertainty.

"Why do you say that?" she asked. "Nicky, has anyone said anything to you at school about this?"

"No," he replied.

"You sure?"

"Yeah, I'm sure."

She didn't quite believe this. Then again, her fellow teachers weren't exactly saying anything to her either, yet it was evident that they knew something.

"Are you just...afraid?" masking her own fear in the moment, to which he could only reply, "Kinda'."

She took his limp hand and gripped it, before he eventually did the same.

"It's all gonna' be fine," she promised.

With the house momentarily saged, Peggy jumped back into proactive mode, driving Vic, Elaine, Luna and Nicky to *Harbor by the Bay* for a nice lunch as they watched the boats dock and set sail while the sun's light formed little stars on the water, which often had a medicinal effect on Peggy. Having the kids there enabled Vic and Elaine to stop being inept pseudo-defense attorneys and just be grandparents, which was all the distraction Peggy could have asked for, as she watched the water and then closed her eyes to embrace the soothing squawk of seagulls.

As she allowed herself to fade into her ambient surroundings, with Luna distantly holding court with her grandparents and the near-silent clicks of Nicky playing a game and lazily explaining the inane goal of it to Vic, Peggy would suddenly be awoken by a soft young female voice; "Mrs. Bubone?"

She opened her eyes to find Tricia Wentworth, her favorite though almost catatonically shy student, standing over her, "Oh, hi, Tricia. What a nice surprise. What are you doing here?" she asked.

"Having lunch with my parents. I'm sorry if I interrupted you.".

"No, not at all. It's nice to see you. Let me introduce you

to my family, okay?" Peggy went around the table to introduce Tricia to everyone, hoping even to impress Elaine and
Vic a little more, since Peggy's career never really seemed to
be much of a reality for them.

"Where are your parents?" Peggy asked.

"They're over there. My father wants to take us out on
his boat, since it's warmer than usual today, so we're going
now."

"Oh, how nice. Well, it gets a little cooler out there,
so bundle up," Peggy smiled, never failing to be a mother on
some level.

"Will you be in school tomorrow?" Tricia asked, remembering that Peggy had needed to miss a couple of days
over the last few weeks, though having no idea why.

"Um, no, actually, I'll be out tomorrow," she replied,
masking any severity.

"Oh no. Really?!" Tricia exclaimed with more aggression than Peggy ever witnessed in her. Peggy felt a momentary sadness, but was equally moved and elated to know that
her presence appeared to mean something to Tricia.

"Just some family matters. I'll be back soon, I promise," she assured, having tentatively put in for the week off,
but hoping to be back sooner given a quick and positive trial
result. Tricia feebly attempted to mask her disappointment,
said goodbye and left. Her sad walk was always the same
regardless of the environment or how bright the sun was
shining, as Peggy watched her go to her handsome and well-
dressed parents' table, deducing in that moment that Tricia
was likely adopted. *What did she come from?* she thought. Almost suspecting that she and Tricia came from similarly dysfunctional roots.

"She's a mousy one, huh?" Vic snickered, thrusting
Peggy out of her pensive state and into the annoying realm
of geriatric adolescence. Something inside made her desperately want to say – *"Well, Vic, they can't all have tits for an
IQ,"*…but she thought better, opting for a bite of her artichoke

quiche,...as she stared back out at the stars on the water.

As they walked to the car, Luna pulled on Peggy's hand somewhat aggressively, "Isn't that Aunt Claire?" Peggy's heart momentarily went to her throat, as she looked across the parking lot to see what looked like Claire with her kids. She removed her sunglasses, took a few unassuming steps closer to see what type of car they got into and, once she saw that it was a candy-apple red Toyota Camry, she was almost certain. The distance across the parking lot was a bit awkward for her to navigate quickly without screaming Claire's name, and she didn't want to simply bolt away from the kids, Vic and Elaine. Instead, she quickly opened the doors for everyone to get in, dialed Claire's cell and looked to see the reaction of the woman across the parking lot. The phone rang...and, in the distance, she saw the woman look at her phone for a moment, then click it off before getting into her car and driving off.

Peggy watched her, her optimism suffering yet another deflation.

"Everything all right, Peggy?" asked Vic from the passenger seat. She barely had the energy to respond, now leaning against the car, thinking "*With friends like that...*" Her hurt was quickly becoming anger, as she watched Claire drive away in the distance.

On the drive back, Peggy was again hoping not to crash into a mailbox, let alone the occasional pedestrian. She continued to process how Claire could just brush her off like lint; the friend that Claire had confided so much in; her personal insecurities, issues with her kids despite all her relentless helicopter parenting, her fear that Albert would grow up gay, Peggy and Mike's own godson. Not to mention a general depression that she refused to see a specialist about for fear of being like her mother, who was still alive and still in her life with regularity despite Claire's copious admissions of despising her. Even her admitting doubts about the durability of her marriage to Ray. And yet, the arrest of Mike and the fact that Claire happened to be a patient seemed to sever the loyalty without so much as a word;

Did it ever dawn on her that this is a mistake? How could she not even call or at least send a text? It wasn't as if we just met, for God-sakes. We've been friends for years. All the times at the country club, all those trips to the park, just the two of us with our kids. All those depth-filled conversations about her fucked up parents...?

And how one-sided, Peggy thought, since she never went into much detail regarding *her* fucked-up upbringing. Admittedly, this may have been more out of fear given the elite circles she rotated within, but still – Peggy remained Claire's most reliable sounding-board, and was happy to be. Even right up until Mike's party, the way Claire clutched Peggy's arm, desperate for her encouragement, despite her trust that Mike would rescue her from the early throes of cancer. Claire was an only child like Peggy and looked at her as a sister, so what did it say about her that press and rumors would take precedence over Peggy's own words? What did it say about Ray, Mike's good friend?

Not a word? Are they really going to wait for a verdict before concluding if they should continue their friendship with us?! How fucking dare she – ?!!!

"My God, LOOKOUT!!!" screamed Vic, the car now going 85 in a 55 mile an hour zone and heading straight for a propane truck. Peggy had two choices in the blink of an eye; T-bone into its side, resulting in a certain explosion, likely killing everyone involved, or what she opted to do – take a very sharp right into some thorn-bushes, narrowly missing a light post, sliding down a 4 foot hill, getting stuck in a two-foot ditch,... culminating in both airbags exploding into the faces of herself and Vic.

There seemed to be few things less depressing to Peggy than watching her car being towed out of a ditch, no less because it was a result of her own mental lapse. The one consolation was that everyone was fine, save for Luna biting down on her tongue upon impact, giving her a subtle lisp. That aside, the only real inconvenience was hearing Elaine's histrionic display – practically equating their survival to living through a terrorist attack. While she couldn't blame *this* on Muslims, as she was apt to do when so much as a blender broke, she was nevertheless shaken; "What the hell happened?! What on God's earth happened, Peggy?!!!" she exclaimed for about the 50th time. Peggy managed to blame it on the brakes momentarily locking, with her eyes internally shifting as a result of this lie.

A pleasant and diverting lunch soon-after became a doleful trip to the nearest auto shop where, for $545.00 for the mechanic to do little more than rub his grease-laden hand along the hood and trunk,...the car was deemed fixed and drivable. *Fucking Claire!*

That evening, Peggy, aided by her sous chefs Nicky and the now-lisping Luna, managed to put together the ultimate feast for everyone, as if it was *the Last Supper*. The incident with Claire compounded by driving the car off the road could have been too much for Peggy to surmount, on top of the larger issue, but the upshot was that no one died, and she didn't hit another car. But once again, she had the opportunity of creating a festive environment and would be firm in that the evening would be all about the general support of Mike, despite any uncertainty as to what was to come; particularly not knowing what was to be expected from the prosecution tomorrow. As wouldn't be unusual for a criminal defense attorney, Larry would have an idea of who would be brought forward, but could also be surprised - and it was that very element which was troubling. But Peggy wasn't a lawyer, nor was Elaine or Vic (*thank God!*), nor was Nicky or Luna. Collectively, all they had was their hope and their belief that the outcome would be in their favor, and swiftly at that.

They ate and drank, with the over-all conversation being relatively low-key and mundane. Vic and even Elaine were unusually soft-spoken; Elaine's heightened abrasiveness left at the auto-shop. All were acting as if speaking too loud now would somehow break the crystal. Mike was sedate, reserved but reasonably upbeat. Perhaps the near-accident even gave him a greater need to embrace this moment with everyone, since they very well could have all been incinerated. They had coffee and, while the plan was for everyone to retire early, Peggy made it a point to have the family gather around in the living room to hear Luna's poem, which she had never heard herself. She had only hoped that it wasn't about a family who killed themselves after the patriarch was wrongfully sent to prison.

It even crossed her mind; *perhaps this is to be the last event of our previously normal lives.*

Luna was void of her usual confidence when at the center of attention. Her now Elmer Fudd-like delivery had something to do with it. But, like Nicky, she also seemed to have somewhat of an understanding as to the fact that their father was being judged on whether he should be a free man or taken away from them for a time.

She pulled out a folded piece of paper on which she had written her poem in longhand, delivering each line as an emotional lisping hiccup:

"*My Father –*
I know him,
I luff him,
He's given uff our home.

I know him,
I luff him,
He'd never leave uff alone.
I know him, I luff him,
I want him home every day,
No jail cell bars,
No poleef cars,
Just home with uff - to stay."

Soon after there was collective sniffling among Vic, Elaine, Mike and Peggy, with moisture from their tear ducts illuminated by the ceiling track-lights. Nicky was generally not one to express emotion at this stage, especially anything by way of his little sister, but he appeared close, seeming to restrain himself as he stared at a faded wine stain on the carpet from Mike's birthday party.

Peggy had a variety of feelings in this moment; anxiousness for what lay ahead, pride at Luna's ability to convey her feelings, even jealousy at the fact that she could do so creatively when Peggy was still unable to, even if she could not help but still find the poem a bit trite; paling in comparison to Luna's earlier opus, *"The Hyena Ballerina"*. Ultimately, however, she was pleased that the day at least ended on a better note than it seemed destined for. And as she and Mike looked at each other, there appeared to be something unspoken that was nevertheless clearly understood by the two of them.

She just wasn't quite sure what it was.

7

They all took Mike's Chrysler minivan to the courthouse after breakfast, saying very little on the way. It was hard to believe that all 6 of them could be crammed inside with only the sounds of the engine being heard. Peggy didn't know what to think or what anyone else was thinking, as she looked out at the overcast sky, but her exhaustion led her mind to venture to a future dinner party at their house where she was holding court – a circle around her clasping bubbling victory champagne, all idolizing her and Mike for navigating through such an arduous period unscathed and already able to spit in the eye of the unfounded accusations with the usual elegance. Queen's "We Are the Champions" loudly echoed off the walls and high vaulted ceiling, laughter abounded, and she could even smell and taste Le Sec's famous crab-stuffed mushrooms being doled out by hired caterers, drowning out the remnants of the coffee on her taste buds from earlier, before "We're here, honey."

Peggy replied, "I know, and it's wonderful, isn't it?" her eyes closed, speaking to Mike atop the granite coffee table, before their adoring throng.

"Peggy, we're here. We're at the courthouse," enunciated Mike, waking her up to their current reality.

After Larry met up with them, Mike kissed and hugged everybody tightly before he, Larry and Larry's assistant took their seats at the defense table. Peggy could barely observe Nicky and Luna embracing their father without losing it, but it appeared that Mike was confident; at least he appeared so to the family. Larry undoubtedly was at the peak of his lawyerly assurance, undaunted by anything that could be brought forth by the prosecution; to the extent that Vic and Elaine believed that he could disprove any claim based purely on his immaculately ironed and color-coordinated suit and tie combo, perhaps more than his actual experience as a lawyer. Peggy wanted to equal their level of confidence, but a part of her could not overlook the fact that some things were simply out of their hands, regardless of Mike's innocence. It would come down to a jury – and a judge – potentially coerced by a fiery prosecution team that would be going for the jugular; any mistake Mike possibly made, any unconscious errors, could be blown up to Nuremberg-level proportions. *And then what?*

She took a breath, realizing she had seen far too many courtroom movies and television shows, which were certainly infusing her mindset. To counter this, she tried desperately to think of exercises from her yoga class; mind-cleansing acrobatics, downward-facing dog-like perception changers, anything that could ease her hyperventilation, as she clasped the hands of Nicky and Luna while sitting a few rows behind Mike and Larry. Finally, she started to count the hairs on the back of Larry's head which, for the moment, did the trick,...as if she were counting sheep in order to sleep. She separated the natural gray strands from the ones tinted by coloring, which had become a sort of burnt tangerine, making her secretly hope that Larry's half-ass dye job would not be something the jury would be asked to consider in their verdict.

Soon after, the bailiff said something, the judge entered, and the lawyers spoke – much of this blurred together for Peggy, almost as if she were watching golf or some other inane sport which she didn't know the rules to. She would watch Mike periodically to try to assess how she should be absorbing all this, but couldn't make the distinction on his handsomely neutral expression in between his occasional whisper to Larry or his assistant. *What's being said? Are we winning this?*

Eventually someone took the stand that Peggy faintly recognized, though, at first, she did not know from where... until she spoke. She was a temporary receptionist who filled in for Monique for about 2 months when she went on medical leave about a year and a half ago. While it was rare that Peggy came by the office, she made an appearance a few times during this period and remembered exchanging pleasantries with her, though Peggy also remembered being somewhat intimidated. Her name was Violet Summers, and as if her stripper/porn star name wasn't enough, she had (and still had) a most curvaceous figure – the kind that the average heterosexual man with a pulse could not be oblivious to. Since this period preceded Peggy's return to teaching, it was a particularly vulnerable time for her. Therefore, Violet's presence eventually gave way to thoughts that Peggy had never concerned herself with regarding Monique, whom she always took great comfort in, not only because of her generally sweet nature but also the fact that she was a rather frumpy, pear-shaped, flat-chested woman who put make-up on as if applied by a funeral director. To be even more blunt, she could not have been less likely to end up blowing Mike under his desk. However, Violet's presence had brought forth a disturbing array of infelicitous possibilities, especially during a period where Mike and Peggy had very little intimacy outside of the obligatory Good morning/Good night pecks that could have just as easily come from Elaine. Now this voluptuous, thick-lipped, sultry-voiced siren was breathily giving testimony against Mike, but it was not as a result of any sexual advances Mike had made towards her.

Violet was up on the stand for an exceedingly long time, and while Peggy initially wanted to attribute it to a male prosecuting attorney simply wanting to have her cleavage in view, she ultimately deduced that Violet was not only a witness brought forth by the prosecution – but was, in fact, the very reason this trial existed in the first place. It was then that a very strange feeling started to develop in Peggy's throat; a nervous tightening that felt as if she were being strangled by a ghost. She never felt this before, but it seemed to indicate that Violet was not merely an opportunist looking to make a name for herself as a well-endowed whistleblower. She *appeared* to have information. She *seemed* to know details, and was able to convey these with an authority that would appear tough to challenge. But she also wasn't Larry. And her only hope was that after she had her lengthy say for the prosecution, Larry would reduce this big-titted pseudo-Erin Brockovich's IQ to all but a babbling bra size. But first, Violet would be given carte blanche to say all that would prompt her accusations and, thus, this potentially life-changing trial.

In short, Mike had hired Violet Summers from a temp agency, not knowing at the time that Violet's skills extended beyond the administrative – she was actually studying dermatology. She now claimed to have knowledge of the skin and, with such knowledge, would know what would constitute a cancerous or non-cancerous mole, birthmark, et al. In sending and receiving X-rays, in addition to submitting insurance claims, Violet said that she was able to make her own deduction on what could be perceived as cancerous, and that it was when she brought up two such cases, which she believed Mike had "mis-diagnosed", that she was soon after contacted by her temp agency and informed that her services were "no longer requested". When Violet asked why, the agency said this was attributed to reports of her tardiness.

Mike would end up hiring another temp for the duration of Monique's medical leave.

It was then that Peggy had recalled Mike mentioning that Violet was *"not working out"* and was *"irresponsible"*, and further remembered the exhalation she felt that Violet's physical assets would no longer be on carnal display in Mike's office.

The mousse-laden prosecuting attorney continued to

allow Violet to divulge the alleged details of what prompted her to report Mike, which she indicated stemmed from nothing else but her simply wanting to do the right thing out of protection for the misdiagnosed patients and her sense of integrity for the profession, while shrewdly minimizing that any such initiative came from her "wrongful termination", which the prosecution shrewdly submerged.

After all, this trial was not about the latter; Mike could not go to prison for simply ceasing someone's temp assignment prematurely, even wrongfully. And yet tardiness did warrant such action, especially as her absence resulted in Mike, however briefly, manning the front desk and thus resorting his professional and respected practice to that of a mom'n pop operation. This would be a point that Larry would re-enforce in his cross examination, to which Violet asserted that she was only late twice and that, regardless, her removal was not what prompted her to report him.

"Ah, I see," Larry said, dripping condescension like honey off his tongue. "So, just to be clear, you're not here because you are bitter over being let go prematurely, correct?"

"No, of course not," Violet replied.

"But nevertheless, you *were* released prematurely, yes?"

"Yes."

"And you were released as a result of dissatisfactory service provided to your temporary employer, Dr. Bubone, yes?"

"They said it was because I was late," she assertively noted.

"Well, attendance is included in the services that you were hired for, yes?"

"Yes, but – "

"So in being late, you were faulty in your services for which you were retained by Dr. Bubone. That's certainly fair to say, correct?"

"That's...yes, but – "

"And it's certainly valid for a doctor with a sole administrative person on staff, that being *you*, to terminate the services of someone, that being *you*, who, as a result of her tardiness, puts her employer in a position of professional embarrassment. Correct, Ms. Summers?"

"I was late 10 minutes – "

"Ms. Summers…"

"Twice. I was late on only – "

"Ms. Summers, please answer the question. It's not the amount of times, it is the fact that you were *in fact* late *multiple* times, to the potential detriment of your employer's professional reputation. Correct?"

Violet began to stammer and, to Peggy's ears, it was almost musical. Larry worked masterfully at reducing a confident and intelligent woman to a shy schoolgirl within minutes. Suddenly, eight questions in succession made Violet less attractive. Even her boobs appeared to shrink, beads of sweat began to form and liquefy her once immaculately applied make-up. With a seeming last gasp, Violet asserted that she did not have her services terminated until she had questioned Mike as to his diagnoses.

Larry took a lawyerly pause, smiled, "Ms. Summers, you were let go for the reasons noted by your temp agency. So what proof do you have from the agency that contradicts the very reason you were removed?"

"I…none, but – "

"Ms. Summers, in truth, wouldn't you say that it was a gift?"

"A gift? I don't know what you mean."

"The fact that Dr. Bubone gave as an excuse for your removal your tardiness? When, in fact, he could have informed them that it was for a much more severe reason. Yes?"

Violet was uneasily clueless as to Larry's line of questioning here, "I'm not getting what you're - "

"Alright, let's try *this* approach, Ms. Summers. At the time of your employment with Dr. Michael Bubone, were you a licensed dermatologist?"

The prosecution objected, to which the judge blessedly

overruled.

Violet took a hesitant pause, "I was a student of dermatology."

"Well, that's all well'n good, but the answer to my question is that you were not a *licensed* dermatologist at the time of your employment, correct?"

"That's...yes, that's – "

"Therefore, does it make sense that Dr. Bubone would jeopardize his own career by heeding the wisdom of an unlicensed pseudo-skin expert?"

"I knew what I was talking about – "

"Answer the question, Ms. Summers. Would you expect any doctor worth his salt to allow their experienced diagnosis to be usurped by that of a glorified administrative assistant?"

"I knew what I was talking about – "

"No you didn't, Miss Summers. And it speaks volumes to the kind of dermatologist you would be if you would think that a veteran of Dr. Bubone's caliber should defer to someone like you. It would have been careless! It would have been irresponsible! And it would have been wrong! And could have resulted in the loss of his license. Are you so arrogant to believe that Dr. Bubone should have taken your advice?"

"I knew what I was talking about – "

"YOU WERE A STUDENT!" Larry bellowed, with everyone in the courtroom appearing unquestionably rapt. "Students are not doctors. Students are students, Miss Summers. Do you know what could have happened if you were wrong, and Dr. Bubone took your advice? Would you have had the responsibility of facing that patient in a few months to find that he or she *did* have cancer, and it was now inoperable because YOU, a student, in your infinite wisdom, concluded the contrary?"

"I felt that – "

"Miss Summers, answer the question. You have initiated a major allegation against my client and it is unfounded. It's unfounded because you did not know for a fact that a patient or patients did not have cancerous or potentially cancerous moles and you were not licensed to make that conclusion nor attempt to coerce Dr. Bubone. You did not have authority. You did not have that right. You did not have that expertise. You were not a dermatologist! Correct?"

Violet was all but a shaking mass, barely clinging to her convictions, "He was wrong..."

"Miss Summers, answer the question, please. You were not a dermatologist, correct?"

A nearly defeated pause, before finally, "No,...I wasn't."

Larry let the moment air out, before concluding, "So the gift that I was referring to, the one that Dr. Bubone so generously gave you, was that he didn't tell your temp agency the *real* reason for your removal because he didn't want to not allow you the opportunity of getting work elsewhere. After all, you can still get work if tardiness is in your file. But how much work could you get if you were labeled as insubordinate? And that's what your actions here were, weren't they? A subordinate questioning a doctor's authority, his decision making, his professional integrity... That is the definition of someone who may not be long for temp work, at least with *that* reputation."

Larry took a few steps, looked at the jury, looked back at Violet, "Miss Summers, may I ask today if you are currently a dermatologist?"

There was another objection from the prosecution, another overruling... "Miss Summers?" followed Larry.

At this point, it appeared that Violet was battered; two or three tears had cascaded down her face, "I had to temporarily drop out due to finances..."

"You had to drop out of school. I'm sorry to hear that, Miss Summers. However, for the court, please respond to my question so there is no remote uncertainty among anyone within these courtroom walls," Larry was about to stick the spear into the bull like a seasoned matador. "Are you currently a dermatologist?"

Violet looked at Larry with disheartened resentment, as if he was the reason for whatever failings had led to her current status; that of a drop-out who actually had to move back with her parents due to financial struggles precipitated by a recent divorce, and having a 6 year-old son in her custody. To everyone, at least to Peggy, it appeared that this young 28 year-old woman's life was reduced to a single word in response to Larry's final question for the day – "No."

"That's right, you pathetic witch!" yelled Vic, for the moment somehow thinking that he was an audience member on the *Maury Povich* show, to which the judge slammed his gavel. Nevertheless, Violet's response drew audible reactions from the jury, and Peggy looked at Nicky and Luna to assure that this was a good thing, even at the expense of a woman's public humiliation.

This woman was out of her bounds. She had delusions of grandeur. Aspirations that in no way met her actual achievements. A woman living with her parents, incapable of taking care of her own child? This bitch couldn't have less of a leg to stand on. How this even got to this point is absurd.

Court was adjourned for the day.

Despite the seeming success of the day, there was still a sense of caution among most of the family. The adults appeared to grasp that Mike was not out of the woods, for there would be another day of testimony, more witnesses who could pose a greater threat, but it was all speculation as to how much so. Nevertheless, Mike felt reasonably confident based largely on the strength of Larry's high-octane performance, especially compared to the prosecution's much more subdued approach. This of course fed into Vic and Elaine's general belief that a jury would respond more to courtroom histrionics, and that advantage alone would bode well – not to mention Larry's suit and $500 Ferragamo loafers. Larry would speak in some detail with Mike afterward before seeing everyone off, though he would remain at the courthouse for a while and call Mike later to discuss the next day's proceedings, but, at least at this point, there was still a belief that whoever came forth from the prosecution could very well suffer the same embarrassing fate as the voluptuous Violet Summers.

As he drove, Mike even confirmed what Larry had alluded to in his cross, as he stopped at a light; "I knew she had a kid. I didn't wana' put the kibosh on her getting more work. I just couldn't have her work for me. That's why I said it was tardiness. And she actually was about 20 minutes late at least 4 times. I mean, I knew she was juggling stuff, but..."

"You have an office to run, f'Godsakes," Vic bellowed. "She had ya' mannin' the front desk like you were runnin' a damn bodega. You're a doctor!"

"I know, dad, that's what I'm saying. Once, okay. Three, four times in a week, I mean... I had patients waiting." Mike seemed as though he was trying to curb the distaste he must have had for Violet by lightening his tone and even indicating some sympathy, which Vic and Elaine were not about to offer in the slightest.

"An opportunistic little bimbo, is what she is," said Elaine, seethingly.

"Larry even found out that she did work elsewhere afterwards through that same agency, so...it's not like she had nothing," Mike followed.

"Right, so what does she want? Her name in the paper?" Elaine replied.

"A centerfold in Playboy, for Godsakes. That's all they want," Vic followed. "There's no damn morality here. You're known n'respected, n'she's nothin' but a pair a' gunboats with horn-rimmed glasses."

"Vic, alright. The kids..." Elaine admonished...

Peggy didn't have the energy to interject amidst Vic and

Elaine's strident indignation, though it was clear that everyone was running on fumes after a long, intense first day – *courtlag* would be an apt description, since the feeling was that of having just gotten off of an international flight. To further the exhausted analogy, it would only be a matter of minutes before Vic, Elaine, Luna and Nicky would doze off in the car like a snoring choir secretly shot by an elephant tranquilizer. The stress was with everyone equally and, with the trial day concentrated with such tension, combined with everyone's lack of sleep the previous night, the only thing left to do was to venture into a state of slumber.

It also gave Peggy some needed time with Mike, which was harder to obtain now, especially with Vic and Elaine omnipresent. She was somewhat assured that Mike had conveyed the legitimacy of what Larry had mentioned with regards to terminating Violet, and the fact that she was now unemployed, living with her parents and not even a dermatological student, let alone a doctor, certainly further diminished her credibility.

Peggy then noted to Mike that she had received reassuring texts earlier in the day from the likes of Judy, Gwen, her colleague Cinda, some other more distant acquaintances wishing Mike and the family well during this time, and Mike had received similar cyber support. However, when Peggy asked if he'd heard from Jack, he revealed that he hadn't, which didn't necessarily surprise Peggy since she had grown skeptical of him. *If he was such a friend, why couldn't he be at Mike's trial, let alone reach out?* And again, nothing from Claire, nor from Ray. *And they must have known that the trial started today. I'm sure the whole town did.* As they passed Ray & Claire's house on Cordelia Street, Peggy mused, "I can't believe how they've just cut us off, Mike."

"And we're godparents to Albert. Some friends, huh?" he replied, with a certain fatigue in his voice.

They glanced at each other with a mutual disappointment about this, but it just as soon appeared that Mike had moved on, resigning himself to the fact that they were out of their lives. The longer they had chosen to remain M.I.A, it was as though the years of shared holidays, lunches, parties and weekend getaways barely ever happened – yet Peggy could not get past feeling cast off by them. It was an unsettling feeling that lent itself to one of her worst fears for as long as they had been a family of some wealth; a sense of being found out, not one of *them*; linked to her not uncommon internal mantra - *If they only knew what I came from.* At the same time, there was something about seeing Violet Summers again that, in Peggy's recollection of her jealousy towards her, now in turn gave her a sudden moment of clarity with regards to Claire:

Maybe Claire had a thing for Mike and it was the awkwardness that resulted in her sudden absence. Maybe she told Ray something and, as a result, they were both passively cutting us off. And, as a result of that, perhaps Ray felt inferior to Mike now – maybe a financial analyst being compared to a doctor suddenly reduced Ray to a mere grifter, of sorts.

It was then that Peggy recalled a telling conversation that she and Claire had had just weeks ago while having brunch at *Harbor by the Bay*. At that point, Peggy was just a couple of weeks into teaching again and her youthful excitement at this new phase in her life was a contrast to where Claire was at. Claire had been working in banking for a couple of years since venturing back into the workforce and it was clear that, not unlike Judy and Gwen, her career was not a source of inspiration for her. This career ennui only exacerbated a larger problem for her:

"I think Ray's seeing someone," she said in a hushed tone, as though the table were wiretapped, while her elegantly long fingers clutched around a vodka & tonic.

"What makes you think that?" Peggy asked, if not excessively surprised by Claire's suspicion.

"Well, for one, he's not interested in me. How's that for starters? He's focused on his work. Works late all the time. He comes home, he's tired, he's this, he's that…"

"Well, alright, but he's doing it for you guys, right?"

"Doing what? We don't need it at this point. We're doing better than he ever dreamed, Peg. And I'm working too. It's not all on him now."

"Alright, so he's a workaholic," trying to put the best face on Claire's chagrin.

"I think it's something else."

"Why?"

"Peggy, come on, he has a secretary. He has other good looking little chickadees on staff. He has money, they're flirty. I'm not blind to the temptations. I just… I don't know."

At this point, Peggy and Mike had rekindled a vibrant intimacy, and while she didn't like to reveal such details, Claire had a sense enough of it to be envious;

"You guys don't have these issues. I know that," she said, half-joking, half-lugubrious.

"How the heck do you know, Dr. Phil?" joked Peggy.

"Oh, c'mon…"

"What?"

"Ugh, you sicken me with your modesty, you know that?" Claire laughed, as did Peggy, but while Claire appeared to be momentarily diverted by this, looking back, Peggy clearly saw her resentment.

She then remembered Claire looking at the large boulder-like engagement ring that she always wore, gazing at it like a marital crystal ball, probably displeased at the future she saw, "You're lucky you have someone like Mike who still shows that he loves you, y'know?"

Peggy took this in, before feeling that it was the time to reveal what she normally would never tell anyone, "I know, honey, but it wasn't always like this. We've…y'know, we've had our phases."

"Peg, c'mon, there's phases and there's infinity," Claire snickered. Peggy couldn't help but grin at Claire's occasional gift with a good T-shirt phrase, but Claire wasn't looking for laughs. She appeared consumed by what her past may have done to manifest what was occurring in her life now, "You know, my father never had to screw my mother to make her come. All she needed was a rave review...and when those stopped, it was just self-medication between meals," she sipped. "My father cheated on her my whole life, Peg. It was only after her career waned that she was even suspicious, but it was the most obvious thing in the fucking world," Claire looked at her glass with unusual pensiveness. "I don't have her diversions. Y'see what I'm saying?" She sipped her drink again, gently rattled the eroding ice cubes, then under her breath, "At least we have the kids."

Peggy knew then that that wasn't enough for Claire. And for as much as Claire despised her mother, perhaps even more than Peggy did hers, she saw that Claire struggled with the possibility that maybe they weren't that different. And maybe her marriage wasn't that different either. Now it started to make sense to her. Maybe that's why she decided to go to Mike's office in the first place. Not just because she was 41 and it was an appropriate time for a woman of her seasoning to get a skin screening – but maybe it was also an easy way for Mike to see her naked. And maybe she took Mike's half-ass country club brunch diagnosis of one of her moles as a sort of subliminal hint. Maybe she played up the severity to Peggy as a ruse for the barely restrained lust she had for Mike. And maybe Mike's lack of reciprocation prompted her to fade into the ether in their time of need.

As awfully Danielle Steel-ish as any of these possibilities were, they were actually preferred. For it meant that Mike was innocent,...and that Peggy needn't be ashamed.

They arrived at home and there was no question that no one was going to be cooking that night, at least in Peggy's mind. They would order Chinese delivery and then urgently shed themselves of their court clothes like snake skin, before Peggy went to her private office to check in with her substitute regarding her classes that day. It was less a concern of the substitute's ability than Peggy's need to make her presence known, even from afar. The substitute said she followed the lesson plan to a tee and assured that she had read the cliff notes for *The Bell Jar* so that she could continue leading discussions in class. However, Peggy became instantly disheartened when she had asked if she had received any contributions from Tricia Wentworth, whom the substitute failed to recall. Peggy found it hard to describe her in any other way but as the quiet girl who blends in with the walls. Regardless, she would take personal responsibility for any relapse in Tricia's classroom performance.

I can't be gone too much longer, she thought. *She'll regress, just as she was starting to make progress with speaking in class.*

No sooner did she get off the phone than would she log on to her computer to check e-mails; something she always did at the end of a school day anyway.

Then something strange happened in the house.

There was an energy shift that almost seemed like a spiritual force concentrated into one consolidated moment. In the span of seconds, the landline would ring in the kitchen, an e-mail alert would ding once Peggy logged into her account, the doorbell would chime and reverberate and, to underscore it all, a distant sound of thunder,...despite rain not being in the forecast.

Luna would pick up the phone in the kitchen, but there would only be silence on the other end. "Hello?" she asked again,...then there was that cigarette-sucking sound that was only familiar to Peggy. "Who is it?" asked Luna, nervously...

At the same time, Elaine answered the front door. It was Larry.

While all this was happening, Peggy discovered an e-mail sent from Claire, titled simply *"from Claire"*, which, while somewhat cold, at least was accurate.

Now her concern with who called the landline or who was at the door or why a storm was coming was silenced. Similar to when she first heard the news from Jocelyn about Mike's arrest, it appeared that Peggy had temporary deafness – a high-pitch whistle-like sound that could summon their old dead lab Lucas from the grave, if he hadn't already been cremated. But, at least for the moment, she only needed her eyes:

Peggy,

I know you must be wondering why you haven't heard from me. Admittedly, I was stunned by the accusations against Mike, and was in disbelief. After all, we have all been friends for years, haven't we. For that reason alone, I found myself wanting desperately to believe him (and you) but as he gave me a severe diagnosis, one that wasn't fatal, but horrifying and life-altering nevertheless, I felt I needed to get another opinion. My hope was that Mike's diagnosis was correct and that, with that confirmation, I could support him and be there for you both during these times. We've been there for each other over the years and, while I have valued our time together, you must understand that this is an issue of my health. An issue that not only concerns me as an individual, but also as a mother and wife.

I was scared to death at Mike's diagnosis of benign cancer, Peggy, and was just as quickly assured that he would be my savior.

However, in my not one but two subsequent screenings with different dermatologists since Mike's arrest, it was concluded that I do not have cancer, and that the mole did not even warrant much concern.

What does this mean, Peggy?

Does it mean that Mike simply made a mistake – an award-winning doctor with years under his belt?

Was his arrest just a coincidence, and a mistaken one at that?

Two weeks ago I happened to speak to our mutual acquaintance, Margot Kutschner. I don't know if you were aware, but she

*was a patient of Mike's a couple of months ago. She too was told by
Mike that she needed a mole removed, but she balked and got a second
opinion – no cancer. A third – no cancer.*

Is that also a coincidence, Peggy?

*Margot had actually been referred to Mike by a woman
named Jennifer Wentworth, whom I don't know and not sure if
you do. Nevertheless, she recently found out through her general
practicioner that she had an irritation attributed to Exzema that
Mike had first cited as "possibly cancerous".*

Was this also a coincidence?

*I don't think so, Peggy. I think Mike simply lied to me...and
others. Many others.*

*I have been betrayed beyond repair, and cannot separate you
from this.*

I'm sure you can understand why.

Before Peggy could finish, let alone connect that *"Jennifer Wentworth"* may well have been the mother of her student
Tricia, there was a tap on the door; one that was almost certain to have the adverse result of recent door knocks.

Mike sheepishly came into her office with a tear in his
eye. Behind him was Elaine primal screaming into Vic's armpit. Behind *them*, a perplexed Chinese delivery man with two
bags of Chow Fun. She heard Mike begin speaking, "Peg,..."
which then quickly devolved into a sort of bizarre cacophony
of words that made as much sense as an auto-mechanic's assessment of an engine. Later, she would be able to better comprehend everything after several explanations from Larry.

The gist was that Mike would be advised to plead guilty
at the encouragement of Larry. Apparently, there was going
to be too much insurmountable evidence against Mike for it
to be worth proceeding with the trial, and could result in
a longer sentence for him if convicted. There would be the
results of agency findings in his x-rays, testimony of other
professionals in his field and the possibility of patients who
would confirm a misdiagnosis of their own. Claire's e-mail

would confirm some of this, aside from closing the door on their friendship forever. The question for Peggy now was how long this had been going on, in addition to quite a few other questions that circulated within her: *how long was Mike going beyond the realm of medical ethics in the name of greed? Why did he feel compelled to do so? Was he trying to make up for the short-comings of his older, ne'er-do-well brother? How could he lie to me?*

It then dawned on her – *Sylvia Plath didn't require nearly as much of a rationalization for sticking her head in the oven.*

In the end, Mike would be sentenced to 4 years in an upstate minimum security prison in a town called Hawking; known primarily as a town wherein a prison was located, a couple of auto-shops and a diner which was known to have decent rhubarb pie.

He could possibly get out in two, which Larry would work to negotiate, but it was certainly fair to say that the damage was sufficiently done.

As a result, the following happened in relatively quick succession:

1.) Mike's assets were seized, which were also predominately Peggy's, since most were under his name.
2.) The house was seized.
3.) Mike's minivan seized.
4.) Peggy was fired from Cold River High School, and given no severance of any kind, and wasn't even there long enough to collect unemployment insurance.
5.) Peggy had to pull Nicky and Luna out of school, for a variety of reasons;

a.) She could no longer afford to keep them

there.

b.) She could no longer afford to stay in Cold River

c.) They had all become pariahs.

8

The erosion of much of their possessions took place in time for Peggy and the kids to be effectively homeless just a couple of weeks shy of Christmas Eve. The upshot, albeit a needle-sized one amidst a haystack, was that there would soon be a Christmas break, which would ideally buy Peggy more time to get settled somewhere else and enroll Nicky and Luna in a new school for the second half. The pervading question, of course, was just where this would be when they were currently vagabonds.

All of a sudden, Violet Summers seemed very stable by comparison.

After all was said and done, aside from their clothes, some electronics and a few other necessary items, Peggy would have only the mere content of her personal checking account, which contained the few payments she had received from teaching, as well as her own car, which had started to make unsettling clinking sounds again as a result of driving into a ditch just weeks prior. *Fucking Claire!*

To say that the roof caved in was an understatement. The sky had fallen and crashed around them – leaving them surrounded by thick clouds. There was no clarity. Friends were no longer friends. Colleagues were no longer colleagues. Calls stopped – texts stopped – e-mails stopped, except for Spam or the occasional hacked e-mail address of an old acquaintance that would include a link for a prescription drug; Peggy was almost desperate enough to reply to these. The exception here was Monique, who was almost equally traumatized by Mike's actions and, as a result, needed to go back to temp work after years as Mike's loyal administrative assistant. She also could have held a grudge considering Mike's actions may have sent her to prison by process of association, but it was clear that Monique was oblivious. If she was ever suspicious, her loyalty to Mike and her assumption that he could not have been capable of such an offense took precedence. Though she may very well have resented him now, that did not transfer to her feelings for Peggy, whom she had always liked. Nevertheless, it was a surprise to Peggy when they spoke that Monique would offer her home, if it was needed.

This moved Peggy beyond words, but it also greatly unsettled her – *how bizarre that someone who once was employed by Mike is now offering us shelter.* It was a jarring twist of fate and one that, at least at first, was one that Peggy felt she was able to gratefully yet politely refuse, even while paying an exorbitant daily rate at the Heston Inn – a 5-star hotel just on the edge of the Cold River border.

What would have been the most logical option was staying with Vic and Elaine down in their West Palm Beach townhouse temporarily. This would have given them the option of being clearly out of the eyeshot of their former Cold River neighbors and friends, while giving Peggy a little time to get her head together before resettling back up north somewhere. Of course, returning would enable her to be closer to Mike for visits with the kids while he was serving time. But a phone conversation with her in-laws would prove the undoing of this plan, which Peggy recalled as she drove the kids on her way to a modest *mo*tel in Moss Creek; a somewhat sterile in-between town just outside Cold River, as the snow descended on the windshield:

"Everything'll be fine. The kids'll be fine, Peggy."

"I appreciate that, Vic. I'm afraid that's the only option that I have now".

"I still can't believe this," said Vic.

"It's a Goddamn nightmare," Elaine added, on the other

phone.

"I know," as Peggy tried her damnedest to avoid even the slightest crack in her voice.

And then there was this...

"You want me to get their tickets?" Vic asked.

"Oh, no, that's okay, Vic. I can – "

"Y'sure?"

"Yeah, I can take care of that."

"Well, if you get 'em and change your mind, I'll send a check up to you, okay?"

Peggy was now hearing certain words that she found unsettling...

"Vic, I'm not... What do you mean send a check to me?"

"Well, you're gonna' find a place, right? You gotta' find a job."

"Vic, you know that I was planning to come down *with* the kids, right?" surprised that she even needed to state this.

There was an odd silence on the other end.

"Peggy, we don't... We thought you wanted to be up there."

She then lost a breath, "Vic, Elaine,...did you really think I would put Nicky and Luna on a plane by themselves so they can stay with you without me?"

"Just temporarily, Peggy. We know it's not forever," Elaine responded.

"Until you get stabilized up there," Vic followed.

"We would be up soon anyway to see Michael. You'd see the kids then."

"Um, no, that's not... That's not what I wanted at all," Peggy exclaimed.

"Peggy..." Vic feebly attempted...

"No, I'm not... I'm sorry, I thought there was an invitation to let us *all* stay there temporarily until we...until I had a chance to figure some things out. A way station, that's all. I mean,...I don't have the money to throw away. I needed your help."

"Peggy, we're giving you help. We're taking the kids off your hands until you can get settled without havin' to worry. And we said we'd buy their - "

"I'm their mother, Elaine. Of course I'm gonna' worry if they're not with me."

"But they'll be with us," Vic asserted.

"Vic, Elaine,....I'm not getting this, okay? Are you... You have room. You have a couch I can stay on. I mean, we're talking days, a few weeks..."

"No one's turning you away, Peggy. We just didn't think that'd be what you'd want to do, for the sake a' the kids," Vic again tepidly attempting to console.

"They need stability."

"I know they need stability, Elaine. You think I need you to tell me that?"

"So that's why we offered to have them while you can focus on yourself."

"What the hell are you talking about? Focus on myself? How can I focus on myself when my kids aren't with me? You think that'd be stable for them?"

"Right now, we think it would be," Elaine slipped, now sounding more like the rigid head of a convent than a supportive in-law.

Peggy's chest was expanding. She had never hyperventilated before, but an asthma attack for a non-asthmatic appeared to be on the horizon. She tried to clear her mind to not say the wrong thing, but dealing with Vic and Elaine now was like trying to scream with a mouthful of marbles.

"I appreciate you wanting to take them, but I can't be apart from them," she said, nearly broken. "I really had hoped that we would be all equally welcomed. I mean..."

"You'd want to live in Florida?" Vic asked, with feigned innocence.

"No, not *live*... As I said, just a safe haven. I mean, we can't stay in Cold River. You know we lost the house, right?"

"Aren't you staying with somebody, Peggy?"

"Staying with somebody? Vic, we're in a hotel."

"Oh, my God, these kids are being raised in a hotel, f'Godsakes?!" Elaine shouted.

"Well, where else do you think we could go, Elaine? We're pariahs. Pretty much everyone we knew wants nothing to do with us."

"Dear God, Vic, what *hasn't* this woman done..." Elaine followed, in a hushed tone that she could have only known would be overheard...

Peggy lost her breath again, "What *I've*...? What?!"

There was an unsettling silence once Peggy questioned if she heard Elaine correctly, but there was little doubt.

While Vic was at least making an effort for this to not be apparent, Elaine was incapable of maintaining a façade. By contrast, Elaine's tone had been leaning increasingly towards blame, and now her words had finally caught up. Now there seemed to be very little reason for this conversation to continue. But as much as she wanted to with every fiber of her frail being, telling Vic and Elaine to fuck-off simply was not something she could do. "Vic, Elaine, I'm...I'm sorry to stress you out here. I'll be in touch soon, okay?" she said through a cracked voice...

"Peggy,..." Vic started, but she knew it wouldn't be anything that would save them, and, frankly, their mere voices were now making her sick to her stomach.

"Take care," she managed, before clicking off.

She stood there, clutching her phone, hoping beyond all hope that she would not need to call them until they were settled somewhere, but more accurately desired to never have to call them again.

Her desperation in this moment would be in sync with a call from Larry, who had been checking in on them periodically and appeared genuinely concerned about where they would end up, knowing well that Peggy was uncharacteristically vulnerable. He obviously knew what transpired, what they had lost, though he didn't necessarily foresee Peggy and the kids as actually being homeless as a result. He probably too thought that Vic and Elaine were an option, not realizing the tenuousness of their relationship, and was also not in the know regarding Peggy's side of the family, of which there was none; an estranged mother whose name he never heard mentioned.

But he would call in a moment of Peggy's unequivocal despair, where she saw little option but to pick up – *What can it benefit me not to answer?* she thought, knowing well that Larry had essentially been the symbol of hope in all this. There was hope in his defense of Mike that he would be exonerated. Hope that he was innocent. Hope that belied a miscarriage of justice and an utterly wrong obstruction of their lives. Without Larry, it seemed that things may have fallen apart the moment of Mike's arrest – but there was hope, because Larry was there. An old friend to both of them, who believed and who knew the law like a neurosurgeon knows every aspect of the human brain. No crevice would be overlooked. Yet even in Mike's ultimate guilt and prison sentence, Peggy, with her resistance significantly lowered, could ill afford to not believe that Larry's presence still rendered hope. Things wouldn't be too bad for Mike in prison, because somehow Larry would see to it. And his knack for allaying Peggy's fears was something that she simply needed. A warm blanket, of sorts. And so, at this emotional moment on a fragile precipice, when Larry asked how they were holding up, Peggy simply broke down...

"Larry, I'm...I can't believe we have nowhere to go. We're homeless, Larry. I have no family, my in-laws blame me for...and I... I just don't know what to do. We're at the Heston Inn and...and...and it's expensive..."

Larry interrupted Peggy's mucus-soaked admission with his own surprise. She could not ask anyone they used to know, for they were, in essence, the enemy of the people. It made sense to him, considering how wide a net Mike's practice had cast among their social circle, and yet he was still surprised that it came to this. Nevertheless, without batting an eye, he threw a rope for Peggy, and thus, she would be pulled out of the quicksand...

"Peggy, listen, you can't blow your money on staying in a hotel, okay? I'm your friend. I look at Nicky and Luna as my own kids, and I want you guys to stay with us, okay? We have the carriage house in the back. You can stay there, we got two extra beds for the kids, so...come over. No arguments."

Peggy's pride could not even appear in this moment. This was, without question, the best option for them now. Larry had space, she knew his wife, Carole, remotely but always pleasantly, and Nicky and Luna knew their two daughters. To know that she could conceivably stay there for a couple of months just to get her head on straight and come up with a foreseeable plan was invaluable, and so all that could be said was "Thank you so much, Larry."

For the next few days, there was the vague illusion of Peggy and the kids being on a sort of extended vacation. They were in comfortable surroundings, not far from their old house, and, for now, they had everything that they needed. But the lack of stability was too apparent for her to take any enjoyment in Larry and Carole's ridiculously gorgeous home. To offset how utterly strange it was to have most of an entire family staying with another family, when they used to live 10 minutes away, Peggy insisted on getting groceries and that Nicky and Luna assist Larry and Carole's daughters in household chores, such as taking out the garbage and walking their dogs, Crosby and Nash (Stills was hit by a car a couple of years ago.) It couldn't disguise the fact that they were still taking up space, but at least it was something for Carole to observe. In truth, their residing there felt very much like an audition for Carole, since Peggy never really had the opportunity of knowing her very well. When Larry would show up at events or get-togethers, it would often be solo. And when she did join Larry for the occasional dinner party, Peggy tended to be among the more socially extroverted Claire, Judy or Gwen.

However, what Peggy *did* know of Carole was interesting; she co-managed an art gallery designed to showcase works of little-known New York-based artists. In recent years, she relegated herself to part-time status in order to focus on raising the kids and her own painting. It was clear that whatever money she made was no more than Peggy made as a teacher, but she had long been lulled into the comfort of the large net provided to her by Larry and his incredibly successful practice. Peggy's fear now was feeling in any way that they were a nuisance, and anticipated a moment when Carole would show signs that enough was enough. In actuality, Peggy appeared to be a pleasant diversion for Carole, since they shared a similar cultural sense; discussing art or books over coffee in the morning or after dinner. It even brought to Peggy's mind her relationship with Cinda, a friendship that she regretted would likely fade now, as did her friendship with her college roommate, Tina.

Peggy managed well enough to make sure that the kids, or she, in no way imposed themselves on Larry's family's day-to-day life, though it did appear as if no one was complaining. Larry and Carole seemed happy to have them, and their daughters (Brittany and Miley) enjoyed having Luna. They were only a year apart and they even attended the same school, though it only became awkward when they would leave in the morning, with Luna staying home. Nicky was certainly the least able to maintain a façade, and was at his most introverted during this period, which was saying something. This was not made easier by Peggy's attempt to act as an interim teacher for both Nicky and Luna. She'd set aside 2-3 hours for each and patch together a very makeshift lesson plan which, admittedly, was wanting, since she barely knew what they were being taught. If nothing else, she felt it was something to help offset the diminishment of brain cells while they were residentially adrift. Of course, where Luna would indulge Peggy's efforts like the dutiful daughter she could often be, trying to get Nicky inspired was akin to emoting to a clam; he was nearly unresponsive and often resistant of Peggy's efforts.

After their first week, Peggy largely gave up trying to teach them, realizing the distraction of their environment and situation was inevitable. But she did assign them books to read and wanted to have them write a report after they were finished, in an attempt at being somewhat progressive. *It's a fast world out there*, she thought. *It doesn't take much for the kids to be set back.* But with not having a home, their father being in jail, the structure of a once indestructible family having eroded, they couldn't help but be set back. They all were, and there was little denying it.

She also spent much time on her laptop computer scouring for teaching work like a hermit crab on a beach, calling schools for the kids and, quite simply, trying to keep her blood circulating for fear of becoming encased by their currently undesirable circumstances.

While Peggy was not making much headway, she took some solace that at least she was not rushed by a hotel's daily billing hacking away at her credit cards. They were in safe surroundings, and while urgency was palpable, she was breathing better. The carriage house was adorable, and she felt younger simply by its size. It was like a dream doll house she would've loved to have had as a young girl, immaculately decorated with a cultured woman's touch; charming quilts and hand-sewn pillows on the bed. The walls were adorned with Carole's artwork which, to Peggy's surprise, was actually decent and even lovely; largely naturalistic and unobtrusive landscapes. Places that appeared to have an aversion to people, and perhaps even symbolic of Carole's social desires.

Even in the carriage house, there were photos of their family, as if the huge main house could not even contain all the wonderful memories; trips to Disneyland, Disneyworld, the Grand Canyon, Hoover Dam, Mount Rushmore, Niagara Falls, the Alamo, Camden Yards... Many of the places Peggy and Mike had been to, minus the taintedness that would infuse any family photo of them now. This was the only real challenge of staying there; the fact that looking at a family that looked so much like hers at one time (as many families in Cold River did) was almost too much to bear. She would avert her eyes to these photos, and even resort to placing the ones on the dresser and end tables facing down.

One night, on one of many where Larry was working late, Carole, Peggy and the kids finished dinner, which they all made together. Luna was effectively diverted by being in the company of other girls, with whom she felt somewhat impressive. And, in truth, she was – though her precociousness would sometimes usurp her cleverness, in Peggy's eyes. But Peggy needed to keep one eye on Nicky. She was concerned for him. No male role models around, for Larry was so often working and meeting with clients. Nicky could barely feign a modicum of enthusiasm in his assigned culinary chore of dicing shallots, which he hated anyway. The only thing that was tethering him to any sort of structure was the book that Peggy assigned him – *The Grapes of Wrath* by John Steinbeck. A book that was not only one usually required in school curriculums, but was also nostalgic for Peggy. It was the book that, in her estimation, broke her out of her shell. Perhaps it was the fact that such an undesirable family would be the protagonists, combined with her sense of alienation aided by both her home life and her peers, who she often felt at odds with. Nicky may not have found identifiability with the novel as yet, but somehow, someway, as depressing as the subject matter was, she hoped it might have a similarly profound effect on him.

After dinner, the girls hung out in the grand den, while Nicky went to his guest room to read. Peggy and Carole remained, drinking wine and discussing recent exhibits at Carole's gallery. While Peggy was vocal in her not wanting Carole to feel that she had to play host, Carole expressed in so many words that she was grateful to have someone to share cultural experiences with. It also now made sense how Carole sometimes didn't appear with Larry at social events, for she wasn't the most gregarious and, perhaps, it took someone to be with her in a less performative environment to get the best of her, as Peggy was enjoying. Carole didn't have to be "on" for Peggy, especially in the way that Judy, Gwen and Claire had a knack for being, *and perhaps "on" was ultimately all they really were anyway.*

By contrast, Carole appeared to simply want to be as she was before she met Larry and not feel beholden to being a type of presentational wife; she liked to wear jeans, didn't care for much make-up or a diamond below every knuckle. So it was an awakening for both of them that, although their husbands were friends for some years, they now had the opportunity to forge a real friendship themselves:

"Let me take you and the kids to the gallery tomorrow," Carole suggested, as she sipped her Merlot.

"Oh, Carole, that'd be wonderful. Are you sure?"

"You deserve a little culture after what you guys've been going through. It'll be like a field trip for the kids."

"Oh, they'd love it!"

"Yeah, give yourself a break. Take tomorrow off and let's just have fun. We can go to this nice little café' nearby for brunch. You shouldn't see anyone you know, since it's pretty remote. You know Packinsau."

Packinsau was a quaint little town about 20 minutes south of Cold River and, indeed, despite it being a relatively short drive away, managed to be quite a different social climate than Cold River. Packinsau was more middle-class, and known to be more of a fishing town that in recent years sparked the interest of various not-for-profit organizations due to low rents. While it was far from a budding metropolis, the downtown area had become sort of a best-kept-secret among bohemians and art lovers, as it now contained a few nice brunch/lunch places, a few galleries and even a small community theatre company, the Packinsau Players.

Carole continued, "Right now, they're exhibiting these photos from this woman who lives upstate. They say she's pretty much been a hermit for decades, so no one's heard of her. This is her first exhibit, so you may get a kick out of it. It's not mind-blowing, but good work. Straight forward."

"How did they find her?" Peggy asked.

"Y'know what, I have no idea. Our curator has a knack for finding these people. As I said, these aren't famous people. They're sort of plucked from obscurity, which is basically the theme of the gallery."

"Well, I'm intrigued," Peggy smiled, as she sipped her wine and, for the first time in over a month, was almost relaxed as she let her spine ease into the couch in Carole's den.

They spoke into the wee hours, largely about art that they loved of late and what inspired them, how Carole got started painting only after she became a mother and, admittedly, needed a creative catharsis to deviate the constant label of motherhood. "I'm sure you've noticed that I don't paint people," she joked.

"Actually, I have," Peggy smiled.

Carole knew inherently that she didn't need to say more, that Peggy understood that many artists (be they professional or a decent amateur) emanate a certain idealization of the world in which they wish to see. She knew in that moment that Peggy not only understood but appreciated that she simply was not the standard affluent Long Island socialite. She liked solitude, creativity, silence and the company of the like-minded.

Carole's post-natal creative burst was, of course, a stark contrast to Peggy's who, upon becoming a mother, would actually become creatively inhibited. It was only by aid of the wine that Peggy would go into as much detail as she did regarding how, at this point in her life, she had hoped to have a few books of poetry and at least 3 or 4 novels. Not only had she not come close to such achievements, she also couldn't recall where any of the writing that she was proud of was. At the same time, she rationalized that if she did come across any of it, she'd very likely be dissatisfied.

"You'll write something soon. It'll come," Carole said, with relaxed assurance.

"I don't know, Carole. I don't know where we'll be in a month, let alone think of when I'll be able to sit down and write."

"Who says you have to sit down? You write when something comes to you."

"But I don't think anything can."

"There's your block. If you're sure nothing can, it won't. But just leave yourself open. Maybe one day you'll be in line at the grocery store and you'll see a pregnant woman, or a fat man with a cane, and it'll trigger something. Then maybe you'll pay for your groceries and be so inspired, you'll be writing on the receipt on the roof of your car."

Peggy was not in the best state to be inspired, but was nevertheless moved by Carole's words. At least it made her feel as if her life was not over because of someone else's actions. She could exude some control and somehow, through the barrage of obstacles, come through on the other side as more-or-less what she aspired to be in college. At least, in that moment, there was a faint glimmer that this could occur and, with it, something that would give her momentum for tomorrow, aside from the responsibility she had for Nicky and Luna to not have a complete nervous breakdown.

By the time Peggy and Carole decided to retire for the night, Peggy marveled to herself at how long they could talk without mentioning their husbands. She even wondered if Carole went out of her way to not discuss Larry in her presence in order to avoid drawing attention to the current imbalance of Peggy's relationship with Mike. But somehow it didn't seem like Carole was making such an effort. It was more like she had the natural ability to not speak about Larry with veritable ease. Perhaps this was the secret to their connubial success after 24 years together.

9

—

The next morning, Carole drove Peggy, Nicky and Luna to Packinsau. Weather-wise it was a day almost identical to the day when Peggy brought the kids, Vic and Elaine to *Harbor by the Bay* prior to Mike's trial. The sun exuded the same peaceful brightness that, as a kid, Peggy remembered blanketing her like a light from heaven. At this point, she and Carole talked almost in an unbroken stream, with Luna occasionally interjecting an observation somewhat beyond her years.

"Do you know Diane Arbus?" asked Luna of Carole.

Carole looked at Peggy, both impressed and stunned that Luna would know of Arbus, the photography pioneer of the far less desirable side of urban life.

"Wow, you know Diane Arbus?" beamed Carole. "You're so cultured, Luna."

Peggy could only smile, since she knew Luna would be bound to impress Carole at her knowledge of that name.

"I know her work, sure. How do you know about her?" asked Carole, with an impressed smile to Peggy.

"My mom took me to see an exhibit of hers in the city."

"Oh, the one at the Met?"

"Yeah."

"Oh, I saw that one too. What'd you think?"

"Kinda' depressing."

Carole smiled, in partial agreement, "A lot of her stuff is, yeah, but you can still like it, right?"

"Yeah, she's interesting. I guess she had a lota' problems, and it sort of shows in the work."

Of course Peggy did not bring up the details to Luna of what befell Arbus in her life at the time, but touched upon her struggles with depression. Peggy was also attempting to nurture Luna's fleeting interest in photography and give her a sense of the artist's catharsis – a subliminal way of noting that true art is often beyond the surface of things; *it is often a tragic excavation,* Peggy felt.

Nevertheless, in Luna's response she was reminded of Tricia Wentworth's observation regarding *The Bell Jar,* which floored Peggy less than two months prior. But as was the stage Luna was at, and what she was exposed to in her heretofore young and fairly privileged life, it was understandable that she would have a hard time connecting with such an artist – and yet, it was still impressive to Peggy that Luna would get enough from her to know that no one could take such photos without their being some sort of scarred person behind the lens, just as no intelligent person could read Plath or Anne Sexton or Charles Bukowski or Jim Carroll without sensing a similarly damaged soul; a sort of tortured creativity that Peggy secretly envied.

It was also interesting in that Peggy realized she had never voiced her admiration of such artists to her Cold River clan, who she knew, despite their educations, would dismiss such artists as depressives, opting instead to engage in, what Peggy would deem, the more surface veneer of culture; Andy Warhol paintings, Bronte novels, etc. She even once attempted to fruitlessly explain to Claire, Judy and Gwen what appealed to her about having her class read *The Bell Jar,* which appeared to go so far over their heads that her explanation may have ended up in the Long Island Sound.

Still, it was a moment of pride for Peggy that she would have a daughter en route to being a woman not unlike herself, except now there was a potential for the trauma of Peggy's childhood to manifest somewhat in Luna by what they were going through in the present, which she feared might ultimately prove more damaging. This was more evident in Nicky who, being a boy, felt all the more excluded in their temporary, female-dominated surroundings. She could barely look at Nicky and not see Mike – which made it all the more difficult for Peggy to keep his spirits afloat, let alone her own. For now, at least, Peggy owed a debt to Steinbeck, whose *Grapes of Wrath* was serving as a pacifier to Nicky as no book had had since he was a toddler glued to *You Stink and Other Smells*, which had virtually no text. And at least it momentarily would ween him away from his video games.

It would also help offset how he might have been acting out otherwise, thus affecting Luna and then eventually creating an unsightly display before Carole, Larry and their kids. But as the remaining pages that Nicky had to read of *Grapes* dwindled, she knew their facade could not last for long.

Regardless, the day that Carole had generously laid out for them was young, and Peggy was as welcoming as she could be of the diversion.

They arrived at the Feldman Gallery, which was currently closed but since Carole had a key, they had exclusive access to the current exhibit, entitled *"The Photographs of Evelyn Morse."*

"Who's Evelyn Morse?" Luna asked Carole, as they started to peruse.

"Evelyn Morse, Luna, is a photographer. She's not really known. She lives in upstate New York somewhere, but she's sort of a secretive person, so not much is known about her."

"Is she gonna' be here?" Luna asked.

"We wanted her here, that's for sure. Our curator who organizes all of our exhibits, he was trying to get her to come down, but she didn't want to have much to do with it."

"That's odd," Peggy chimed in. "She's an unknown photographer getting an exhibit of her work, and she doesn't wana' see it?"

"That's the thing. She told Bruce, *'I know what the photos look like'*. Real character," Carole laughed.

"Sounds like the Emily Dickinson of photography;

she'll do the work, but won't leave the house," Peggy added with a smile, as her eyes moved on to the next photo. At first glance, it appeared that Evelyn Morse was a photographic kindred spirit to Carole's work, in that a person was nowhere in sight of the many landscapes, hills, abandoned cabins, armories, mills and factories she photographed in or near her very remote town.

"Whata' y'think, Nick? Not bad, huh?" Carole asked Nicky, whose expression had morphed into a scowl of indifference.

"s'okay," he barely uttered. Peggy eagerly inserted herself to deflect any lack of appreciation Nicky would exude, even if Carole seemed to have enough of an understanding as to why he could not just forget that his father was in prison.

Peggy escorted Nicky by the hand to a photo that did not create much of a different vibe from the previous one, "This is kinda' cool, huh? That's a cannon."

"I know it's a cannon," he replied.

"But the way the camera's inside it, and the sunlight. It gives it kind of a nice effect, doesn't it? I think it's pretty cool," Peggy boasted, not really impressed by it herself, but clearly attempting to arouse Nicky's emotional state at the mundane. Of course, this was no small feat for someone who had been exposed to one of the most legendarily violent photos in history.

"Anyone can photoshop that. It's like such a generic image. If you google *cannon*, like a million images like that'll pop up," Nicky snarled, sounding more like a tech-savvy curmudgeon.

Luna, on the other hand, had voluminous commentary on every photo, imposing more of her own need to be heard than perhaps any real understanding that she had of a piece. As she and Carole looked at a photo of a dirt road, Luna rewarded herself with every observation, "See that one dandelion? That's so cool how it just sits there alone, right? It's like you think there's like nothing happening but that dandelion says there's life. And the bee. See the bee?!..."

"It's a dirt road, Luna," barked Nicky, fed up with Luna's narration.

"Nick, stop that," as Peggy corralled him away from Carole's earshot. In a hushed tone, she continued, "If Luna sees more than a dirt road in a photo of a dirt road, then that's fine, okay? I know you're not in a good mood, but try to just...make the most of this. Carole's taken time out of her schedule to treat us to this beautiful day. She doesn't have to."

"I didn't ask her to."

"Nicky, that's it. Enough. You hear me? Be nice. We can't afford to not be nice when we don't have a Goddamn home of our own."

"That's not my fault."

"You think it's mine?"

"No, but - "

"None of us asked for this, okay? We're all learning something from this and, right now, I'd like to know what the hell that is but, regardless, you need to keep it together. I need you to be the man here. As much as you can be. Okay? Please, Nicky."

Carole continued to guide Luna to each photo slowly, before she would peek over to see how Peggy and Nicky were doing.

"These are quite nice, Carole. Very pleasant," as Peggy and Nicky made their way back...

"Yeah, I think you're right. They're pleasant. Some a little more illuminating than others, right? Not Diane Arbus," Carole winked at Peggy, indicating that she could give or take some of what was on display, yet seeming more impressed by Luna's enthusiasm;

"Mom, did you see this beautiful deer!" Luna exclaimed, as if on cue, as she pointed to a sole deer next to a decaying barrel alongside...*another dirt road.*

Peggy continued to delicately guide Nicky along with her as they looked at each photo. She would no longer try to engage much with him now, thinking it better to resign that if he was to be remotely impressed by anything, he would be so without coercion.

Eventually Peggy came upon the only photo of a person in the entire exhibit, which stood out for her. It was a woman with a large sun hat gazing out at a calm ocean near dawn, though the woman's face was completely obstructed by the largeness of the hat rim. It was appropriately called *Woman in a Sun Hat.* For some reason, Peggy was comforted by the mystery of this, perhaps because she could place herself in the photo, and imagine how glorious it would be to have nothing on her mind but an ocean's tide. Suddenly she was breathing a little better. She could sample the simplicity of this moment, and even block out all that was clouding her mind, including her very recent spat with Nicky.

Her definition of bliss was now that, one day, she would be able to simply look out at the water, as this enigmatic woman was – *a clean slate untainted by life, if only for a moment.*

After a savory brunch, Carole drove everyone back; the day serving as much of a distraction from the obvious as Peggy could have asked for, though no sooner did they enter back into Cold River than would reality begin to set in. For starters, a walnut that Luna bit into at brunch would exacerbate issues with her back tooth, which had been subtly bothering her since Peggy drove into a ditch weeks prior. *Fucking Claire!*

The thought of bringing Luna to a dentist, especially since this would likely be an out-of-pocket cost, was some-thing that Peggy desperately wanted to put off so long as Luna wasn't wreathing in pain – which, if she was, without question Luna would let it be known as loudly as an air raid siren, given her low threshold.

Peggy asked Carole to stop at the next drugstore so that she could get some items which she hoped would at least numb Luna's discomfort. After such a diverting day, Peggy momentarily lost her inhibitions regarding the possibilities of running into anyone she knew;

"Peggy?" a male voice asked, stopping her heart; *this cannot be good,* she thought. She quickly grabbed a handful of Anbesol, inadvertently knocking over several bottles to the floor in a nervous panic, as the voice got closer to her - "Peggy?"... She reluctantly looked to her right to find Jack approaching, Mike's friend and cross-town dermatological rival. Since Peggy was now on Jack's side of town, it suddenly made sense that she would bump into him, as she internally kicked herself for lowering her guard. Had she thought ahead, she would have at least sent in Carole or created a make-shift burka out of her scarf to avoid being recognized.

"How are you?" asked Jack, with concern in his voice that Peggy instantly resented.

She had somewhat suppressed how she felt about Jack, since his friendship seemed to more-or-less match the fair weather of pretty much their entire social circle. However, in this moment, it was resurged within her how she had been highly suspicious of him and his possible role in Mike's arrest. She would then recall the last phone exchange they had;

"Do you know who reported him?" he aggressively asked, to which she could only respond, "I don't know." "Is it a patient? His old partner, maybe?" he continued, before Peggy followed, "Jack, this has all just happened, okay? I can barely remember my name let alone absorb all of this." "But someone has to know *some*thing. I mean, they arrested him!" Jack continued, sounding impatient by her lack of knowledge.

She remembered getting off of that call with a distinct feeling that Jack was fusing concern with paranoia; as if more preoccupied with how any contributions he could've made to this situation would come back to bite him.

Now Peggy looked at Jack, whom she had not seen nor heard from since that call, feeling strongly that he knew every sordid aspect of the Bubone family's stark descent, contemptuous of his façade of concern.

"Do you really care how I am, Jack?" she rhetorically asked. Jack's face revealed obvious surprise, "Of...of course, I care, Peggy."

"Well, not showing your face while we were going through absolute hell is a heck of a way to show it, don't you think?"

"Peggy, I – "

"Look, I didn't ask to run into you or have a conversation with you, okay? I came to get Anbesol. Alright? I'm in this store to get Anbesol for my daughter because we are fighting to maintain our lives, despite what you pulled."

"What I...? Peggy, what'd I – ?"

"Don't even try it, Jack."

"Try what? Peggy, I'm – "

"You reported my husband. I know it. You reported him and then called me and acted concerned when you were only concerned for yourself.

"Peggy, wait - "

"You were always jealous of Mike and you fucking know it. He couldn't just be a better dermatologist, right? No, it had to be illegal, and so you...you...you fucking blow a whistle on a dear friend just out of your own ego, because you couldn't be bettered, right? You had to be king, you sonofabitch! And now you wana' approach me with...with that bullshit concern in your voice?!"

"Peggy, calm down, okay? You're making a – "

"YOU RUINED OUR LIVES!!!" she bellowed, which effectively turned the heads of the dozen or so customers on the floor, as well as the two cashiers up front.

Jack was clearly stunned at her accusation, before she stormed out of the store...

As she approached Carole's car, "Mam?!" emanated from a man with a deeper baritone than Jack's. Evidently this was someone who did not know her personally, but perhaps gathered who she was by her outburst and had two cents to contribute. She sped up with the anger now aided by fear that this could be another disgruntled patient of Mike's seeking to expel his own ire – "Mam, stop, please!!!"

She stopped and turned sharply, ready to unleash her unhinged emotions at this badgering stranger, only to discover that it was the store security guard; in her hostile state, she unknowingly had left with a handful of Anbesol bottles without paying.

She stood there in the parking lot, so shaken by her display that she barely managed to be properly embarrassed in front of him. She had debated whether to give the bottles back to the guard or go back in and pay for them, while risking seeing Jack's face again. "Peg, is everything okay?" as Carole stepped out of the car, having observed the security guard chasing her down.

"Ye...it,...Carole, it's fine. I got distracted and forgot to... Stay with the kids. I'll be right back, okay?"

Peggy sheepishly trailed the guard back into the store, which immediately descended to hushed tones upon her entrance; the sudden whispers instantly filled Peggy with the worst possible belief that everyone, including the pharmacist, knew exactly who she was. She paid for the bottles, left quickly, only to be stopped by Jack just outside of the store; "Peggy?" he asserted, as she attempted to walk past. "Haven't you done enough, Jack?!"

"I defended him, Peggy!" he proclaimed.

She stopped, turned to him with audacity, "You what?!"

"I defended him," he repeated. "Just so you know. I had a hunch about what he was doing and I lied about any suspicions I had when the commission approached me, okay? I put myself in jeopardy for him, 'cause we were friends. And I wasn't M.I.A. I called Mike and he never called me back, so I assumed he was embarrassed or didn't wana' hear from me, for whatever reason, so I just let it be. I knew you were all going through a lot. But I didn't ruin your lives. Just for the record."

He walked to his car in the distance as Peggy watched

him, at a loss for words. It was easier to hate him, regardless of if what he said were true. It was easier to feel victimized, as if to somehow offset the fact that Mike was unequivocally at fault. It was easier to look at Jack as someone who was only looking out for himself and simply didn't want to be touched by the scandal. And what proof would Peggy ever have of anything that he just said? He could've rehearsed that speech to his medicine cabinet, then just waited for a prime moment such as this in which to recite it, thus allowing him to exit off into the sunset, cleansing his own delusional conscience with his steadfast denial of having any hand in his good friend's public demise.

Or it could've all been true.

"Peggy?" Carole yelled, as she pulled the car up to her in front of the store. "Are you okay?"

Peggy stood there a moment, took a breath,...then got into the car.

"Is everything okay? Who was that?" Carole asked.

"Are you okay, mommy?" followed Luna from the backseat.

Peggy sat there a moment, gazing ahead, recalling her envy of that mysterious woman in the photo looking out at the calm waters as dawn fell,...but only managed to see a shopping cart in front of Carole's car.

"So what'd you guys think of the gallery?" asked Larry, making a rare appearance at a traditionally-timed dinner with the family that night. It was the first time he had done so in the few days that Peggy and the kids had been there, and his presence seemed to be the one thing that was oblivious to the cloud that had infiltrated the remainder of the day. Peggy still had residual effects from her encounter with Jack and was distressed at how a largely delightful day could become so unhinged so fast. Luna appeared to be distracted by what she sensed in her mother but was more preoccupied at how her own pesky tooth issues forced her to chew on the least favored side of her mouth. Nicky remained like a turtle, his head barely peering out of his shell enough to eat the veal scallopini Carole and Peggy had made. Carole, of course, was aware of all this and was gingerly in her tone so as to keep all emotions in check, while attempting to not reveal anything adverse in the presence of her daughters.

"The gallery was really beautiful. And what a nice location for it," summoned Peggy.

"Yeah, not bad for an old fish market," as Larry cut his veal.

"Really?" Peggy asked, with some genuine surprise.

"Oh, yeah. Carole didn't tell you? Yeah, what, about 16, 17 years ago."

"Well, we talked about a lot of stuff," Carole added.

"But it's quite an interesting nugget, wouldn't you say? God, I went there for the first time when Carole started there. It'd been there a year, and damn if you could still smell it," he continued.

"That's funny," Peggy forced a chuckle.

"That's a cultured man for you. He doesn't remember the exhibits, but he remembers the smell of fish," Carole half-joked.

"Hey, come on. I'm just saying, you had pictures up, sculptures on the floor, and there was old sturgeon seeping out of the walls. It's hard to forget."

"Luna really had a good time, right, honey?" asked Carole, navigating away from Larry's aromatic preoccupation.

"Yeah, there were some nice things," Luna politely concurred, through her discomfort.

"Yeah, my God, she was just all over it. I'm so glad," Carole beamed.

"I wouldn't say *that*. I liked *some* of them. Some were okay," Luna audaciously replied, which halted things for the moment. All of a sudden, Luna was displaying a side of herself that would only come out in the rare instance when she would mimic her big brother. Perhaps being unable to ignore his heavily dour state made her somehow realize that she shouldn't be enjoying herself either.

"Luna, why would you say that? You were going on about all the photos. You told Carole as much," Peggy said.

"It's okay," Carole followed, unable to mask her subtle embarrassment.

"I'm just saying..."

"Luna, you don't *say* anything else but that you loved the exhibit and how appreciative you are to Carole for taking us around today. It was a beautiful day. Remember? It was a beautiful day. From beginning to end. Look at this meal. How nice is this? Everything!"

"Peggy, it's okay..." as Carole attempted to calm her....

"No, Carole, that's very unlike Luna, and I'm sorry. I don't know where that came fro..." Peggy looked at Nicky staring at his barely touched plate, across from Luna, and in that moment, understood what was seeping into Luna's skin. Perhaps it was more honest to be as Nicky was, clearly in mourning, clearly confused, clearly out of balance with the world he once knew, which he was now looking at from the outside, as if a vagrant. But their survival could not be represented by such dejection. It took all of Peggy's efforts to maintain a façade of normalcy, knowing that the world does not endear itself to the distraught. It was all she could do to not scream at both of them in the middle of their dinner and summon thunder to make them see that they needed to dig deep and be strong for each other. There was no foundation other than the one that would be built again someday; one that could not exist unless they survived together.

Everyone went back to eating soon enough, as Larry, with his usual lawyerly levity, picked up pretty much where he left off;

"It's funny how these towns get so resistant to change. When the fish market left, you wouldn't believe how many people still showed up there lookin' for a good deal on scallops. Right, Carole?"

Before Peggy faded into her carriage house for the night, and would soon be halted by the dormancy of the weekend, she wanted to speak with Luna and Nicky together. It felt that since they had been at Larry and Carole's that she had not been connected to the kids as much and desperately wanted to let them know that she was still their mother. That she wasn't going anywhere. That they needed to try with every fiber of their being to be "pleasant", especially in front of their hosts.

"I know this is tough. And I know you miss your dad. We're going through something unusual. It's unusual for... most people, not just people who had a lot, like we did. But... life...sometimes...throws us a curve and we...y'know...."

"We what?" asked Luna.

"We have to keep swinging. It's a bad metaphor but it's...it's true here, okay?" Peggy assured. "Nicky?"

"Yeah?" he glumly mumbled. "Is there anything you're feeling that you want to tell me? Get off your chest? I know you're really sad now."

"I'm fine," he slurred, his eyes gazing out the window.

She knew better, but it was fruitless to push. "Luna, honey?"

Luna looked at Nicky, then back at her mother. Once again, seeming to fall under the influence of Nicky's stoicism, though softening. She concurred, "I'm fine, mommy."

Peggy wanted to ask again, but resisted. She was afraid their answers would change.

She sat in her single bed in the carriage house, gazing up at the artfully plastered ceiling, her list of to-dos already written out on the adorable boutique desk nearby:

1.) *Breakfast*
2.) *Ask Carole/Larry if there is anything they need (groceries/ etc)*
3.) *Follow up with schools for midseason openings, substitutes, etc.*

While she would still look up apartments and schools for the kids after the holidays, it would not be as productive to do so until she knew how she would be making a living. It even dawned on her, with the lack of response she would be getting with the holidays approaching, that she may need to at least temporarily conceive of doing something else altogether. But it was hard to think outside of the box, which she felt very much within. Having worked only one type of job since giving birth to Nicky did not help, nor did the fact that the ceiling was so close to her face in this carriage house that it all too accurately represented the very box she was within.

Such preoccupation all but erased the day that preceded it, much to Peggy's regret. She could not think past her run-in with Jack, then the overcast dinner, how Luna responded, how Carole tried to offset the awkwardness, how Peggy was so consumed with surviving that she didn't want to hear the truth from her kids, even if they were not at the age where they could properly verbalize it anyway.

And then there was a knock on the door...

Peggy was thrust up, instantly seeing a silhouette at the carriage house door. It was too big to be the kids, so she assumed it must be Carole checking up on her, which would be a pleasant surprise considering the dour note that dinner was left on. But it was Larry.

"Larry, hi," she said, with genuine surprise.

"Hey, sorry, did I wake you? I saw the light on..."

"Uh, no, I was...I don't...I haven't been... I was thinking, that's all," she replied. "Is everything okay? I'm so sorry about dinner."

"Sorry about what? The veal was great. You and Carole make a helluva a cooking team. You're spoiling me."

"Oh, you're funny. I mean, the kids. I know they're..."

"Peggy, they're going through a lot. It's hard for them to be 'on'. Believe me, I get it."

"But you guys have been amazing and I don't want you to think that it has anything to do with anything else but..."

"They miss their home. They miss their dad."

"Exactly," Peggy breathed a sigh, always assured by Larry's understanding. Whereas Larry definitely had a veneer in larger groups, and one that was not that dissimilar to his more commanding courtroom presence, he managed always to be a soothing balm when speaking to Peggy solely. While he wasn't present for much of their current stay, she would be in a hotel room if not for Larry and that was never lost on her.

"Are you okay in here?" he asked.

"Oh, God, you guys're spoiling *me*. It's adorable."

"Oh good," as Larry made his way in. "Yeah, this little house's come in handy."

"Yeah, I know. Carole said she used to use this as a studio."

"Yeah, she did. She did," he noted, but there was something weighted about how he said this. It then became clear that there had been a specific reason why this ceased being an art studio for Carole.

Before Peggy knew it, Larry was sitting on the small love seat by the entrance, a glass of bourbon already clasped in his hand. With Peggy having not seen Larry for much of the last few days, this was the first opportunity for them to talk at any length and, while it was not the best time for her, she was certainly not in a position to ask Larry to let her get some sleep, which she was hardly getting anyway.

"Sorry, is it a bad time?" he asked, already immersed in the cushions with a naturalness that indicated many previous immersions.

"No, Larry, we've hardly seen each other. It's good to see you," which she nearly meant.

"You too," Larry smiled at her, took another sip, then looked around. "Yeah, she did," he repeated, now oddly out of sequence.

"Oh, you mean...Carole...?"

"Yep," he took another sip, started to giggle. "This was my room for a stretch. Y'believe that?"

"Wha...I... Really?" almost embarrassed at his admittance.

"Yep," he took another sip, laughed a little more. "A bad stretch, that's for sure. You know, you wonder why so many divorces happen in this country? It's because the average couple doesn't have the room to retreat. It's something you think about, sad to say. But couples can suffocate each other, y'know? One room apartments, forget about it. A death knell. I think...when you have space,...you can breathe a little better. Sometimes it saves a marriage. And sometimes...it puts off the inevitable." Larry sipped his bourbon again, looking around, before taking notice of a family photo that was placed face down by Peggy, along with all the others.

"Where's the...?" Larry asked, before Peggy seized the photo of Larry, Carole and the kids at Carlsbad Caverns. "Oh, yeah, I must have knocked the photos down, somehow."

"The others too?" Larry asked, genuinely amused at the sight of about a dozen framed family photos lying face down.

"It...um...I don't know, I got...I think I was a little dizzy or something, and then forgot to put them back up..." Peggy continued to pull a bizarre excuse out of her ass for why every family photo in the room was capsized, while every figurine around them was miraculously upright.

"I know. It's tough," Larry said, his unsettling if slightly inebriated comment about divorce having instantly faded into his keen sixth sense for what Peggy was going through; not only deducing that she intentionally placed the few standing family photos down, but the why of it.

Peggy's instinct was to continue the ruse that she inadvertently knocked over the photos in a sudden fit of benign vertigo, but it felt better to admit to it. Larry had seen a lot professionally, dealt with a lot of people and, like any good lawyer, she imagined that he wasn't a bad psychoanalyst either. It was easier to be revealing, since Larry was also being so. And since he was, it would appear demeaning for her to deny the obvious.

Before long, Peggy was on the couch beside Larry, and they spoke not unlike they would have at get-togethers in the past, especially ones hosted by her and Mike;

"You didn't ask for any of this, Peggy," as he sipped. "You were a wonderful wife, you're a wonderful mother, a teacher..." While Larry's words were consoling, the past tense of having been a wonderful spouse was nevertheless dispiriting, even if Larry didn't intend this. The life she knew was gone, but she still clung to hope that it would return somehow. Since this was so new, it seemed rash to think otherwise.

"I'm still thinking this has to be a bad dream, Larry. It doesn't seem real."

"I know."

"And when I realize it's real, I guess it's silly but...I can only think that the same life we had is just around the corner. I just don't know how to get there, y'know? I'm like... I guess I just have to find a decent place for us and another job, ideally teaching, and hope that Mike gets out soon enough so that we can...start again, I guess."

"Peggy, I don't think it's silly but, at the same time, I think you have to just focus on starting again now."

"What do you mean?"

"I just mean, even if I can get Mike out in 2 or 3 years, that's a long time for you to be in limbo, right?"

"I'll be in limbo anyway, Larry. No matter where we end up. He's still my husband. Still the father of my children," she answered, if tepidly now.

Larry nodded, sipped again, "So you'll wait."

Larry's question/statement now opened up a Pandora's box of speculation on her part, "Are you saying I shouldn't?" she innocently asked, with a gentle smile.

"I'm not saying that. And I'm not saying that I'm not gonna' do whatever I can for Mike. He's my friend and he's a client that I intend to do right by,...but I also am a friend of yours."

"I know, Larry, but...I'm afraid I'm a little confused. I mean, we know now that Mike made a major mistake. A major error in his professional judgment, and I'm angry at him for that but...he's gonna' serve time, many people will be compensated and he'll...we'll have a right to..."

"Peggy, I'm just saying this is all very new. Very new. For all of you. It'll be different in 6 months. It'll be different in a year. How you'll feel. How you may feel about him. Yes, he'll still always be Nicky and Luna's father, but...other things can change."

The more Larry spoke, the more Peggy started to see Mike through a telescope that appeared to be pulling away, like a sort of hypnotism. Suddenly the difference in this conversation with Larry and past ones was stark. Of course, it was different because Peggy was now homeless. Different because she had never felt so unstable in her life and had two kids to be responsible for. Different because her husband was 5 hours away in an upstate prison in a town where a diner's rhubarb pie had more distinction than any of its residents. Different because the trajectory of her life was being questioned by pretty much the only person whose questions she would heed.

Different because...Larry's hand was now on her knee.

Peggy noticed this, at first vaguely, but was more consumed by doubts about her life than the current reality that Larry was navigating towards a region where he had not ventured before.

"You're a lovely woman, Peggy. You have a right to think for yourself," his hand moving up slightly into the vicinity of her thigh... "You know, the master plan is that we marry someone and it's perfect and nothing goes wrong and we're always happy, or happy enough to not notice the imperfections, ..." his hand inching up ever slightly,..."but reality is different. We can grow to delude ourselves for whatever reason until, one day, we realize that we haven't been doing ourselves any favors."

As Peggy was now aware enough of Larry's roaming hand to be unsettled, it finally dawned on her that he was speaking about himself and his own dismay over his marriage, while strategizing that their collective unhappiness with their spouses would justify a torrid roll in the carriage house hay. *Where else could we go?* she thought, if she resisted Larry's advances. *Is this something I could actually do?* On one level, she would admit that Larry was not unattractive, but had never thought he was attractive enough to rival Mike in any amorous way, and yet Mike was so remote, so tainted and stripped of the confident Italian-American veneer she had fallen for, that Larry's slightly-buzzed vulnerability and baritone cadence made him almost appealing. But this was not two people of equal stature meeting privately outside of their respective abodes for a fling that neither necessarily felt would last – there was an unsettling imbalance here, and it was that very imbalance that would place Peggy in a precarious situation;

"Larry..." she delicately uttered...

"Peg, I think...I've always thought..."

"Larry, please..."

"No, I have to be honest here..."

"Please don't. I really appreciate where you're going..."

"Where am I going?!" he joked, followed by a slightly drunken giggle...

"Larry, I think we need to –"

"Peggy, please...," unable to maintain the slow, confident build he was attempting, Larry leaned into her aggressively with his tongue extended out like a desperate cobra, before Peggy thrust herself up off the loveseat...

"Larry, please, you're a dear friend. I really need your friendship. Both you and Carole. I can't...I can't do this."

"Do what, Peggy?" he asked pointlessly.

"Wha...? *This*, Larry! I can't. *You* can't."

"Why can't I?"

"Larry, ...Carole!" exclaiming as loud as she could through a hush.

"Peggy, have you been hearing me? Just a few months ago I was living here."

"And now you're not."

"And you think that means anything's better? You think it means we so much as touch each other?"

"I can't do this, Larry. Please understand."

"Because of Mike."

"Well, yes, he's my husband, Larry."

There was now a cavernous silence which sat like an intermission amidst their rapid exchange, as Larry took a sip from his glass. He looked just away from her eyes enough so as to indicate he knew something that he intended to begrudgingly reveal;

"You think you'd be doing something that Mike hasn't done, Peg?"

In a near instant, Peggy swung from anxiety to astonishment at what she thought she heard, but hoped, as she had hoped when she heard similar bits of devastating news, that she simply was mistaken.

"What are...what are you suggesting, Larry?"

He appeared to just as quickly regret using this card as pretty much his best and last chance to coerce Peggy into a tryst, yet he still hoped that his revealing Mike's infidelity would enable her guilt to fade and perhaps be supplanted by sexual justification. Perhaps he thought she may have had *some* idea of this but, in actuality, this news would be as stunning for her as hearing of Mike's initial arrest or the ultimate admission of guilt.

"I just know that he had...been seeing someone."

"Seeing someone? Who?"

"I don't know. I never met her. Never saw her..."

"But he told you this?"

"He mentioned her, yes. Peggy, listen..." as he rose to try and comfort her...

"How long...? You...? How long was this...?"

"Peggy,..." he moved closer, as Peggy stepped back, her shock replacing her fear... "How long was this going on, Larry? And please stay there!"

"Ssssssh, Peggy..." as he continued to move towards her...

"Larry, I'm politely warning you, please, stay there and answer my..."

"Peggy - "

"ANSWER   MY   GODDAMN   QUESTION, LARRY!!!!!!!!!!!!!!!!!!!!!"

Larry all but jumped into the air, as the family dogs Crosby and Nash began to bark from the house. Even the relative soundproofing of the carriage house could not completely drown out Peggy's piercing volume which, up until then, she had been struggling desperately to suppress.

Larry held up his hand gently for Peggy to calm down, while remaining in place and breathing somewhat heavier now... "Peggy, I think it was about 6 months in that he mentioned her. And that was about 6 months ago. She's not from here. She's from somewhere else. Ohio, I think. I think he met her during a conference or something. That's what I know. I'm sorry that I... I didn't mean to bring it up like..."

Peggy continued to watch Larry's lips move, but only heard a piercing whistle-like sound and expected any second that Crosby, Nash and the rest of the neighborhood's dogs would come crashing through the carriage house door and finally devour her. If what Larry said was true, then there was ultimately very little that was real about much of what she thought was a successful family life.

There was a knock on the door, and with it, Peggy and

Larry had to wonder what the consequences could be, based on who was on the other side. If it were Nicky or Luna, they may find it strange that Larry was there, and the same if it were Miley or Britney, ...but if it were Carole...

Larry walked to the door and opened it to reveal Carole in her bathrobe. She was there upon hearing Peggy's scream, but did not necessarily think that Larry was there too until she saw him. However, she never would get as far as vocalizing any actual question once she was greeted by him. She saw Larry at the door with bourbon on his breath and Peggy standing a few feet away; her vocal chords all but strangled by a sudden reemergence of anxiety that had almost set the equally sudden emergence of anger, depression and despair to the side... Carole looked at them both, emitting a palpable air of disappointment, and saying without words that, in essence, her marriage and charitable indulgence were at an end,...as she walked back into the house.

Peggy's heart was beating as if she imbibed a dozen cappuccinos, as she looked at Larry near the door, gazing out sheepishly while holding his snifter. She hadn't a clue what action would be most appropriate for her to take. She wanted to punch him in the stomach for his inappropriate advances, for putting her in a position where Carole even conceived that Peggy was reciprocating of them, for dropping a colossal bomb about Mike. And yet, he was still the only one who could get Mike out of prison sooner than later. But did she even want that now? Did she care? It would just be easier to cut Larry off, cut Mike off, file for divorce and leave not only Cold River, but Long Island – for being anywhere on this island was too close. If only she could leave the planet and teach Martians literature. Or at least, if she could be born again, and out of a different mother, perhaps on the west coast or somewhere in France. *A clean slate.*

But one thing was for certain; that night she would not sleep. And by morning, she, Nicky and Luna would be on the street,...with Christmas just days away.

10

The recent memories of both her last call with Vic and Elaine conjoined with Larry's advances nearly forced Peggy off the road, yet again, as she drove herself and the kids to a motel in the nearby town of Moss Creek. The motel, incidentally, was a $140 per night savings off the previous *ho*-tel they were staying at prior to moving in with Larry and Carole. Snowflakes continued to descend on the windshield, void of the charm they once had for her; now merely representing the coldness of the world as she had come to know it, aided in no small part by the clinking of her car's engine, which now made it sound like a diminutive locomotive. *Fucking Claire! Fucking Larry!*

After Peggy checked them into their adjoining rooms, as before; one she would share with Luna, the other which she would allow Nicky to have for himself,...she looked off of her balcony at the barren parking lot. She could hear the oceanic sounds from the morning rush hour of the nearby Long Island Expressway, and embraced what felt like her first breath since the previous night's incident with Larry. The morning leading up to this moment had Peggy discretely gathering the kids at about 6am, with Larry asleep in the den and Carole blessedly so in the upstairs bedroom. They tiptoed through the darkened house to avoid arousing Crosby or Nash. She then told the kids to wait in the car before placing an envelope on the dining room table with $300 cash – far in excess of any food they consumed or electricity they may have used, accompanied by a brief note:

"Thank you so much for being such gracious hosts, but we cannot impose further. We'll be in touch. – Peggy and the kids."

While the money may well have proved unexpected, it was important to her that she maintain some dignity, even in her sheepish departure. As for the words contained in the note, what she would place on the table would be the last of 57 drafts she composed amidst an arduously insomniatic night, opting for a cordial neutrality over more incendiary versions, which included such prized lines as *"So sorry, Carole. Larry tried to jump me"* or *"Carole, it wasn't what you thought."* And even with all the time it took her to come up with a final version, she still pondered if there were any other words she could have included that would somehow evict the toxicity from the previous night, but ultimately resigned that there was little else she could do other than get the hell out of there. Larry would certainly have the opportunity to defend himself how he saw fit, perhaps even putting the blame on Peggy somehow, not unlike Vic and Elaine. *Hell, he's an attorney – he's sure to come up with something.*

The disappointment in Larry's advances combined with what seemed to be the end of her newly burgeoning friendship with Carole, would take a back seat to what Larry would reveal about Mike's affair with a nameless/faceless woman from *possibly* Ohio. *But was this actually true? Did he just say this in order to allay guilt?* It was certainly possible, as he was admittedly anxious to get into Peggy's pants, *and what wouldn't a man say if he was, in fact, drunk and horny enough?* Further, it was just one more thing to cloud Peggy's mind that she did not need and so, again, with every fiber, she attempted to clear her oppressive brain fog as best she could.

Realizing that it was only 7:30am, she would attempt to take a much needed nap before taking the kids out for breakfast. She came back into her room, averted her eyes to the blinding canary yellow walls and embarrassingly faux impressionistic prints, which insulted her cultural intelligence more than she expected, especially when recalling some of the artwork that used to adorn their house which was eventually seized in the federal compensatory grab bag. *Fucking Mike!*

"Luna, let's get some sleep for a couple of hours and then I'll take us all to breakfast, okay?" she said in an exhausted mumble.

"Mommy, Nicky won't let me in his room," Luna said, from her own single bed alongside Peggy's, already adorned with a pad which contained some ill-conceived lyrics and girlish doodlings of cats and dogs. This was beside the book that Peggy had assigned her to read, *Bless the Beasts and the Children*.

"Honey, let Nicky be by himself, okay? You know how he is."

"Why does he get his own room?"

"He's older than you and he's a boy, that's why. Now did you hear me? Let's get a couple of hours."

"I can't sleep."

"Alright, then wake me up at 9:30am, if I'm not already up. We'll go out for a nice breakfast, okay?"

"My bed is uncomfortable."

"Well, we have to make do for now, okay?" as Peggy elongated herself on her bed, "Oh my God, this bed is like a sleeping on plywood. How the hell can they charge $135 a night for *this*?"

"Why did we leave Larry and Carole's?"

Peggy stared up at the chipped white ceiling, taking a moment before turning to Luna, "We just did, Luna. Now let me take a nap. Mommy didn't get any sleep last night."

"Why not?"

"Luna, I just didn't. Read your book or do your doodles and just give me a couple of hours."

"I don't like what they do to the buffalo in that book."

"They do a lot of bad things in the world, Luna. You need to be aware of it sooner than later. Now let me get some sleep."

Peggy rested her head on her pillow, closed her eyes... and soon heard the ocean...:

There was a rumbling from a silhouetted cluster of people in the distance, voices that she recognized but that were hard to distinguish. Occasionally, she'd hear her name mentioned, amidst other garbled words... As she appeared closer to the sounds, she would only hear her name said louder, but much of everything else was unintelligible; "Peggy garbonzaconsuelaretorka – Peggy lefrienziasticpatrayusbeyonsunset – Peggy garbonzaconsuelaretorka..." She would continue asking "What?" fruitlessly, as the silhouetted cluster remained unacknowledging... Suddenly, something scurried across her feet, which was so fast, she couldn't quite make it out. The oceanic sounds continued, as did the utterances - "Peggy" - amidst a wave of pig latin... She saw a man standing on a small table in an orange jumpsuit, not unlike Mike proposing a toast at his birthday party, but she couldn't tell if it was him nor make out what he was saying... "Mike?!" she desperately called out. "Mike, are you okay?!" she continued, attempting to walk towards him, the cacophony of sound growing more ominous, the mentioning of her name barely audible amidst a sea of angry inaudibility, the ocean's tide coming closer but sounding less like water and more like taps on a stage. She soon became encircled by faces she began to recognize, albeit briefly; Larry was there with bourbon in hand, Judy with a large tray of ill-formed cupcakes, Vic and Elaine gawked from a distance, Claire would briefly extend her head out from the crowd; giving Peggy a bone-chilling death stare. "Peggy! Peggy!" would be squawked as if from an abrasive parrot that sounded oddly like her mother, with that unmistakably sandpapered Jersey cadence of hers... Something again would scurry across her feet, but she was afraid to look down this time... Vague images of people who appeared to be composites of those she once knew encircled her, appearing somewhat worn and hollowed out; their skin gray and damaged, their clothes from another period... Something else scurried across her feet, then something else, then something else... Now she felt gentle nibbles, which paralyzed her, as the largely darkened mob caterwauled and then dispersed… She looked down and saw her feet lost amidst a veritable sea of armadillo-sized rats, before looking up to see a giant bell jar descending over her. She saw Carole in the distance looking at her in the same disappointed way as she last saw her, before fading out of sight…as the glass jar covered her and muffled the external sounds. "Mommy?" Peggy desperately tried to lift her feet out of the sea of rats while hearing Luna's voice again… "Mommy? Mommy?"…as she continued to lift her bloodied feet desperately, crying and yelling, "Luna, where are you?!" – "Mommy! It's Nicky!" - "What about Nicky? Luna, where are you?!!!" "Mommy…" "LUNA, WHERE ARE YOU…?!!!"

...as Peggy shot up from her motel bed, where Luna stood pulling on her arm eagerly – "Mommy, get up. It's Nicky!" she repeated, near tears. "Luna, what? Oh my God, what's wrong…?" as Peggy started to the door connecting to Nicky's room, "He's not there," Luna cried.

"Whata' you mean he's not there?"

"He's gone."

"Gone? Wha… Luna, what do you mean he's gone?!"

"He said he didn't wana' stay here, and he left. But I didn't think he meant for a long time."

"When did he say this?"

"About 2 hours ago."

"Oh, my fucking Go… 2 hours ago…?!" as Peggy marched into Nicky's room to find his bed barely touched, his own roll suitcase and bagpack gone, and his copy of *Grapes of Wrath* resting atop the night table. "Luna, why didn't you wake me up? Why the hell didn't you…?!!!" as Peggy ran outside, looking desperately off the balcony.

"I fell asleep," Luna said, shameful and near tears.

"My God… Did he say where he was going?"

"No, he just said he was leaving. I asked if I could go with him and he said I should stay with you."

"Oh, my God… What time is…?" as she picked up her phone, "11:45?! Jesus Christ…" Peggy stood on the balcony, her feet moving in a pointless circle, before running back to her phone on the bed to attempt to call Nicky, under the assumption that he had his with him.

"Maybe he's on his way back..." said Luna, with feigned belief, as Peggy dialed. The phone rang before going to the automated outgoing message – "Damnit!"

"Did you call him...?"

"Yes, I called him, Luna. Wait here."

"Where are you...?"

"Luna, just stay in your room and shut the door," as Peggy stormed downstairs, her mind at a speed far faster than her bare feet could take her, before twisting her ankle halfway down... "AHHHHHHHHHH!" she bellowed, as she tumbled down the last few concrete steps, before hobbling to the front desk with bleeding knees and elbows, gasping for breath...

"My son...my son, Nicky... Nicky Bubone. Is he here somewhere?"

The pockmarked young man at check-in, seeming put-out by the vagueness of Peggy's question, while oblivious to her blood loss, "Who's Nicky, mam?"

"My son! MY SON! He left his room. He was asleep!"

"He was asleep and left his room?"

"I mean *I* was asleep, okay? You know what I mean!"

"No, I really don't, and I think you should calm down, okay - ?"

"Don't tell me to calm down! It's enough I'm even staying in this overpriced hovel! My son ran away while I was taking a nap. Have you seen him? He's 13, brown hair, about 5'5"..."

"No, I haven't, mam. Are you sure he ran away?"

"Yes, I'm sure. He took his bags. He left. You didn't see him leave?"

"No, I just said, I didn't see him..."

"Don't tell me what you just said. I can ask twice. This is my Goddamn son!"

"Mam, please don't take your frustrations out on me,

okay? I just work here."

"Do you even do *that*, you sarcastic asshole! You should be ashamed of yourself."

"Um, excuse me, I'm not the one who lost my kid, okay?"

Peggy saw red in this moment. It was even amazing to her that, despite all she'd undergone in the last couple of months, she hadn't managed to kill someone. But in this moment, she felt that she was capable of bludgeoning this obnoxious desk clerk until he was in a puddle of the condescension that coursed through his veins. Instead, she froze, realizing that her being arrested for assault would lead to nothing but the possibility of Luna and Nicky ending up in foster care or with Vic and Elaine. All of a sudden, that awful story from *American Sleaze* that both Gwen and Vic had recalled to her rushed through her head, along with a vision of Nicky and Luna dangling lifeless from a pipe.

She continued to gaze at the clerk intensely, before she stepped outside and gasped a needed breath. Her heart beat rapidly to where she needed to sit on the pavement, as blood continued to stream down her knees and elbows. An incoming family about to check in unsettlingly gawked at her as if she were a macabre exhibit...

"Mommy...!" Luna yelled from the top of the steps...

"Luna, please go inside your room! I don't want you out!"

"Oh, my God... Are you bleeding?!"

"I'm fine, just...just...just go inside!" Peggy gasped. Her lack of sleep, blood loss and adrenaline rush were slowly sapping her to where she could barely stand, but she managed just enough stamina to dial 911:

"My son ran away while I was taking a nap. He's 13, brown hair, about 5'5"..."

"Mam, are you sure he ran away?"

"Yes, I'm sure! He took his bags. He left!"

"How long has it been?"

"My daughter told me he left 2 hours ago."

"Left where?"

"Left our motel.   We're in a motel – the Moss Creek Motel."

"And you're saying she saw him leave?"

"Yes, she said he left."

"You have no idea where he would go?"

"No! There's nowhere he *could* go. We're in the middle of nowhere. He doesn't drive, we don't know anybody around here..."

"Do you know why he would leave and not come back?"

"I...yes, there are many reasons, which I can't get into here. He's missing. Please put out an alert for him, okay...?"

"Perhaps he just went for a walk, mam. It's only been 2 hours."

"Whata' you mean? Did you hear me? He took his bags. He's 13! He's off somewhere. Can you please put out an alert of some kind. He's a minor, for Godsakes..."

"Mam - "

"WOULD YOU PUT OUT AN ALERT FOR HIM, PLEASE! He's sad, he's depressed...   We have no home, we have no friends, we practically have no family... He has every reason in the fucking world to run into the Expressway, okay? WOULD YOU PLEASE – ?!!!"

Just as Peggy felt her exhausted rage consuming her to the nth degree, she heard a car pull up. She lifted her perspiring head from her phone to see that it was a police car and inside was Nicky in the back seat – gazing out, numbly.

She dropped her phone, rose from the pavement like a welterweight boxer, dazed and barely ascending from the canvas, and hobbled towards the car. There was now dried blood on her knees and elbows, sweat seeping through her shirt, her hair was unkempt from her recent nightmarish nap, and yet she was oblivious to how unbalanced she must have looked to, of all things, a police officer...

"Oh, my God, Nicky...!"

Nicky remained in the car, as the officer quickly emerged from the driver's seat...

"Mam, are you this boy's mother?"

"Yes, yes, oh, my God, thank you. Where...where was he? Nicky, why did...? Where were you...? Where was he, officer? Thank you for..." Peggy wildly babbled, through the burnt fumes of energy she had left...

"Mam, he was hitchhiking near the entrance ramp to the expressway."

She looked at Nicky, "Oh my..."

"Mam, are you alright?"

Peggy stood dazed as she looked at him in the back seat, staring ahead...

"Mam, are you alright? Can you step away from the car for a second?"

"Can I... What? Yes, I'm fine. I just... I was sleeping and..."

The officer approached Peggy, deducing from her physical state that Nicky was perhaps fleeing from an abusive home life...

"Mam, can I talk to you for a second, please?"

"I, yes, but...my son..."

"He's not going anywhere. He'll be fine. Can I ask you a few questions, please?"

"I..., yes, of...of..."

"Are you okay?"

Peggy took a moment, finally realizing that the officer was now questioning her own mental stability, "Yes, officer, I'm fine. I just...I was napping, I woke up, my daughter told me that my son had left, and I panicked and fell down the steps to...to get to the front desk..."

"You haven't been drinking?"

"I...no, God, no... Why are you asking...? No, I just fell down the steps. I was panicked. He's never done this before."

"Never?"

"My God, no. No, we're just...we're just going through a

bad time right now."

"Do you know why he would want to go to Hawking, New York?"

Peggy took a moment to digest this, "Wha...where?"

"Hawking, New York."

As tears began to form in her baggy eyes, she looked over at her son, then softly, "Yes,...I know why."

An hour later, Nicky and Luna sat across from their mother in a booth at a nearby *IHOP*. Peggy managed to bandage up her elbows and knees, but did little else in the way of freshening up. Her hair, always immaculately brushed and shiny, now appeared hardened and spikey; a combination of the annoyingly firm motel pillow and the frayed nerves that were aggravating her follicles. She was still collecting her breath from the recent events stemming from Nicky's attempted departure, but at least could take a modicum of solace in the fact that she was not taken into custody for child endangerment, or some other germane offence.

It was the lunch rush on a Saturday afternoon, and so there was no shortage of families with their miscreant children tossing fruit from their half-eaten waffles at each other – *the epitome of Long Island white trash* - but they had little choice. Peggy was exhausted and refused to superfluously drive around Moss Creek in pursuit of an elegant café, which likely did not exist there anyway.

As they waited for their food, Peggy looked at Nicky, who had not spoken a word since being returned to her by the police, resulting in Peggy having to order for him. "Nicky, I want you to talk to me, okay? Why did you feel you needed to run away like that?"

He gazed out at the parking lot, not unusual behavior when he was in full-on clammed-up mode.

"Honey, this...this is big, okay? You can't not discuss this with me. I'm your mother. I love you. Your sister loves you. We're all going through the same thing here, okay? We can't... I can't... We're a unit, okay?"

"What's that?" Luna asked.

"That's...that means that we're a team, okay? It was...it was the four of us, and now it's the three of us for...for a little while. Not forever, but...a while. And our strength is in each other, okay? That means that if we're...if we're all willing to work through this and work together, then we can...we can come through this okay. But if one of us wants to leave, then that makes the unit weaker. It gives us less of a chance to... to... We're a family, okay?"

"Dad's not family?" Nicky tersely retorted, as he continued to gaze out.

"Nicky, I...I can't... I'm not saying that. He's your father. He's my husband. That hasn't changed. But he's not here."

"And I wana' see him."

"You can't just go see him like that."

"Why not?"

"Because he's in prison!" Peggy exclaimed, just as a pocket of silence occurred around them, causing a few patrons to glance over. She smiled weakly before resuming in a hushed tone... "You cannot just hitch a ride to your father's...current residence...and see him. That's not how this works. We will see him together. But we have to get ourselves settled first."

"When's that gonna' happen?" he snapped.

"Honey, I'm doing the best I can to make that happen. It's a bad time of the year, unfortunately. Christmas is approaching, so finding a job and then finding a school nearby for you guys to go to is challenging, but trust me, I'm doing my best."

"Are we gonna' live around here?" Luna asked.

"Oh, God, I... No. I mean, I hope not. If so, it'd be temporary, but... No. If there's a God, we'll be in a nice neighborhood."

"Cold River?" followed Luna.

"*Like* Cold River, hopefully, but not Cold River."

"Why not?"

"Because we can't move back there, Luna. That's why. Too many...things have happened. I've explained this. We need to start fresh."

"Can't we see our friends again? My friends Kathy and Kim... They keep asking me when I'm coming back to school."

"Luna, you're not going back to Cold River Middle School."

"Why not?"

"Luna, we all need to start fresh, okay? It's just easier that way."

"Easy for you," Nicky sniped.

Peggy instinctively wanted to smack Nicky across his face, but somehow resisted. Her exhaustion and hunger made it more challenging to comprehend the mutual struggle that they were all experiencing, but perhaps the fact that she also announced that someone was "in prison" made her realize that coupling that with smacking her child in a public establishment would only serve to draw more eyes to them.

However, her physical restraint did little to curb her hostility, "How dare you!", lowering her hushed tone to a brooding guttural rasp. "I want you both to understand something here, in case there is any question why we are where we are. Your father made a mistake. He knows he made a mistake, but it was a mistake, nevertheless. As a result of this *bad* mistake, not only does he have to serve time, but it's also put us in a bad situation as far as my job and our old friends are concerned. They know what your father did and so they don't want anything to do with us. And if they don't know, then their parents know. And chances are if their families knew that they were in touch with you, they would not be pleased. And, no, this is not just about me, Nicky. Don't you remember how the kids started to ignore you? Your own friends? Is that what you want, to go back so you can be humiliated? I don't want that for you, and I don't want it for any of us. And hitchhiking like an idiot 5 hours up to some hick town by yourself is not gonna' help anything. Look what happened. You worried your sister, your mother almost got arrested... Was it worth it?!"

He remained still, looking down at the table setting and poorly acting like he was preoccupied with the inane puzzle within the placemat. Nevertheless, he was red. He was embarrassed. But, hopefully, something got through.

She leaned back in the uncomfortable booth, as the food came. "Here we are!", said the waitress, her buoyancy being what Peggy both envied and was sickened by, as she feigned her most appreciative smile, "Thank you."

"Anything else I can bring you guys?"

"I think we're all set. Thank you."

The waitress left, and for a while the only sound among them was the clanging of silverware against their plates. She could pretty much conclude that Nicky would not speak for the duration of the day, which she would not object to at this point, considering all the energy he had caused her to expend. But there was still Luna:

"Are Larry and Carole not your friends anymore?"

Peggy stopped cutting into her french toast, in an attempt to formulate a careful response... "They're... Yes, we're still friends."

"Then why did we leave?"

Again, Peggy took a beat, sipped her coffee in the hopes that more caffeine would help jog a proper answer, "I didn't want to overstay our welcome."

"But I thought they liked having us there?"

"They did, Luna, but...they had a lot going on, and it's a lot for a family that has their own issues to be dealing with another family and *their* issues."

"What issues are they having?" Luna probed, as she picked at her blueberry pancakes.

Peggy looked at Luna, barely indulging her youthful Diane Sawyer impersonation now, "It's personal, Luna. And I don't know all the details myself but it's not anything that you need to know, okay? Now why don't you eat your pancakes."

Luna begrudgingly went back to her food, while Nicky continued to pick at his; his face remaining focused nowhere outside the periphery of his plate. Peggy sipped her coffee and gazed out the window at the gray Saturday, relishing the momentary silence between them:

"Mommy, do we have any other family?"

She looked at Luna, then at Nicky, then back at Luna, again attempting to formulate an answer before gulping more coffee. It dawned on her that this question had never come up, since the kids had only known Vic and Elaine as their only real extended family, aside from their great aunt and uncle, Vic's brother and brother's wife, who lived in Colorado. They barely knew of their Uncle Vic Jr whom they never had occasion to meet, and he was brought up so rarely that he was all but forgotten by them anyway.

"Um..., no, we don't. Your grandparents are in Florida. Your great Aunt Josephine and Uncle Jim are in Colorado. You have some second cousins scattered around somewhere, but we don't have anyone close, I'm afraid."

"Shouldn't we have more?" Luna inquired.

"More what, honey?" Peggy hesitantly asked.

"More family? Like...how come you never mention the family *you* came from?"

Peggy was suddenly wishing that Nicky would say or do something, anything to alter the line of questioning that Luna had opened up.

"Honey, our family is...what you've known as family. Your dad, myself, Nicky. Your grandparents, obviously," though Peggy barely had any stock in the latter, at this point.

"Those're daddy's parents."

"Yes, that's right."

"What about yours?"

"Well, my father... He...died when I was very young. That would be your grandfather, on my side," Peggy sheepishly divulged. In truth, she wasn't certain if her birth father was dead. She only knew that he had left when she was a barely a toddler. But death was an easier explanation.

"What about your mother?"

Peggy's subconscious plan, since her children had entered into the world, was for their contentment with who they were exposed to as their family. The older they got, it would be enough to simply let them believe that Mike's family was enough, coupled with the friends they would make, to create a sense of familial fullness. This seemed logical enough, since Peggy had long believed that a blood connection did not by any means oblige any contact if that relationship was deemed unhealthy. Claire didn't have the courage to cut off her mother, for she was too much like her in the end and may have ultimately feared severing ties, and so their dysfunctional co-existence would no doubt prove ongoing for as long as her mother would live. As for Peggy, it was less out of embarrassment and more out of a mental survival that she severed ties with her mother. They stopped speaking just prior to Peggy's wedding, and once Peggy and Mike moved out of their New Jersey apartment to their first house in Long Island, it seemed that Peggy's mother would not have an easy time tracking her down, provided that she cared enough to do so. There was never a forwarded letter in all those years and, since their communication had ceased prior to the ubiquity of e-mail or texting, she would never receive correspondence that way. However, there were those recent phone hang-ups on their now-disconnected landline which Peggy started to speculate could be her; that cigarette sucking sound still etched into her brain that sounded so similar to the sounds her mother made when Peggy was a child, with hostility in every puff.

If there came a time when Peggy would somehow reconnect with her mother, then she concluded that, at that point, she would explain things to Nicky and Luna. Yes, they were now at the age where, together, they could at least absorb the surface details, if not understand how a mother and daughter could not speak for almost 20 years. But up until now, it was easier to rely on the belief that such a reunion would never happen. That Peggy would be encircled in such affluence and success, that she would be all but untouchable to anyone from her past, especially her mother, and would then choose to bring her past up with Nicky and Luna as adults; when there was nothing at stake but simply letting them know a bit more about their roots.

Yet now, given the apparent barrenness of their options, her precocious daughter was asking why their family was so small, and particularly why Peggy never mentioned much about where she came from. As depressing a time as it would be to address this, it made sense that, since it hadn't been broached before, it would come up now. For Peggy's life had become like *The Emperor's New Clothes*; when all was stripped away, what was really there?

But just how much was beneficial to divulge? Would it add anything other than gloom to their current misfortune? There was a certain déjà vu in this moment, as she pondered how to respond, similar to when she first revealed to the kids at dinner of Mike's arrest:

"Nicky, Luna,...listen to me for a moment. Stop eating, please."

They both did. Nicky remained looking down at his waffles, while Luna looked directly into her mother's eyes...

"I realize that...I've never told you about my mother and...maybe you've wondered why. I hadn't... Well, I hoped there would simply be a time to tell you this when you were older, and when things were...more stable for us, but since... I actually think it's a good time to let you know about...my mother. Your...other grandmother."

"Is she alive?" Luna asked.

"Yes, she's alive."

"Why haven't we met her?"

"Because... Well, she doesn't live... Because we don't speak to each other."

"Why not?"

"Because...we had a fight many years ago. Before I married your father."

"And you haven't spoken since?"

"No, we haven't."

"Has daddy ever met her?"

"He, yes,...when we were engaged. He had met her... once."

"Did he like her?"

"Well,...he wanted to but, I'm afraid, my mother didn't

like *him* very much."

"Why didn't she like daddy?"

"Because she didn't know him. She was... I don't think she wanted to."

"Why?"

Peggy took a breath, since this was the first time in years she actually gave this any thought, and with good reason, "I guess she felt...suspicious, maybe."

"She didn't want you and daddy to be together?"

"No,...not really." As Luna's questions continued, Peggy began to recall exactly what was the catalyst to their relationship's ultimate demise. It was never far below the surface in her mind, no matter how far away she was geographically.

"So you had a fight and that was it?"

She looked deeply at Luna, then over at Nicky, whose head was now tilted up ever so slightly, indicating that he was at least cognizant of what was being said, even under his usual façade of indifference.

That wasn't it, she thought. There was more to what had happened that would end their relationship in seeming perpetuity, but this just wasn't the time nor the place to delve that deeply. For now, what they needed to know was just what Peggy had revealed.

"It's complicated, honey,...and not something for us to discuss right now," she evaded as honestly as she could.

The kids resumed eating, as Peggy stepped into the ladies room, simply needing to throw some water on her sagging face and wash herself of the mental corrosion that had been accumulating since last night.

She looked in the mirror, the cold water dripping from her face, and suddenly began to fear what would happen if the very bane of her existence were to become their only option.

11

Days went by slowly as the money quickly dwindled. Peggy looked at her bank account online from her drab Moss Creek motel room, as panic was beginning to take over. The $300 she placed in an envelope for Larry and Carole, once faux symbolism for the dignity she wanted desperately to maintain, now was money she cursed herself for dispensing with so easily. *Fucking Larry!*

She hadn't made any headway with obtaining teaching work, even as a substitute, given the proximity of the winter school break, and could not even collect unemployment since she hadn't managed to work the minimum number of weeks required. Days were spent with Peggy trying desperately to divert Luna and Nicky's attention from how perilous things were becoming as the holidays approached. While Nicky and Luna's reports on the books Peggy assigned were initially serving as educational diversions, they were also illuminating their own insecurities. For Luna, she could not get past the treatment of the buffalo portrayed in *Bless the Beasts and the Children*, and would even start to exhibit pre-teen anxiety attacks, coupled with increasing discomfort as a result of what now clearly appeared to be a cracked tooth stemming from Peggy's plunging the car into a ditch weeks prior. At the same time, for Nicky, the parallels to their life now and the life of the nomadish Joads of *The Grapes of Wrath* were almost too on the nose.

Peggy would now question what inside her prompted her to assign these books to the kids, other than the convenience of her owning them. Was it simply because she felt they were good books for their age, or was there something in her that wanted them to better understand experiences that were the opposite of the insulated world they had previously known, just as she had selected *The Bell Jar* for her privileged students? In any event, it was backfiring – and badly.

She now went to bed every night needing to calm Luna from crying. She missed her father. She missed her friends, and her tooth was now causing her increased discomfort. Peggy continually feared that she would wake up one morning to discover that Nicky had run away again. The Dali-esque dreams that seemed to arrive the moment her eyelids lowered now included images of him strewn out on the Long Island Expressway. In her weakest moment, she even began to ponder the upshot of Nicky fleeing; *it wouldn't be the worst thing if it were just Luna, but the embarrassment of dealing with the police again, and God forbid he died. The soap opera of this family would continue in the news…*

Being the best parent possible, even in the most hellacious of circumstances, was the only option here and that meant being more clever than anything, given their fiscal limitations. She curbed their eating out and started to stockpile dried goods in their motel rooms. She would basically encourage Luna to consume only yogurt, pudding and other soft foods that were least likely to cause her further discomfort. But the writing was on the wall; she needed to see a dentist. And yet there was no way that Peggy could go back into Cold River to see Dr. Kim, their family dentist. He was in the heart of town, and the likelihood of seeing several people that they knew was far too great. *Not to mention that he also was a former patient of Mike's!*

As she looked online for local dentists, she noticed the date on her computer screen and was crestfallen to discover that it was Christmas Eve. *Jesus Christ!*

The three of them sat around the small circular table in Peggy's room, as they lugubriously ate bowls of cereal while rain washed away the previous days dusting of snow. Peggy barely endured a cup of dreadful coffee from the miniature Moss Creek Motel coffee maker that was incapable of making anything stronger than beige bath water. While this hardly gave her enough of a caffeine jolt to stand let alone think of how they would get through this day, she knew that Luna and Nicky were aware of the obvious – that they would be spending their first Christmas without Mike, and their first without a place to call home.

As she watched Nicky and Luna eat and blankly gaze at their phones, there was a sinking feeling within her. Yes, this sinking feeling had very much become as regular as a bowel movement, but this went deeper as she recalled a particularly disastrous Christmas with her mother when Peggy was around Nicky's age.

Peggy, her mom and her mother's often inebriated boyfriend at the time, Clyde, arrived at Peggy's grandmother's house in Baldwin, about 15 minutes outside of Kelp Stream. When they arrived, Clyde, already hungover from the previous night, became impressively *re*-drunk within the first hour. Peggy's mom, Grace, was keeping pace, as she liked to take pride in the fact that no man could drink her under the table. The problem was that Grace was taking medication for a work injury, so it took even less for her to become slurrily confrontational. Peggy recalled how Thanksgiving and Christmas had come to be like stages of Dante's hell; mainly existing as a build up for an eventual drama of Greek proportions. And so, on this day, and not unexpectedly, Peggy's mom and grandmother would go at it.

"You've got some nerve comin' here with that drunk bastard and gettin' drunk yourself."

"It's Christmas! We're being celebratory, for Godsakes!"

"You're being what you always are! A Goddamn spectacle."

"And what the hell are *you*? You're holier than thou? If I hosted Christmas this year, *you'd* be the one drunk off your ass."

The words and volume would continue to climb like a ladder of unbridled hostility until they (mother and grandmother) would lunge at each other as if in a steel cage. Within minutes, they were rolling on the table containing a just laid-out Christmas dinner with all the trimmings of stuffing, salad and yams, which would soon be reduced to abstract art... By the time the turkey hit the floor, they were separated like rabid dogs by the local neighbors.

The next thing Peggy knew, she was in the backseat of her mother's car nervously watching her expertly drunk-drive, before she would be pulled over and arrested, along with her boyfriend Clyde, who thought it would be a chivalrous display to defend her honor by attempting to punch a female cop.

The car would be impounded, as the police drove Peggy home where she would spend Christmas with her dog Wojo, eating a peanut butter sandwich and watching *It's a Wonderful Life* on channel 11.

She now looked at Nicky and Luna and, once again, dug deep for inspiration, as she had had to do so many times recently; attempting to float a rose on the surface of refuse.

"We're gonna' go shopping today," she exclaimed, with forced ebullience.

"Shopping for what?" Nicky moaned.

"It's Christmas tomorrow. We've gotta' go shopping, like we do every year!"

"Can we do that this year?" Luna asked.

"Of...of course, we can. It's Christmas."

"But we're not home and daddy's not here," Luna followed.

"I know, sweetie. But we can't just wait for the day to pass. It's a special day, right? One of your favorites. It's always been special for us. This year it'll be a little...different, but we're gonna' make the most of it. And tomorrow we'll talk to Daddy, okay?"

"Can we call him today?" asked Nicky.

"We can't call him, Nicky. Your daddy has to call us."

"Why? You can't just call him?"

"Nicky, don't you think I would if I could? They have rules. There's all sorts of procedures."

"Why can't he call when he wants?" asked Luna, innocently enough.

"Because he's in prison. He doesn't have a choice."

"Has he called you?"

"No, he hasn't. Because he can't. They don't let prisoners make outside calls except on holidays. At least that's how it is now."

Luna began to cry again, which was becoming more of a reflex...

"Honey, but you'll speak with daddy tomorrow."

"Are you sure he'll call?"

"Yes, I'm sure. That's why we need to get our gifts today and then tomorrow we'll wait for his call."

"When?" asked Nicky.

"Tomorrow," Peggy responded.

"When tomorrow?" Nicky harshly followed.

"It's scheduled for 10am, so we'll make sure that we're up and all together to speak with him and then I'll take us out, okay?"

The kids remained silent, having already forgotten the plan for the day that Peggy proposed.

"So let's get cleaned up and go to the mall."

"What mall?" asked Nicky, impatiently.

"Whatever mall they have around here. There's gotta' be something. We'll shop, have a nice lunch. It'll be fun. Okay?"

"I don't wana' go," Nicky retorted.

"Why? You don't want to get gifts?"

"Gifts for who?"

"For your sister."

"With what money? We don't have anything, remember?"

"Nicky, I'll buy everything, okay? All you guys have to do is pick out something for the other."

"But we're already gonna' see each other's gift," Luna asked practically.

"No, you'll give them to me, and I'll have them wrapped before the other sees it, okay?"

"And what about *your* gift?" Luna asked.

Peggy was touched at the mere thought of her thinking of this, "Don't worry about me, honey."

"You should have a gift too, mommy."

She needed to take an emotional breath before she replied, "Just worry about your brother, okay? And, Nicky, you just worry about your sister."

"This is ridiculous," he murmured under his breath.

"Nicky, what's ridiculous?" though Peggy already knew.

"This! Being here. Eating in this crappy motel. Going to buy crappy gifts for each other."

"Stop it right now."

"No!"

"I said stop it, Nicky! This isn't helping anything! Now enough!"

With that, Nicky rose and started for the door...

"Where are you going?"

"To my room."

"What're you planning on doing in your room, Nicky?" she probed, with some paranoia as to his intent.

"Not be here."

"Nicky, wait. Come here."

"I wana' go to my - "

"Nicky, come here! I'm not asking you!"

Nicky stood there a moment, not moving. He was already exhibiting a resistance to Peggy's demonstrative tactics, which she was not the best at anyway. However, every time Nicky would rebel now, something within Peggy would be ignited; a reminder that she needed to overcompensate for the absence of Mike.

She stood up and walked from the table to him.

"I can't keep repeating the same thing to you. Things are what they are, but we have to make the best of it. This is not my fault, do you understand?"

Nicky remained looking out the window.

"Look at me."

Nicky remained...

"NICKY!" she bellowed, enough to make Luna flinch. Nicky restrained himself from the same, though he'd never heard Peggy yell at him like this, aside from the night she went off on him for displaying the graphic Viet Cong photo to his grandparents and Larry. He faced her with audacious slowness, as she resumed, "Tomorrow is Christmas...and we're not just going to spend the day staring at the crappy art on the walls. We're going to make the best of it. That means that we're going shopping and tomorrow we will have Christmas together. This is not an invitation. This is not a question. This is an order. We will be together because we only have each other, and if you think for a second that it's better to hitchhike to your father's prison, you're in for a rude awakening. You know how your father's spending Christmas tomorrow?"

Nicky did not reply, but Luna would ask instead, wearily - "How?"

"Without us - for the first time in your lives. And don't think that doesn't weigh on him too. Don't think he doesn't think about how his actions have put us in this situation. Don't think that he doesn't feel sadness and regret. And don't think he doesn't at least feel gratitude that we're here together, because if *I* wasn't here, where do you think you'd be?"

"In Florida," Nicky whispered, as if it wouldn't be the worst thing.

"Yeah, in Florida. Farther from your father. You think that'd be better?"

"At least we'd have a home."

"It wouldn't be your home. We lost our home, Nicky. That's your grandparents' home, and we're not welcome there, okay?"

"Grandma and Grampa don't want us there?" Luna innocently followed.

She looked at Luna, loath to nuance her response so that it was more accurate; that the kids were welcome but not her.

"We can't go to Florida. That's the point. The point is that we're here – together. The point is that you both have had everything since the womb and now you're just getting a small taste of all that I knew in my life before I went off to college. You've known nothing else but having everything. So now we have some adversity. It's bad, yes, but...this too shall pass. You know what that means?"

"No," Luna said, barely curious.

"It means...this is only momentary." She looked at both of them to gauge their level of absorption, becoming exhausted already at the start of the day. She took a lengthy breath so as to diffuse the tension, "Tomorrow's Christmas. So, Nicky, why don't you finish your cereal, then we'll all get cleaned up and head out. There's gonna' be a lot of traffic today, so the earlier we move the better, okay?"

"I'm not hungry anymore," he mumbled.

She looked at him for a moment, debating on what order to give him next, "Then get cleaned up and we'll leave soon."

He walked into his adjoining room, before Peggy made her way back to the breakfast table.

She stuck her spoon back into her cereal, distressed that her corn flakes had become a disgusting pile of papier-mâché. She leaned back into her hard chair, rightfully repelled at the sorry excuse of a breakfast before her, internally cursing the fact that even *IHOP* had now become an expense that challenged their day-to-day budget. She could only close her eyes in the hopes that the day would improve from here.

"I wrote a new poem. Can I read it to you?" Luna asked Peggy's closed eyes.

She had rarely discouraged Luna from impromptu readings, as she never felt it was a bad time to hear words that her daughter had created, but *life* was a bad time now, so she seriously contemplated declining. Yet the moment the thought crossed her mind, she recalled her own mother's frequent lack of interest in her work. At best, Peggy's mother would listen and her responses ranged from middling to confused. She'd more often ask Peggy to read something *"after her shows"* and then forget, and soon Peggy would simply get tired of having to follow up. Now as a mother, there was a fear within her that if she put off Luna's readings too often, it would somehow become habitual.

"You wana' read it to me?" she said, if a bit forced.

Luna went to the writing pad on her bed, and came back

to the table:

"I'm still working on it, so it's not perfect," as she read...

"It's cloudy today like many days
Why isn't there sun?
Is it hiding because it's afraid?
Is it because the snow will come?
We're in a motel today like every day
My mother, brother and me
My father is somewhere else right now
So now it's just us three.
Soon it will be Christmas and then the New Year
And someday it won't just be us three
Because my father will be here.
And then maybe the clouds will part
And good luck will soon come
Maybe things will be like they were before,
With the return of the sun."

She and Luna looked at each other, each mirroring a slight smile, but even that Peggy could not savor without envying Luna, resenting the fact that her daughter did not need to be responsible for them and could, therefore, focus on coming up with such a poem. But it was good. It was art inspired by life.

At the same time, Peggy felt that material was now swimming within her in an unfocused fragmented stew, but wondered if it ever could become anything else but fuel for a breakdown. Would she ultimately need to resign herself to the fact that Luna would be "the writer" and Peggy just the nurturer?

In the moment, that seemed to her to be a worse nightmare than the one she was living now.

12

On Christmas morning Peggy's phone rang louder than Quasimodo could ignite the bells in *The Hunchback of Notre Dame*. Everyone stopped picking at another subpar motel room breakfast to brace themselves as she answered. An automated outgoing message responded – *"Call from Hawking State Prison from...Michael Buh-bone";* the machine pronouncing the last name with an incorrect shortened "u" sound, making it less a name and more a percussive accent after a punchline. Nevertheless, it was him, as Peggy's heart raced at a pace beyond her expectations:

"Peggy?"

"Mike? Oh my God..."

"Hi, honey. I miss you so much."

"I miss you too. We all do."

"Merry..." Mike suddenly stopped. It sounded as though the phone might have initially cut out but, in fact, it was simply him having difficulty speaking, given the circumstances...

"Mike, are you there? Mike...?"

"I'm here, honey. Sorry, I'm just...I..."

"I know," as Peggy struggled to keep it together herself.

"I miss you very much."

"I know. We do too. Are you okay?"

"I'm...I'm okay, thanks."

"Are you sure? Is there... I mean, I don't know what I can do, but is...?"

"It is what it is. We're working on things. You know."

"Working on what?"

"You know, honey. Larry. He's trying to reduce my time. Trying to work out an appeal. Hasn't he been in touch with you?"

Peggy balked at this, for obvious reasons. "Um, yeah, he...yeah, it's just that I haven't spoken to him in a few days, and we've been dealing with trying to get situated, so I'm not up-to-date on everything, but I knew he was trying to..."

"Where are you?"

"Well,...we're in a motel."

"A hotel?"

"No, a *mo*tel. It's...not quite as glamorous," she tepidly snickered.

"Jesus Christ, what're you doing in a motel?"

Suddenly, Nicky's impatience with wanting to hear Mike's voice interceded, "Let me speak to him. He doesn't have a lota' time, right?"

"Nicky, wait..."

"Can you put daddy on speaker, mommy – ?" Luna followed.

"Guys, one second, okay? I need to just...speak with daddy a second first, then I'll put him on speaker, okay?

"Peg, is everything okay?"

As soon as she revealed where they were, the surface desire of wanting him home and genuine concern for his health and well-being faded behind her resentment. Now the 10 minutes that they would have would be nowhere near enough to cover topics ranging from where they were living, why they were there, why they weren't staying at Larry's, or at Vic and Elaine's, Luna's troubled tooth and sporadic panic attacks, Nicky's attempted AWOL and obstinate behavior, Peggy's daily struggle to not hoist herself onto the Long Island Expressway, barely having money for gifts, let alone many more nights at this fleabag, canary yellow shoebox of a motel, let alone pancakes at *IHOP*, let alone...

"Peggy, are you okay?" Mike followed, unaware of the medley of misery flashing before Peggy's eyes.

She restrained from making this call be about her trauma and what this was doing to the kids, and opted to click the phone on speaker in order to change the trajectory...

"Hey, guess who's here?" she forcibly exclaimed.

"Daddy?!"

"Hey, Dad!"

Luna and Nicky respectively spewed over the phone now resting in the middle of the table...

"Hey, kids. I miss you guys."

"We miss you too," Luna said, beginning to choke up, as Nicky suddenly appeared at a loss of what to say to his father.

"I love you, my little Luna."

"I...I love you too, daddy."

"Nicky? Are you there, buddy?"

"Yeah,...I'm here, dad. Are you okay?"

"Yeah, I'm okay, son. It's okay."

"Are you eating?" Peggy followed.

"Yeah, yeah, I'm eating. I wish they made your parmigiana, but it's... It's okay," he managed a laugh, indicating just how remote the cuisine was in quality to what he was used to.

There was a silence, as Luna and Nicky gazed at the phone, perhaps blocked with their own ill-formed questions, leading Peggy to realize that she could no longer yield the floor to them. There was too little time, and there was much Mike didn't know. But what exactly was beneficial for him to know? *What could he do?* For so many years, Mike was her net – the security blanket which wrapped the Bubone household like the most reliable quilt, and yet now they were exposed to the most undesirable of elements with Mike now bereft of his once formidable powers; no money, no medical practice, not even a cigar to chomp on. She could picture him on the other side of the phone in his prison-issued haircut and jumpsuit. His name now a number. He even sounded less attractive. Powerless. So what good would it do to enable his weakness further by revealing such debilitating news? He needed to be strong in prison, as Peggy needed to be strong on the outside.

She quickly brightened her tone, "The kids miss you so much. We're all sitting around here about to open our gifts, but this is the best gift we could have. Right, kids?"

The kids mutually agreed; Luna now tearfully, Nicky

introvertedly.

The euphoria that had entered the room all of minutes ago like a surprise guest now was sufficiently usurped by more of what had been.

Mike forced a laugh, "Ah, you guys are about to open your gifts? How cool. You have to tell me what you got the next time we talk, okay?"

"When's that, daddy?" Luna asked, a question they were all unsure of the answer to.

"Well, honey, right now, I'm only able to call out on the holidays so...I guess that means New Year's. And that's just, what, a week away, right? So we'll be talking soon."

"When can we see you?" Luna followed.

"Well, um, Peg?" Mike answered.   "I mean, you can see me...when you guys get settled, I guess."

"We need to find a new home and I've gotta' get a job and, once we do that, which'll be soon, we'll drive up to see daddy, okay?" she followed, asserting that these were not exactly choices within her control, at the moment.

"We were staying with Larry and Carole, daddy, but we left," Luna blurted, to which Peggy shot her an angered glare.

"What?" Mike asked.

"Luna,... Um, yes, honey, we were there for a bit."

"Because you had no place to stay?" Mike summoned the energy to express his concern over their residential in-stability.

"Well,...no, we didn't."

"He didn't even mention that. That's odd."

"Well, you know Larry, Mike. He's busy. And he was hardly there when we were."

"Well, why did you leave? Larry and Carole wouldn't mind you being there longer. They got enough space."

"Mommy didn't want to..."

"Luna, let me talk, okay?" Peggy snapped.

"Why didn't you want to stay, honey?"

"Mike, let's not take up this call with this, okay...?"

"But Peg, I'm sorry, but you're in a hotel."

"A *motel*," Nicky interjected.

"Nicky, please!" Peggy again snapped.

"Jesus Christ, a motel, Peg? And that made more sense than staying at Larry's? I don't – "

"Mike, I just felt like we were putting them out a bit," she delicately balanced her untruth. "They were very nice about everything, but it just seemed easier to not be there."

"These rooms suck," Nicky abruptly chimed...

"Nicky, stop it!" as Peggy's impatience built...

"Jesus Christ, where the hell are you staying, Peg?"

"Mike - "

"Moss Creek," Luna interjected.

"Luna, that's enough!"

"Moss Creek, Peg?!" as Mike's frustration grew, however audaciously. "You're in a motel in Moss Creek?!"

Peggy abruptly picked the phone off the table and took it off speaker, as she walked outside to the cold balcony..."It's temporary, Mike. We're not living here. It's a way station until we find a place."

"Well, when do you think that'll be?"

"When's it gonna' be? Mike, I need to find work. And until I find work, I can't get us a place. I can't put the kids back in school."

"The kids are out of school?!?

"Yes, they're out of school."

"Why the hell are they out of school?"

"Because I lost my job at the school! And Nicky went to the same school, if you recall. Everyone in Cold River knew what happened, Mike, so we had to get out of that town. We had no choice. And if I had my druthers, do you really think I'd have us staying in a shitty MO-tel on Christmas fucking day!"

"Peg, alright..." his indignance gradually receded while Peggy's hostility grew...

"I mean I know you're closed off to things being in fucking prison, but can't you at least gather how things would follow after all this?! I have no job, and because I have no job, we have no money and, because we have no money, we have no place to live. *That's* what's happening, Mike. You wanted to know? There ya' go!"

Mike was ill prepared for such unfiltered words from his once adoring wife, which led to the considerably humbled silence of crow consumption; his tone shifting now from a semblance of his usual authority to one of a beaten man. Then, softly, he inquired, "What about my folks?"

She took a breath, desperately not wanting to go down this road, "What about them?"

"You can stay with them. That makes the most sense, right? You're out of Cold River, you can recharge and then…"

"We can't, Mike."

"Why not?"

She was far too fatigued to indulge this line of questioning, but had hoped that perhaps Mike would understand on some level. She did not want to relay that the last conversation she had with them was laced with suggested blame, as if Mike would not be in prison were it not for him trying so hard to be the perfect, affluent husband to Peggy.

And then there was what Larry said in his desperate attempt to mount Peggy like an inebriated jackrabbit; *was there, in fact, another woman?*

The automated voice came on to announce that there were seconds remaining on this call, as Peggy rushed back in to put the phone on speaker for the kids.

They conveyed their love in their own ways, and they would note how they looked forward to hearing his voice again on New Year's Day, but the phone call did little to buoy anyone's spirits.

Peggy and Mike then exchanged tepid *I love you*s before the call was over.

There was silence among them when Peggy clicked off. She looked at Nicky, then at Luna – then hugged them both. Nicky was quick to let go, whereas Luna clung to her like a koala bear.

Eventually, they would open their gifts. Not out of excitement or anticipation for what was beneath the wrapping, but simply because…they were there.

She walked along a seemingly endless path and, in the distance, she would see aged homes - feebly erected domiciles that had a loathsome look of familiarity to them. In the further distance were sounds of a gathering, with indiscernible voices stacked atop each other. An occasional word or cadence would stick out, which at any point could have emanated from Mike, Vic, Elaine, Larry, Carole, Gwen, Judy, Claire, Cinda, Jocelyn, even snippets from the testimony of Violet Summers, among others. Peggy strained to make sense of this, but her attempts were futile, but it quickly dawned on her that this was the soundtrack of her recent past, which eventually led her to a vast parking lot, populated by obscured faces walking at a leaden pace, oblivious to her presence. There was all but one whom she clearly recognized – her mother, as she last remembered her. Her mother looked past her, appearing at first to be a statue of herself, as Peggy coasted by. But after several steps, Peggy could not help but stop and turn to make sure – and, in turn, so would her mother.

They gazed at each other within a now barren landscape, as if they were the last two individuals on earth.

The furrowed look on her mother's face said "Don't I know you?"...

"AHHHHHHHHHHHHHH!!!! MOMMY!!!!!" Luna shrieked, having inadvertently enhanced the crack in her tooth while brushing.

Peggy gasped as she woke up from her dream to the writing on the wall, which may well have read - *You can't afford to stay in this Godforsaken shithole much longer.* And now the piercing sound of Luna's scream not only conveyed her pain but, more painfully, what this would cost.

There had only been a one-way cash-flow for weeks since her dismissal from Cold River High School, and a very warranted fear of running out of money and maxing out her credit cards was something Peggy needed to offset in some way. No job that she could obtain quickly would make a dent in their expenses, given her limited qualifications for doing anything else but teaching. She had only ever worked in an office part-time, answering phones for Mulveck Plastic Tubing. But, of course, that was over 15 years ago, when she was also teaching and solely paying the rent while Mike was in dermatology school. Therefore, she couldn't be said to have had much of an administrative history. She started to consider waitressing, but the thought of herself in an *IHOP* uniform with a dutiful fear-of-getting-fired grin, shuttling from table to table to make sure the syrup bottles were full, seemed a fate worse than death. *Fucking Mike!*

Every dentist within a reasonable radius was on vacation through New Year's, before Peggy managed to come across a dental facility just south of Moss Creek in an even more attractively named town called Wauphaug (pronounced like an insult to Italian immigrants, *Wop-hog.*)

"What's that sound?" Nicky scowled from the backseat.

The sound was the car; the clinking that had steadily ascended since its pseudo-repair weeks prior now had escalated to that of a full-scale high school drum corps. The combination of what the motel was costing her each day, combined with what this dental appointment could cost combined with needing to repair whatever in God's name was wrong with the car left her stomach in knots, as she carefully made her way to the parking lot of *Shetler Dentistry of Wauphaug, Long Island.*

When they arrived, Peggy was given the standard paperwork. She filled it out with insurance information she wasn't even certain was valid, since it was Mike's plan through his practice, but she basically hoped for the best. Even with insurance, she was fearful of what it would cover, as this was not a routine check-up. Luna clutched her hand, with a sustained pout that had managed to go unaltered since the morning. Nicky sat beside them, attempting to get through the final third of *The Grapes of Wrath*, which Peggy insisted he finish, if only out of principal that he started it, if certainly not as an extension of hope.

She went in with Luna as Nicky remained in the waiting room.

"Please try and just focus on the cracked tooth. Nothing else, okay?" she requested.

"Well, when was the last time she had a cleaning?"

"A year ago. She's fine with that."

"Well, if it's been a year, you may want to let us – "

"No, I don't. She's in pain. I just want you to take care of that tooth. That's why we're here."

The dentist, Dr. Shetler, a portly, diminutive man, was slightly offput by Peggy's insistence, but nevertheless proceeded to analyze the extent of the damage.

"AAAAAAAAAAAAAHHHHHHHHHH!" Luna screamed, gripping Peggy's hand like a miniature vice.

"It's okay, honey," Peggy assured.

"We'll just need to take an x-ray of the tooth to get a better idea of the damage."

Peggy began to mentally calculate what this could possibly come to in her head, instantly assessing what would be absolutely essential to alleviate Luna's pain.

"Is an x-ray necessary, doctor?"

"Well, yes, it is."

"Can't you just... look and see with your own eyes what the damage is?"

"I'm afraid my vision's not quite that acute, Mrs. Buh-bone..."

"Well, it's evidently cracked, so can't you make an assessment based on that?"

"Based on what, exactly? I can't see the tooth this way, Mrs. Buh-bone..."

"Okay, first of all, it's 'Boobony', not Buh-bone, okay...?"

"I'm very sorry, but, in any case – "

"She is in pain and I can't afford bells and whistles. What can you do?"

"Mrs. Boobony, an x-ray is neither a bell nor a whistle. It's necessary for us to assess the damage to the tooth. Now if the damage isn't so severe, we can save the tooth. If it's severe enough, we may have to remove it entirely."

Peggy wasn't quite sure how to proceed in her argument, so she relented; electing to trust a doctor whom she had never met and would likely never see again. As they took x-rays, Peggy began to panic. Whatever the result of this and how much better Luna felt once whatever procedure was completed could not allay the potential sting that would come from this, especially if there was an insurance issue. As Luna was cringing in pain with every oral maneuver by Dr. Shetler or his assistant, Peggy was cringing at dollar signs, balancing between economy and trying not to appear like a welfare case.

"The tooth is severely damaged, I'm afraid. But at least it's in the back. It's one of her molars, so you may want to look into replacing – "

Before the doctor could finish his post x-ray analysis, Peggy agreed to have the tooth removed, while bypassing any additional procedures. However, another dilemma arose when the doctor suggested anesthesia.

Peggy looked at Luna in the chair and could barely fathom that she could endure the doctor's chubby, hair-knuckled fingers in her mouth much longer, let alone endure this procedure without anything to numb the pain. Alternative methods raced through her mind, including suggesting that she run to a local liquor store to get her some brandy as a numbing agent. But it was clear before she could suggest this that proposing that her 11 year-old daughter get slightly inebriated in order to save a few dollars was not a viable option. She relented again, if begrudgingly.

Before the procedure began, Peggy went out to the waiting room to make sure that Nicky was still there. He wasn't.

"Nicky?!" Peggy yelled, in an instant panic before the startled receptionist. "Where's my son?"

The receptionist stammered at the question, "Your...? I'm not sure, mam..."

"What do you mean you're not sure. He was right here and now he's not, for Godsakes...!"

She ran out into the hallway, "NICKY?!!!" then into the parking lot to her car to find that he wasn't there either, "Jesus Christ!!!" She stormed back into the office. With images of him hitchhiking alone on an L.I.E. entrance ramp or strewn out dead on a barren road somewhere, she was ready to audibly take the head off of the receptionist for letting Nicky walk out of the door unimpeded,...only to find him now sitting in the waiting room - "Oh my... Thank God. Where the hell were you?"

"I was in the bathroom," he said, undaunted as to Peggy's fears. She could now only be embarrassed that she didn't think to check there before assuming the worst, as she displayed a weakened grin to the receptionist in an attempt at downplaying her histrionic display, "I'm sorry for... He's had a history of... Well, I overrea.... Well, you know,...motherhood."

"Is that what it is," she tersely responded, as she went back to her paperwork.

Peggy looked at Nicky, sheepishly, before returning to Luna's room.

A half hour later, Peggy's hand remained in a sweat-laden clench with Luna's, as the fractured molar was successfully removed.

"So, Mrs. Buh-bone, the insurance company is saying that your insurance has lapsed," revealed the receptionist who Peggy had previously chastised for not keeping her eyes on Nicky.

"What? I thought it was... It should still be active," though Peggy was not completely surprised by this. In fact, it was her worst fear realized.

"Well, you might want to call them," the receptionist tersely responded. "In the meantime, we would need to have the balance paid in full. It's $1,692.00."

"What?! What's that for?"

"It's for the service that was provided, mam."

"What service? She got a tooth pulled."

"Yes, exactly."

"Well, that's ridiculous."

"I can show you an itemization."

"I asked for no bells and whistles. I asked for the basics of what was needed so that my daughter wouldn't be in pain."

"Well, I'm afraid that this wasn't a basic procedure. It

wasn't a check-up. It was a tooth extraction."

"And so he sticks his fingers in my daughter's mouth, pulls out the tooth and that's considered complex?"

"Mam, – "

"I mean, give me a break. What option did we have here? She's in pain and the tooth was cracked. So I need to be absolutely stung for almost $2,000?"

"Mam, I can't make any alterations on the work that was done that you're now responsible for, okay?"

"Who knew I'd be responsible for this? You think if I knew I'd be responsible for paying you almost $2000, I'd even come in the door? I would've just gotten some pliers, a bottle of bourbon and done the job myself."

"Mam, I really can't – "

"Let me speak to the doctor, please."

"He's in with a patient."

"Fine, then deal with my insurance company."

"Mrs. Buh-bone, your insurance company is claiming they are no longer your carrier."

"Well, that's their own bureaucratic ineptitude. Who were you talking to?"

"A representative of the company."

"What was her name?"

"I don't remember, but she – "

"Then how can you give credence to what they're saying? You call a number, give my name, they say *"no, she's not with us."* Anyone can give misinformation. Find someone with information and give me a name."

"Alright, if you'd like to wait here, I will call them again."

Peggy took a beat to figure out how far she wanted to pursue this line of deceit, before she managed, "Fine, call them."

The kids gazed awkwardly at Peggy, as she paced in a small nervous circle before the receptionist. She fleetingly heard the receptionist provide her name over the phone, which then led to the receptionist summoning, "Mrs. Buh-bone? I have a Darla who will be happy to speak with you."

Peggy nervously took the phone, now knowing full well the information that she would be provided;

"I'm afraid you were covered under Mr. Michael Buhbone, but the plan was terminated upon his business's closing, mam" said Darla, in a sort of Alabaman twang.

"Well, that's...that's news to me," with feigned indignance.

While Peggy's instinct would normally be to probe blindly or at least defend herself, something else took over, as she eyed the somewhat distracted receptionist, "Are you sure you're spelling it right? People always misspell it."

"B-U-B-O-N-E. That's what I have, mam."

"Oh, well, you see? I knew it. It's B-U-B-O-N-**E**," Peggy exaggeratedly stressed.

"Well, that's what I just said, Mrs. – "

As Peggy looked at the receptionist, who was now occupied with another incoming call, she further animated her tone:

"Oh, so you found us under the correct name now, yes?!"

"I'm sorry, mam – ?"

"Oh, that's wonderful. Okay, I'll put you through to the receptionist and you can get all this settled, okay?"

"Mam, I'm afraid you're not understa – "

Peggy discreetly disconnected the call outside of the sightline of the receptionist, before putting the receiver back on the hook, just as the receptionist turned her attention back to Peggy.

"Okay, so it appears they were looking under the wrong name. We're all good," as she started to walk away, while guiding the kids...

"Mam, what happened to the call?" the receptionist asked.

"Oh, I'm sorry, I meant to put it on hold for you. In any case, just call back and they'll have record of our conversation."

"Alright, well, can you wait, please, so I can confirm - ?"

"All of our information is there. You have our home address, if you need to reach us. Have a good day! Thank you!"

...Peggy grabbed Luna and Nicky by the arms and hurriedly escorted them to the parking lot. Her heart was racing as if she pulled off her first bank robbery. While there was something unsavory to her about leaving there without paying, she took a certain gratification in somehow managing to create the scenario that she was disputing an unlawful charge. Further, she would be hard to trace, given that she put down their old residence and now disconnected landline number. *But where did this sudden burst of savvy come from?* she wondered, as her hands rested upon the steering wheel. A bill had never gone unpaid in her adult life. Her lifestyle and affluence, of course, allowed for this without a second thought. And yet, in that moment, she reverted to a type of behavior that she had never been called upon to summon. But then she recalled a time as a child, when she was 12:

She remembered coming home to a ransacked living room with her mother. Various items were missing; most notably the television, stereo, some jewelry, and the sliding glass door to the backyard was open. Within hours the police came and inspected, and then wrote up a report for the insurance. One thing that Peggy clearly remembered was an unbroken spider web that was across the opening of the sliding glass door. Even then, she remembered wondering how a burglar could've gotten in and out of the house without that spider web breaking. Weeks later, after the sudden reappearance of much of the "stolen" items in the house, she would eventually connect that it was Grace, her mother, who set up the scene in order to defraud the insurance company. Everything was just a little too convenient, looking back. It wasn't as if her mother was a career criminal, but she did recall Grace often complaining about the mortgage around this time, which she paid herself; no thanks to Peggy's long-absent father or the few ill-equipped boyfriends she had had since his departure.

Regardless of the source of Peggy's current deception, it dawned on her that she may need to delve into this reserve more if they were to survive.

After the palpitations rendered by the dentist experience subsided, she felt they were owed a nice brunch out – or at least *she* was. She thought fondly of the days where she could do this without so much as blinking at the cost of three mimosas and a piece of spinach quiche accompanied by a seasonal salad. Except the drum corps-sounding engine had now escalated to a sort of tribal exorcism.

"You've gotta' be kidding me," she muttered as she nervously sped along the desolate road, occasionally looking into her rearview mirror to be assured she wasn't being followed by the receptionist.

"This car's gonna' break down," Nicky scowled.

"Mommy, whass wrong with the car?" asked Luna slurrily, still somewhat distracted by the numbing in her mouth.

"I'm not sure. Just let me focus here, okay? I just wana' get us to the restaurant and we'll figure it out from there." Peggy was committed that the problems with the car would not usurp their having a decent meal.

But apparently, even this was too much to ask...

KA-CHONK! KA-CHONK! KA-CHOOOOOOOOOOOOOOOOOO-OOOOOOONKKK!

The car suddenly gave out like a dying donkey; or what was more accurately to be the sound of the other shoe dropping.

13

A half hour later, a tow truck was driving them back into town, with their car seemingly on life support behind them. Nicky begrudgingly scrunched next to Peggy in the passenger seat, as Luna sat in Peggy's lap, much to the chagrin of the tow driver who argued that he could get a ticket if pulled over. But his conceit could hardly be called a victory for Peggy, who was still incensed that their avalanche of ill-fortune could not take an hour's reprieve to allow them a proper brunch in a restaurant. To enhance the sense of growing misfortune, as she observed *The Grapes of Wrath* in Nicky's hand, she couldn't help but further draw comparisons now to the nomadic Joads of John Steinbeck's creation. The way they were now piled into this rickety tow-truck with the building winter wind was akin to being piled into a wagon during a dust storm. Her nostalgia for what this book once did for her as far as bringing her out of her shell in Mr Gadds' English class was now replaced by her very real belief of being cursed by it, as if the repercussions resulting from Mike's offenses weren't enough.

The car was dropped off at the repair shop, which was at least a walking distance from the motel; "Call tomorra and we'll have an assessment for ya'," the grease-laden mechanic grunted, looking uncannily like the previous mechanic in Cold River, which did not bode well.

After waiting another 40 minutes, amidst the grating barrage of metal clangs and drilling sounds, a taxi finally arrived to take them to the closest thing to a Shangri La they had come to know - the *International House of Pancakes*. It was a wonder to Peggy that she was surviving this day, born out of a literal nightmare of her and her mother being the last two people on earth, dovetailing into Luna's oral surgery and the whopping bill, and now the car breaking down – all without the aid of even a terribly weak cup of motel room coffee.

They sat at what had become their favorite booth with a view of the parking lot and dumpster; a far cry from the scenic views Peggy was used to at *Harbor by the Bay*, *Le Sec* and any number of places she and Mike used to frequent. She began to do budget calculations on the paper placemat – something she hadn't had to do since she worked two jobs right after college, while Mike was still in school. She configured the daily motel rates they were paying along with the basic costs for food, cell-phone bill, laundry, along with a worse-case scenario estimate for what the car repair would cost, provided it was even salvageable. But her math could not result in any numbers that were of help to her. She only knew that the checking account was barely over thousand, and the 4 or 5 credit cards were nearly maxed.

What else can go wrong? Can anything else? It felt like it really wasn't possible, and yet that seemed like wishful thinking. *I mean, we're almost really homeless,* she thought. *Not living-at-a-hotel-or-motel-homeless, but real no-options-but-a-shelter homeless.*

Her anxiety was now quietly filling her stomach before her mushroom omelet even reached the table.

"Will there be anything else?" asked yet another benignly smiling waitress.

"Yes, can I get a drink?" Peggy asked.

"Sure, what can we get ya', hon?"

"Is it possible to make a mimosa?" Peggy asked, trying to mask a desperate plea.

"A what?" the waitress sincerely inquired.

"It's... I know it's not on the menu, but it's champagne and orange juice."

"No, I'm afraid we don't have that. I'm sorry. Would you like a Strawberry Lemonade?"

"Does that have alcohol?"

"Um, no, it's just...a strawberry lemonade."

"Is it possible to just get a drink? A scotch? A brandy?"

"I'm sorry..."

"Really? Nothing?"

"I'm sorry, we - "

"There's not a busboy back there with a flask of something?"

The waitress weakly chuckled, "'fraid we only have what's on the menu."

Peggy was almost desperate enough to keep pressing, but thought better of it, absorbing the awkwardness now in the poor waitress's eyes, while Luna appeared to take notice of Peggy's eagerness.

"What's the matter?" she asked Luna tersely, as she aggressively stirred her coffee.

"Nothing," as Luna cut into her waffles ala mode.

Peggy was not having even a hint of judgement regarding her display, even if her requests were obviously beyond the bounds of an innocent pancake waitress's capabilities. In the moment, she couldn't even care to consider if Luna was looking at her that way because she recalled, even in her youthful innocence, that her mother once drank too much; a fact that Peggy felt only *she* was really aware of.

And yet, in Luna's eyes, Peggy began to see herself at that age; perhaps at a point where her own mother's eccentricities were still surprising to her.

Why does it seem like we're no longer among the living world? she wondered. No e-mails of note, no texts from anyone except reminders of bills that needed to be paid. No calls. Larry had been M.I.A. since Peggy and the kids fled their abode. It was obviously out of embarrassment, awkwardness, what have you. But while she could not bear to speak with Larry the bourbon-sipping horndog, she felt she could at least tolerate Larry the lawyer. He was still working for Mike, after all, and no one really knew more as to the progress of Mike's status or lack thereof than Larry. But she didn't feel right about initiating a call to him, especially with how things were left off. It seemed easier to wait, and it wasn't as if she didn't have other concerns.

As she sat by her motel room window and chain-smoked as she hadn't in years, she was sick to think that she had all of two things to look forward to; a call from the mechanic about the status of her car and a call from her husband in prison on New Year's Day. Other than that, there was nothing. Vic and Elaine had not called since the last hostile exchange just prior to them moving in with Larry and Carole; another fact that she had avoided bringing up with Mike in the limited time they had to speak. What good would it do him to know that his parents harbored unwarranted resentment towards his wife to the extent that they would only take her kids but allow the wolves to devour her? Just as what good would it do her to mention that Mike's most trusted friend tried to jump her?

Her phone rang, forcing some of the elongated ashes from her cigarette to descend onto the asparagus-green carpet. Something in her still recalled how nervous she had grown with answering the phone in recent months; expecting that pause - that cigarette sucking sound. But that was only ever on the landline, never on her cell,...so at least *those* fears were pretty much unfounded now. It was the auto-shop:

"Thecorpuselleftcylinderisimpairedduetotherig   ht-crankshaftdamaged..." the mechanic spewed in a rote mono-tone, or it at least sounded like this.

"How much is this gonna' come to?" she asked, de-featedly.

"Well, sincetheenginesleftcylindercrankshaft - "

"Please, no more auto-lingo, okay? How much is this gonna' cost me?"

"$3,255, with labor."

Peggy began to hear that piercing whistle-sound again, expecting any neighboring dogs to bust through her motel room door. *We can't not have a car. We at least need a damn car.*

"How much for me to be able to drive it out of there?"

"Whata' y'mean?" asked the mechanic.

"You're telling me how much it costs to fix everything. How much for the bare essentials, just so I can drive it?"

"Mam, if ya' don't take care of the other issues, you still could end up with the same problem..."

"Look, do you want me to get the Better Business Bureau on your back, sir...?!"

"Look, mam, I know from experience that you need – "

"HOW MUCH TO DRIVE IT OUT OF YOUR SHOP, PLEASE?!"

The mechanic took a pause, as the metal clangs behind him continued...

"$1,250."

"With labor?"

"Yeah, with labor."

She was still leveled by this. It was still far too much. It was still going to devastate their finances... And they offered no sort of installment plan.

She needed to pay this to have a car, and had no idea how long it would last, but she had little choice, unless they were to exist on taxis or infrequent local buses. *And what kind of people take the bus in Long Island?*

The end was nearing.

They arrived at Monique's home, which appeared to be smaller than Larry and Carole's carriage house. Peggy gazed at it from the curb, a sigh taking over her breath: *How the hell are we gonna' fit in there?*

It had come to this, cashing in on Monique's offer from weeks prior. Her once affluent and respected husband's ever-reliable receptionist, who Peggy enjoyed for brief exchanges and hugs whenever she stopped by Mike's office, whom Peggy comforted in the parking lot when Mike was arrested. The net that Mike had all but swore he'd be for Peggy and the kids was now in the hands of his formerly underpaid administrative assistant.

They were greeted by Monique and her 3 kids in an endearingly respectful line to welcome Peggy, Nicky and Luna at the door, as if they were long-lost relatives.

"This is Jason, Michelle and Richie," Monique introduced, in the order of their height and ages, which was from 7 to 10.

"Oh, how handsome you all are. Monique, they're beautiful."

"And who are *these* handsome ones?" Monique asked playfully.

But she was not completely kidding, for it soon dawned on Peggy that Monique had never met the kids in person. She had only seen their pictures in the office, and perhaps through the car windows as they were driven out of the office parking lot. She was never at the house, not even at Mike's 40th Birthday party, and it saddened Peggy to question if Mike ever even invited her. And even if he did, it made her feel equally bad to not have asked him at the time. *What was it to ask, "Did you invite Monique?"* But then, they lived an embarrassment of riches. Friends were like the ocean. Everything was in abundance, even if it was ultimately vapor. And now, here was their saving grace, Monique, taking them in to her house like orphaned cats.

The house was a fraction of the size of their Cold River home, which was a continent by comparison. The place was well-kempt but cluttered with family photos adorning every table and bookshelf. There was a man in some of them, but not many. Peggy assumed this was the husband, or ex-husband. She wasn't exactly sure, as he was not mentioned, nor was there a sense of one being around. It appeared that this may well have been a post-marriage house that Monique could barely afford on her own, and which was already stretching it for a mother and 3 kids - now there was another mother and 2 kids. *Where could we go in this place?* she wondered.

"So I have the kids in one room and basically made the boys' room for you guys, okay? It's still a little messy, but you guys should be comfortable enough there."

The room was a slightly enlarged broom closet. *The tomato section of our garden was bigger than this.* Yet on the outside, Peggy kept her best face on and was firm about Nicky and Luna doing the same. Again, they were to be appreciative. Grateful. At the mercy of another family bailing them out of indigency. And yet the rooms were getting smaller and smaller, like a *Twilight Zone* episode or some such thing. There was barely room to have a nightmare.

"We can't all sleep here," Nicky spewed, as the three of them stood in their new luxury suite. "Ssssh, Nicky. What's the matter with you? They can hear you," Peggy chastised, in what would be a consistently hushed tone.

"Well, look at it. It's too small."

"I know it's small. An elf would know this place is small. We don't have a choice."

"My bedroom was the size of this entire house."

"Nicky, put a sock in it. Right now! We are guests."

"We're *always* guests."

"When're we gonna' have a houfe again?" Luna slurred, the effects of the recent surgery and anesthetic still with her.

"Honey, do you think I know that? Your mother doesn't know how she's gonna' pay for the phones, let alone when we're gonna' own a home again. Now I know this sucks..."

"Duh!"

"Nicky, that's enough! The walls in this place are probably made with paper towels, so if you have the urge to say something sarcastic, you better keep it to yourself. Do you hear me? Now we...we obviously are not gonna' be able to stay very long..."

"I miff daddy," Luna began to cry.

"I know you do, honey..."

"Why're we even staying in Long Island anymore?" Nicky spewed.

"What?"

"Dad's upstate, grandma and grandpa are in Florida, you don't have a job and we're not in school, so – "

"So what's your solution, Nicky? You always seem on the verge of having an answer. Give me one. What, you wana' move to where your father is? Well, y'know what, they don't have accommodations for entire families in prison! Okay?

You wana' move with your grandparents? Well, y'know what, your grandparents hate your mother. Okay?"

"Why do they…?"

"They just do, Luna. I'm not gonna' get into all this, except that they are not an option for us, unless I wana' send you down there to live with them for a while, which is not going to happen."

"Why not?" Nicky blurted, with momentarily blind courage, before just as quickly bracing himself for Peggy's ire. She gazed at him intensely, on the verge of a violent outburst for what seemed like a short, frozen lifetime…

"Because you're *my* fucking kids."

This sentence managed to hang in the air, creating a pin-dropping silence, as her eyes remained fixed on her son who, again, she was oh so very close to slapping. She even hated him in this moment. *The gall of him to even suggest that they'd be in better hands with Vic and Elaine.* He still hadn't a clue what this experience was doing to her, and what she was doing just to keep them afloat. And if she ended up being a waitress somewhere just so that there was a modicum of income, he would never comprehend the nobility of her efforts.   All he would ever know, at his dim-witted 13 years of age, would be that he once had everything he needed without comprehending it – and now he didn't. Now he was forced to share a room with his mother and little sister. He'd have to wait 40 minutes to use the only bathroom. He couldn't raid the refrigerator whenever he wanted. He would be going into the New Year knowing only that his mother had failed them all.

She continued to gaze into Nicky's eyes, and became all the more enraged when she saw Mike in him and all the similarities he would grow to have; the charm, the arrogance, the natural talent, the possible infidelity,…perhaps even the greed. What was sliding off of him and what would stick throughout all this? Would he be doomed to repeat his father's sins?

And this little bastard thinks I'm to blame?

Then there was a knock. Monique's voice bled through the door, as if sensing the tension on the other side:

"Hey, guys. Sorry to bug you, but if you'd like to join us for dinner, we'd love to have you, okay?"

After dinner, the kids dispersed into their ultra-cramped quarters, as Peggy and Monique remained, sipping coffee. It was a strange sort of déjà vu, for she remembered not long ago being at the table alone with Carole after the kids had left, sipping coffee, talking about all things aside from Peggy's circumstances and, in hindsight, Carole's disintegrating marriage. Monique did not have the same sense of culture as Carole had, so there was little to discuss there beyond anything impressive her kids had done in school. She also didn't have an interesting vocation to share, such as co-managing an art gallery, nor could they even discuss interesting books they had read, since Monique's tastes were fairly low-brow, judging from what cluttered her shelves; romance novels, shlock mysteries or true crime stories, which more or less centered around a rich wife who had her rich husband killed or vice versa. Monique admittedly would read this sort of crap because, by comparison, it made her life seem enviable, as one would suspect made up much of the intended audience for the genre.

In actuality, aside from owning a home and having a job, her reality was not much better than Peggy's, and so it proved difficult to navigate their conversation in any other direction than the present tense:

"I'm just thankful there's an income, Peggy. Knock wood, y'know?"

"I know."

"I mean, it's hard when you're in the administrative world to be at one place for so long, and then one day - blip! - you're not there," she weakly snickered, as she sipped.

"But at the same time, it must look pretty good to have 7 years at one place, right, Monique?"

"*8* years, Peggy," Monique said with emphasis, which took Peggy back a bit. "8 years. And sure, you'd think, *oh yeah, 8 years of experience in one place.* Sounds good, right? But no, they look at it like it was 8 years in one place doing one kinda' thing for one doctor. And then technology changes, so if you're gonna' do somethin' new, you gotta' learn somethin' new. You go from being a seasoned veteran to a rookie over-night. Startin' from scratch. And then you gotta' be grateful for anything that comes your way. Anything. I was dealin' with 3 or 4 different agencies, workin' 2-3 day weeks as a temp when people are on vacation or out sick. Then gettin' desper-ate enough, God forgive me, to even hope someone got the plague or somethin' so I'd have a long term assignment," she laughed with embarrassment.

It was hard for Peggy to hear this and not have tremen-dous guilt. The very reason that Monique was going through all that she was describing was Mike, plain and simple. And what was even sadder for Peggy was how Monique looked at having any job now as a success. Even with having no job, no prospects and no income, Peggy could not envy this. She hated this life she was witnessing, even though she was at the mercy of it. Where else could they go other than a cheaper motel for a couple of weeks before the money ran out?

She could say very little in consolation other than com-mend Monique for her endurance, before eventually Monique, perhaps self-aware of what she may have been inadvertently giving off, extended her encouragement:

"Maybe it'll be to your advantage to not have been at one place for so long. I don't know how it is for teachers."

"Well, I'm afraid it's different for teachers who aren't substitutes."

"I guess so."

"Yeah. They expect substitutes to bounce around, not full-time teachers of Literature or English. All they'll see now is a teacher who hadn't taught in over 15 years getting let go after 3 months. But I'm mainly speculating now because I can't even get an interview anywhere with the holidays. It's like *All Quiet on the Eastern Front.*"

Monique laughed, "You're clever. That's a good title for somethin'."

Peggy wanted to savor her diverting laughter, but could

only be distressed that Monique didn't know that this was her humorous variation on Erich Maria Remarque's classic, *All Quiet on the Western Front*, though it was hardly worth the effort to note this.

In the end, Peggy resigned that it was simply going to be far too difficult to be there very long. And while the duration of their stay was not discussed, it didn't take a tree to fall on her for her to realize that this sort of diversion was not something that was needed by Monique. Whereas Carole ultimately had grown to relish Peggy's presence, as it likely served to divert the distance in her marriage to Larry, it seemed it was all Monique could do to simply feed her kids and pay her mortgage with as little outside distraction as possible.

And what the hell are we going to talk about aside from our miseries? They didn't know each other outside of the 10-minute office stop-bys or the 2-minute phone exchanges. Monique was content to work to survive every day and have little else in the way of a life, aside from maybe occasionally masturbating to her romance novels or going out to see a terrible Hollywood movie at the multiplex. But this was who she was. She wasn't stupid. She was smart and had good survival instincts, and Peggy could tell that, while she may have had bad taste in men, she was a good mother - perhaps better than Peggy would ever be. She was proudly from Jamaica, Queens, and it seemed that while the girl left Queens, Queens never left the girl. On the other end, Peggy had spent most of her life fleeing from everything she came from, re-making herself from scratch as a shy, vulnerable girl to an outspoken student who adored books, art, good films, confessional poetry, with dreams of writing novels, book tours and network interviews. That was the dream, sidetracked by way of marriage and motherhood. And yet even that digression was what still made her appear successful to Claire, Judy, Gwen and pretty much everyone who knew the Bubone family, especially Monique.

And now she was here, even farther from her original aspirations. Having to be content with gratitude for having shelter, for being alive, for not holding up a convenience store or resorting to prostitution...

She was so low that failure was almost a complement.

14

There was an azure sky – the clarity like nothing she ever witnessed in her life. So quiet; a peace that she fleetingly experienced during moments of yoga class, and yet somehow she was experiencing this bliss now. She wasn't even thinking to ask herself how her mind was finding this solitude. Soon there were distant sounds; not voices, but something strangely percussive. The louder it got, the clearer the source – a shovel coming in and out of the ground. Suddenly, the tranquil blue sky was being gradually obstructed by dirt descending upon her. She couldn't move. She began to wonder where she was, why was she constrained and being hit by shovel-fuls of black soil.

As the dirt continued to rain upon her, it became clear...that she was being buried alive...

She woke up, hyperventilating alongside a barely sleeping Luna, with whom she was sharing a twin bed.

It was morning of New Year's Day.

"*Call from Hawking State Prison from...Michael Buh-bone*"; the automated outgoing message again saying the last name as if a drum accent after a punchline.

"Hey, Guys!" emanated from Peggy's phone, which laid on one of their beds, surrounded by Peggy and the kids.

"How are you daddy? We miff you!" yelled Luna, louder than necessary.

"I'm ok, honey. No better or worse, which is a good thing. Don't worry about me. How are you? Did you get something nice for Christmas?"

"Um...yeah, I guess."

"You guess? I'm sure it was somethin' good."

"I got a new drawing pad,...and a new journal to write in."

"Okay, cool. Did mom take you guys out?"

"Um...yeah, I guess..."

An awkward silence, which Mike could deduce conveyed a general dissatisfaction...

"Well, I know it was a little different this year but..."

"A lot's happened, Mike. I don't think the kids really remember Christmas."

"What's happened in a week?"

"We're staying at Monique's," Luna inserted.

Peggy looked at Luna, saying without words that she wanted to divulge their current circumstances to their father at her own pace. But since there was such an utter lack of other news to reveal that wasn't horribly bleak, it seemed that that was all that could be brought up. Nicky at least appeared well warned by Peggy to not regurgitate his criticism over their current residence, but he also wasn't saying much of anything else.

"Monique's?! Are you serious?!"

"Sssssh, Mike, she's here, okay? She can hear."

"Whata' you mean she can hear? Is she in the room?"

"Mike, Monique...Monique has been nice enough to take us into her home. It's a little small and the walls are not... Just, yes, we're at Monique's. I'll tell you more at another time."

"I thought you were at a hotel."

"We were at a *mo*tel, and we couldn't afford it."

"So now you're at Monique's?"

"Yes, we're at Monique's, Mike. Why is that the biggest issue for you? First it was the motel that you had issue with and now this. Yes, okay?"

"I can't... I mean, how... This was the only option?"

She took a breath, reluctant to continue this particular exchange in front of the kids, "Yes, Mike. It was."

"Peggy,..."

"Don't fight, please," Luna ordered.

"What, honey...?" Mike asked, unclear...

"No one's fighting, honey. It's... Mike, let's just... Can we just...be together with the kids and...and...?" She looked at Luna and the sulking Nicky, and simply could not sell herself on the benefits of wasting a phone call with Mike by acting as if nothing was wrong. She grabbed the phone...

"Can you guys leave me in here to speak with your dad a second?"

"I wana' speak to him. I WANA' SPEAK TO DADDY...!"

"Luna..." Peggy could barely console...

"Peggy, look, I wana' be with the kids. Is Nicky there? Nick?"

"I'm here, dad," Nicky mumbled under Luna's tears...

"I'm sorry, we have to talk," Peggy insisted. "Kids, go in the living room and watch TV or something."

"Her kids are out there already," Nicky protested...

"So be out there with them. They're not lepers."

"No. I don't wana' go out there. *You* go!"

"Peggy, just let the kids be here, okay? I can't call every day – "

"I know, Mike! But we need to talk, okay?!!!"

She grabbed the phone and left the room. Since it was New Year's Day, everyone was home, so there were even less options of where to have a private conversation in this mini-abode. She stepped into a small pantry closet adorned with boxes of Fruit Loops and rolls of paper towels and attempted to close the door for privacy...

"Mike, can you hear me...?"

On the other end, the phone was breaking up, "Pe...it...ot...Pe...it...ot..."

"Shit!" she yelled loud enough for Monique and her kids to hear, as she raced out of the house until the reception improved, but continued down the block to allow herself room for a panic attack...

"Mike, we're in trouble, okay? We're at the end here."

"Whata' you mean? The end – ?"

"THE END!!!! NOTHING. WE HAVE NOTHING!!!"

"Peggy, my God, calm - !"

"Mike, I can't. Okay? This is too much. We have hardly any money left. I spent over a thousand dollars to fix the car, which can still konk out with a slight breeze. We couldn't afford to keep spending money at the motel... I have no prospects. I don't know when I'm going to get a job. I can't do anything else but teach and I just started doing that again – "

"Peg, calm – "

"I got into it for 3 months, Mike! All of 3 months before I was fired, Mike! I can't do anything else, okay?! For almost 15 years, all I was was your wife and their mother. And you know what? They don't pay you for that. And we have nowhere else to go while we're breathing through straws and standing in a flood, okay? That's it. You wana' metaphor? There it is. We're drowning!"

"Peggy, please, just calm down, okay..."

"Mike, this is how things are, do you understand? I'm telling you where we're at."

He took a breath, "Peg,...why did you leave Larry and Carole's? They would love to have you and they have the room..."

"Mike, I'm gonna' scream right now."

"Peggy, don't screa... Why're you gonna' scream...?"

She managed to restrain herself, but conveyed severity with her intense enunciation, "We-cannot-stay-at-Larry's!"

He took a moment, "Well, what happened? He said he hasn't even heard from you."

"Mike,...it didn't work out," it was all Peggy could do to not reveal the truth. As frazzled and emotionally unstrung as she was, she at least was cognizant enough to know that impairing his relationship with Larry would affect what Larry could do for him. Mike would at least be prideful enough to tell Larry to fuck off if he believed that he came onto Peggy while he was imprisoned barely a month.

"Why...what didn't work out? Was Carole put out? I know she can be a little anti-social."

She took a moment, before taking the opportunity to

use the excuse that Mike readily provided, "Yeah, she,...we just sensed it was a little much for her. Larry's probably a little embarrassed about it, so I...I wouldn't mention it to him."

Mike absorbed this, realizing their time was dwindling, "Well, at least pick up when he calls, okay? He says he can't reach you. It's important that you be in touch. Especially if there's news."

He can't reach me? She indulged Larry's blatant lie of having called her, even once, since their last encounter by acting as if she didn't hear it, "Is there anything new that I should know about, Mike?"

"Well, not really. I'm just not sure right now when I'll be able to call next. They're doing some permission restructuring here, and so it could be a couple of weeks, a couple of months. And I know it's not practical to come upstate now, but why don't you just stay with my folks. It's a cheap ticket to Florida, and they'd love to have you and the kids. And then you can all come up together."

She knew this would be brought up, and again she debated revealing anything, but her contempt for them and the situation had now become insurmountable, "Well, they'd love to see the *kids*, I know that."

"Why do you say it like that? They'd love to have you too."

"You really believe that, Mike?"

"Yes, I do. My God, of course I do."

She found it hard to believe that Mike bought this, but understood that his denial of their questionable character could render such conviction. He was their favorite son, after all. Nevertheless, she couldn't contain her skepticism, "Have they said as much to you?"

"What...? They don't have to. They're practically your parents."

She took a quiet, resentful moment at just the inference of this, "They're not my parents, Mike."

"Why do you say that, Peg?"

"Because they're not."

"Peg,..."

"Mike, you think I'm Little Orphan Annie? I should just be grateful to be taken in by whoever wants to adopt me?"

"I'm not saying that. I'm saying that they care about you."

"You're saying they're like my parents and I'm saying that they aren't."

Mike took a moment, "Well, who is, then?"

"What does *that* mean?"

"I mean if you're alienated from everyone else in Cold River, if you can't stay anywhere else that you can afford, if you don't want to go to Florida, I mean...what other option? *Your mother?* You're gonna' reconnect with *that* pieca' work? I know hell would freeze over before you'd even consider that, so...that's what I'm saying. My parents will be there for you. I know they will."

In her dreams and in faint flashes, her mother had crossed her mind. She still knew the number like her social security number. She could call and try and act composed and not desperate; a guise of being the bigger one who reached out first after 17 years. But would this really be better than sending the kids to Vic and Elaine's and focusing on just trying to get herself on track? What was of most importance here; that the family just do what it needed to do to survive until the fog somehow cleared? *And how would it?* It now seemed so clearly foolish to think that life should be on hold until Mike was free. He would be different somehow. He would feel different. And she would see him differently. Kissing on their marble coffee table with her heal in the pâte was a memory that all but belonged to another couple now.

And while it was clear that Mike genuinely felt terrible about not being able to do anything to help his own family, Peggy was not endeared to him anymore by having to stay with Monique. It was a perspective that, for the moment, somehow veered Peggy away from the current subject and brought other things into question. They may have been misplaced now, but they somehow still mattered to her:

"Mike?"

"Yeah."

"Did you ever invite Monique over?"

"What? Why're you asking such a thing?"

"It just dawned on me. Your 40th birthday party. We had everyone there, except her. Did you ask her?"

"Peggy,...it's all I can do to survive right now. Thinking back to the guest list of my birthday party months ago is the last – "

"You don't remember asking if she'd like to come?"

Mike let out a frustrated sigh, "I probably did, and she probably couldn't make it. She's got 2 kids."

"Three."

"What?"

"She has *three* kids."

"Okay, so, there ya' go."

There was an odd silence, with Mike clearly being thrown by the course of the conversation...

"What, did she mention this to you?"

"Of course not. It's just...something I've been thinking about."

"Why?"

She wondered if she would've given this a second thought if she wasn't staying there,...but she was.

"Honey,...you know, we're gonna' have to wrap up soon and I'd rather just focus on you and the kids, okay? I wana' know you guys're gonna' be alright. I know I made mistakes and I'm responsible for this, but it'd break my heart to hang up and not know you guys are safe. So, please, just get an airline ticket and stay with my parents right now. You have no ties in Long Island, aside from Larry, so it makes sense. Doesn't it?"

She stood in the middle of the quiet road, under-dressed on a 42 degree New Year's morning, and looked at her phone, aware of their time dwindling...

"Mike?"

"Yes, honey."

She swallowed, "Do you know anyone in Ohio?"

"Do I know what?"

Suddenly the automated outgoing message interceded, as if on cue – appearing to bail Mike out, and possibly saving

Peggy affirmation of what Larry had reluctantly divulged.

They rushed their goodbyes, before she clicked off. "You son of a bitch," she whispered in the cold, in earshot of Luna now standing beside her, crestfallen at missing the opportunity of saying goodbye to her father.

"Were you fighting?" she asked.

"No, honey."

As she looked at Luna before gently walking her back to Monique's house, Peggy mused over what this latest exchange with Mike accomplished. She could not reveal all she wanted to reveal or ask all that she wanted to ask, but perhaps the one thing that got across was her lack of confidence in relying on his parents; something she never even dared to suggest before.

But, of course, this mainly served to bring into question just who else there was.

15

That night her phone trembled in her hand as she dialed from memory. She wouldn't speak if anyone picked up, but simply wanted to know at this point if her mother would. Peggy felt strongly that her mother was alive and still living at the same home of Peggy's up-and-down bringing. Even though she had no connection to her mother for 17 years, she felt some sort of intuition would let her know if she had passed; a sort of internal sensor that could only reside within one's offspring.

The phone clicked on, and Peggy gasped, ready to click off,...but not before hearing that unmistakable voice... *"Hey, this is Grace and Joe and little Pearl. We're not home right now, but leave a message..."*

Peggy hung up, her heart palpitating like a thousand drummers. It was her mother, alright. She didn't even need to hear her name, with that raspy cadence wrapped in Central Jersey that was most undeniable, and barely altered from years of Benson & Hedges. *But who's Joe? And who's Pearl? A daughter?*

Am I no longer an only child?

It seemed already that the house may have been fuller than Peggy anticipated. She assumed that Grace would be alone, as she always had the tendency to end relationships before they started. And she didn't necessarily see that changing with age.

But perhaps she *did* change. Perhaps the quiet domestic family life that was undesired throughout Peggy's childhood finally became appealing, aided in no small part by the hole left from Peggy's estrangement.

She decided to not wait for opportunities to appear. Instead, she would be the aggressor, propelled by her desperation that she attempted to mask with confidence and a seasoned professionalism that belied exactly how seasoned she was. Over the course of the next week, she would drive through a half dozen neighboring towns, and would simply walk into high schools and private schools that she managed to find, requesting an interview with anyone with enough administrative clout to hire.

"Hi, my name is Peggy Bubone. I was wondering if I could speak with the Vice Principle or Principle or anyone in a decision-making role regarding any openings you might have for teachers," was her introductory sentence to the average secretary or front desk person. She would often be greeted by an expression that conveyed,*"This is not normally how things are done here,"* but Peggy was not surprised by that, nor was she deterred. Yes, she knew that you didn't just walk into a school coldly like a pock-marked teenager walking into a Starbucks looking for a summer gig as a barista, but she was a Joad, she rationalized. No one was going to hand her anything, nor was anyone going to care about her well-being as much as she. Thinking outside of the box had clearly become the only option.

She appeared to get lucky and garnered a meeting with Janet Bergen, the principle of Massapauke Highschool, a respectfully-rated public school;

"Peggy, may I ask why you left such a prestigious school as Cold River?" after already meeting with Peggy for 30 minutes and seeming to be warmed by her humor and the remnant of her persona that she was able to summon for this interview.

"Well, I..." Peggy had attempted to rehearse the answer to this question, which she did to the medicine cabinet at Monique's before leaving that day. To her reflection, the answer came out like this:

"That's a good question, and I'm happy to answer. Actually, I very much enjoyed my duration at Cold River, and I was in very good standing with those on staff and had established an excellent reputation among my students. But, to answer your very astute question,..."

However, when in the room with Janet Bergen, she somehow blanked on exactly what she had dutifully rehearsed. Instead, her response came out as such:

"Well, I... That's, yes, that's a very good question, Janet. Thank you. Yes. I was...I was... Well, to be honest, which is I know all you would expect from someone in my position, I was a very good teacher. I was in very good standing with... My students loved me. Most of them, *many* of them. They... I was getting through to many of them, I felt. Tricia; Tricia Wentworth. This very plain girl. I looked at her every day and saw myself. I saw this shy girl. Misunderstood by the world. I saw myself in her because I *was* her. And I was waiting for someone to tell me, *'You're smart. Don't be afraid to be smart. To say what's....what you think is....'* And I was able to be that for her. It was one of my greatest victories. I know teachers who had been in the field far longer than myself and I can tell you that they didn't have a story like that. They didn't have that...that victory with a student, and *I* did. I was winning with her. It was...it was...it was... And I could've done more. I knew it. I know it. I can do more. I want to...to be victorious for these... I have kids. And I sometimes don't see how I can be that for them. I'm just their mother. I'm just the one who cares for them. I'm the one who tries to stimulate their creativity, their intelligence... I'm the one who tries to keep them focused when the world that they knew has... has...eroded. I can't...I feel I can't be victorious for them because they just assume I *have* to do these things. Their heroes need to be someone who hasn't seen them in their underwear. Who hasn't potty trained them. The external world is what... is what they admire because it's outside of the one who gave them life. I only gave birth to them, you see?"

Janet Bergen was beginning to get that unsettled glaze, like a dismayed doughnut, but somehow it was not enough to slow Peggy's verbal avalanche:

"I mean, I went to Princeton, for Godsakes. I got a scholarship. You can't understand how much of a dichotomy I am compared to what I came from. *Dichotomy*, my God. If I said that in my hometown, they would think I was talking about something prehistoric. My husband has ruined my life!"

A moment sat, as Peggy looked at Janet as if just remembering why she was there and suddenly realizing how inappropriate such revelations were.

"Okay, well, Peggy, thank you for...coming in and telling me a little about yourself. I have your resume here, so should anything open up..."

Her voice faded away... Peggy knew she blew it. She knew Janet wouldn't so much as hire her for a janitorial position, given her display. Not only that, she realized that her vomiting up such details may as well have placed Janet Bergen into the vast category of those who had ostracized her.

She walked numbingly to her car and thought about some of what she'd said to Janet. While her determination was there, it occurred to her that she simply was not equipped to represent herself professionally until she could overcome her sense of feeling outcasted. *How ironic*, she thought. She recalled what Tricia Wentworth had said in class, about Esther Greenwood's sense of alienation; how it wasn't so much a sickness as her feeling removed somehow. While Peggy's reasons for feeling this way had greater clarity than Esther's, it no longer seemed that the solution for her state resided in simply getting a job and an apartment. She was being engulfed by a lack of identity, and was only certain that she needed to move out of Monique's house soon and have an income and do whatever she could to avoid having to call her mother, now residing with "Joe" and "Pearl"; a new family that could perhaps null and void any connection she had.

She drove silently to Monique's small home with the kids distracted by their gumdrop/balloon-type games. Luna would occasionally throw up an unhelpful sentence, as she had been doing a lot of lately; *"I miss school"*, *"I miss my friends"*, *"I miss daddy"*, *"I miss our home"*... Peggy ignored her now. She had exhausted her optimism or even parental rationalization. She was not a teacher now, she was not a wife now, she was barely a mother and, perhaps, not even a daughter. She drove as if waiting for a head-on collision to erase these earthly issues, and then perhaps she'd come back as a Koala bear, with little responsibility aside from consuming eucalyptus leaves.

She started to think more about the infamous story of the wife and kids who all killed themselves while their once wealthy husband and father was in jail, which constantly appeared in re-runs on shows like *American Sleaze*. It did not help that Monique often watched these shows, which she allowed herself to be addicted to along with her hideous romance novels. The irony of what led to her unemployment did not seem to deter her from enjoying various flim-flam artists getting their comeuppance. Peggy's paranoia even led her to think that Monique's very intent was to remind her that her husband was a greedy, selfish fucker.

"I couldn't conceive what he was doing with all those poor people's money," a tear-struck wife exclaimed on the latest episode.

"What a shame, huh?" Monique repeated, as she voraciously wolfed down a box of caramel corn. Peggy sat beside her on the couch, barely listening, but feeling obligated to be an ear when it appeared one was needed. At the commercial, Monique would continue on the subject of infamous criminals and their offspring, "Madoff's kid offed himself too, and maybe he really was clean. Hell, Charles Manson had a kid. D'you know that?"

"Um...no. Really?" Peg replied.

"s'what I heard, yeah. I jus' found this out after Manson finally died. Had a kid, Charlie Manson Junior. Tried to change his name, this'n that. Whata' y'think happened? Killed himself."

"Oh God."

"You know why? 'Cause they were contaminated. Mighta' never intended to do a bad thing in their lives, but the ghosts of their evil fathers were already in them. You can't outlive somethin' notorious. Right? It's within you. People think you can outlive it. You can't. Maybe it doesn't mean you're gonna' be evil too, but evil is hard to outlive when it's what you came from. Y'know, Peggy?"

As Monique continued to speak, and unusually aggressively for someone with a mouthful of caramel corn, Peggy was all the more weighed down by all this talk of "fate". *And whose fate?* Her own for marrying Mike? For being born from a boorish mother? Were Nicky and Luna fated to be doomed as a result of this?

Just what do we have control over in this life? she wondered.

She stared at plasma screen and saw her life, which was a barely preferable re-run to this depressing episode of *American Sleaze* that Monique was now hypnotized by.

And when her recollections finally returned her to the couch beside Monique,...she would only have the strength to retire for the evening.

Nicky was asleep, while Luna scrunched beside Peggy on their own twin bed. She gazed up at the ceiling, praying for her mind to clear so that she could possibly have a few hours of stress-free rest.

"Mommy?" Luna softly whispered.

"I thought you were asleep."

"I can't."

"Well, try."

"What are we doing tomorrow?"

"I don't know, Luna."

"Do you have another interview?"

"Not that I know of, but we'll see."

"Why won't anyone hire you?"

"Because it's...it's a tough time of the year to be looking for work. The holidays just finished. I've told you this."

"What are we gonna do? How long can we – ?"

"Luna, you have to stop with these questions, and telling me what you miss. I can't explain things any more than I already have. We're here now and when we're not here, you'll know. Now your brother is trying to sleep and so am I."

There was silence, but Peggy still felt Luna's unsettled eyes upon her.

"What, honey? If you have something to say, then say something new, okay? Just don't tell me what you miss."

"It's hard not to."

"I know it's hard, but complaining about it isn't helping. Go ahead then, what else do you miss. You miss homework?"

"Yeah, I do."

"Well, then what about that book report you were supposed to write for me? There's your homework."

"I thought you didn't care."

"Who said I didn't care?"

"Well, you haven't brought it up."

"Right, and why have I not brought it up? Because your mother's had a few distractions, okay? But now that I *have* brought it up, get it on my desk by Saturday."

"You don't have a desk."

"I meant in my hands. It's a meta... Just have it for me by Saturday."

"Nicky too?"

Peggy remembered in that moment that, shortly after their car was towed, she had secretly tossed Nicky's assigned copy of *The Grapes of Wrath* into a garbage can at the auto shop. Her reasoning was that she was beginning to believe the mere presence of the book was further fueling their instability.

"Don't worry about Nicky. I'm talking to you now. You're two separate people. Worry about your responsibilities here, okay?"

"Okay."

"You probably didn't even finish it."

"Yeah, I did."

"What happens in the end?"

"It's depressing."

"That's not an event, Luna. What's the event that happens in the end? What's the lesson that's learned by the principle characters? *That's* what happens. *'That's depressing'* is not what happens."

"But it *is*, mom…"

"Luna, I'm gonna tell you something. If you're going to go through life thinking the happy ending that you want is what's real, you better think again. And true art is not like that. True art will make you think, will make you feel sad. Diane Arbus. Yeah, the photos can be a little depressing, but that's not a valid critique. What else do you get from her photos? Google some of them and really look at them. The same with the book. What's the message? What comes off to you? Don't just look at a sad event as being sad. Look at it for what else is being said."

"You mean like what it stands for, maybe?"

"Yes, like that. You've even done it in your own writing. You remember your *Hyena Ballerina*? It's not just about a hyena wearing a tutu, is it?"

"Not at all."

"Right, it's about what? It's about – "

"It's about how being different changes her relationship to her fellow hyenas. And how they look at her differently."

"They look at her differently because she's different from *them*. Right. So it's about how a hyena follows her dream despite the pressure to conform. So if someone read that and thought, oh, this is just about a hyena dancing to *Swan Lake*, you'd say they didn't understand it, right?"

"Yeah, I guess."

"So think about that. Think about what the author's taken the time to say. What'd the book mean to you? What'd you like? What didn't you like? Re-read it if you have to. Okay?"

"Okay."

"Alright?"

"I'll start working on it tomorrow."

"Good girl."

Peggy went back to looking up at the ceiling, then slowly began to close her eyes…

"Mommy?" Luna whispered.

"Yes, honey."

"Do you think you might get the job you interviewed for today?"

"I don't think so, honey."

"Why? You were a good teacher. Why wouldn't they hire you?"

"I don't know, honey. It's just how things go sometimes. When you get older, you...you develop a sense for these things."

Luna appeared to be out of questions, as Peggy attempted to close her eyes, yet again...

"Mommy?" Luna whispered.

"Yes, honey."

"Kathy and Katie stopped texting me."

Peggy sat with this, "Since when?"

"A couple of weeks now. They were telling me what was happening in school and then they just stopped answering me."

"Well,...it's not your fault." These were the only words that Peggy could come up with regarding this. She was surprised they hung on this long. It was probably less them and more their parents who finally got wind of their correspondence with Luna. In any event, this was another lesson Luna was learning – *friends can fade like the tide.*

There was silence again, though Peggy still sensed Luna's mind momentarily racing...

"Mommy?"

"Yes, Luna."

"That poem I wrote about daddy. That's another example. It's not just about the weather. It was about how much we miss him."

Peggy took a moment to absorb this, then reluctantly, "Yeah, that's... Right, honey."

As Peggy attempted to drift off, Luna could not help but recite the last portion from memory:

"And then maybe the clouds will part
And good luck will soon come

Maybe things will be like they were before,
With the return of the sun."

Luna's half-conscious recitation lulled herself to sleep, as Peggy stared up at the ceiling. A tear somehow appeared down her cheek, which she was now too tired to decipher if it stemmed from her being moved or in despair.

It all blurred together now.

◆ ◆ ◆

Friday morning came. Monique and her kids had already left for work and school, respectively, and it was assumed that Peggy would take the kids for the day to wherever she would attempt to drive for interviews, and maybe she'd splurge for lunch at an *Arby*'s or some such place.

"I don't wana' go," Nicky snapped.

"Nicky, I have to try and find work, and I can't leave you here by yourself."

"Why not? I'm not gonna do anything."

"Nicky, this is not our house. And I only have the one spare key that Monique was nice enough to give me."

"So?"

"So, if you go out, you can't get back in."

"So I won't go anywhere. There's nothin' to do around here anyways. It's friggin' boring."

"So, what, you're just gonna' sleep and play games all day?"

"What else am I gonna do in the car?"

"You'll get some sort of...of stimulus, okay? Being out in the world. You can't just incubate here."

"I can't what?"

"You're not staying here by yourself. And we should be together."

"I wana' be by myself. We're together enough, don't y'think? We're in a ten foot room together, we're in a car together. Can't I just have some time to myself? I'll read that book, okay?"

"How?"

"What do you mean?"

"Because..." Peggy hesitated. She could not very well admit that she ditched the Steinbeck classic in an auto-shop trash can because she began to think the book was a hex on them. "I haven't seen it around, that's all. So I thought you lost it."

Nicky looked at her oddly, "I'll look, okay?"

Peggy was, of course, keenly aware that there was nothing for him to find. At the same time, she could not leave him there without some sort of assignment, and realized that, in this instance, the internet actually could bail her out. "Well, if you don't find it in an hour, you can find it online. You were almost done anyway, right?"

"I think I had like 30 pages or somethin'."

"Alright, well, find it online. There's a site called *Classics for Free*. You can download it. Okay?"

"Okay."

She looked at him, trying to will that he would behave. In actuality, he had only been introverted or verbally sassy in his recent years, at worst. And it just seemed easier to let him have his way, as the three of them had been in such ridiculously close proximity of each other since leaving Larry and Carole's; between the cramped motel rooms, the bedroom they were now sharing at Monique's and the car, it actually felt like a good idea to give Nicky some space. And having time with just Luna wouldn't be the worst thing either.

She and Luna drove around much of the morning as if waiting for good fortune to descend on them like rain. But it was a desert; dry as the opportunities. "Where are we going?" Luna whined.

Peggy stopped the car, as she noticed that she was about to enter Cold River. She had literally called or visited every middle and high school within a half-dozen towns of Monique over the course of the last week. If she went further west, she'd practically be in Queens, and the furthest she could go east meant that she'd have to go through Cold River. This meant she'd have to endure about a 30-minute drive through bad memory lane, which she wasn't sure she or Luna could handle.

"Are we going to Cold River?"

Peggy looked at the welcome sign to the town, "Welcome to Beautiful Cold River, Long Island". *Even the sign is haughty*, she thought. She gripped the wheel, hoping it would give her strength to step on the accelerator and forge ahead. But in that moment, it seemed like it would end up feeling like a drive through nuclear waste. A sunny day appeared to become overcast as she continued to gaze ahead.

"Mommy? What's wrong?"

She was about to turn the wheel back and take them for a cheap lunch at a *Sonic* they had passed by. She saw how the day would end up, from that point. A couple of hot dogs and Cokes, then driving in circles as if to justify being out of the house, before returning to Monique's depressing, overcrowded home, only to indulge her, yet again, as she watched back-to-back episodes of *American Sleaze* after dinner, then listening to her condemn the evil-doers of the world as she gagged on Jiffy Pop or Pringles or some other highly caloric snack that Peggy was starting to become addicted to.

She stepped on the gas as if being chased by her second guess...

"My God, mom! What're you doing?"

"We're going to lunch, kiddo," she exclaimed with a grin, as she plowed passed the Cold River town sign on the way to Peggy's favorite eatery, *Harbor by the Bay*, where she had so many lunches with Claire, Gwen, Judy; where she and Mike would go for Sunday brunches with the kids, and where Peggy would take Vic and Elaine in order to shut them up for an hour. They passed by shops Peggy so-often frequented; including *Dispiace's Gourmet Market*, and, of course, *Le Sec*, another favorite place that catered Mike's 40th birthday party. She was prepared to see a face she knew but, for the moment, was fearless.

They arrived only for Peggy to be reminded that, since *Harbor* was largely outdoors, they were closed for the winter season.

"Fuck!" Peggy exclaimed.

"Mom, you cursed."

"I know I did, Luna. Sometimes people... Damnit."

"We can go somewhere else," Luna suggested, rationally.

"I know we can go somewhere else. I wanted us to eat here, for Godsakes!"

She looked at Luna the moment after she said this, realizing how childishly adamant she was being. Somehow, she probably rationalized that eating there would be a small victory, especially if others she knew saw her. Word would then perhaps circulate that Peggy was in town. And then what a gloriously unsettling box of questions would emerge and maybe even get back to Judy and Gwen; possibly leaving them rattled at the prospect of bumping into her after all the scandalous things they were likely saying about her.

She touched Luna's leg, "I'm sorry, honey," before she turned the car around. Upon heading out, she came across *Borgon's*, a tiny French bistro that Peggy and Mike would occasionally go to by themselves, since it had such a romantic vibe; dim lighting, walls adorned with Cezanne and Van Gogh prints and such. Since the kids never came with them there, this would be a new experience for Luna, which probably was better than it being a place that would bring back memories for her, like *Harbor by the Bay*.

The place was open but empty, as if they were even expecting a pariah for an early lunch. Thanks to Luna's moment of adulthood, Peggy now had less of a need to prove anything to anyone, except to herself. She was in Cold River, a town she swore she would be far too ashamed to ever come back to, and yet here she was, on a random day having lunch with her daughter in perhaps the quietest and most intimate place in town.

"*Starry Night*, right?" Luna said, as she pointed to a classic Van Gogh that they sat under.

"Yes, that's right."

"That's not the real one, I know that."

"No, that's a print. We saw the real one, remember? At the Museum of Modern Art."

"That was the original?"

"Yeah, it was. At least I assume so. Sometimes you don't know."

"Why?"

"Well, there's forgers and sometimes they fool people."

"You mean they paint the entire painting themselves and then act like a famous painter did it?"

"That's right."

"Why? That's a lot of trouble to go through."

"Money. That's the reason most people do a lot of things, honey. Now let's figure out what we're eating."

Inadvertently, Peggy initiated the subject of greed with Luna, not realizing that her resentment was so close to the surface that it could appear at the most inopportune times; ...her recent disastrous interview at Massapauke High School being a prime example.

Unfortunately, she was not easily diverted of this topic by the prices on the menu. Four months ago, she wouldn't have blinked at a salmon and caper-stuffed crepe at $40, but any price tag now instantly became the subject of strained number-crunching; *if we just drank water and maybe split a... Well, maybe if we just had water and a cheese and fruit plate... Alright, well, how about we have a small... Jesus Christ!*

"Mommy, can we afford this?"

She looked at Luna, smiled weakly, appreciative of the moments like this when Luna was almost like a younger friend. Not in terms of acting as if she knew more than she did, as she was quite prone to do in groups, but simply by her being aware of something outside of herself. She could tell her mother was stressed by the menu, and also that her mother wanted to will a good time for them, even if it was truly beyond their means now.

"Would you be okay if we split a nice salad?" Peggy asked sheepishly.

"I'd be ok with a hot dog. I like *Sonic.*"

"You do?"

"Yeah. Don't you like them?"

The waiter approached, "Good Afternoon. How are we today?"

"Fine, thank you," Peggy responded.

"I'd be happy to tell you our specials, if you'd like to hear them."

"Um, sure, yes," as Peggy looked at Luna.

The waiter ran off a list of six succulent entrees, which Peggy estimated would be well out of their budgetary realm for lunch, but gave a feigned smile for his efforts.

"Would you like a minute to decide?"

She looked at Luna again, who appeared willing to go along with what Peggy decided, but this all seemed like a forced attempt at being something that they no longer were.

"Yes, I think we'll need a little more time. Thank you."

"Of course. It's good to see you again, by the way."

Peggy was taken aback, not realizing she had been there enough to be recognized by the staff – and she barely recalled this waiter.

"Oh, well,...thank you."

"It's been a while, yes?"

"Um, yes. We've been...yes, we've had a lot to keep us busy."

"I'm sure. And this is your lovely daughter, I assume?"

"Yes, this is... Yes, this is my daughter," Peggy catching herself before giving the waiter Luna's name.

The waiter left them to decide, and their decision would be to discreetly leave *Borgon's* and Cold River and, instead, have a couple of hot dogs and Cokes at *Sonic.*

"That was odd," Peggy said, more to herself, as they ate in the car.

"What?"

"That he acted like he knew me."

"Well, you said you came there before with daddy, right?"

"Yeah, but we hadn't been there in months. And when we *did* go, it was maybe three or four times, I think. I mean, who was he talking to?"

"He was talking to you, mommy," Luna said with a laugh.

"No, I mean..." she didn't bother to finish, choosing to distract herself for the moment by removing a strand of sauerkraut from the corner of Luna's mouth, the heat barely keeping them warm enough. What Peggy meant was just how this waiter recalled her. Was it in fact the few times she had dined there, or was it something else? *Did he connect me to the scandal?*

"Mommy?"

"Yes, honey," as she snapped out of her momentary paranoia.

"How much longer do you think we can stay at Monique's?"

"Not long. I mean, I don't want us to. There's no room for us."

"Will we have to go back to a motel?"

"We can't really afford to."

"Why do you think grandma and grandpa don't like you?"

"Because... It's complicated, honey. You're too young for it to make sense to you, and maybe when you're old enough, it won't matter anyway. Just... Your grandparents love you and Nicky, but we see things differently."

"Is it daddy?"

"What do you mean?"

"Are they upset about what happened?"

"Of course they're upset. We're all upset by this, honey." And then she couldn't resist to add, "They're upset at *me*, more than anything."

"Why would they be upset at you?"

She looked at Luna, wiped a splotch of mustard from the corner of Luna's mouth, then took a breath, feeling perhaps that it would be a healthy purge to explain this to her, even if it was beyond her to truly understand, "I think they feel that what your father did, what put him in prison, was... because of me."

"They think it was your idea?"

"No. They...they think that... Luna, your father wanted the best for us. That's what... That's what I *want* to think, honey," she took a moment, looked out the front window, then back at Luna. "We had a very nice house, then moved to an even nicer house. He took us on trips. We had everything because that was what... He thought that was what would keep us happy. And to keep that up, I guess, he felt that he needed to...to do what he did, which was a crime. But I never asked for all that we had. We didn't have to live so grandly, but that was what he wanted for us. You and Nicky have really only known this. You've only known having a huge bedroom, having a nice backyard, going on trips, going to special schools..." she took a breath, trying not to get caught up with how much Nicky and Luna had compared to what little she had at their ages. "I'm saying that I didn't think we needed all that we had, but I got used to it. And I enjoyed it. And maybe there were times where I did ask for more of something, especially when I wasn't working and had nothing else to do but make sure you and Nicky were taken care of, but... The long and the short of this, honey, is that I didn't ask for all that we had. I just thought I got extremely lucky. I loved your dad and knew he would be successful, and he...whisked me away from everything I thought I wanted for myself. I thought that was my fate, and going back to teaching would be gravy. I mean, God knows, no one gave much thought to it, especially your grandparents."

"Why?" Luna asked, trying to absorb all of this.

"For the same reason."

"What reason?" Luna followed, almost defensively.

"Everything that I've been telling you. The reason why they blame me," as Peggy found herself becoming agitated.

"But I don't under -"

"They think your father felt that he had to make a lot of money to keep me, just like they thought my job was just a diversion to hide the fact that I was a rich housewife. That's how they saw me. And they'd rather blame me than blame your father, because they're more responsible for how he turned out than anyone, and they can't face it. *That's the reason!*"

Peggy bit into her hot dog as if it was the exclamation point. She chewed animatedly as she gazed out, committed that revealing all this to her 11 year-old daughter was healthy, perhaps more for her than for Luna. Luna, on the other hand, sat with this, visibly confused. It would be hard to turn her from her grandparents. They were always the special guests, after all. The ones who she saw every few months, received gifts from, was doted on by. She would never be remotely aware of the flaws in their character. And what would she do with this information? Of what benefit would this be to her, aside from letting her know that people can be assholes? Ultimately, Peggy knew it was a selfish act, but she needed to reveal this to someone. She couldn't afford a shrink and couldn't very well talk about this to Monique. Yes, Nicky was older, but his struggle with all this seemed greater, so it made sense to confide this much to her daughter, and the fact that she was able to get it out as succinctly as she did lent greater clarity to exactly why she had grown to hate Vic and Elaine. If this scarred Luna somehow, so be it. Better she learn early that deceit comes in all forms – especially family.

Peggy soon after felt a relief as one does after they've vomited to rid their nausea. As she chewed, she even noticed the hot dog was becoming a succulent filet of sole. The Coke had become a room temperature glass of Pinot. She felt the sun coming through the clouds even as it was setting on the day.

And then her phone rang. It was Monique, unusually serious:

"Peggy, you need to come home - *right now*."

16

————

"I haven't touched a thing because I wanted you to see what I came home to," as Monique intensely greeted Peggy at the door, her hands glued to her hips like a displeased middle school teacher.

She would not reveal anything by phone, but when Peggy nervously arrived at Monique's it was clear what had happened. Among the highlights of the mess was the precious plasma TV on the floor with a California-looking crack along the screen, framed family photos shattered and ripped throughout the living room, many a crappy romance novel strewn about, a gallon of whole milk on the kitchen floor, broken dishes and cups afloat within it, and melted Fruit Loops from a torn-open box creating a rainbow river which oozed into the dining room carpet...

"Oh my..." Peggy frozen in shock.

"And that's not all," declared Monique, her hostility seeming to feed off of Peggy's disbelief. "Look at Richie and Jason's room!"

The room in which Peggy, Luna and Nicky were staying was effectively turned upside down. The mattresses of both twin beds capsized, the mirrors shattered, presumably by Richie and Jason's Track and Field trophies, which appeared decapitated as a result.

"Monique, I...I... Was the door left open?" Peggy could only meekly ask.

"Was the door left open? You think this was a break-in?"

"What do you mean?" Peggy braced herself. If it wasn't

a burglar, then...

"IT WAS YOUR SON!" Monique howled. "IT WAS NICKY, PEGGY! HE DID THIS! LOOK AT WHAT HE DID TO MY GOD-DAMN HOUSE!"

The high-pitch whistle-like sound was ascending within Peggy yet again, as she attempted to wrap her mind around how Nicky could cause such destruction. She could only act as shocked as she genuinely was, and be equally clue-less at how he could find it within himself to destroy much of Monique's home. She was unquestionably engulfed by the enormity of this situation, and how she was ultimately re-sponsible; *the one time I elected to leave him alone since we've been here...* In looking around at the catastrophic surroundings, previously ominous signs would impede her vision, especially the photo of the North Vietnamese prisoner getting his head blown off that Nicky had doctored with colored blood and brain matter. She had submerged any concerns of how this would affect Nicky's stability because she simply did not have time nor the patience to address it. And now here it was; his potential.

She watched Monique's lips move with venom, and could tell she was repeating the same thing over and over, but could not hear her. Monique had lost any reverence for Peggy as the wife of her former employer, but did consider her a friend on some level, even a sounding board. But now any such feelings were incinerated. Monique even appeared on the verge of getting physical, making Peggy fear the possibility of her picking up a shard of broken mirror and slicing her throat.

Peggy clutched Luna's frightened hand, and could only ask where Nicky was, as she trembled...

"He should be in jail, like his Goddamn father!" Monique spewed. This sentence appeared to cut through the piercing whistle that Peggy had been hearing. She looked at Monique, wanting to defend her son, but it was hard to be righteous as she stood amidst such devastation.

"Do... I... Monique, I'll help..."

"You're not doing a damn thing. I'm calling the police."

"Monique, I... He's a kid. I'll take responsibility for..."

"For what?! You don't have anything! That's why you're here! That's why you needed me to take you in, right?! The great fucking Bubone family!!! You owned that Goddamn town, and you needed *my* help? And I fuckin' gave it to you, didn't I?"

"Monique, I'm so very – "

"Save your sorries! I took your entire family in 'cause you had nothin' because a' your scumbag husband. Do you know how much he was taking in and what he was paying me?! While he took you on trips, while he ordered fucking lobster for lunch at the office! Fucking lobster! And I could barely pay my fucking mortgage!!!"

"Monique, I know you're upset..."

"You know?! What gave it away, Peg?! WHAT GAVE IT AWAY!!!"

Peggy backed up a few steps, as Luna began to cry...

Monique continued, "Your family destroyed my life once, and I take pity on you and you do it again!"

"Monique, he's not himself. This has all been – "

"*Not himself?!* He's a little monster, is what he is. If my sons were home, I'd let them kick his obnoxious ass!"

"Monique, please, I'll take care of this. You don't have to call – "

"No, this is what's gonna' happen, Peg," Monique took what appeared to be her first breath. "You're gonna' leave and I'm gonna' call the cops. I'm gonna' tell them that my home was vandalized and I don't know who did it so that I can at least get the Goddamn insurance money, which is more than I would get from your broke ass. "

"Monique, please – "

"All I want from you is to get outa' my life! I don't ever wana' see you again, and if I do, you better run the other way. Do you hear me?"

Peggy stood there, the intensity of the situation taking

precedence over any comfort she could take from Monique not pressing charges. Nor could she waste time crediting her for having the wherewithal to say that a stranger broke in and ransacked the house. For now, Peggy simply needed to not be there.

"Monique, just tell me where Nicky is. I need to know where my son is."

"I don't know and I don't care!"

"Please, Monique, if you know, can you just tell me where he is, please, Monique...?!"

"I DON'T KNOW WHERE HE IS, PEGGY! HE RAN OUTA' THE HOUSE! DO YOU THINK I SHOULD FUCKIN' CARE?! HE'S YOUR RESPONSIBILITY, NOT MINE! WHERE DO YOU COME OFF ASKIN' ME WHERE YOUR IDIOT SON IS!!! HE'S A GOD-DAMN CANCER, JUST LIKE YOUR HUSBAND!!! NOW GET THE HELL OUTA' MY HOUSE!!!"

Peggy was now awash in panicked tears, which appeared to shower Luna as they fled, "Oh my God, oh my God...," Peggy chanted, as they ran down the driveway, clutching clothes and suitcases that they quickly grabbed from their room...

"Mommy, I'm scared. What are we – ?"

"Luna, just get in the car..."

"But mommy – "

"Luna, get in the car!!!"

Luna got into the car, her frightened tears still flowing, as Peggy began a terrified trot around the outside of Monique's house, then up and down the street hysterically, "NICKY!" she continued to scream, as the few neighbors who were home began coming out of their houses, uncertain if she was crazy or if they should band together to help her...

"NICKY, WHERE ARE YOU?!!!"

She continued to run aimlessly, flop-sweating despite the 32-degree temperature. Doors continued to open, some people shouted something which Peggy couldn't decipher. The dreaded whistle was back, which she tried desperately to scream over, "NIIIIICCCCCKKKY...!!!!"

She soon ran back to the car, with Luna crying so animatedly that she looked like a wounded animal. Peggy stepped on the gas and proceeded to drive in circles around the neighborhood. The sunset and the limited street lighting made searching for Nicky that much more difficult, as she continued to caterwaul his name out of the open window. A good samaritan neighbor would yell from his lawn, "What does he look like?!"

"Like...like my son! He's white, 13. Brown...brown..." she could barely describe him through her unhinged emotions, as she continued driving and muttering under her heavy breathing, "Oh my God, Nicky. Nicky, where the hell did you go? Where the hell did you...OH GOD....!" Suddenly, Nicky appeared within the headlights, as she slammed on the breaks before nearly running him over – *certainly a temptation*. Nicky stood there, looking at the car, knowing it was his mother. She was unsure if he would try and flee, just as he seemed unsure of what she would do to him.

Peggy came out of the car, as they looked at each other. He appeared vulnerable, as he never had before. Almost like a stray, distrusting of any contact with others. She took a breath, "Get in the car." He remained a moment. "Nicky, we need to leave," she followed, with softened urgency. After another moment, he slowly made his way to the backseat, as if knowing he might not have much time left. Upon him entering, Peggy noticed a reddened handprint on his left cheek in the mirror. "What happened?" she asked.

Nicky looked out the window, afraid to answer.

"Nicky, what happened to your face?"

Just as it appeared as if he might not respond, "She hit me," he mumbled.

"Who?"

"Monique."

"When she came home?"

He only nodded, as he faced the window again.

Peggy could barely absorb all that had occurred up to this point, but now she would also have to contend with another woman smacking her son. This was something Peggy never had done. And while she knew full well that he was responsible and punishment of some kind would be forthcoming as soon as she could get her head on straight and find out where the hell they would be spending the night, the fact that Monique took it upon herself to take such action against her son, and usurp her authority as a mother, seemed to be a worse offense.

She sat there a moment, then slowly started to make her way out of the neighborhood,...before abruptly turning around and heading back to Monique's. The police hadn't arrived yet, so she stopped the car a couple of houses away, walked rapidly towards Monique's house, grabbed a large rock from a neighbor's gravel path, positioned herself on Monique's lawn and, as she flashed back to her brief stint on her high school's shotput team, hoisted the rock through Monique's living room window – *Add that to your insurance claim!* she loudly thought,...as she ran back to the car and sped out of yet another neighborhood...for the last time.

◆ ◆ ◆

They drove in silence for some time. Luna's crying had subsided, though the tears were dried and cold on her reddened face. Nicky appeared cautiously numb – waiting for when his mother would decide to pull over and finish what Monique had started. For the moment, Peggy drove only with the intent of being a considerable distance from the scene of Nicky's crime. *Another motel,* was all she knew. *One night, two at the most. We can't afford to blow any more money on these places.*

Even after throwing a rock through Monique's living room window, she knew that Monique was not a bad person.

She was someone who had been screwed over, probably more times than Peggy would ever know. She also questioned how well she would respond if *she* came home to find that someone else's child had destroyed her house. It made sense. It's just that Peggy could barely live with herself as things were, but having someone else slap her child, when she never had the honor herself, was a new low; one that she could not just walk away from. She rationalized that Monique's anger was mainly at Mike anyway, and that she was just waiting for the excuse to release it.

Fate was in the air again; what Monique was jabbering about during *American Sleaze*. How one attached to the ill deeds of another could only have precipitous effects. *Is Nicky fated to be a criminal?* And not just the white-collar kind, as Peggy might've hopefully assumed – *this was violence*. She wondered where such an outburst came from. Yes, he was obviously depressed; he missed his father, his friends, his home, his school, his cherished sense of privacy... *But destroying someone else's property?* And the utter selfishness of such an act, where he would've had to have been aware that it would leave them homeless, yet again. Then again, Nicky wasn't always one to think ahead. Peggy tried to curb her burgeoning rage by thinking of him in better times. Of course, he was never a social butterfly, but he would sometimes initiate a kiss or a hug from his mother. Sometimes he conveyed vulnerability and confided in her, as with when Mike was about to go to trial. She wanted to remember this creative young man who had a soft spot and ultimately seemed to know the value of family. She wanted to understand that no 13 year-old boy who seemingly had everything could adapt to living like a vagabond with no place to call home, with only his digital gadgets and a dog-eared depression-era novel to keep him occupied.

But she couldn't,...perhaps because this was *her* fate.

She also couldn't help but note the odd synchronicity, having just run out on the dentist's bill, then recalling her mother's staged home burglary almost 30 years ago. Now Monique, though certainly more within legal bounds than her mother was, was planning to attribute Nicky's devastation to an unknown criminal in order to get more from the insurance company than much of her damaged items were likely worth. It made Peggy even recall those episodes of crime shows that she was forced to watch in Monique's company, which often resulted in one's desperate attempt to exceed the income they actually earned; she was among such desperation now.

She turned into a strip mall parking lot and parked in a darkened area that had no nearby cars. She sharply got out of the car, went into the backseat alongside Nicky, placed the suitcases that were on the back seat and slammed them onto the roof, before getting in and closing the door. She could sense Nicky's fear, as he discreetly scooted from where Peggy now sat. Right now, this was to Peggy's advantage. She looked at him penetratingly, between understanding and something considerably darker.

"Nicky," she intensely whispered, aware that they were still in public, "why did you do what you did?"

He sat there, as expected, appearing to struggle for an answer that would justify his actions, but knowing that they were beyond this. He weakly shook his head, gazed down at his knees...

"Look at me," she said, with restraint. Nicky slowly turned to her.

She took a deep breath, then spoke slowly and methodically, "Do you know that you put us in a very bad place? Do you? There's no one, Nicky. No one else that we can turn to. This is it. We're at the end. Are you aware of this?"

He turned his head, unable to continue looking at his mother and endure the ferocity of her glare, "LOOK AT ME!" she roared. He did, slowly. She sensed Luna turning to face them, "Luna, do not look back here. Face the front."

"Mommy, please don't hurt – "

"DON'T YOU TELL ME HOW TO BE A MOTHER! FACE THE FRONT!"

Luna did so quickly, as she began to cry new tears atop the dried old ones, while beginning to subtly chant *"The Mole on the Mohel would fall into the soil..."*, which she created years ago inspired by one of Mike's more notable diagnoses. She only revived it if she was unsettled about something, which was rare as it had been at least a year since Peggy heard her recite it – when their beloved dog Lucas passed away.

"Luna, stop!" she ordered, sharply. Luna did.

Peggy resumed her glare at her son, her eldest offspring. She could barely conceive that this human before her emanated from her womb. This would not be the first time she was tempted to slap him. She was close when he ran away, closer when they first arrived at Monique's... Had Monique eclipsed the seeming inevitability that this would happen, since this was by far the apex of Nicky's rebellious displays? If Monique had not already physically reprimanded him, would Peggy have had any reservations now?

It was something that the Cold River mothers surely would never resort to, but of course many of them medicated their kids or had them seeing shrinks practically in infancy. These were actions Peggy would never conform to, but what she was feeling now had been within her before – just not to this degree. Her son really deserved a *'good beatin'*, a phrase sometimes heard from certain parents of her friends in Kelp Stream, New Jersey. There was never any artifice there, and maybe that was to be commended. But it was also another era. God knows Peggy took some lickings in *her* time, but never for anything nearing the scope of what Nicky had done here.

Fate? she thought, as she continued to burn holes into Nicky with her eyes.

She continued to force him to look at her for what seemed like an eternity, which eventually made her believe that this was more impactful than anything she could do to him physically.

She left the car, closed the backseat door, then took out

a cigarette and tried to withstand the bitter cold night air. After three emphatic puffs, she tossed it away and came back to the driver's seat.   Luna was sniffling, but had stopped crying. Peggy then looked in her mirror to see Nicky with a single tear descending down his cheek – an emotional miracle akin to blood flowing from a stone. But she would not console either of them.

She would only drive.

17

The machine picked up again – *"This is Grace and little Pearl. Leave a message."*

Peggy anxiously hung up, her heart still beating rapidly just from the sound of her voice. She wished she could be thankful that her mother didn't pick up and also that, in her not doing so, it somehow meant that their situation wasn't so desperate – but this was delusional thinking. In truth, there was really no one else. She had put off seeking any other kind of work, out of fear and also out of the knowledge that she would likely not be hired for any respectable position without a modicum of experience. Waitressing was an option, but when she pictured herself smiling forcefully like one of those *IHOP* waitresses, she began to get nauseous. And what could she do in an office when she hadn't been in one in over a decade and a half? And any such job that she *could* obtain would be too little too late anyway. She would never make enough money to even keep them in a motel let alone allow her to save towards a cheap apartment. She had crunched the numbers so hard, there was little else but crumbs now.

She then suddenly realized something after clicking off – the outgoing message had changed from just days ago. There was no mention of "Joe". *What happened in the span of 3 days that could warrant such a revision?* In any event, it appeared that the house was now less occupied; there was only her mother and "little Pearl", whoever this was. It was odd.

But then, so was her mother.

She left the cold balcony that oversaw the pool with

a slushy tarp over it, and went back into their latest motel room in a town called Friggingham, still in Long Island but just about 30 minutes from Queens. The lights were dim in the room with Nicky and Luna asleep in their beds. She looked at them and, for the moment, realized that she could just leave if she wanted. *Someone would take them, right? Would they really be in worse hands without me?* At that moment, she could not see how her dragging them around would serve as any benefit to them other than to increase their potential for psychosis. It just all seemed to be a mistake now; *meeting Mike, let alone getting married to him, let alone having children with him, let alone sacrificing any sense of independence to just being a wife and mother...for years!*

Who the hell was this person? she thought. Whoever it was, it didn't seem to be anyone she knew now.

She soon found herself behind the wheel of her car in the parking lot, gazing up at their motel room window on the second floor. She envied how the kids could sleep so soundly, and how children didn't seem to take stress to bed with them the same as adults. She felt that her being gone could only help this. Yes, they might initially panic, Luna for certain, but they'd come around with a new family. And, in time, would come to know that they were not mistakes; it was just who they came from that were. They were offspring born not from a marriage but a mirage. *It was a miracle, really,* she thought, that they could be flesh and blood while coming from a father and mother who now appeared to exist as a vaporous façade. *Another good title for something,* she thought.

It increasingly made sense to drive away, change her last name back to her maiden name or something else altogether, shred her identification and just drive as far as she could, and then live the rest of her life in a small apartment above an aged general store in a small town out on the West coast. She wouldn't need to live on much, for it would just be her. No husband. No children. No responsibilities except to work a simple job and write at the local diner over tuna salad on her lunch break each day. And then after a few years, maybe she'd amass enough pages to have a great novel – her magnum opus.

In the end, she would have come to find herself; all that she was and all that she wanted to be, in all its clarity.

She could then one day go to a quiet beach, look out at the water at dusk, just like the mysterious women in that photograph from the Feldman Gallery, where Carole worked.

Yes, that would be the plan.

Yet, by the time all these thoughts ran through her head, the sun was beginning to rise. She had literally been in the car contemplating this for about 5 hours. The darkness of night seemed to have given her permission to flee, but with the daylight came the guilt at even considering the abandonment of her children. It was too late. She had to stay.

Now what?

With the car again packed to the gills with their luggage and little else, they drove en route to the Garden State. She hadn't been there since the apartment she and Mike shared after college, but that was worlds away from where they were going. Kelp Stream may have been just about an hour or so from Princeton, but it was more like another universe, and from where Peggy had been for the better part of the last two decades, it was even beyond that. This gave her the false sense of having all the time in the world to rehearse just what she would say to Grace, her mother. But in truth, she could have been coming from Mars in a helicopter and still would not have had enough time to formulate words that would make her arrival appear anything less than ridiculous. What the hell would she be doing surprising her mother like this? How could she soft soap their desperation for such a trip? Would her mother actually be glad to see her? Or would she pick up where Peggy left off with Monique; bitter and even vengeful?

When Peggy last spoke to her mother, it was by phone.

She couldn't quite remember the last words she said, but she remembered her mother's: *"You think you built yourself into something, don't ya'. Ivy League college, now this big shot who thinks his shit don't stink? You think you'll have a family and live the high life and you'll be everything but what I know you are."*

She got chills recalling this, which came to her as if it were a cassette stored in the attic of her brain. She'd tried to tune out this last exchange for much of her adult life, but realized now that it was always there in some way. It was with her on their wedding day, as she looked at Mike at the altar. It was with her when she was alone in the house as the kids were growing and Mike was working or at conferences. It was with her when she started to drink in the morning. It was with her when her "inner Jersey" came out, as Mike would jokingly refer to it. It was with her when she was in the company of her elite Cold River circle.

And it was with her when it all came crumbling down. This force was what she had been keeping at bay, and now she would be facing it head on, as if standing in front of a massive wave and knowing for certain that it would crash down upon her, yet somehow hoping to remain dry. *The definition of madness.*

On the verge of a panic attack, she pulled over on the side of the road and realized that she could still not put herself through this. Her mother didn't even know she was coming, after all. Peggy could save face. She could eat a modicum of crow and put the kids on a plane to Florida and figure things out for herself...or simply flee. Wouldn't that be better than going back to her mother with her tail between her legs? And would her mother even welcome her?

But she'd been calling, right? Peggy knew that must've been her. That cigarette sucking sound, unmistakable and unaltered from her youth. Her mother was trying to reach out. *What other reason for the calls?* She knew she wasn't getting any younger. She just couldn't form the words. *She was never what one would call a gifted linguist, after all.* She had given birth to a sole daughter who elevated herself beyond where she could ever fathom. Getting a scholarship to a major college was already beyond what Grace could wrap her head around. Then going to Princeton? Living there? Getting her degree? Then moving to Long Island and marrying a soon-to-be dermatologist?

Peggy realized that she should really try to speak with her mother by phone first before just showing up at her doorstep. *Wouldn't that be too much for everyone involved?* She parked on the shoulder of the turnpike, exited the car and slowly dialed...

"Hello?"

Peggy gasped at the sound of her live voice.

"Hello? Who is this?"

"Mu...mu..."

"Who the hell is this?" the voice barked.

"Mom, it's me," Peggy hiccupped. "It's Peggy."

There was a silence, which Peggy could not have dreaded more, since she could fill the time with the worst possible thoughts running through her mother's salty mind.

"Peggy?"

She gasped again, then a breath, "Yeah."

"Well,...I didn't see this comin', I'll tell ya' that."

"No?" Peggy innocently asked.

"Why would I?"

Peggy wasn't quite sure how to respond. Her mother was not welcoming, nor unusually off-putting. She was, actually, not unlike how she always sounded, or so it seemed from these few words. "I was... Well, first, how are you?" Peggy asked.

"I'm fine." Then a long silence. "Where are you?"

"Huh?" Peggy acted like she didn't hear, secretly not wanting to reveal that she was about 40 minutes away from the Kelp Stream exit.

"Where are you? Sounds like you're on a highway," Grace enunciated.

"I'm... Well, that's sort of a long story."

"What's *'at* mean?"

"Look, I'm... I'm not far from the house. Do you mind if I stop by?"

"Whose house? *My* house?"

"Yes."

"What a' y'doin' around here?"

"I'm... I just happen to be in the area."

"You just happen to be in the area? What would bring you back here?"

"Well, I just wanted to see you."

"But why're you here?"

"I just told you. To see you."

"You said you happened to be in the area, so what's 'at mean?"

"I'm in the area because...I wanted to see you, okay? There's no other reason."

Grace took a moment, "Okay. So why didn't you just say that?"

Peggy grasped for words, "I just... I don't know. We haven't spoken in a while, so I guess I'm... I don't know."

"So, what, how far away are you?"

"Um...about an hour. I'm on the turnpike."

"Jesus, you're an hour away and *now* you call?"

"Well, I tried before."

"You didn't leave a message."

"No, I didn't."

"I mean, I got errands to run n'stuff to do. What was the plan? Come here and just assume I'd be home to greet ya'? I've got a life too, y'know."

"Well, I'm sorry. I'm calling you now."

"And why are ya'?"

"What do you mean?"

"I mean, what is this? I haven't heard your voice. Haven't heard hide or hair and now you're callin'."

"It's complicated and...I'd rather not get into it on the

shoulder of the Jersey Turnpike. Will you be there in an hour? Can I come and see you?"

There was another disturbing silence, "You're not with *him*, are ya'?"

Peggy's heart went into her throat, "*Him?*"

"You know. Your boyfriend or husband. You still married?"

"I..., yes, I'm married, but Mike isn't with me, okay?"

"He throw you out or somethin'?"

"No, I... He didn't... What kind of thing is that to ask me?"

"Hey, you're callin' *me*, okay? You're askin' to come over outa' the blue. I'm jus' tryin' to make sense of all this."

"I'm your daughter," Peggy spewed defensively, and instantly regretted it, especially since it never meant much to say it before. But it seemed like the one thing that would cut through Grace's suspicions, which it did little to sway, "So that's it. 17 years goes by and that jus' dawns on ya'?" Grace answered.

The one consolation Peggy took thus far was that it appeared Grace knew nothing as far as Mike being in prison, or the events that led to it. Therefore, she knew that her mother's contemptuous tone stemmed from when she and Mike were engaged, and with such contempt appearing to have gone unaltered from nearly two decades ago, Peggy needed a moment to figure out the words that would not lead the phone call to end as it did then. - "It's taken a lot for me to make this call, okay? But I did. Do you mind if we come by?"

"*We?* Who the hell is *we?*"

It was not intentional that Peggy would change her phrasing from "I" to "we" during this phone call, but now that she did, it obviously needed to be addressed. "Nicky and Luna," she even attempted to brighten the sound of their names, as if Grace might actually find the news pleasant. "Who are *they?*" she chirped.

"They're my children." Then with reluctance,..."Your

grandchildren."

There was another long silence. Peggy expected to start hearing the infamous cigarette sucking sound that was practically Grace's breath, especially when she was angry or stressed,...but there was nothing. Pure silence.

"Really," Grace noted, not particularly impressed.

"Yes."

"You brought 'em to meet me."

"Well,...yes. And...I wanted to see you too."

"Really," Grace replied, with the same identical slant-eyed skepticism as the previous *Really.*

Again, silence. And the worst kind. It was not easy to get a handle on how to respond to someone she had been estranged from for so long, especially someone she never really got along with. But this was the worst. She recalled her last conversation with Vic and Elaine and how, with her every fiber, she had to restrain from telling them off. Now Peggy was in need of her mother's help in order to avoid having to turn to Vic and Elaine to take the kids. It appeared to be the ultimate Catch-22.

Still, she could not appear desperate. And tears would not help. She needed to be tough with her mother, but had to avoid being accusatory. It was a fine line. Her mother also had a pretty good bullshit detector, to the extent where she thought most people were full of it, and Peggy, for all she knew, had become one of those people; someone with an agenda. And it also wasn't like Peggy felt she could trust her mother.

Regardless of their stances, after 17 years, they probably had a right to share a mutual skepticism of each other, but time was of the essence. If nothing else, Peggy needed the opportunity of speaking with her mother in person. What would actually be accomplished by this? Peggy wasn't even sure anymore. She knew, as Thomas Wolfe once said, that you can't go home again.

But, at least in Peggy's mind, she could visit...for as long as she could stand it.

Finally, Grace managed, "Alright, well, give me 90 minutes. I've got some stuff to do." This was as close to an invitation as Peggy could ask for, based on how this conversation had been going. And still, this didn't remotely mean that they would have a place to stay for any length of time. It only meant that she was going to see her mother for the first time in 17 years,...and Nicky and Luna were going to meet their grandmother for the first time in their lives.

18

They pulled up to the house, the same as they had pulled up to Monique's just a couple of weeks before. A similar dread was there, but it was enhanced by a knot of nerves in Peggy's gut. Memories came flooding back of the last time that she was in this very spot, which immediately made her breathing labored. The feelings of the past merging with her undesirable present suddenly wrapped their hands around her throat and dared her to leave the car and knock on that brown door.

She took a breath in the hopes that her brain would somehow clear and allow her to speak lucidly. But one was not enough.

"Are you okay?" asked Luna, growing nervous through osmosis.

"I'll...ye...I'm...ye...just give me..." Peggy held up a finger, assuring Luna that this sudden hyperventilation would cease, but her finger seemed to remain up for minutes before this occurred.

"Okay, now...I don't know exactly how this is going to go."

"What do you mean?" asked Luna.

"I mean, that this will be the first time I've seen her in a long time. We had a bad falling out and so I don't know if she'll be willing to let us stay. This is... Well, it's a gamble and it's... very difficult for me. But we don't have a choice. I'm just hoping she'll want us to stay and wana' get to know you both."

"And if she doesn't?" Luna followed, as Nicky remained

insular, gazing out at the pot-holed Morgan Street.

Peggy looked at Luna, squeezed her knee as if to say "Let's hope," and stepped out of the car. She walked on the eroded cement path leading to the same shit-brown door, chipped and faded from years of the weather's flagellation. She took in the same red bricks, even noticed an etching she had written in the corner when she was 9, *Peggy lives here*, which even surprised her in its banality. She gazed at other bricks, then at the living room window, which appeared to have new curtains. The fact that there would be a semblance of remodeling after nearly two decades was a surprise to her, though much of everything else appeared frozen in time. At least the roof was still on the house.

She stood in front of the door, and just before the last few months would again flash before her eyes, she heard an intense growl from behind her... She turned around suddenly to find none other than a salivating pit bull with its fixed gaze on her. Peggy had not been this close to an unleashed pit bull in her life, nor had she actually seen one up close. Nevertheless, she knew what this was, knew their reputation from many a *People's Court* episode, and knew that once they locked their sights on prey, their goals of decapitation and maiming were hard to impede unless you had a gun.

"Oh my God..." she softly uttered, the dog holding its ground between her and the car.

Luna rolled the window down, "Mommy...?"

"Luna, stay in the car!" Peggy ordered, as the dog's growl escalated slightly. "It's okay, it's okay..." she whispered softly, as if this canine rhino could remotely comprehend her courtesy.

They were at a standoff for what felt like an eternity; Peggy standing in front of the door, the beast staring her down with a steady growl that began to sound like a funeral dirge, obstructing her path to the car from where Luna and Nicky watched nervously... Perhaps Peggy wouldn't mind conceiving such a dramatic scene so long as she wasn't *in* it – but this was reality. The days of her standing atop their granite coffee table before their adoring throng in one of many elegant cocktail dresses was laughable by comparison to this scene from *Cujo*.

She suddenly realized that knocking on the door would now be the wise thing to do; her trepidation regarding seeing her mother now was a distant second to her fear of having her throat ripped out. As she urgently knocked, the dog came closer, its growl more menacing... Their eyes remained locked; Peggy's revealing unequivocal fear, the dog's nothing less than murder...

She turned towards the door as much as she could so as to bang on it as loudly as possible, while trying to keep an eye on the dog, whose heightened growl conveyed clear disapproval of Peggy's attempts to save herself. "HEEEELP!!!! HEEEEELP!!!!!" The dog continued to approach her, while Peggy fleetingly could hear Luna and Nicky calling for her. She heard a screen door from across the street open, yet she was not in the position to grasp the irony that she was yet again drawing the attention of neighbors who may have been questioning her sanity. The whistling in her ear began tuning everything out, though she hoped the dog couldn't hear it for fear that it would launch it into full on attack-mode. She continued banging and screaming, "HEEEEELP!!!!! MOM, OPEN THE GODDAMN DOOOOOOOR......!!!!!!!!"

Then, from that sand-papered cadence, "Little Pearl, get back here!" It was Grace, now standing beside the dog. She came around the back of the house, not realizing that "Little Pearl" had gotten out through the fence. It was now clear; Little Pearl was not a new little sister or some such thing. She was Grace's pet – this monstrous mongrel with a jaw like an unremorseful vice.

Within seconds, Little Pearl was reduced to a squealing baby who meekly ambled to the backyard, as if such intense drama never occurred. It took more than a moment for Peggy to finally realize that she was now ten feet from her mother.

They looked at each other, not unlike the dream that Peggy had months ago, when they stood in what looked like a vast, empty parking lot - *the last two people on earth.*

For a moment, it still felt that way – that is except for Peggy's hyperventilation. "She got out. Sorry," Grace chirped, without much concern.

"That's...that's Little Pearl?" Peggy rhetorically asked, still gasping.

"You okay?"

"Yeah, I'm... Just give me a..." She, again, held up the same finger, clearly needing to regain her breath after appearing at the doorstep of death. When she managed to regain a semblance of her normal heart rate, she took in her mother – Grace. The same, pretty much. The skin a bit saggier and world-worn. The eyes a bit squintier, but still piercing. The hair silver now, but cropped and brushed in that 1980s feathered way that only a hair stylist in a boondock town like this could get away with without losing their license.

She looked at Peggy, barely above a mumble, "Well, look at you, huh?"

Peggy cracked a tepid smile, "Maybe I'm not the best thing to look at right now."

"Don't worry. She's a good girl. Just protective."

"I thought she was gonna' kill me."

"No, no. She jus' doesn't take to strangers right away."

"My God, that's an understatement."

"Hey, you just met 'er and she just met you. Cut her some slack."

"It's hard to cut an animal slack when she was seconds from taking my head off."

Grace was quickly done with defending Little Pearl, and was now back to questioning Peggy.

"You wana' tell me what this is about?"

"I told you what this is about. I wanted to see you."

"You didn't tell me why. There's a reason, right? You wouldn't just come back."

"How do you know? Maybe I - "

"Who the hell d'you think you're talkin' to? You think I got dumber since you been gone? I don't drink and don't smoke. My mind's as clear as it's ever been, so don't think I've become some Goddamn meek little old lady who don't know better."

She resigned that Grace would not allow herself to be mentally swindled by anyone. That much had not changed. And maybe what she was saying was true - she may've looked older, but perhaps she was as healthy as she'd ever been. Between the dog and her, Peggy didn't have the strength to be self-righteous. She could only yield.

After a moment, she looked at the car where Luna and Nicky warily looked out. Seeing their other grandmother was like seeing an exotic animal at the zoo. They had heard things from Peggy and, since what they heard was minimal and not particularly flattering, there was an expected reticence.

Grace turned toward the car as well and squinted at Luna and Nicky like a hardened sea captain, "So that's them, huh?"

"Yeah. That's Luna and Nicky."

Grace continued to look at them, and they at her. Eventually, Grace turned to Peggy, "They wana' come in or what?"

After such a rigid invitation, Peggy looked back at the kids, wondering if it was better to just keep them in the car until she had effectively surveyed the terrain. Instead, she walked to the car and, with a forced smile, signed for the kids to come out and meet their grandmother

The moment Peggy walked into the house, it was as if she stepped into a depressing dream of her childhood. The oppressive brown that adorned the walls remained, offset only slightly by cream-colored drapes that looked to have been purchased within the last 5 years or so. There were

some other mild upgrades, like the ash-stained leather couch was now gone – replaced by an aqua-green velvet one, which clashed with the walls like nails on a chalkboard. The coffee table was even new-*ish* – a glass topped table on gold-plated legs in place of the 2-ton wooden coffin-looking one that Peggy remembered her mother constantly stubbing her toe on and cursing to high heaven. While Peggy could not absorb everything upon her much belated entrance to this house, it appeared that Grace had made a half-hearted effort to develop a modicum of domestic taste, perhaps from watching all the many household makeover shows that were ubiquitous over the last 15 years or so.   However, judging from what she was seeing, it was clear that if Grace did watch those shows, she turned them off before the "after" segment, which usually would depict an improvement.

One thing the house was surprisingly bereft of was the familiar smell. By the time Peggy went on to college, the home had the embedded aroma of an illegal basement casino – one would practically be susceptible to lung cancer just by entering. Yet the smoke scent was all but gone, and replaced by an acrid raspberry-scented Renuzit dispenser that was almost more offensive.

There wasn't enough time for Peggy to adjust to the new/old surroundings, soon becoming aware that this was, in fact, not some bizarre time travel dream by the presence of Nicky and Luna, who meekly attempted to take in their latest stopover, while appearing wary of when Little Pearl would re-emerge.

"Have a seat," Grace chirped, bereft of welcome.

While Peggy and the kids sat on the couch, Grace stood for the moment, needing to take in both her nearly 40 year-old daughter and the two strange bodies that emanated from her during the course of their estrangement. Throughout, the TV played a re-run of *American Sleaze;* this one about the Manhattan bonds trader who moonlit as a pimp. It was little surprise that Grace watched this type of show, for her cultural taste was a notch or two below Monique's. Even as a child, Peggy remembered her mother watching the closest things there were to sordid television; *Sally Jessy Raphael, Jenny Jones, Morton Downey Jr, the Richard Bay Show* – all precursors to *Jerry Springer* and the more current *Maury Povich* and *TMZ*.

A moment sat in the air not unlike their recent phone call, only this time Peggy needn't imagine what was going through Grace's mind. She could see it clearly, as she eyed the kids like they just landed from another universe, before coming back to Peggy, who gazed at her meekly; her resistance lowered, aided by her recent near-death experience at the jaws of Little Pearl;

"So...is this all a' yas?"

"What do you mean?" Peggy asked.

"Just these two? No more kids?"

"No. These are my only two."

"I see," Grace turned back to the kids. "Nicky and Lulu?"

"Luna," Luna replied, softly.

"Luna. What's that, the moon?" Grace observed.

"That's right," Peggy replied, with a tepid smile.

"You kids wana' - ?" – suddenly there was a thunderous bark from the back yard that bled through the windows like a giant reverberating bell, as Nicky, Luna and Peggy jumped about a foot off of the couch.

"PEARL, HUSH UP!" bellowed Grace, without moving an inch from her spot in the living room.

"You kids wana' soda or somethin'?"

"No, thanks," replied Luna.

Nicky said nothing.

"You talk, kiddo?"

"Yeah," he reluctantly mumbled.

"Well, you wana' soda or what?"

"s'okay."

"Nicky, no thank you," Peggy gently scolded.

"No, thank you," he followed, looking at the glass coffee table.

"Well, look at you. What the years make us, huh?"

This last sentence resonated unsettlingly with Peggy, before she suggested, "Can we talk in private, please? Maybe the kids can watch TV in here while we go somewhere else?"

"We can't just talk in here?"

"Well, I thought the kids could just divert themselves, while we..."

"Well, I like the TV too, if ya' don't mind. My show's comin' on."

"Your...? Well,...can it wait? I mean, we drove all the way here to see you."

Grace looked at Peggy, clearly letting her know that this was putting her out, before reluctantly giving the remote to Nicky, who barely reacted to it. She mumbled, "I ain't seen this one before, even though it's a re-run." Before leaving the room, she looked at the set one last time, as a bald 47 year-old man named Herb Schberger recounted his double life as a trader/pimp while draped in the requisite orange jumpsuit. Grace gave one last chuckle, "What a prick," before heading into the dining room. Peggy followed, reluctantly, after glancing at Nicky trying half-assedly to figure out the remote while Luna gazed helplessly around the ill-matched living-room, then out the sliding glass door at Little Pearl, who gazed penetratingly inside.

They sat at the dining room table. Peggy placed her hands on the wood and recognized certain indentations like braille from her adolescence; familiar marks from Grace's fallen ashes, even a chip young Peggy accidentally put into the table with a steak knife, which drew Grace's ire. The memory of her mother's slap shortly thereafter, as if the indentation would upstage all the other marks, momentarily distracted her from the present, until she looked up to see Grace at the end of the table with a cup of coffee, waiting...

"So? What happened?" Grace asked.

"Well,...we've hit...a bit of a bad patch, I'm afraid."

"Whata' y'mean?"

"I mean, that..." Peggy was distracted by the increased volume of the TV from the living room, "I mean, that...some unfortunate things have happened and...we're not in a very good place. It's...it's temporary, but..."

She was halted by Grace's expression. It was clear that Grace was not going to fill in the blanks for her. A universe had elapsed since they were last in each other's company and there appeared to be no reason to assume what had happened, given that they were virtual strangers to each other. Grace was not remorseful about this and, if anything, seemed to thus far insinuate that this was due to Peggy's actions. If anything, one thing that Peggy could be almost certain of was that divulging Mike's own actions and subsequent downfall would only incur vindication within Grace. She hated Mike. Peggy knew this all too well. It was the catalyst to the demise of their relationship, and the catapult that would enable Peggy to discard her childhood so swiftly and ultimately land in the cushy confines of an elite Long Island town. And yet, here she was.

But how could she not tell the truth, especially since she didn't have the energy to lie?

"He cheated on you, didn't he," Grace said, with predictable relish.

Peggy simply sat there, stunned at such words, "I don't... No, that's... That's not why I'm... He made mistakes."

"Yeah? And what were those?"

The line of questioning was a worst-case scenario for Peggy, because there was no getting around the inevitable. She couldn't admit to Mike's infidelity because she was still clinging to the probability that it didn't happen. She didn't know firsthand, at least. She only heard it from Larry, and what stock could she put in him now, especially after he tried to jump her in his carriage house. But she needed to admit what led them to this.

She braced,..."He's in prison."

Grace remained for a moment, looked out the window,

glanced in the vicinity of the kitchen entrance, not far from where the kids were, before coming back to Peggy, "Well, isn't that somethin'." It was almost as if she were surprised, which, in turn, surprised Peggy. "What'd he do?"

"It had to do with how he was conducting his... It was related to his business. Insurance."

"Fraud?"

Peggy took a beat. She saw in Grace's expression that she knew this kind of story based on what she likely indulged in on television. She loved *American Sleaze* and all that other crap that seemed to cater to those too impatient to follow fictional narratives.

She looked at Grace, gazed out the window at the quiet street,... "Do you have a cigarette?"

"Told you, I quit."

Peggy did not absorb when Grace stated this initially, since it was just moments after her near homicide at the hands of Little Pearl, but upon hearing this now, she was incredulous - "Really?"

"Yep. Coffee's it now."

"What made you stop?"

"Nothin' made me. Jus' decided."

Peggy sat with this, both surprised that her mother exhibited such will-power while, at the same time, almost admiring how she could turn off a major compulsion like a faucet, without being goaded by a bleak diagnosis.

But this was all a digression to Grace.

"So was it fraud?"

She looked at Grace, beyond angry with Mike at this moment. What a position he had put her in, at the mercy of her mother – long despised by both of them.

She still couldn't bring herself to answer.

"Can we just...? We won't stay long. A few weeks. I just... I just need to stop moving for a few weeks and decide what's best."

"What's best for who?" Grace chirped.

"For the kids. For myself. If I should let the school year go out, if I should enroll them somewhere here and find an apartment."

"And what about me?"

"What...what do you mean?"

"What's best for me? You think being a den mother is where I wana' be at this point in my life?"

"I'm not asking you to be that."

"It sure sounds it."

"This was where I grew up, and it's the only place I could think of to come."

"Why not *his* parents? Where the hell're *they*?"

"They're in Florida."

"So? What's wrong with Florida?"

"Mike is upstate. I don't want us all to be... We have to visit him soon."

"So why don't you move upstate?"

"Jesus, I'm asking for a few weeks, okay? I don't know anybody upstate and we need to save money."

"Hey, I didn't put you in whatever the hell situation you're in, understand? You gotta' gripe, talk to that felon of a husband of yours. Don't bring it here. I have a life. I have a way I like things, y'understand? You come on in here outa' the clear blue sky after God knows how many years and you want me to bail you outa' somethin'? Then you show me some a' the respect you haven't shown me since you had a ponytail, otherwise get the hell out. You hear me?"

Grace slammed her coffee cup on the table, tightly folded her arms as if strengthening the fence that prevented any sympathy from seeping through. Peggy could only swallow every feather of the crow which now seemed to be half-way down her throat.

She took a breath, then forced a smile, "I'm very sorry, mom. It's just been...a very difficult period. It's not your fault, okay? I'm just asking for us to have a place to put our heads down and figure things out for just a few weeks. I know you have a life. You...you have the house, the dog, your... You have stuff, I'm sure. We won't be in your way. We just need a roof for now. Okay?"

Grace's aggression appeared to allay ever so slightly, but it was obvious that she wasn't going to waste the years of resentment she had built up and the opportunity of looking down at her only offspring.

She would yield enough to let them stay on a day-to-day basis, with the understanding that if she became dissatisfied enough with the arrangement, she had every right to kick them out.

And if it appeared that Peggy had forgotten this proposal, there would be little doubt that Grace would remind her.

19

It was several glorious seconds after she opened her eyes before she would recall where she was, and the avalanche of unfortunate events that would lead her back here. It was the sad reality that was her, at 39, staring up at the taped, yellowed photo of Sylvia Plath still encrusted on her childhood ceiling, which had now become one with the burnt orange paint of her youth. Sylvia once looked down at her on her bed as if giving her creative inspiration like an eccentric aunt – yet now Peggy only saw a manic depressive who put herself in an oven like a lugubrious meat loaf.

"Oh, God, make this be a dream," she begged internally, still hearing that knock on her classroom door from back in early November, only now it was actually her bedroom door, ...followed by the sandpapered cadence that could only emanate from the one person she had tried to keep a distance from since childhood. This was not a dream.

"YOU UP?!" Grace barked through the door.

"Oh, God..." Peggy said to herself, as the reality slowly sunk in...

"WHAT?!"

"I... Can you...? I'll be out in a few..."

"You plannin' to eat?!"

"Was...? Yeah, we...we'll figure something out, okay? Just..."

"There's cereal n'bread for toast. Don't go nuts with the eggs."

"That's...that's fine, we'll – "

"I suggest y'get groceries for yourselves today. I only got enough for me'n the dog. Wasn't plannin' on a full house."

"That's...that's fine. I'll get some stuff later today," she was already overwhelmed by such a high energy exchange before she even could get her morning eyes opened.

It amazed Peggy that her room was preserved as it was – or, more accurately, ignored after all these years, as if the house knew she'd be returning someday. She could barely process Grace's statement about not going *"nuts with the eggs,"* like they were some sort of sacred commodity, before her attention was usurped by seeing Nicky and Luna awkwardly lift their heads from their twin air mattresses that she had gotten from a local *K-mart* the night before. These pretty much covered the entirety of her small bedroom's floor, making standing and leaving the room an act of circus-like navigation.

As the kids slowly ascended from their half-deflated beds, Peggy looked at the door, her neck already tense from the anticipation of Grace's unwelcomed return, before her head dropped on the pillow like a boulder. She continued to look up at the ceiling and desired nothing but a few more minutes to shut her eyes, but felt odd about her kids being up and about in the house by themselves, especially with Little Pearl roaming around. Yet no sooner did she motion to rise before her phone rang.

For the last few weeks, at least, the ring tended to symbolize nothing of positive value. She had even begun to loath looking down at her screen to see who was calling, as it was sure to be nothing to add hope to her current existence.

She wished Mike would call, of course, but his phone time was handcuffed by Hawking State Prison. She wished Larry would call with an update, but since his sexual advances, she knew he would find it awkward to speak with her and, while she could call him, it would nevertheless do little to diminish the awkwardness.

Aside from Mike or Larry, it appeared that any incoming calls could only amount to the bleak or the mundane, and so it ran through her head what this call was; a cell phone bill notification, perhaps that rip-off dentist's secretary somehow found her, or her bank letting her know which credit cards were maxed, or Monique cursing her for the broken window, or being badgered for a platelet donation – *if they don't want money, they want blood.*

But this was a number she hadn't seen before, and it wasn't an 800 number either. She was reluctant to play the message back, having been so conditioned to adverse news that she felt as if every new revelation was eroding her somehow. She had even become a bit hunched in the last few weeks. Her toned arms had begun to sag. At 39, she was now feeling closer to 59, and it wouldn't take more than a stiff breeze to push her to 60, especially now that she was living with an animal who had come within seconds of ending her life. *No more news*, she thought:

"Hello, this message is for Mrs. Peggy Bubone. This is Jane Madden with American Sleaze. *In case you're unfamiliar, it's a reality-based television news show that airs nationally, but we're based in New York. I don't want to go into detail on your voicemail, but we'd be interested in speaking with you and providing more clarification, if you'd like to give me a call. I'll be in most of today until about 4. Again, my name is Jane Madden, and the best number to reach me is –"*

The rest of the message was inconsequential, for the moment. For now, she could only remain stunned that this tabloid news show that followed her of late like a bad odor would now be calling to, assumingly, feature Mike.

Could this get any worse?

Peggy navigated through the kitchen, as Luna and Nicky sat at the table, unusually dutiful. She expected to find the same items from 17 years ago in these same cabinets. As she opened one, she remembered the Cocoa Puffs that used to reside there, and how quickly crestfallen she'd become when she picked up the box to discover there was barely enough left for a bowl to start her youthful day. But now there was nothing but stockpiled *Nutri-System* boxes and bowls, which appeared to be ignored and almost dusty.

As an old morning re-run of *American Sleaze* bled into the kitchen, she eventually came upon a prescription bottle of Levothyroxin. She wasn't clear what this was for, but wasn't shocked to think that it was Grace's. Perhaps it was blood-pressure medication, or something for weight, which no doubt would have contributed to her stockpile of *Nutri-system* in the cabinets. But at a closer glance, she saw that it was a prescription for Joseph Zelansky – *the "Joe" from the earlier outgoing voicemail message?*

She had not inquired with Grace if there were any other inhabitants to be concerned with, aside from Little Pearl, as she had basically put the memory of hearing Joe's name out of mind, just to simplify things. But now her questions resurged; *Who is this guy? Is he coming back? She didn't so much as mention him yesterday.*

Peggy assumed he'd need his meds, whoever the hell he was.

The volume soon raised from the living room, *"...and when I found out that he was extracting diseased organs and selling them to hospitals, I just about collapsed,"* said some shocked wife speaking about her husband's get-richer-fast scheme. While Peggy's forced exposure to this insipid program had not warmed her to it, she could not help but be lured to the kitchen entry way to listen in a bit more, but out of eyeshot of Grace, who seemed to be doing her best to resume her daily life, unfazed by the three new occupants. *"I was just... disgusted that he would do this,"* continued the tear-stricken wife. This episode Peggy even recalled seeing with Monique; a podiatrist, of all people, sold his practice to buy a funeral home and subsequently began to sell organs from the people he was being paid to bury. Of course, it was one thing to loot the organs unbeknownst to the families who were paying him to inter their loved ones (as a whole) – and even replace pilfered bones with pipes, but it was another to take cancerous kidneys, livers and other infected organs and sell them to hospitals for use in implant procedures.

When Peggy first saw this in Monique's tiny living room, as they shared a bag of caramel corn, she nearly threw up. She even remembered running to the bathroom and standing over the toilet, just as a precautionary measure. Yet now, she could not separate that the producer of this show just left her a voicemail message – and she knew exactly why. *I could never be that woman who sits their glistening from my shameful tears, spewing on about the sins of the man I love,* she thought. Love was still in the present tense, despite all the known and unknown facts of Mike's behavior. What would change this would be a confirmation that there was, in fact, a woman in Ohio who Mike would "see" when in town for conferences. *If that were true, then...* But this was still connected to her belief that it was all just a desperate falsity by Larry to mount her like a Clydesdale.

"Mom, is there something here to eat," asked Nicky, who sat glumly at the kitchen table. Peggy was thrust back into the present, and resumed looking for something to make the kids, while Grace remained transfixed by the morbidity of *American Sleaze*.

Eventually, Peggy came upon some instant oatmeal, which required no more than boiling water. As she waited for the water to simmer, she looked for a coffee maker. This would ultimately require her to inquire with her mother, since the thought of getting through her first full day in that house without coffee was a fate worse than death. She entered into the living room, "GRRRRRRRR...."

"AHHHHH!" Peggy jumped back into the kitchen...

"Pearl, hush up," mumbled Grace.

Yes, there was Little Pearl, apparently in her usual spot, wedged beside Grace on the couch, as Peggy remained pinned in fright to the refrigerator. "Does she have to be there?!"

"What?!"

"I said, does she have to be right there?!"

"Where else she gonna' be? She lives here, for Godsakes!"

"You can't put her out back? I need to ask you some-thing!"

"I'm not gonna' keep her out 24/7, if that's what you're askin'. What is it?!"

Before Peggy could respond, she looked at Luna and Nicky, who had both of their spoons frozen in the air, as if to brace themselves for a pending attack. She took a breath to recall what she needed to ask Grace – "Where's your coffee maker?"

"Coffee maker. Just use the instant in the cabinet."

Peggy hadn't had instant coffee since...well, the last time she was home. It then dawned on her that her mother never had a coffee maker. Why bother, when she usually never had to make more than a cup at a time. God knows she rarely had visitors. *And maybe this Joe guy wasn't much of a coffee drinker.*

She gulped and moved on from her disappointment, seizing the jar of Maxwell House and filling the same pot with more water. For the first time since they had arrived there, she, Nicky and Luna were at the table together. It was almost like things were months ago in their own home, except that the rooms were getting progressively smaller and less stylish. Little could be said, at this point. Peggy was almost impressed by the fact that Luna and Nicky just ate, as if they understood that silence was more reassuring. As Grace's program con-tinued to blare throughout the house like a megaphone, Peggy tried to focus on what the next step should be.

It was at that point that she realized the kids couldn't stay there.

And if the kids couldn't stay with Grace, and Peggy couldn't stay with Vic and Elaine, then, sooner than later, Peggy would need to let the kids stay with their grandparents.

There was a deep sadness in this sudden realization, but also a sort of invigoration – for it cleared the fog of all that was overwhelming her, what was becoming so amorphous. But there it was, certainly helped by the death-simmering growl of Little Pearl.

But before she could think of putting them on a plane to Florida, she wanted to at least take them up once to visit Mike – and now was as good a time as any.

20

――――

Not trusting her car to make the 7 hour ride to Hawking State Prison, Peggy opted to bring the kids by train and then grab a car service once they arrived at the train station to take them to the prison. The train ride wasn't so strange to Peggy, as she had taken the train into the city on occasion from Long Island, and often brought the kids. But, of course, those were better times. Then they took the train because Peggy was scared to death of driving in the city, not because the old donkey car with an engine that was practically glued together was incapable of surviving the trip. She tried to avoid thinking of her past and, instead, tried to simply enjoy the ride. As Luna and Nicky looked out the window, taking in an occasional farm adorned with cattle or horses, Peggy attempted to embrace not having to worry about keeping her eyes on the road, or Grace barking through the door, or Little Pearl staring her down with her dirge-like growls.

Sleep had been hard to come by, but maybe she could catch an hour or so on this trip. As she started to fall into the zone of deep slumber about 2 hours in, her phone rang. It was that number again, which she now recognized; Jane Madden, producer of *American Sleaze*. This would now be the second call in three days, which was beginning to give the illusion that Peggy was in some sort of demand:

"Hello, this message is for Mrs. Peggy Bubone. This is Jane Madden with <u>American Sleaze</u>, just following up on my call from a few days ago. I'd really appreciate speaking with you with regards to appearing on our show. I'll be in most of today until about 4. Again, my

name is Jane Madden, and the best number to reach me is – "

There was no way Peggy was going to return the call on the train, in earshot of the kids. And, frankly, she still didn't have much compulsion to return it at all. She knew enough about the show to know that she definitely didn't want to be a part of it. And cashing in on their plight was all but unthinkable.

"Who was that, mommy?" Luna asked.

"Nothing important," Peggy mumbled, as she closed her eyes and attempted to fade away.

They arrived at Cucklesby Station, which was the nearest town to Hawking. Since Hawking didn't have the honor of possessing its own station, this was the closest they could get. As they stood outside, Peggy called a local car service advertised by 20 scotch-taped, dog-eared business cards on the wall – *Chatty's Taxi*. How fitting the name would be.

"How long you in town?" said Chatty, a heavy set, ever-gregarious man in his late 50s, as he drove them through the bleak town.

"Um, just for the day," Peggy indulged.

"Yeah, not surprised. Usually people that take the train to Cucklesby are visiting the prison. They're not exactly here for the scenic elements. I'll tell ya' though, the foliage here in the fall is a sight to behold. Say what ya' want about it bein' nowheresville or whatever, but to see the trees around here in October is really somethin'."

"How nice," she could barely say with sincerity.

"The orange, the yellow, the red. It's like a beautiful fire."

Yeah, this town would be better burned, she thought to herself.

"You kids get foliage down where you are?" he boisterously asked.

The kids looked at Peggy, both on the exact same page of dumbfoundedness, before Peggy forced, "Uh, yeah, we get foliage where we are."

"Yeah, but not like up here. I'm tellin' ya', come on up to Cucklesby in the fall. You won't believe it."

"Thanks for the tip."

"Oh, and you can't leave without grabbin' some rhubarb pie from *Chubby's*. Have you ever been there?"

"Uh, no, this is our first time up, but we've heard things."

"Yeah, on the way back, you might wana' hit it. It's almost as good as the foliage, I'm tellin' ya'. If you need a ride back, just call me and we can stop there first, if you have time before your train."

"Oh, well, we probably won't have time for that, but thank you for the offer."

"Hey, sure thing. It's real good though, I'm tellin' ya."

On one hand, it was all Peggy could do to not tell the aptly named Chatty to, well, stop being so chatty, as she could barely absorb that she was taking her kids to see their father in prison. But on the other, she appreciated the fact that Chatty, knowing full well where they were going, didn't inquire as to *why* they were going there. How many families had he driven there over the years. He probably heard all he could, and now was content to divert the focus by selling this sad little town. She was almost grateful to him.

They waited in the Hawking State Prison Visitor's Room. Since it was minimum security, they could actually be in the presence of Mike without protective glass between them. They could hug and kiss minimally but, of course, were under watch.

As a brawny, buzz-shaven guard looked on from the corner of the room, Mike gazed at his family and they at him with similarly moistened eyes. How long it had been. Of course, their time was limited, but there was clearly an unconscious need to just take everything in before words were spoken. Peggy was overwhelmed inside; seeing Mike, watching the kids see him and him seeing them. He was thinner, of course. The food played a role, no doubt, though not as much as the stress.

"Daddy, you're so skinny," said a tearful Luna.

"I know. I haven't had home cooking in a long time," he said. "Mommy's such a good cook. It's not the same."

"How are you?" Peggy asked.

"Better now," he said.

As Luna clutched her father's hand, and Nicky tried to keep from crying, "They've missed you."

"I've missed you guys. Oh my God..."

"Are you okay?" Peggy asked, redundantly.

"Honey, I mean, I'm as good as I can be in here, y'know? I don't wana' go into details with the kids here. But I'm okay. I'm good. I just wana' get outa' here and come home."

"We're with Grandma Grace," said Luna, which halted the emotions in the room.

Grandma Grace? Peggy thought. *Where did Luna get that?* To anyone else, it would sound endearing, but to her and, especially to Mike, it was ulcer-inducing. Mike's look to Peggy conveyed as much.

"You're with your mother?" he asked under his breath.

"Where else can we be?" she discreetly responded. "Not now, okay?"

Mike let this pass for the moment, and tried to focus on interacting with his kids. It was clear that he felt he needed to play catch-up as much as he could, having been out of their impressionable lives for months now. Peggy watched much of this with a running commentary in her head, as if watching a depressing home movie:

I know he feels so bad about this. He wants to cram all these months into this visit. I can see he's particularly worried about

Nicky, his only son. He feels how I've felt. This will have an adverse effect on him. Not so much now. Now he's acting like a 13 year-old who's been forced to experience something that he shouldn't have to. But he knows. He'll be in here for at least 2 years, even Larry couldn't get him out in less than that. That was always the best-case scenario, once he pled guilty. Two years for a young teen age boy to not have his father. I'm worried, but I'd be more worried if he stayed in Kelp Stream. Better he be with Elaine and Vic. Even if they sabotage my parental authority and turn him away from me, the real damage started here – and Mike knows it. It's what's made him thin.

Mike struggled to give equal attention to both Luna and Nicky. Luna, as she was always prone to do, could not help but monopolize the time. Nicky seemed too weakened to compete, as Mike gazed into his eyes, "Talk to me, buddy. I haven't seen you in a while. I wana' hear how you are."

"There's not much to tell. We're living with mom's mom," Nicky mumbled, again bringing Mike's greater concern back. It wasn't enough he fucked up as bad as he did, but now a woman who he deemed to be dangerous was housing his family.

There weren't many places the kids could go in the visitor's center without being in earshot of Peggy and Mike, but they definitely needed to speak among themselves. Peggy made certain that they had enough time to do so, especially given how their phone calls would always end so abruptly. There was a row of seats near the entrance where the kids sat, as Peggy and Mike spoke in hushed tones:

"Why are you staying with her? I thought you were at Monique's."

"It didn't work out. I don't wana' get into it."

"How did it not work out?"

"Mike, I don't wana' – "

"They didn't work out with Larry, they didn't work out with Monique..."

"Are you forgetting *why* I had to stay with Larry and *why*

I had to stay with Monique in the first place, Mike?!"

"Alright, I just – "

"Are you?!"

"Take it easy. The kid's are right there."

"I know they're there. I brought them to see their father in prison."

Mike sat back in his seat. This wasn't the first time, since his incarceration, that he was put in his place by his wife. It was impossible to sustain a sense of righteousness in a jumpsuit. She now looked at him like a timid boxer that she socked in the jaw. She had remorse in seeing him like this, but it was short-lived.

"Why the hell did you do it?"

He sat there, tempted to ask what she meant, if just to stall, but just as quickly realized that, in her physical presence, it was harder to conceal that he knew exactly what she was asking.

"I...," his voice sounded lost, as if searching for words that could do justice to such an overwhelming question. "Peg, honey, I... It just... I wanted us to have...everything. And... I mean, it's not easy to do everything in this world by the book. It's just... When I was in school, I thought the possibilities were endless; the American Dream, all that shit, but they're not when you do everything by the letter of the law. I learned that as I went along, with taxes and equipment and insurance, and paying for... I thought, just a few little... Just to help with the house and... It just...got outa' hand."

"We didn't need any of it, Mike."

"But you liked having it, didn't you? The kids – "

"Mike, we're not gold-diggers, for Godsakes."

"I know that."

"I never asked for this. The kids never asked for this. If they had less and we lived in a smaller house, no one would've cared. You think this is preferable? You being here and us being...?" she stopped herself, before stating the obvious.

He sat back, let out a deep breath, then looked at the

kids across the room, knowing that he couldn't argue.

It was amazing to think how much she idolized this man once, to the point where she threw her aspirations aside to be a wife and mother, thinking it would be just a few years before she could resume her path. But it turned out to be almost the entirety of their marriage. And just as she set foot back on the course she had initially planned for herself,....that knock at the door came. Now she was speaking to her husband who looked like a tangerine with a bad haircut. She always wanted to say so much to him, but was trying not to spill her grievances to the point where he would be debilitated, especially in a place where he could ill afford to appear weak and vulnerable. For the remainder of their limited time together, she tried to convey only the most important information:

"Mike, I'm gonna' have the kids stay with your parents, alright?"

"Whata' y'mean? Aren't you going too? That's what I-"

"No, it's just gonna' be them. I'm gonna' stay with my mother. It's just...easier that way."

"How is it easier if you hate that woman?" his energy suddenly resurged.

"There's nothing for me in Florida, and I can be closer to you. Just don't push this, Mike. I'm not going to stay with your parents."

"It just seems strange to me that you'd stay with her."

"Well, she is my mother."

"Yeah, and she tried to kill me, remember? My God, she's lucky *she's* not in prison."

Peggy looked over at her kids, who were momentarily diverted by two crows fighting through the window; perhaps a more entertaining battle than what was happening inside. *Thank God they didn't hear,* she thought.

But yes, it was true.

She took a breath, "I don't have a choice, Mike. And you need to understand that."

"Don't worry about being closer to me right now. I'd

just rather you be with the kids – "

"I've been with them, Mike. It's not permanent. I just need to figure things out, and it's harder to do that if I have to care for them. They need to be in school, not following me around. And I don't want them going to school in Kelp Stream. They can finish out their school year in Florida and then, I'm sure, by the summer, I'll be able to bring them back up to wherever I am."

Mike took a similar breath, defeated, "I'm just… Jesus Christ, Peggy. I know I did all this. I know. I can't apologize enough. I just… Never in a million years did I think this could lead to you and the kids being…"

She nodded understandably, but was nevertheless surprised by his reaction; "Mike, it's not like I'm selling our kids to strangers. They're gonna' be with your folks."

"Without you."

"Mike, there's no other way, if you want me to survive this."

"What does that mean?"

She finally had to increase her candor, "Mike, it'd kill me to live with them," her eyes locked into him in a way that could not be questioned by him. "And they don't want me there, anyway."

Mike made a feeble motion of denial, but her determined expression halted his attempt to deflect this. She knew that he knew. It wasn't like he wasn't speaking to them too. God knows what they were saying.

"Peg, I told them from the beginning this was all on me," a feeble attempt to ease her resentment.

"But you know it doesn't matter, right?" she followed, with a pained smile. Not disbelieving his words, but also not convinced that his defense of her in any way altered his parents' steadfast belief; *it had to be someone else's fault.*

They sat there a moment, looking at each other. Mike again weakened. Peggy attempted to subtly shift gears:

"What's Larry saying?"

"You still haven't heard from him?"

"No, and I don't think I will, Mike."

"What happened over there? He's supposed to keep you apprised."

"Well, I'm here with you. Tell me what's happening."

Mike sighed, "Nothing. I'm stuck at 2 years. And I'll still have reparations to pay when I get out. Who knows how the hell I'll do it? I won't be able to practice in New York again. I'll only be able to give what I can give. That's the least of my concerns."

There was more silence between them, as Mike again looked over at the kids. Peggy tried to let him have as many moments uninterrupted by adverse news as possible, but also knew that their time together was dwindling...

"I got a call from a tabloid show, if you can believe it," she couldn't help but divulge this with a weak chuckle.

"Why? What show?" as he sharply turned back to her.

"*American Sleaze.*"

"What the hell do they want with you?"

"Mike, what do you think? It's all about stories like this. People who live these seemingly respectable lives who're also involved in some..." She stopped herself, barely resisting the word crime or any variation of it.

"So, what, they want to do a thing on me? This whole mess? Jesus Christ..."

"Mike, I haven't even called them. I wasn't even considering it, okay? But I know why they're calling. -I've seen the show. Monique watched it, my mother watches it... It's... sordid."

"It just gets deeper and deeper, doesn't it," he asked himself, softly and rhetorically.

"I don't think they can do anything if I don't agree, so don't worry about it."

"They'll pay," he suddenly blurted, not looking at her.

"What?"

"I said...they'll pay you. You need the money."

She almost gasped at this, "Mike, there's no way…"

"If they'll give you a decent amount of money for it, you should do it. I'm in here. Everyone who knows me knows. What the hell's the difference? As long as you can get some money for it…" He became choked up as he looked at the kids, who were now looking at him from the corner of the room. Peggy looked back at them as well, her eyes remoistening.

She then saw the guard approaching, which signified their time being up, but it was nowhere near enough…

"Kids, c'mere!" Mike exclaimed through a cracked voice… Luna and Nicky rushed to him…

"No, there's… Just another few minutes…" Peggy pleaded with the guard, who would be undeterred.

She looked to see Mike hug the kids so tight that they would normally cry out in pain, but their pain threshold seemed to be increased for this occasion. They could endure it if this was the last time they were going to see their father for a while.

Mike and Peggy quickly kissed and, within seconds, he was gone. Luna and Nicky were now audibly crying, as Peggy looked at the door where Mike had exited through. She was surprised at his willingness to let her pursue speaking to Jane Madden, and saddened by how defeated he was by her being separated from the kids… And yet, she wanted to speak with him about the woman from Ohio – *if there really was one*, but it seemed fated that she not know for certain, at this time. Maybe her assumption would have to be enough. Maybe her hope that it was just a lie Larry told would need to sustain her, so that she could still love this man. What was she if not his wife and the mother to his children? Especially when it looked like the only way she could make an income at the moment was from profiting from her husband's crime.

She still was not planning to return Jane Madden's call, but at least Mike appeared to give her his blessing to pursue this avenue, in the interest of giving her a fraction of stability.

How much do those shows even pay? she wondered.

When Chatty arrived to pick them up outside the cold, sterile fence of the prison, with just less than a half hour before the next train back was leaving, he had a box for them in the backseat. It was the famous rhubarb pie from Chubby's Diner.

"Wasn't sure you'd have the time, so I picked it up for ya'. My treat, okay?"

Peggy held the pie on her lap, and tearfully whispered to the kids to thank the nice man.

They did.

"You're welcome," he said, as he drove them back to the station, barely uttering a word this time.

21

There was hardly a word spoken on the train back, but many things were going through her mind; like how sad it was seeing Mike. How sad for the kids, who still looked so crestfallen. She also was concerned with how the conversation would go with Nicky and Luna about living with their grandparents, provided they weren't all killed first upon entering the house by the relentless jaws of Little Pearl.

At least there's the rhubarb pie.

Before they got back to New Jersey, Peggy decided to listen again to Jane Madden's message. For some reason, she wanted to hear it again, despite the lack of detail. Perhaps it was just nice to hear someone who was interested in her for something other than paying a debt. It took so little time for Peggy to feel unwanted by the world after years of seeming adoration. She still clung to Mike's love. She believed it perhaps more than it was actually true. Maybe what she was interpreting for love now was his desperation to have anyone on his side. Maybe it was just guilt. But he was in prison and certainly not in the position to carry on an affair. The reverence that once adorned him was long gone, and there was only room for the family that he and Peggy created. His adoring parents aside, it was clearly the only thing that would get him through the next 2 years.

They arrived at Grace's that night, both fatigued by the long trip and emotionally spent. As they gingerly stepped towards the door, Little Pearl's sixth sense kicked in, as she emanated a nerve-rattling bark that sustained itself like a long demonic note. Through the door, Peggy heard Grace admonishing Little Pearl, as Peggy stepped back and pressed the kids against the brick behind her as Grace's steps approached.

"Jesus Christ..." she muttered, clearly annoyed, her dimly lit frame through the screen door, "It's late."

"Well, we travelled far. I told you."

"What do I know what you told me? You said you went to visit 'im."

"He's in upstate New York."

"Okay, so he's upstate."

"Can you put her out back, please? I just want to get upstairs."

"She ain't gonna' attack you now."

"Mom, please. I've got the kids here. I don't wana' take chances."

Grace looked at Peggy, again, clearly resentful that whatever televised inanity she was indulging in was getting interrupted.

"Alright, hold on. Jesus Christ..."

Peggy's fear was supplanted by the resurrected feeling of being unwanted in her childhood home. Even if this seemed like a stranger's home now, and even if she felt no deeper connection to Grace than she had before their arrival, it was exhausting to continually be perceived as an inconvenience. At least she knew the kids would not have to experience this much longer.

"SHE'S OUT BACK!" Grace yelled from the living room, not wasting the steps back to the door.

Peggy and the kids crept in like cat burglars, almost in disbelief that Little Pearl was out of jaws reach.

"Okay, why don't you guys get cleaned up and get ready for bed. I'll be up in a bit."

Peggy felt odd about just continuing on upstairs, and came into the living room to check in on Grace.

"Is everything okay?" she asked.

Grace's eyes remained fixated on the TV, watching an

episode of *Dateline*. "Huh?" she muttered.

"I'm just...checking in. We were gone all day, so I just wanted –"

"Hold on a sec, I wana' hear this," she snapped, her eyes unmoved from the TV, as she watched a surveillance interview with an apparent murder suspect.

Peggy thought to walk upstairs, but begrudgingly remained. *"I wun't there, I'm tellin' ya. I was at my brother-in-laws, jus' like I tol' you before. I had nuttin' to do with it,"* proclaimed a burly southern man, accused of hacking an ex-girlfriend to bits and putting her remains in his meat freezer.

How could she watch this crap? she wondered. But, of course, she knew now that *many* people watched this crap. Many people's barometer for morbid curiosity was seemingly boundless. Particularly people that had little, like Monique and Grace. To such an audience, watching other people experience tragedy was an equalizer – especially for a show like *American Sleaze*, which particularly focused on the fall of the wealthy, be they lawyers, doctors, politicians, hedge funders... She wouldn't even bring up Jane Madden's call with Grace, which was easy enough to do, since she and Grace hadn't managed a conversation of any length in the three days that she'd been there.

Still, she wanted to keep Grace abreast of her plans, thinking she would be relieved to not have Luna and Nicky there anymore, not that their presence altered Grace's habits much.

As the show went to commercial, "There's rhubarb pie in the fridge, if you want some." She thought it was best to warm up with an offering.

"Okay. Is that what you wana' talk about?"

"No, I... It's there, that's all."

"Okay," Grace retorted, clearly not impressed.

Peggy took another breath, which it seemed she needed to do anytime she spoke to her mother, "Anyway, so I just wanted to let you know what's happening," as she sat at the end of the couch, a considerable distance from Grace.

"What's happening?"

"Well, I've decided to send Nicky and Luna to be with their grandparents."

"You mean, *his* parents."

"Yeah."

"What, you don't want 'em around me?"

Peggy was stunned at the question, "I just...don't feel it's fair. To you. Or to them."

"Why ain't it fair to them? 'cause I'm not like your Long Island friends? They scared a' me or somethin'?"

"Mom, it's not... It just makes more sense right now, that's all. It's nothing personal. They know their grandparents a lot more. They've been in their lives."

"So why ain't *you* goin'?"

"Well, I... I just want to be closer to New York. Where Mike is."

"That sounds kinda' fucked up, dontcha' think?"

While Peggy didn't necessarily expect gratitude from Grace, she also didn't foresee being questioned regarding her parenting skills.

"What do you mean by that?"

"You know what I mean, Peggy."

"The idea was that this would only be short term, okay? Just until I got on my feet. And I realized it'll just be easier if I do that on my own. They'll be with their grandparents, they can finish school down there, and by the time they're done, I'll be in a position to bring them back up."

"So you're sayin' it's jus' gonna be you here now?" Grace knowingly asked.

"Well, not for long, but yeah. I mean, it's not like you expected the kids."

"Expected the kids? I didn't expect *you*, for Godsakes."

"Look, I already explained that we hit a bad patch, okay? It took some time for me to consider you as an option. It's not like you were first on my list." She very quickly realized it was audacious to say this.

"I tell ya' what, how about you join 'em."

"What?!"

"You heard me. You wana' give me shit about me bein' a last resort? Fine, go to your ritzy in-laws. Let them deal with ya'."

With that, *Dateline* returned from its commercial break, as Peggy remained, agape.

"Can you mute that, please, so we can talk?"

"I told you I hold the cards here, okay? This is my God-damn house. My name's on the deed. You got issues with anything I do, the door's right there. Now let me watch this."

Peggy wanted to seize that ridiculously oversized remote from Grace with every fiber of her being, but knew that the mere attempt would result in nothing less than her eviction. Instead, she merely sat there, watching Grace watch this drivel until the next commercial break...

Once it came, she would resume, "I just wanted to let you know that I plan to tell them tomorrow."

"That you're sendin' them off?" Grace said gruffly, sounding as if Peggy was placing them on the black market.

"It's not like I'm sending them to live with strangers. It's their grandparents. And they'd love to have them. I just need to focus on how I'm going to make a living and then get a place."

"Yeah, how *are* you gonna' make a living?"

She took a beat, trying not to be insulted, "Well, I was a teacher."

"Oh, that's right," Grace scoffed, as she turned back to the Metamusil commercial that was currently running.

"Yes, that *is* right," she said, with restrained adamance. "That's what I was doing before... I mean, that's what I went to college for."

"Right. You were gonna' be a teacher and a writer. Right?" Again, Grace's question was continually in the form of judgement, as her eyes remained away from Peggy.

"Yes, exactly." She looked at Grace with resentment, which was getting harder and harder to suppress, especially being so drained from the day. Grace wasn't even aware that Peggy, prior to her brief stint at Cold River High School, hadn't worked for years and hadn't written a thing, yet it felt as if she knew the dormancy of her career aspirations somehow. Then again, it could've just been the contempt she always had for Peggy's desiring to further herself. This began to be prevalent when Peggy applied to colleges outside of the local community college in Kelp Stream, and developed significantly once she got a scholarship to Princeton. When she met Mike and announced their engagement, it was the icing on the cake.

She continued, "Look, I'll get out of your hair as soon as I can. We needed to make this trip today and...I'll be talking to Nicky and Luna. Once they're in Florida, I can focus better and I'm sure I'll... Well, I'll find something."

"Around here? What, you're gonna' teach at the high school?"

"I'm...gonna' try and find something elsewhere."

"Yeah, figured. You always wanted to be elsewhere."

"That's what a lot of kids do, mom. They aspire to leave the only thing they've known."

"Do they, now?"

"My kids will be on their own one day too, and I'll support what they want to do."

"You sayin' I didn't support you?"

Peggy was astonished at the mere hint that Grace actually cared how Peggy perceived her, "I never felt you wanted me to leave."

"Who told you that? I never told you that."

"No, you... I really don't wana' get into this now, mom. I just wanted to let you know that I'll be getting their airline tickets and they'll be in Florida by next week. And I'll try and be gone in a couple of weeks myself, if that's okay."

Dateline came back on, as Grace's eyes shifted to the screen. She turned up the volume, which was as close to a response as Peggy expected to receive. They spoke enough, she felt. Conversations were never going to be longer than a couple of minutes before they risked delving into the disturbing core of what led to their estrangement.

She lumbered upstairs to her old childhood room. She looked down the hall at the closed bathroom door, with light bleeding out from the bottom. She thought she heard odd sounds emanating through the door, as she approached. As she pressed her ear against it, it was clearly Luna crying...

"Honey?"

She didn't respond, but the hiccupped sobbing continued...

"Honey, are you okay? Can you let me in?" as she twisted the locked knob.

Luna kept crying, unabated, as Peggy tried more desperately to open the door, "Honey, open up, okay? Everything's gonna' be fine."

"No, it won't!" she barked.

"Of...of course it will, honey. Why do you say that?"

"Because you're sending us away!"

Shit, she thought. She didn't consider that the kids would be in earshot when she told Grace. She had so wanted them to get through this day with the ample amount of emotion that came with seeing their father in prison. *Now this.*

Before Peggy spoke to her again through the door, she of course wondered if Nicky knew what Luna now knew. Or did Luna just hear this herself and was so stricken by the news, that she could only lock herself in the bathroom. Peggy peeked into her bedroom to see Nicky sitting at the end of her bed, gazing at the wall solemnly. *He knows.*

"Nicky, are you okay?" she superfluously asked.

He didn't answer. With that, she went back to retrieve Luna from the bathroom and reconciled that she would need to speak with them both together that night. Once she did, the most challenging thing would then be making the call to Vic and Elaine, who she had not said a word to since their last memorable exchange, which led to Peggy accepting Larry's offer to stay with him and Carole.

She finally managed to corral Luna out of the bathroom so that she could have, what felt like, the umpteenth morale-building huddle with the kids inside of someone else's small bedroom – yes, technically, this bedroom was hers when she was a child, but it was hard to consider it her own anymore.

"It's only gonna' be temporary, but I think it's best that you stay with Grandpa Vic and Grandma Elaine for a little while."

It sickened her to say their names that way, but it sounded a little more reasonable than *"Grandma Grace"*. Luna remained crying, as Nicky simply appeared lost, which was a contrast to his usual glum indifference.

"You know it's not because I don't love you, right?"

"Then why?" as Luna wiped her snot-laden nose.

"I was going to explain this to you tomorrow. I wanted us to just rest tonight, because we've had a hard day. But since you overheard, we may as well get this out in the open." She took a breath, "It'll be easier for me to set us up in a new home if I can just focus on getting work. And having all of us here is gonna' be too much of a distraction."

"Why? We were with you at Monique's, and Larry and Carole's."

"That's because we didn't have a plan, honey. We were just staying with people because they invited us, and we didn't have a choice. And we're here now because we don't have a choice, but it's different. I just... This is the end of the line, okay?"

"What's that mean?" Nicky mumbled.

"It means that...I can only go up from here. It means that this is not a good place for us to be together as a family. It's one thing if it's just me, but I don't feel it's safe for you guys."

"Because of Little Pearl?" Luna asked.

"Well, she's one reason, yeah."

"But can't Grandma Grace just keep her outside?"

"She's not gonna' be happy about doing that, Luna. Listen, it's hard for me to explain this in a way that you guys'll really understand right now. Yes, she's technically your grandmother, but she and I have been out of each other's lives for a very long time. Longer than you both have been in the world. And it's for a very…sad reason. And we have to work through it, and having you both here will add complications. So as much as I don't want to be apart from you, please know that it's because I love you that I'm doing this."

Luna and Nicky looked at their mother blankly. It wasn't clear if they really understood what she was saying, but it was as much of an explanation as she could summon for the night. It was a long day.

Enough was enough.

22

————

This was going to be a difficult day, that much was clear. Peggy's stress-induced dreams conveyed as much, as she sat on the side of her musty childhood bed. She looked down to see the kids on their small, inflatable beds that were slightly less inflated by dawn. It was early, so they still were asleep, as was Grace.

Peggy crept down the stairs, with the first creak of the steps prompting a nerve-rattling bark by Little Pearl through Grace's closed bedroom door.

With her housecoat thrown over her nightgown, she went downstairs, sat at the dining table and started looking at airline ticket prices on her phone. It was Florida, so it was a bit more economical than flying anywhere else in the country, but given the fact that she was looking to put them on the plane within a few days heightened the cost a bit. And yet her newfound frugality that had developed into a well-honed new muscle over the recent weeks guided her to the plethora of discount sites. She whittled down the options to one decent price for two one-way tickets for minors, though it was still a fiscal stinging given the space that remained on her one un-maxed credit card.

She still hadn't called Vic and Elaine yet, but didn't want to lose these low-price tickets, so she purchased them for next Monday, which would at least give her the forthcoming weekend with the kids before their undoubtedly emotional departure. Just as she finalized the sale, she was startled by an incoming call. It was Jane Madden, producer of the notorious *American Sleaze*. This time she would pick up.

"Hello," she nervously uttered. Just as Jane Madden was about to speak, a door slammed open from upstairs, and the horse-hoof stomping on the thinned carpet from Grace's morning venture to the bathroom would reverberate throughout the old, small house.

"Yes, is this Mrs. Bubone?"

...Peggy rose and urgently motioned for the front door, "Yes, one moment, please," as she bumped into a kitchen chair on her way out, prompting a distant howl from Little Pearl, which only accelerated her momentum. She closed the door behind her, but was greeted by a ferocious waft of bitter cold air. It was still winter, after all. But her desperation to have this call be as clandestine as possible took precedence over the fact that she was in pajamas and a silk robe in 32-degree weather.

"I'm sorry if I've been a little aggressive in my reaching out, but time is always of the essence when it comes to programming," Madden opened. "But, to sound like a cliched producer, I'd like to save you time and cut to the chase here. We're interested in your story."

Peggy knew why she was calling but, nevertheless, played as ignorant as possible. "When you say 'my story', I assume you mean...my husband's, right?" She didn't intend to be defensive as she asked this, and yet it came out a bit more assertive than she had anticipated. Perhaps this was because she had a resentment for being used in this way. Perhaps it also had to do with the fact that the cold air made her feel virtually naked.

"Well, I wouldn't say it was *his* story alone, Mrs. Bubone. I mean, you're his wife. I assume this has affected you. You have kids, yes?"

"How did you find out about all this?"

"This is what we do, Mrs. Bubone. We're a news show. We have researchers. Story editors. Sometimes we have to look a little harder for stories in other areas of the country, but you being in Long Island put you sort of in our backyard here. And I live in Long Island so, in this case, I was the first to discover this and found that it would be perfect for the show."

"You're aware I've had to live this, right? I don't see this as being entertainment."

"Peggy,... I'm sorry, may I call you Peggy?"

"That's...yes, that's fine."

"Thank you. And call me Jane, please. Peggy, please know that I know you have been through a lot. Just as our show focuses on crime, it also focuses on the results that have come from it."

"I know what your show is, Jane."

"So you watch the show?" as if it was a compliment.

"Yes, I've watched the show. I'm not particularly proud of it, I have to say, but I have. I know what you focus on and, I have to be honest, I'm not interested in being portrayed as a grieving, beaten wife."

"Well, no one is saying you have to be that."

"How can I not be that if that's what I am?"

Jane seemed taken aback by this, "I'm sorry, I'm not –"

"I *am* grieving and I *have* been beaten down by this, okay? I am living it right now, but I don't need to have that be exposed to the world. And I can't do it to my husband."

There was a considerable silence, and within it, Peggy was all but sure that the opportunity had dissolved. "Peggy, ...I hear you. And would you believe that pretty much every distraught, disgruntled, devalued spouse we have had on our show in the 6 years that we've been on has said the exact same thing to me?"

Jane's attempt at easing her despair or quelling her trepidations only incurred in Peggy an unsettling sense of being indistinguishable; a deceived wife merely among the masses of other deceived wives, piled atop each other like feminine slabs. This only gave her more of a sense that this was wrong. They couldn't pay enough to make this seem like anything else but selling out. And it's not like it would be selling out as some sort of artist – it would be selling her life. Cashing in on her and her family's tragedy. *Could a price really be put on that?*

And yet, at the same time, she couldn't help but be curious, "How much are you offering?"

"Well, Peggy, how we work this is we'd pay you a flat rate of $5,000 for the episode, which would not include syndication. This would actually be for you to come into the studio in New York for an interview segment. We'd only need you to come in once, but we'd need you to commit a full day. You'd sign a release to appear, of course. And it would be exclusive for a year."

"What does that mean?"

"It means the only thing we ask is that you not sell your story to another television show, specifically on a major network, for a year. However, you keep film rights, book rights, etcetera."

"So basically one flat rate for a show and you own the television rights for a year."

"Yes. Of course, there will be some nuance in the contract, but we can send that to you and, of course, if you have any questions before you sign or want to consult with an attorney, that's completely up to you."

It suddenly unsettled Peggy that, no sooner was she fairly assured that she would turn this down, she found herself talking money and contract details. Before a disturbing feeling engulfed her more than the cold air sweeping down Morgan Street, she put the breaks on, "I'm gonna' have to think about this, okay? This is new for me and, frankly, I just...I never saw myself... I don't see myself as someone who would do something like this."

"Peggy, I respect your feelings, but just remember, you're entitled to be upset. You're entitled to be appalled at what was thrust upon you. And you're also entitled to share your story. And sometimes the latter justifies the former. That's why we do this. This is a show about shedding light. It's a show about justice."

While Jane was, in essence, elevating her tabloid show to that of a Ken Burns documentary, Peggy knew what she was selling. Her eyes didn't deceive her, nor her ears. Yes, the stories may all have been true. But, in the end, the show was cashing in on American schadenfraude – that German word that best summed up the joy that one derives through the misfortune of others. It was guilty candy, plain and simple. And it was not a mere one-off interview she'd be getting paid for. She'd be signing off permission for this show to run until the end of time.

"I appreciate your time, Jane. I'll get back to you if I'm interested."

"Thank you, Peggy. If you have any questions, just let me know. I'm happy to allay any concerns."

With that, Peggy clicked off...and gazed down the potholed street. The gray sky and bitter wind magnified her sense of being alone in an increasingly lonely world. Before she could even recap some of what was said by Jane Madden on the call, she looked to where Ms. Dulcy's house used to be and noticed it was gone. Not refurbished or rebuilt, but gone. An empty lot of weeds and overlong grass stood in its place. Peggy remembered it was there the last time she saw her mother, 17 years ago, and had presumed Ms. Dulcy was still alive. While she wasn't surprised that she would have passed on by now, as she must have been in her early 70s back then, the mere weeds that were in the place of where her home once stood struck her as both sad and eerie. There were a lot of myths that came with that house. Peggy and her friends all believed it was haunted, and even suspected Ms. Dulcy of being a witch – mainly because she always looked so old and so pale, and she rarely spoke to anyone. Grace always thought she was weird, and probably never said a word to her in all their years as neighbors. Of course, Grace wasn't chatty with neighbors in general, and her finding someone to be weird could by no means be considered an objective judgment.

Before Peggy knew it, she was coaxed by the wind to the now vacant lot where Ms. Dulcy's home once was. She remembered where her nice garden used to be, which had inspired Peggy to create her own small patch in the backyard. It made her realize that she hadn't had a chance to take in much of anything in her childhood home because of the kids and trying not to invade Grace's space. She hadn't even seen the backyard since being back, but knew the remnants of the garden were long gone.

She slowly walked on the tall strands of grass and weeds in the now vacant lot, oblivious to the fact that she was wearing slippers while holding her robe tightly closed. Each step was careful, as if she was walking into Ms. Dulcy's home without knocking. It still felt invasive and even dangerous. Her emotions were manifold, as she continued; overwhelmed at the thought of Ms. Dulcy killing her husband and how she may've done it. Then again, there was always the possibility that she was merely a lonely woman who lived the only type of life she seemed fated for. Was she offended by the scared looks of kids who could never walk past her house without trying to peer through her windows? In the end, she was gone from the earth, in all likelihood. A woman, like many in this town, who would never leave. Who never remotely aspired to anything but owning a shitty home and dying in it.

That certainly appeared to be Grace's fate, which would be easier for Peggy to conclude if she wasn't now forced to live with her.

And then she remembered Jane Madden's proposal, which suddenly didn't seem like the worst idea.

After breakfast, Peggy decided to take the kids for a day trip to the site of the few pleasant memories she recalled as a child; the boardwalk at Ocean Bay. Ocean Bay was about an hour east of Kelp Stream and it would be the closest proxim-

ity to a natural body of water. Granted, it was late January
– cold, gray, windy and…utterly not the best day for such a
venture, but this was to be their final weekend together for
a while, and so Peggy felt that there would be some benefit
in taking a trip to a place that still held some nostalgia for
her. Luna and Nicky were silent, gazing out the window as
they exited out of Kelp Stream, passing nothing of distinction;
barren fields, old houses; some dilapidated. *Prager's Ye Olde
General Store* still stood, which would be where Peggy would
likely get cigarettes as soon as she ran out, along with other
household basics. It was where Grace also got her cigs, which
she often used to send Peggy in for while she waited in the car.
It was significant that the store remained and had the same
name, but she couldn't imagine the friendly owners, Mr. and
Mrs. Prager, weren't retired by now. Maybe one of their kids in-
herited it. Or maybe new owners were too lazy to change the
name.

They arrived in Ocean Bay which, considering the time
of year and the type of day, was as barren as a town could be.
People did live near the ocean, but not nearly as many as when
Peggy was a child. No doubt Hurricane Sandy had something
to do with that. It made it seem even more depressing than
Kelp Stream, with the presence of the Atlantic Ocean looking
misplaced and unworthy of such a melancholic environment.

"Why're we here?" Nicky asked from the backseat, as
they all stared at the boardwalk just about a half block from
where they were parked. Peggy couldn't answer this too
quickly, for she also started to question why she thought to
bring them there. *My God, I'd've been better off bringing them to a
morgue,* she thought.

"Well,…this place was where I had a lot of good times
when I was your ages."

"*Good* times?" Luna asked, almost as if this were a
thought that slipped out inadvertently.

"Well,…I mean, in the summer. That's really when I'd
come. But even in the fall I came here."

"Why?" Luna followed, still looking out the window in amazement of its bleakness.

"Luna, you... You have to look beyond the surface of things. I've told you this before."

"Told me what?"

"Like with the book. *Bless the Beasts*. You can't just look at what's easy to not like. You have to... I'm saying, I didn't just come here to swim or to get a tan. I came to think. There was something that it always did for me that I couldn't really find anywhere else. And I know this isn't the best weather for you to understand that - "

"There's no weather in the world that'd make this place look good. This is a hole," Nicky spewed... "Nicky,..." Peggy turned to him, determined to not lose her patience, given the circumstances... "He's right. This is depressing!" Luna followed.

"Look, we have to make the most of our time together."

"Right, because you're sending us away," Nicky said, with an unusual conviction, as if this was the one thing he was most certain of in his young life.

"Nicky, Luna, I didn't drive us out here to argue. I wanted you to experience...as many nice things as possible before you go to your grandparents, which is only temporary anyway."

"This isn't nice," Luna said, near tears...

"Well, it's nicer than being in that house, that's for sure. And I don't think you'd disagree, right? Do you wana' stay in that house 24/7 until we go to the airport on Monday? *I* sure don't."

"I don't wana' go anywhere," Luna cried. "I don't wana' go anywhere."

"Luna,..." Peggy looked at her, nearly speechless, then back at Nicky, who continued to gaze out. In a matter of minutes, this turned into the most depressing day trip imaginable. But an hour drive here and the gas it took would not be wasted, in Peggy's mind. She wanted them to at least look at the sea that, as a young girl, gave her some sort of amorphous hope. There were no other words she could say. She just wanted them to experience it for themselves, even if this was inevitably fruitless.

She herded them up to the barren boardwalk, in perfect view of the boards nailed over the windows of cotton candy and pizza stands and closed arcades. With the wind increasing its ferocity as they approached the boardwalk railing facing the incoming tide, they stared at the ocean. The waves and wind were so loud that nothing Peggy would say could be clearly heard anyway, as she looked down at Luna shivering convulsively while Nicky tried to appear undaunted by the merciless temperature and ferocious gusts. With her arms around them, Peggy looked out, desperate to recall a semblance of what she felt as a child; her dreams at the possibilities that awaited her as an adult and getting out of Kelp Stream somehow. And then there was the more recent memory of that photograph at Carole's gallery that had such an effect on her; that faceless woman with a sun hat gazing out at the water. The peace she seemed to feel, the contentment with her place in the world... At least, this was the story the photo told to Peggy, and it was the persistent dream to embody it herself someday – *a clean slate, untainted by life – if only for a moment.*

But as she looked down at her shivering offspring, it became all too clear that the moment was not today.

Monday morning arrived, as Peggy, not atypical from her Cold River persona, made breakfast for the kids in Grace's kitchen. Since it was before 9am, Grace was still asleep, though she knew full well that her grandchildren would be departing on a noon flight to Florida. For the moment, Peggy didn't care if Grace didn't want to see them off, as it was all that she could muster to see them off herself without breaking down. Vic and Elaine would be expecting the kids at Palm Beach International Airport, and at least she knew that where the kids were heading would be a place that they were wanted. Regardless, this would be the most painful breakfast of her life.

They sat quietly around the table, the kids barely picking at their bowls of instant oatmeal, as Peggy begrudgingly sipped her cup of instant coffee, which she had not come close to getting used to. It was not much different to meals they had had after Mike's arrest, when silence proved better than fielding questions from the kids who, back then, were very much in the dark on what was happening. Now, barely 3 months later, they knew too much. And while they still resented being shipped off without their mother, they knew it wasn't quite the same as her abandoning them with Grace, who had not endeared herself to them or made much effort to get to the know them in the week and a half that they were there.

They eventually brought their bags to the car, before Peggy sat in the driver's seat with her hands clasped around the wheel. She looked at Luna and Nicky and made a decision to not drive away just yet. She got out and began walking toward the house before noticing the curtains slightly ajar from the dining room window. She was taken aback, and it made her second guess if it were a wise thing to ask Grace if she would like to say goodbye to the kids. *But perhaps she actually cares. Why would she peek out like that if she didn't?* she thought.

Rather than go inside, she instead signaled for Grace to come out, "We're leaving now!" Grace remained for a few seconds at the window, as if contemplating, before the curtain closed. Peggy wondered if this meant that she was actually coming outside, but wasn't sure. This woman was her mother, after all, but she was far from predictable. To avoid freezing (and embarrassment), she went back to the car and waited.

"Are we going?" asked Luna, meekly.

She looked at Luna, almost surprised that she seemed anxious to leave, "Well, I…I thought it'd be nice to have your

Grandma Grace say goodbye to you. You may not see her...for a while." She delivered this with forced authenticity. For one, she didn't think it was "*nice*", but courteous to at least allow Grace the opportunity. She knew that Grace was insulted by her sending the kids to live with the *other* grandparents, and so this gave the impression that Peggy didn't trust her with the kids or the kids with her, which was accurate At the same time, Peggy was the one coming back to live there and so, at the very least, she was hoping Grace would consider this a sign of respect. Secondly, she felt more than likely that this would be the last time the kids would see her. By the time she would be ready to bring the kids back, she anticipated having a place far away from Kelp Stream. Even if it was in New Jersey, they would be closer to the city; a different county. No trace of connection to this town and her roots. And once she moved, she knew Grace would never venture beyond where she was, and this would become even less likely as she got older. She was already almost 70; a retired nursing home nurse. While it was hard to believe she ever really took care of anyone, it managed to be how she made her living. The payoff for her labors was now sleeping until 9 and watching shit television throughout the day and evening, while forging a permanent ass groove on the aqua-colored couch beside her menacing dog. A road trip beyond a visit to *Prager's Ye Olde General Store* seemed all but inconceivable.

After 10 minutes of silence, Peggy gave up and stuck the key in the ignition. Just as she did, she was jolted to see Grace slowly approaching across the lawn in her jeans, Mickey Mouse sweater and worn bathrobe. Peggy abruptly shut the car off, then discretely turned to Nicky and Luna, "Please be nice and say thank you."

"For what?" Nicky gruffly asked.

"You know for what. For housing you. And you might not see her – ever again, so just...be appreciative. And remember I have to come back here."

Grace stood about two feet from the car as Peggy

lowered the window, "Thanks for seeing them off. They really appreciate it."

"No, we don't," Nicky whispered under his breath, as Peggy sharply turned to him, in a guttural whisper, "Nicky!"

She turned back to the window where Grace remained, almost as if waiting for Peggy to move the car closer rather than Grace making the two foot trek with her legs. "I appreciate you coming down to see them. This is tough for them."

"What is?" Grace chirped, while remaining still, arms folded.

"What is...? Well, leaving. Everything, really. It's a lot, and so...it's just... I appreciate you saying goodbye."

"Yeah, you said that."

She looked at Grace, who was still stuck in the same place on her lawn as if her slippers had become cement boots, "Okay, well,... Anyway, here they are, so..." Peggy turned to the kids, then back to Grace, no longer sure who was the bigger child. It seemed that Grace should initiate, since the kids were certainly going through their share of trauma, with leaving their mother and boarding a plane by themselves to a state about a two and half hour flight away, but Grace looked unfazed, which, admittedly, was unsurprising. No one's trauma could ever be worse than her own. Nor could she be relied on to display even vague compassion. She didn't know these kids, in the end. And her sense that they didn't particularly care for her certainly didn't help. It was enough that she was even on the lawn.

"So have a good flight," she finally barked, as Peggy turned to Luna and, with her eyes, told her daughter how to respond, "Thank you for having us," she finally said, in a rote monotone. Peggy then turned to Nicky, who gazed at the street, unmoved to say anything.

"Nicky," Peggy pleaded, in a whisper.

"She isn't even there."

"She...?" As soon as Peggy turned, Grace had vanished from her spot on the lawn and was already entering the house.

She shut the door and, with that, her farewell was given.

    Peggy sat behind the wheel, pained more at the fact that she would be returning to the house than seeing the kids off at the airport. After resting her head on the steering wheel for a moment and taking a needed breath, she sat up, inserted the key in the ignition...and off they went.

23

At the gate, Peggy ran through all the particulars with them, since this would be their maiden voyage as unaccompanied minors, "Be nice to the crew. They work very hard. Listen to the announcements. Pay attention to when they go through the emergency procedures."

"I'm nervous," Luna mumbled, her eyes filled with tears, while Nicky still tried to hold it together with his well-honed scowl and averted eyes. "It's gonna' be fine, honey. You've flown before. So many times."

"Yeah, but this is different."

"I know it is, but it's a short flight. You'll take a nap and, before you know it, you'll be in Florida and you'll see grandma and grandpa. They'll be waiting for you as soon as you get off and they'll take you out to lunch."

"I'm not hungry."

"Well, it's not lunchtime and you're not in Florida yet, honey. By the time you get there, you'll be starving."

Luna didn't know how to respond anymore. She conveyed her dissatisfaction with everything aptly enough and, at this point, could only be what she was – scared and sad. Peggy looked at her, then at Nicky, who tried his damnedest to look anywhere else but at his mother, "Hey," she said gently, while scootching Nicky and Luna toward her. Nicky resisted, as his face reddened. "Nicky, don't do this."

"I'm not doin' anything," a surprisingly choked exhalation, which noted to Peggy that Nicky was no less scared or sad than Luna.

The flight was about to board, but Peggy was trying her best not to rush this moment with them, as she knew that a terse send-off would only magnify their stress. She looked at them both, feeling that she had already said everything that she could say. The weekend was to be a build-up to giving them stability leading to this moment but, of course, that didn't go nearly as planned. The morning adieu from Grace did nothing, nor did it make sense that it would. Regardless of all this, she wanted them to believe that this trip would be the beginning of a return to some sort of normalcy, as much as she grew to despise Vic and Elaine. At least they weren't strangers to her kids.

"This is only temporary, okay? You're gonna' go back to school down there, make some new friends. I'm gonna' get settled up here. Get a nice job, a beautiful new home. When you finish school in a few months, I'll come down and fly back up with you – or maybe we'll even drive up the coast. Wouldn't that be fun? Drive through all the eastern states?" as her eyes started to well up. "We'll see daddy again. And... and...and things'll be...wonderful," she managed, struggling to believe it.

Finally, Peggy dropped any artifice that remained, feeling compelled to be a bit more candid, "There's been a lot of shit that we've gone through, okay? I'm not going to act like this has been anything other than...really unfortunate, but we're all alive. And I think the worst of this you've already made it through. Now I have to continue going through it just a little bit more. That's why you're going on this plane – because I don't want you to go through this anymore. I don't want you to have to endure what I'm going to have to..." She stopped, looked them in the eyes that were now focused on her, as if realizing that this was somehow important, even if it was still beyond them, "One thing has not changed and it won't change. I love you very, very much. Don't let anyone tell you otherwise, okay?"

She expected Luna to understand this a little more than

Nicky, "Who's gonna' tell us otherwise?" he asked.

"Nicky, just don't even give it a thought, okay?"

He took a moment, still unclear, "Okay."

She embraced them tighter than ever. It felt very much like a scene from *Sophie's Choice*; such a supreme sacrifice, and yet she knew the kids would survive. She just wasn't sure about herself and the effect that the ensuing weeks would have on her.

Not too long ago, there was joy in the unknown,...but this was something else.

She drove back to Kelp Stream, having cried most of the way. She could visualize the kids in their plane seats, overwhelmed by all the frenzy that comes with boarding a commercial airline. It felt as if she lost a limb. As she was about to enter town, she tried to think of what she needed to do to be proactive, since it was the beginning of a new week. The second half of the school year was already about 2 weeks in for most high schools, and she held out hope that something would materialize with at least substituting at a local school, though it seemed like such a remote possibility.

The increasingly less attractive trees along Quentin Road signaled that she was close to *Prager's Ye Olde General Store*, which she popped in for cigarettes. As she approached the counter, she was stunned to see Rita Prager, the co-owner, still there, much older and with a slight hunch, but still recognizable. Peggy knew her enough as a child to call her "Mrs. Prager", but she literally had not been in this store in almost 20 years and wondered if it was worth even noting who she was. *And, of course, God forbid she somehow heard the news about Mike.*

"Can I get a pack of Virginia Slims, please?"

"Sure," Mrs. Prager said, as she grabbed a pack and tossed it on the counter. "Anything else, hon?"

She couldn't take her eyes off Mrs. Prager, somehow feeling odd that she was in the store as a stranger, "Um, you don't have any wine here, do you?"

"Wine? I wish. I could go for a glass. No, but you know there's *Barnard's*."

"No, I don't. Is that new?"

"New? It's been there about, what, 12, 13 years. Just 2 minutes south on Quentin. You'll see it."

"Okay, thank you."

"Sure. Anything else?"

"No, that's... Um, are you... Mrs. Prager?"

Mrs. Prager lowered her glasses at Peggy, "Yes?"

"I... It's been a while and I don't know if you remember me. I'm...Peggy."

"Peggy? Do I know you from somewhere?"

"Well,...here. I used to come in here up until I graduated high school and went to college. I used to get... God, what was it now – ?"

"Bubble Yum and 7-Up, right?"

"Oh, my God, you remember!"

"Well, look at that. Look at you. Where've ya' been?"

"Uh, well... I went to college, got married, moved to New York."

"Well, you were a pretty young girl and, of course, you turned out to be a pretty woman."

"Oh, thank you."

"I think I remember askin' your mom about you some time ago."

"Really."

"Well, I don't think ya' said goodbye. I think you may've mentioned about going to college, but that mighta' been it."

"Yeah,...it was a little sudden, if I remember. Sorry. I did miss coming here and seeing you and Mr. Prager. I'm so glad you still have the store."

"Well, Bob passed, Peggy. About 6 years ago."

"Oh, I'm very sorry to hear that."

"Yeah, well, he had a stroke about 8 years ago, and we had a coupla' tough years before he passed. The store's been a nice distraction, y'know?"

"Oh, sure. Well, it's always been such a part of the town."

"Yeah, well, it ain't New York, that's for sure, but it's been ok for us. Not surprised you moved on. You were a smart kid. Always so nice. Always pleasant. Bob liked you."

"Oh, that's... That's nice to hear." Peggy was surprised to hear this acknowledgement of herself as a child, as she never thought of herself as particularly distinguishable before going to college, but was touched by Mrs. Prager's memory, and to learn how Mr. Prager felt about her.

"So where in New York?"

"Uh, well,...Long Island, actually."

"Really. Whereabouts?"

"Well, I'm not there now. We...we moved."

"Oh, okay. Where?"

Peggy did not want to say anything resembling the truth, feeling now was as good a time as any to resort to her newly erected skill of lying on her feet, "Manhattan. We're waiting on an apartment to be finished on Park Avenue, but it's supposed to take a few weeks, so..."

"Wow, look at that. You've done well for yourself."

"Oh, well, uh..."

"Kids?"

"I...uh, yes. Two."

"Oh, how wonderful. Boys? Girls?"

"Both, actually. Boy and girl."

"Look at that. Y'gonna bring 'em in?"

"Oh, well,...they're...uh...they're with my husband. In the city, so..."

"I see. A lot goin' on in your life. Good for you."

"Uh, yes, you can say that," she could only tepidly agree.

"So you're visiting your mom."

"Yeah, I...yes," she said, with barely gritted teeth.

"Well, I'm sure she's glad to see ya'."

Peggy honestly couldn't tell if Mrs. Prager was telling the truth, since she had seen her mother probably every other day for years when Grace came in for cigarettes and essentials. At the same time, Grace was not one to be chatty and may very well have disclosed nothing with regards to their estrangement.

"Um, I was sad to see the Dulcy house is gone. I assume Ms. Dulcy passed?"

"Oh, yeah. Maybe 4-5 years now."

"Oh. Well,...still sorry to hear."

"Yeah, poor thing. Well, she wasn't exactly poor. Had a nice little nest egg, apparently. She sure gave a nice nickel to the library. That ol' library barely had a copy machine all these years. She died, and now they got a whole new computer wing named after her."

"Really?"

"Yeah, i'nt that somethin'? Well, she never had kids or a husband to worry about, so I guess it was a little easier to save. God knows she barely went out for years."

"Well, she *was* married at one point, right?"

"Nope. Never married. Guess they'd call her a spinster. Didn't say much, but nice enough. I know people used to be scared of her, for some reason. Thought she was a witch or somethin'. No, just a single ol' woman. You know she served in Vietnam?"

"Really?"

"Yep. I think she was the first woman in this town to serve. She was a medic. Came back, worked in forensic science, served in the National Guard, then Green Peace. Saw more of the world than most. Did quite a bit for someone who everyone thought didn't do much."

"Wow, I had...no idea."

"Yeah, well, that's how life is. Sometimes you never know what a person really was until you read their obit. Sad to say."

Peggy sat with this and, for the moment, had almost forgotten that Nicky and Luna were in the air to Florida. She now marveled at how she spent her whole life believing the myths about Ms. Dulcy, particularly that she killed her husband and buried him in her backyard. Knowing that there was no husband now sufficiently debunked that theory and much else of what she had heard about her. And then what Mrs. Prager said added even more to her guilt, how sometimes one never knows about a person until they're dead. Peggy wondered, if she were to die tomorrow, just what would be known about *her* – or even what she would write about herself; *a wannabe author, a wannabe teacher, a wife and mother married to a felon, who sent her kids off to live with their grandparents while she died living with her own mother...*

Ms. Dulcy was Joan of Arc by comparison.

As Peggy touched the door on her way out, she suddenly realized that Mrs. Prager could be a source of some valuable information, "Um, Mrs. Prager,...just curious. Do you still sell my mother cigarettes?"

Mrs. Prager took barely a few seconds to digest this, before quickly recalling, "Jeez, think it's been a few years, actually."

"Really?" as Peggy now fully turned her attention to her.

Mrs. Prager looked surprised by Peggy not knowing if her own mother still smoked, "Yeah, s'been a while. I assume she quit. I think I was even gonna mention it one time to her, since she used to always come in for 'em, but thought better. Your mom's always been pretty hi'n bye," she said, with a gentle smile, as if to not give the impression that she was imposing an opinion on Grace's social skills.

Peggy weakly smiled in return, "Oh, I know." Now the information she had just gotten about Ms. Dulcy was sufficiently usurped by Mrs. Prager all but confirming Grace's claim of having quit smoking for some time. And yet Peggy was certain those hang-ups were her this whole time, with those unmistakable cigarette inhalations being the most distinct aspect about them – the closest thing to a word that was ever uttered by this mystery person.

But it had to be her, she persisted.

Who else could it've been?

She turned the key in the ignition, barely having a chance to absorb Mrs. Prager's information, before she was greeted by the return of the car's dying donkey sound – KONK!

"Oh, no…"

She tried it again, as she started to pull out of her parking space, before yet another KONK! – KONK!, followed by a resounding KAPLONK!!!…and then a deep fizz, as if the last breath of a giant machine.

In truth, Peggy should've considered herself fortunate that the car, which had been living on borrowed time anyway since its half-ass repair in Long Island, managed to make it to the airport without breaking down on the expressway. She was only a three minute drive from the house now, but it didn't ease the pain of her having to still call a tow truck and brace for what the cost would now be to repair whatever the hell was wrong.

Fucking Claire!

Fucking Mike!

Fucking world!

It was also of little surprise to her that, even hours away from Long Island, she would still be subjected to the same mechanic-speak, "Looks like it could be the enginemodifier-exhausttrachiodometer," said a local mechanic. "We'll give it a lookover."

With that, Peggy opted to make the 20-minute walk to the house rather than wait almost an hour for the one nearby taxi service that, in all likelihood, was little more than one man and one car. And while it was surely depressing to be sauntering through the bizarrely unchanged town of her youth, it almost seemed better for her to not be behind the wheel. An array of thoughts kept circulating within; how Nicky and Luna were doing as their plane was probably over Virginia by about now, reacquainting with Mrs. Prager and the revelations that came from their brief exchange about Ms. Dulcy and then, of course, the confirmation that Grace was no longer a smoker.

Ultimately, this thought stream brought with it things that she hadn't thought about consciously in many years, like what happened to her own father, whom Grace had said "up'n left" when Peggy was around 4. This was no doubt triggered by Peggy being moved by Mrs. Prager recalling how fondly her husband thought of her as a young girl. Such a moment of warmth from an older couple, who Peggy admittedly never knew very well, seemed now like the closest thing to familial affection she had ever felt. She also knew why she never questioned Grace about her father, or had any desire to find him. She never said he had died, only that he left. And, in the end, Peggy probably couldn't blame him. At the same time, if he was like every other man Grace had had in her life through her formative years, there was little doubt of the type of man he was; hard-living, hard-drinking, loud, of little education and utterly content with his lack of achievements. Peggy never met her latest, "Joe", who it seemed, for a fleeting moment, lived with Grace per the old outgoing answering machine message, but deduced that he was no different.

As she walked near the dumpster behind the local Shop Rite, Peggy knew a plan of action was in order – and needed to be executed as quickly as possible.

By the time she set foot on Grace's driveway and stopped to look at the unaltered house, she knew that survival meant avoiding Grace. Perhaps even locking herself in her room and only coming out for bathroom trips or when leaving the house. This only served to enforce the absurd metaphor that, since her own house was seized, every place she stayed in was getting progressively smaller. Her childhood room was a coffin compared to when she was staying with Monique, to the extent that she felt like her head could go through the ceiling if she stood perfectly erect.

Regardless, her little room would have to be her safe haven for as long as she was there.

24

"Yeah, like I thought. It's the enginemodifierexhaustt-rachiodometer," slurred the mechanic over the phone, amidst the usual clangs and drill sounds. All of a sudden, the palpitations began for Peggy, anticipating just what they were going to try and abscond from her, knowing full well that she wouldn't have a clue what was real and what was simply grease-monkey gouging.

"Can you make it drivable?" she nervously asked.

"Well, yeah, but it's gonna' take us having to dist-mantlethecristenbloweranddetachthehypercontaminator-crank'nflowandmovethecentralhypontenoos."

'How much is this going to cost me?"

She braced herself, before "Twenty five hundred."

Considering the car likely had more damage since its last repair, it didn't surprise Peggy that it would be more than she paid before. Actually, had she gotten everything done then, it would've come to almost $4,000, and allegedly would've been fully repaired. With what she paid before and now this, it would be *over* that amount. She would've kicked herself, except the fact was she didn't have the room on the credit cards for that much back then, and now didn't have room for even half of this round of repairs.

This meant that she would need to leave the car at the shop until she somehow came up with $2,500.

As she stared out of her small childhood window from her old, thin-wooded roll-top desk, still adorned in eroded stickers of The Go-Gos, Joan Jett and Prince, she realized there was only one avenue that gave her the opportunity of obtaining that much money in a short span of time, which would then enable her to, ideally, go about rebuilding her life.

Her call to Jane Madden later that day would very quickly lead to the taping of her interview by the end of the week. She took the train into the city where she was to report to the midtown production office for *American Sleaze*. She still couldn't get over the turnaround time for a primetime television news show. She had called Jane later that Monday after receiving the quote for her car, and by Thursday she was riding to the city to provide her interview portion of the episode that was to air in a month. The brevity of everything was overwhelming. Somehow, Peggy tried to rationalize this almost as if she were applying for a job, which made it appear less psychologically damaging than the fact that she was cashing in on Mike's crimes. She rationalized further that she would not even be considering this had Mike not suggested she do it for the money, and that was solely why she was. There was little catharsis here. She was desperate; desperate to get out of Grace's house and to bring the kids back up.

She entered Manhattan and the luxurious midtown office building, almost awed by how she missed coming to the city, forgetting for a moment why she was even there. It didn't take much for memories to be triggered in the last couple of months, and visiting Manhattan brought with it many of coming in with the family to see a play, having dinner or visiting museums. She took the elevator up to the 12th floor where, upon coming out, she was greeted with the undeniable blood red logo for the show in large obnoxious letters against a sterile white wall. At that moment, Peggy could only laugh at the irony that she was about to visit the Wizard behind this addictive piece of tripe that seemed to take the pulse of low-culture America; one that Grace was watching morning re-runs of on some crime channel right about now, with Little Pearl nestled at her side.

Of course, Grace was still oblivious to what was happen-ing, and Peggy was loath to mention it. Her mother would likely take unbridled glee out of Peggy being on display to admit that her husband was a crook. She was hoping beyond hope that she would be long gone by the time the episode aired, and wouldn't have to deal with Grace's reaction, let alone the rest of the town. In her mind, the fact that she had a month before the episode aired gave her a more focused time-line to obtain some type of work and vacate her childhood premises forever.

"Hi, Peggy. I'm Jane. Thank you for allowing us to do this."

Jane looked as Peggy suspected; attractive, seemingly polite but intensely focused and commanding. It didn't do much to strengthen her resolve to be in the presence of such a woman, with Peggy feeling like Oliver Twist by comparison; broke and almost broken.

"So let me give you the lowdown on everything. Would you like coffee or anything?"

"No, I'm – "

"Y'sure? Did you eat? We have bagels, crullers…"

"No, I'm – "

"Okay, well let me take you on a little tour of things and I'll give you the skinny on how we operate."

The pace of Jane Madden was one of a vacuum all but sucking Peggy along, down hallways, passed recording booths, passed scenic windows of glass-walled conference rooms. Peggy was nearly getting a draft with how fast she needed to walk to keep up with her.

She could barely make out any preparations Jane had mentioned in anticipation of her interview, and was going along purely on the desperate fumes of the $5,000 pay day that was going to come with her telling her story. But with every step, it seemed that the amount of money compared to what she was committing herself to do was unequal. It was $5,000 to sum up her husband and, in essence, her life. She would be asked questions purely as the wife of a thief. No one wanted to know who Peggy was, what aspirations she had. The money shot that she would no doubt be asked to provide was, ultimately, how she felt the day Mike was arrested, and how she felt once she was certain of his guilt. *This is what I'm here for*, she thought.

Before she could have a second thought, she would be sat down before Len Getz, the host and "chief reporter" of *American Sleaze*.

"Hi, Peggy. Good to meet you," he gripped her hand as if unable to distinguish the grip of a woman from a sumo wrestler. "Have a seat."

She shook out her crushed hand as she sat down in a seat directly across from Getz, her head spinning from the rapid pace that was established upon Jane's offer of coffee and bagels. She certainly wasn't timing anything, but was certain that they managed to go from the waiting room clear to the opposite side of the floor in under 30 seconds, which left her breathless and on edge.

"So I know Jane's prepped you. This is all pretty straight-forward. I'm going to ask you a few questions, and you can answer them as honestly as you wish."

"Um, o...okay – "

"Everything's gonna' be edited, so don't worry about droning on. If you feel you have light to shed on something, please, by all means, shed it like a snakeskin, okay?" he laughed, a little too uproariously for someone who was about to interview a woman whose husband was in prison. And the analogy of a snake certainly wasn't helpful either in giving Peggy a sense that she was justified in speaking out. That was Jane's bill of goods, after all; *"You have a right to tell your story"*, she said in their first phone call. Now that stuck with her all the more. She didn't believe it. Why should she? She'd seen enough episodes now. She witnessed how they made these wives look; *always so distraught and tear-driven.*

A make-up person came by to dab her, as Peggy was now sweating, while Getz and Jane discussed the interview out of earshot of Peggy, who was feeling substantially adrift in this sordid world of tabloid television. This only served to bring forth every other concern imaginable, such as if the kids would ever see this, their old friends in Cold River, teachers at Cold River High School, Vic and Elaine, Grace, Mrs. Prager... And then the reruns, which would run in perpetuity on one channel or another, etching Peggy's name in history as nothing more than a deceived wife, powerless to her husband's greed. *All this for $5,000? All this just to get my car out of the shop?*

"We'll do a few practice questions, just to give you a chance to hone your responses and then we'll do an actual taping, okay?" Jane said, with her firm hand clasped around Peggy's shoulder.

"Uh, that's, well..."

"Okay, everyone, quiet! We're going to just do a few practice questions for sound, etcetera," exclaimed Jane.

Suddenly the room was very dark. She could barely see the lips of Len Getz across from her, now seeming like little more than an ambient voice. This resembled nothing so comfortable as Jane had described that it would be. There was no sense that anyone surrounding Peggy, be it the key grip, the boom operator, other random silhouetted bodies that appeared to encircle her, knew who she was or why she was there. It all just appeared to be the usual drill; subject arrives, gets offered bagels and coffee, camera set up, lights, sound, and then the interview...

"So, Peggy, how did you meet Michael?" Getz asked from the surrounding darkness.

She was surprised at this, not quite expecting that this interview would in any way encompass the arc of their relationship. It also was not easy to go into the vault of her memory to recall how she met Mike and all that she saw that was so appealing about him then. She had to think, and in her thinking found that it was akin to digging in the sand and searching for granules that would have any relevance to the question. Before she knew it, nearly a minute had gone by of such excavation...

"Peggy?" Getz quietly asked, attempting to hide his voice...

"Um, sorry, I... It's...it's been a long time. It was college. Before I... Well, I... You see, I didn't intend to... It was a big deal that I got into the college that I did, actually. No one could've fathomed that I would, considering where I... I wasn't there to meet a man to whisk me away, okay? I was there to become a successful writer and teacher. That was always the goal. It just... It got sidetracked."

Getz took a second, seeming to convey with this pause that much of what Peggy was saying would be prime material for the cutting room floor, "Um, Peggy, why don't you tell us the qualities in Michael that lured you in, so to speak."

She found this to be a very leading question, and yet it wasn't necessarily inaccurate to her; *In a way, he did lure me, didn't he.* Of course, this would soon lead her down a different rabbit hole regarding just how he managed to do this. She could not have been more focused about having a career of her own, and knew that only that would justify the scholarship she received. Yet, somehow, it all went by the wayside and she wasn't able to discern specifically why. Did Mike ever ask her to forego her career and just be a mom? Did her first pregnancy dictate everything and, with it, lead her down a path of mere contentment? In this moment, Peggy wanted to be able to place blame, but this period was now like walking through fog.

"Peggy?" Getz followed, again with a tone in his voice that this was not going as it should.

She tried to look at his eyes, but could not locate a discernible face in which to respond. It now just seemed like she was under interrogation in some foreign land. Why she was even there appeared even more remote; *Give us information*, she heard. How easy was this now, to answer a few questions that only she would really know the answers to? It wasn't, in the slightest. If she went through with this, it would equate to her leaving her heart in the chair and walking out emotionally hollowed by the experience; a feeling which would surely metastasize with time.

"Peggy? Wana' try this again?" Getz followed, as there began to be murmurs among the darkened circle around her. She started to tremble and sweat through the dabbed powder on her face, as she questioned if she had the courage to hoist herself out of this uncomfortable chair and walk...

"Peggy?" now coming from Jane, who was standing somewhere behind Getz. Her voice conveying faux concern with a genuine fear that this interview would be a bust.

Peggy clenched the arm of her chair, "I'm sorry, I just... This is difficult."

Suddenly, Jane's voice got closer and warmer, "Oh, I understand, honey. I do."

"I'm sorry, but I don't think you do, Jane," she nervously whispered back.

"Peggy, why do you think I produce such a show?"

Even though Peggy couldn't care less to know, she reluctantly responded - "Why?"

Jane's voice was in hushed tones, with her breath shooting into Peggy's eardrum, "I know of where I speak. I've been here. I've sat exactly where you're sitting now. I created this show so that every woman would have the opportunity of sharing their stories and not be victims. You're not a victim, do you understand? You're not a victim. And this show will let the world know it."

Jane's silhouette soon faded somewhere behind where Len Getz remained sitting. It was clear that this was not the first time that Jane had said these words, as if to comfort someone who clearly was having second and third thoughts,

THE WOMAN IN THE SUN HAT

as Peggy was.

It was also clear that, whether it was true or not, Peggy could not let herself be a lamb led to the slaughter. With that, she hoisted herself out of the chair...and walked.

"Shit..." uttered a clearly irked Len Getz, under his breath, followed by Jane's "Peggy?"

...Peggy walked fast in order to avoid Jane having the opportunity of selling her more snake oil. Her pace was furious, but she wasn't sure if she was going in the right direction. She walked through the hallways hoping to see some sights that she barely observed when Jane brought her in, but the generic nature of the white-walled offices made this journey akin to Jack Nicholson's fatal trek through the maze at the end of *The Shining*. With every dead end, she turned back, made another sharp turn leading to another dead end. Her desperation with needing to get out of this environment was all-consuming, enhanced by knowing Jane Madden was not far behind.

As Peggy embarked on another dead end, she heard "Peggy, please don't leave!" She turned to see Jane at the end of the hallway, with two men who, in all likelihood, were producers on the show behind her. She was reluctant to speak at all, but managed "I'm sorry, I just can't do this. It's not –"

"Peggy, I understand. We've had many people in your position who've felt the same way, but they went through with it."

"No, they didn't."

"They did. And, believe me, they're stronger for it."

"Bullshit!"

"Peggy –"

"BULLSHIT! No one is stronger for doing this kind of crap! Who the hell are you kidding? You've made an empire out of Faustian offers."

"Out of what?"

"*Faust?* You've never heard of – Goddamnit, I was a Literature major! I should already have 5 novels! I should be teaching at a Goddamn university and doing book tours! I should have a life of integrity and respect, instead of selling my soul on some tabloid television show!"

"Peggy, let's go into my – "

"I'm not going anywhere, except out of this building."

"Peggy- "

"GET ME OUT OF THIS FUCKING BUILDING NOW, DO YOU HEAR ME?!!!"

There was a stillness in the air, among the sounds of other hurried footsteps coming from various rooms to watch this unequivocal train wreck. Peggy remained at the dead end of this hallway like a trembling feral cat that, at any moment, could attack. As a result, Jane appeared to finally resign to the fact that the interview was not going to happen and, with such resignation, indicated for one of the men behind her to escort Peggy out. Peggy followed him at about a 5 foot distance, in order to avoid any possible conversation down the narrow hallways.

By the time she made it to the elevator, she was finally able to exhale as she descended slowly to the lobby. Her first instinct, upon exiting the building, was taking a deep breath... and then calling her kids, which she at least felt she could do with a degree of pride.

"They're doing just fine," assured Vic.

"They're eating okay?"

"Yes, yes, jus' fine. They're eating, they're sleeping. They're acclimating jus' fine, Peg."

"Okay, well, put them on, please," she urgently requested.

"Alright, Luna's here. Nicky's on the throne. I'll get him for ya', okay?"

"Please, thank you."

Vic seemed pleasant enough. Peggy assumed his ease

may well have come from the fact that he had the kids with them. She certainly didn't trust him as far as she could throw him, but it was preferable to speaking to the obnoxiously un-filtered Elaine, who would go unmentioned.

"Hi, mommy!"

"Hey, my love. I miss you."

"We're doing okay."

"Well, don't you miss me?"

"Yes."

"Well, you should say it."

"I just did."

"I mean, I shouldn't have to — " she thought better about continuing to guilt Luna. "Alright, so how are you guys?"

"We're good. It's warm."

"Yeah?"

"Oh my God, it feels like 80 degrees."

"Wow. Well, it's Florida. It gets warm there."

"Where are you?"

"I'm... Well, I'm in the city, actually."

"Really? Did you get a job?"

"Well, no, but that's... I came to sort of...explore a possible...opportunity, and just thought I'd call you guys."

"Teaching?"

"Huh?"

"Is it a teaching job?"

Now it felt as if Peggy was speaking to a distant friend whom she was trying to impress. When it came to relating to her kids, the phone put her at a clear disadvantage, "Well, sort of. But, anyway, I don't wana' say too much right now. I just wanted to hear your voices. Where's your brother?"

"Not sure."

"What do you mean? Your grandfather said he was in the bathroom."

"He's not in the bathroom."

"So where is he?"

"Hold on, I think he's out back. Grandma, where's

Nicky?"

Peggy heard the phone being placed down somewhere, with a distant muffle from Elaine in response to Luna...

"Luna? Pick up, honey?!"

She remained, now feeling awkward and significantly removed, as she waited on a busy street during what was now rush hour in the city. The activity around her, and the fact that there were so many people walking with such swift focus, made her envious of where they were going, regardless of if they were simply heading to dead-end, soul-sucking jobs. At least they appeared to be going places where they were wanted. Right now, as Peggy waited for her own son to pick up the phone, especially after her experience at the studio, she could not have felt less so.

"Luna?! Luna, can you please pick up?!"

The phone was suddenly picked up, "Hello?" Elaine asked.

"Yes, I'm still here, Elaine."

"Oh, Peggy? I thought you hung up."

"No, I'm waiting to speak to my son. Where did they go?"

"I think Luna went to get him. He's in the backyard, I think."

"You think? The house isn't that big, Elaine. You don't know where they are?"

"Peggy, don't get testy, okay? Now we're happy to have them..."

"You *want* them there! Don't act like you're doing me a favor!"

"Peggy, look – "

"No, don't pull this, Elaine! You wanted them. They're there. Don't act like you don't know where the hell they are in your little condo. I'm calling to say hello to both of my children and I want them on the phone with me now, do you under – ?"

She abruptly heard the phone thud onto what sounded

like the kitchen counter, followed by the rapid clomps of Elaine's wooden-soled sandals fading out...

She continued to wait, shielding herself from the ricocheting bitter wind off the surrounding buildings, while cursing under her breath; "Dear God, I hate these fucking people," before, eventually, "Mommy?"

"Yes, honey. Is Nicky there?"

"Hi," a morose sounding Nicky uttered from another landline phone.

"Hi, honey. Are you okay?"

"Yeah, fine."

"Are you sure? I miss you guys."

"We're fine."

A brief silence sat in the air, which was odd since there always managed to be some stream of conversation going if Luna was involved, but there was an awkwardness that Peggy sensed among them both now.

"Okay, you guys just sound a little... I don't know. It's only been 4 days, and you sound different. Is there anything you wana' tell me?"

"No, it's cool," said Nicky, quietly but tersely.

"What's cool? Nicky, please, don't use these phone calls to sulk. If you wana' talk, let's have a conversation."

"I don't wana' have a conversation. Everything's fine."

She could hardly force things. By phone, her parental tricks were in sparse supply. She worried about coming off harshly to the point where they would start to dread her calls. She took a breath, "Okay, Nicky, look, before I let you go, I think I'm going to start calling you both directly on your own phones from now on, okay? So make sure you pick up when I call. I don't care where you are. If I call, I want you to pick up, okay?"

"Sure," he said softly.

"I'm paying for them, and the whole reason you have them is so I can reach you guys, so it just makes more sense, okay?"

"s' fine."

"Luna, you there?"

"Yes."

"That goes for you too."

"Okay. But we start school next week."

"I know. I won't call you during school, unless it's an emergency. And, of course, you know you can always call me. Day or night. If you need something, if you want to talk, if you're concerned about…about anything, please call me. I wana' be hearing from you too."

"Okay," Luna said, her more introverted tone now matching Nicky's.

"Nicky?"

"Yeah, I heard you."

With that, Peggy took a frustrated sigh, knowing a cigarette was in order shortly after she would hang up, "Alright, I love you both."

"Love you, mommy," said Luna.

Nicky followed, "Bye," before hanging up.

The dial tone reverberated a few seconds before Peggy clicked off. This somehow felt worse than the experience at the studio, which now was a distant memory.

She had never felt so alone in her life.

25

She remained shivering on the corner of 44th Street and 6th Avenue, sucking down a Virginia Slims as if it were lemonade. She couldn't bring herself to just hop back on the train from Penn Station and sequester herself in her childhood bedroom, especially since she couldn't go anywhere else without a car. At least it made sense to take advantage of being in the city while she was there. She went into a deli, which had a few informal circular tables by the window, and had a coffee while mindlessly gazing at her phone. She hadn't visited the only social media site she had an account with in ages, as it made little sense to, but noticed that she had a friend invitation. She was stunned to see that it was from Tina Collier, Peggy's friend and former roommate from her days at Princeton whom she had all but lost touch with after she graduated and moved in with Mike. She wasn't sure how long this invitation was sitting there, but it was nevertheless a pleasant surprise to hear from her.

Upon eagerly accepting Tina's friend request, Peggy quickly sent her a message, uncertain of how long it would take her to find it:

"Hi, Tina – It's Peggy. I'm sorry if you sent this request a while back. I've sort of been off of social media the last few months, but it's so nice to hear from you. Let me know how you are. Here's my number - ..."

After Peggy finished, she looked at Tina's profile and saw that her location was "New York, New York", which meant that, for all Peggy knew, she could be within blocks of where Tina resided.

With not much money to spend, Peggy finished her coffee and walked about the city, peeking in windows of restaurants that three months ago she would have gone in without blinking an eye for a cocktail and a succulent lunch, but now she was clearly on the outside looking in. The city was more of an exhibit for her now, where she could look but not touch. She killed more time than she normally would have, as she was hoping to hear from Tina while she was there and, perhaps, meet up, if Tina's schedule permitted.

After circling within the same twelve block radius for almost two hours, Peggy resigned that it was a little too convenient for a meeting with a long lost friend to take place on this day, especially when she was there for a completely different reason. Somehow it didn't feel completely wasted though, as it gave a little more credence to what she told Mrs. Prager about eventually moving to a swanky Park Avenue apartment. While she was not there looking for a residence that she couldn't remotely afford, she was at least in the city. That alone was so beyond where any in Kelp Stream would venture, even being just an hour and a half train ride away, that it almost legitimized her lie.

If anything, Peggy could chalk this up to being productive, especially now that she had an old close friend who lived here. And being in the city gave her an energy jolt that the dormancy of Kelp Stream could never provide.

As she travelled back on the train, the modicum of positivity soon faded as the question of *What now?* arose. The goal was to do this interview in order to receive the money needed to pay for the car's repairs. Instead, she was returning empty-handed with no more prospects than when she left.

Strewn out in her undersized bed, she stared up at the

chapped ceiling and the eroding photo of Sylvia Plath, whose eyes stared back at her. It was strange that Grace's attempts to remodel, at some point, seemed to begin and end in the living room, since the kitchen, dining area and most of the upstairs remained oddly the same. Her room had become an unintentionally preserved museum. Though the walls were mainly bare, since Peggy had brought the posters she had on her wall to her college dorm room, it was bizarre to see that most everything else remained, as if Grace never entered the room in all this time.

Had Grace been a social person or one who may have, on occasion, had a friend or relative over, it likely would've been converted into a proper guest room at some point, but her aversion to most of humanity seemed to be all that it took to leave the room as it was. Her lack of friends would go unchanged, matching her lack of familial attachments; there were no siblings or cousins or nieces or nephews. Grace's mother (Peggy's grandmother) had died shortly before Peggy went to college, which was no love loss for Grace. Yet her incorrigible nature made it astonishing that, of all things, she would quit smoking and drinking, which Peggy was still skeptical of. For someone like Grace, whose only real life diversion since retiring appeared to be watching television, it made sense that drinking and smoking would be components of her daily existence. Then again, they spoke so little since Peggy had returned that she was still very much in the dark on anything else that Grace would have going on. And yet, from what she was observing from afar, at least from the earshot of her upstairs bedroom, it didn't appear as if much was. She had been there barely 2 weeks and hadn't heard Grace's phone ring, or Grace speaking to anyone except Little Pearl. The short errand runs appeared to be it.

And while such a life was still unfathomable to Peggy, she was at least grateful that Grace didn't seem very curious about what she had going on. If it didn't require her to be woken up or taken away from her shows, Peggy was able to come and go as she pleased. At least for now. This was also why she wanted to avoid having to ask Grace to borrow her car. She was certain that, even if Grace had no plans to do anything on a given day, she would still act as if it were a massive inconvenience.

Little Pearl's growl pierced through Peggy's door, and she could practically feel her snout at the foot, inhaling and exhaling like a bull. She was almost used to this, since it happened nightly. Little Pearl didn't like closed doors when she knew someone was on the other side of them, which is why Grace always had the bathroom door open when she showered or went to the bathroom. This would not be a practice that Peggy would even consider engaging in.

"Pearl, get down here!" Grace yelled from the couch, as per usual. As the carpeted footfalls of Little Pearl faded down the stairs, Peggy recalled the clomping of Elaine's shoes in the kitchen when she was on hold earlier that day. She sat up with anger at the recollection, too angry to sleep or even productively think about the next day. She found herself sitting on the corner of her bed, as her eyes shifted from the darkness of the outdoors to her rolltop desk. She suddenly remembered that that very desk had been the surface on which she used to voraciously write, and even saw herself there as a girl, observing her past like a curiosity seeker who wanted to peek over the shoulder and see what was being composed. As she snapped out of this momentary recollection, she found herself standing beside her chair; the first time she really noticed it since she'd been back. She gently touched its wooden back, rubbed her hands along the arms and felt the texture of the smooth wood. Eventually, she sat in it, turned on the desk light which, somehow, still worked, rubbed her hands on the desk top, before noticing the drawer on the side. She opened it with some effort, as its metal slats had been dormant for nearly two decades, and was stunned to find an old spiral binder.

She opened it delicately, as if an artifact that could somehow crumble. In truth, it was more the unknown. She didn't understand how this was here, since she thought she'd brought all her valuable writings with her to college, particularly those from her later teen years which she vaguely recalled were more respectable. But this was earlier than that and that was, perhaps, the reason why she left it behind. The cover was simply a crimson color void of any personal scrawlings, but the first page would reveal in crude italics *Poems of This Girl.* She still did not recall this, as apparently this period of her writing was so submerged in her psyche that it had all but vacated. And yet at least she had found some evidence of her past writing, whereas her later compositions somehow managed to get lost between college and moving to Long Island; symbolic of her eventually casting her writing talent aside for the eventual domesticity that was to dominate the ensuing years.

The first page contained a short poem called *Wojo,* named after her beloved mutt:

You don't say much,
but you do,
I know you
and maybe you know me,
or don't you.
I'd like to think you do
and that you're glad that you do.

Are you?

Peggy wasn't particularly impressed. Each poem was hand dated, so she knew how old she was when she wrote it; October 8th, 1989. *Not bad for 9,* she thought, *but strange.*

She started to judge each poem as if she were grading it, weighing in the fact that these were written by a young girl who hadn't been exposed to many mature poets at this point.

She had maybe read a few Plath poems, but that may've been the extent of it.

On the next page was one called *A Fall Day*:

The leaves are turning
and the backyard looks on fire
with yellow and orange and brown
underneath the telephone wire
where the squirrels leap and the birds roost
for most of this fall day,
and they never seem to notice each other,
it's probably why they never play.

She was even less impressed with the structure of this one, but at least could appreciate some of the descriptions. She also found it strangely synchronistic when recalling that the taxi driver they met when visiting Mike, the aptly named Chatty, referred to the Cucklesby foliage as *"a beautiful fire"*. That coincidence aside, while she still had no memory of writing these, it did make her recall how observant she was as a child and how she could make some sort of artistic use of her obvious boredom. This was one thing she managed to pass on to Luna, despite the many diversions that existed in her young life. Even before the devastation, Luna always made time to write or create something. Her many friends and the activities that were always in abundance never hindered her, so there was a victory in that for Peggy. She even could see some of Luna's poetic rhythms in these poems, which she at least found...*interesting.*

She continued to flip through the many pages, taking in each poem and trying to recall what was occurring in her life at that point. But, by and large, these all seemed to be the work of a stranger; a precocious young girl who, if nothing else, tried to create something out of the tedium that surrounded her.

She then heard a ding from her phone. Since this was

a rare emanation, particularly in these times, her curiosity quickly replaced her intrigue at the poetry of her past. It was a response from Tina:

"Oh my God, how wonderful to hear from you. How the hell are ya, Peg? I see you're in Cold River, NY. I think that's Long Island, right? I tried to gather some things from your posts, but it looks like you haven't posted anything in a while, but I looked at the photos of your kids at the Grand Canyon – they're beautiful. Anyway, I don't know if you make your way into the city often, but maybe, if you have time, we can meet up for lunch. I got your number but, since it's been a while, I figured you'd appreciate a message first. We have a lot to cover, I'm sure. Anyway, it'd be great to hear your voice, so, if anything, maybe we can have a phone call soon. I don't want to blindside you, as I'm sure you're busy, but let me know a time that could work, or you can call me whenever. I'm not easy to get a hold of during the day, but try me anyway and I'm sure we'll figure something out. I've missed you. Tina.

She was deeply moved by Tina's message, for a variety of reasons. The most considerable being the fact that there was someone out there who simply wanted to see Peggy for no other reason than to see her. And it was someone who Peggy wanted to see as well. While she still regretted the fact that they lost touch, it wasn't as a result of any sort of profound falling out. At least Peggy wanted to believe so. They had been very tight for much of the 4 years that Peggy was at Princeton, and she even partially credited Tina with broadening her cultural exposure. Even back then, they took trips into the city to see museum exhibits, partake in downtown poetry readings, see Off-Broadway plays and concerts. It may have been the most purely fun period of her life, and one that certainly increased the distance between herself and her roots.

When Peggy started dating Mike towards the end of her 3rd year was when her time hanging out with Tina had begun to dwindle. While it felt like a natural evolution for her to now venture into a serious relationship, it also seemed that Tina was still hoping to maintain what they had. Yes, there was a bit of experimentation in their sophomore year, but they mutually attributed it to a phase, and therefore she didn't think, or want to believe, that Tina could be adversely affected by her growing relationship with Mike. What was apparent was that they just didn't socialize as much, and the circles they were in changed. Peggy's final year went by in a rush, with little memory of any notable events with Tina. Then graduation came and, with it, so faded any connection they had. It was that simple, really. Anticlimactic and unfortunate, but *such is life*, Peggy thought.

But how wonderful it would be to have the friendship again, especially now.

Just as she thought this, she heard the downstairs refrigerator door open. She knew it was just before 9pm, having noticed a pattern that every night at this time, Grace would pop in some miniature pizza bagels which would be ready just in time for whatever next show she was watching. This pattern would also be attributed to Little Pearl, whose collar Peggy could hear gleefully shaking in anticipation of her favorite dog snack that Grace kept below the sink.

Knowing that the distraction would lessen Little Pearl's curiosity, Peggy always took this opportunity to brush her teeth before going to sleep. As she headed back to her room from the bathroom, she would hear Grace and Little Pearl landing back in their couch grooves, as Grace would kick up the volume, *"You're watching American Sleaze. I'm Len Getz. Thank you for joining us tonight..."*

Peggy shuddered at the memory of his voice from earlier in the day, as well as his vice-like handshake. She wanted to feel more victorious than she did for not allowing herself to be subjected to such exploitation.

At least, for the time being, she was still relatively anonymous to the world. This and hearing from Tina were now the incentives for having some hope that with the new day would come possibilities.

26

The next few days went by and rendered little in the way of income opportunities. She continued to visit certain teaching job sites, as she'd often been, but there was little call for local schools looking for Literature or English teachers. She did submit her skeletal resume for the few that looked remotely appealing, but never heard back – which wasn't necessarily surprising given her limited experience and the significant gap that resided in her history. Just to avoid the tedium, she would start taking a daily walk in the afternoon that would at least get her out of the house for about an hour or so. Since Grace rarely left, it was all the more necessary that Peggy have an excuse to leave her tiny room.

She played phone tag with Tina, but they hadn't managed to connect as yet, though Tina had proposed a weekend day for lunch in the city. It appeared that Tina's life was far more active and eventful than Peggy's, and yet Peggy wanted to create the illusion that hers was no less so, which mainly was why she wasn't quick to pick up when Tina called:

"Hi, Tina – Sorry we keep missing each other. I guess we're both busy ladies, huh? Well, Saturday is definitely a strong possibility, if you want to meet for lunch. I may have to shuffle a couple of things, but it'd be wonderful to catch up before too long. Why don't you name a place and a time and...we can go from there, okay? Talk soon."

The ball was in Tina's court, even though Peggy couldn't help but feel a little foolish that she felt compelled to *act busy.* It had been years since they had seen each other and, for all Peggy knew, Tina may have changed. The once culturally savvy and liberated old friend could have become a multitasking, high-powered corporate executive, even though it belied everything that she remembered about her. Of course, Peggy certainly did not want to see her again as a lonely unemployed mother and wife who lived with her mother and pit bull in New Jersey. She had to build herself into something, even if she hadn't revealed anything to Tina as to her profession, where she was living or the status of her family. And then, of course, there was the possibility that Tina knew something. After all, she lived in New York City, but a stone's throw from Long Island, and certainly could've come across something on the news about it or researched it on the internet. Peggy didn't know what she would be walking into and, in truth, it scared her.

"So how much longer?" Grace suddenly yelled from the living room, as Peggy returned from her walk through her bleak neighborhood.

"What?" as she crept into the living room, surprised by Grace's sudden inquiry.

As she sat on the couch with the muted television, "I said how long? It's been about two weeks now, right?"

"Uh, yeah, I guess. It's..." Peggy was at a loss of what to say, now reduced to a stammering older version of her younger self when Grace would question her in a similarly accusatory way. "I'm looking for work and it's just... It's been tough."

"What the hell y'lookin' for?"

"Well, I'm a teacher."

"You mean you're lookin' for teaching work."

She took a moment before responding to this, desperately trying to avoid taking offense, "Yes, I'm looking for teaching work, okay? And it's not easy in the middle of a school year."

"Looks like ya' best look for somethin' else," as Grace

looked at the silent television.

Peggy again sat with this, every question or comment from Grace becoming a weight that was pulling her down further and further, "Well, I may have to, but I don't know what that is yet."

"Hm," Grace uttered, continually looking at the muted screen.

"What does *that* mean?"

"Don't mean nothin' but what I said."

She looked at Grace deeply for the first time since her return; her contempt for her barely concealed, but there was little that she could do. She didn't even have a car to sleep in at this point, if she decided to curse her out and leave. She was almost literally handcuffed by her circumstances with no one to help her. She was in the worst position imaginable with being at the mercy of her mother, who seemed to only want the worst for her, and now reconnecting with her old college friend who once revered her. The former was winning out. Grace could not give two shits about Peggy's degrees. She didn't care then and only looked at Peggy's current situation as affirmation that it was all for naught. *After all, what good is a degree in Literature if it only leads you back to living with your mother?*

Peggy had nothing to add, and if she could leave the living room at that moment without being pulled back further by another inciting comment or question, she would simply continue on upstairs for the evening – which she did; just like a moment from her childhood,…and yet she would turn 40 in June.

On Saturday, Peggy was back on the train to New York City to see Tina for lunch at a café in midtown, not far from where Peggy was earlier in the week for the infamous encounter at the *American Sleaze* studios. It was of some relief that she was going this time to see an old friend, but there still was a sense of nervousness and dissatisfaction within her. If only Tina could have reached out without Peggy having the insurmountable baggage that had accrued from the last 3 months. And so she fruitlessly asked herself the same question as she looked out at the Jersey towns she passed through; *why couldn't she see me when everything was bliss?*

Since they still managed to not speak directly by phone, Peggy was able to remain cryptic on her status, but she would definitely have to be more revealing in the presence of Tina. She wondered how much of a ruse she could keep up for the duration of a lunch.

"You look wonderful," said Tina, with a tear in her eye, as they sat across from each other at *The Gray Strudel*, a modest German restaurant that Tina recommended.

"Me? My God, you haven't aged a day," Peggy quickly replied.

"Stop."

"Tina, I'm serious. You'd think you were still in college."

Tina could only laugh at this, knowing that she was much more lived-in than that, but they both resigned that they could only extend the highest compliments to each other out of the gate, pent up from the years of missing each other.

There would be a variety of strange, small meal courses that would come throughout their conversation which, for much of the time, appeared to go by in an unbroken stream of amusing recollections from their college days. Peggy could barely taste what she was eating while hearing Tina, who *did* look as if frozen in time. *Certainly not a woman who had been beaten by life;*

"So, yeah, when I left college, it was a rude awakening. I

mean, yeah, I wanted to be an artist. I wanted to teach. But life was, well, I'm sure you understand, Peg. You get out there and it's daunting. I mean, I realized that school had been an incubation chamber. And it really is. I mean, not just for us. For everybody. It doesn't prepare you. It doesn't even educate you about life. It educates you on subjects and then, you know, we go out there and we're left to the elements."

"Yeah, that's true," she agreed. Engaged, yet subtly growing more ill at ease with the fact that Tina was still in the dark regarding her current life.

"Yeah. I mean, *you* knew what you wanted to do. I know that."

"How do you mean?"

"Peggy, you *always* knew. When we first met in our dorm room. You don't remember?"

"I... Gee, it was so long ago, Tina."

"Well, you had drive. You had what so many there didn't. Even if they got a scholarship. They were coasting. *You knew*. I mean, don't you remember us eating up poetry books and novels and essays...?"

"Oh, sure, that was - ."

"We read them to each other. You organized reading groups in our rooms. I mean, you weren't just there to graduate college. You were there to envelop yourself in the world you wanted to be a part of when you left. You were there to prepare for your life. My God, you inspired everybody."

Peggy found herself for the first time in this lunch without the ability to immediately vocalize anything. She looked at Tina, then looked down at her plate of what she presumed was a sort of marinated knockwurst, and nearly started to cry...

"Are you okay, Peg? Did I...? Did I overstep or...?"

"Tina, no. Not at... It's just..." Peggy took a breath, then looked at Tina. "It's good to see you."

Tina smiled, as did Peggy. For the moment, Tina believed that this momentary pause in her old friend stemmed more from sentimentality than anything, but for Peggy it was certainly more the result of being confronted by her past – when she had only optimism for life and what lay ahead, and all by her own design. Nothing helped her get to such a point other than her own tenacity, love of culture and encouragement from maybe two or three middle and high school teachers.

How could I work so hard and have achieved so little?

But she hung on emotionally, more than happy to yield much of the floor to Tina. She wasn't quick to speak much herself, for obvious reasons, but also felt Tina was owed the opportunity of being loquacious. *She was back then anyway, so why not now?*

"Anyway, I'm droning on here. What else is new, right?" Tina laughed, as did Peggy.

"Don't apologize."

"It's just... Well, you know, you don't see someone for years and you want to..."

"I know, I know."

"So what about you?"

Peggy gulped, but managed to react with an appropriate reply, "Wait, you haven't even told me what you do?"

"I didn't tell you? I teach poetry at Hunter College. What else?"

"Whata' you mean what else? And you write poetry."

"Alright, well, yeah."

"How many?"

"How many poems?"

"Yeah."

"My God, Peggy, probably thousands."

"Thousands?"

"I mean, believe me, they're not all gems. You have to write a lota' shit to get to the gold. You know that. You still write, right?"

"I...ye...well.. Yeah, I... More short stories and essays, of late," she lied.

"You were an excellent prose writer."

"Really?"

"Of course. You used to show me all your stuff. Don't you remember?"

"I, God, I..."

"I remember you had this one story, it got published in the Princeton Student Magazine. It was amazing. About the... the girl who ran away from home and started working at a homeless shelter as a volunteer and ended up getting adopted by this homeless woman somehow. And the girl ended up living with the homeless woman under a bridge."

"Oh, my God, I barely remember that..."

"How could you...? Well, back then, you were turning them out by the dozen. Oh, my God, it was beautiful, Peggy. What was it called? Do you remember?"

"I barely remember the story. I don't think I can come up with a title."

"Well, anyway...," she sipped her wine. "You know, after college, there was a period where I used to look in the *Times* best seller list and expect to see your name. I mean, your maiden name, of course. I didn't know if you were still married. You're married now, right?"

"I...yep," Peggy replied, tersely, as she sipped.

"To Michael?"

"You remember."

"Well, I knew him too, remember. You have his last name, after all," she smiled, then sipped.

She looked at Tina, not quite knowing what to make of her comment. Tina and Mike never disliked each other. Sometimes, early in their courtship, Tina would hang out with both of them, and he would always treat, until Tina started feeling increasingly like a third wheel. By the time Peggy and Mike got engaged after college, it was becoming less likely that Tina would attend the wedding. An invitation was sent, but she had just moved to Illinois to start a teaching job and couldn't get the time off. This may or may not have been true,...but it didn't matter anymore.

Peggy awkwardly stammered, "I don't really do the social media thing. At one point, I had a little more time for it, but ...it's just depressing."

"Oh, I know," Tina concurred. "Believe me. It's like the one thing that makes us seem modern. I still can't get over what my students can't comprehend about how we didn't have such things at their ages. And it wasn't even that long ago."

"I know," Peggy laughed at the irony.

"15, 20 years? You think it's just a generation, but it's... My God, it's a whole way of communicating. I mean, if I had kids, I don't know how I'd relate to them outside of a class, to be honest."

Peggy was struck by this, "You don't have kids?"

"No. Why, you thought I did?"

"Well,... I mean, it was possible, right?"

"Well, it's possible because I'm a woman, I guess, but... that wasn't ever something I wanted, Peggy."

This seemed to be another telling moment, and perhaps there was something in between the lines of what Tina was saying. She knew that Peggy had kids, but could only assume that she simply had a maternal nature that belied her own. Peggy also took it as Tina somehow knowing, deep down, that maybe she wasn't entirely fulfilled, and yet she still knew so little about her other than that she was married with kids and, not dissimilar to the lie Peggy told Mrs. Prager, was awaiting the completion of a new home.

Tina's cards, on the other hand, were pretty much on the table, despite Peggy acting as if Tina was withholding of her achievements. She was once married (to a man) and was divorced. They didn't have kids, and now Tina lived in a decent studio apartment on the upper west side. She'd been teaching Poetry at Hunter for the last 7 years, after having taught at other smaller colleges outside of New York. The city was where she always wanted to be so, when the opportunity came at Hunter, it was like a dream fulfilled. Though she didn't say as much, it may have been less of a dream for her husband, which may have been what led to their split. Or maybe not. Peggy didn't need to know everything at their first lunch in years.

The lunch tab was insistently picked up by Tina, and their conversation continued out onto the sidewalk. Peggy thrived when speaking about certain memories, but would become noticeably more restrained when Tina tried to bring the subject back to Peggy's family or her career. It was at this point that she couldn't look Tina in the eye. It was easier to fabricate when looking at inanimate objects. As she looked down at the gum-laden sidewalk and off at the architecture of certain older buildings they passed, she would at least find the courage to speak:

"It's wonderful to have the eyes of the impressionable on you. I mean, I go into class and I'm really excited to have them experience these worlds that are unknown to them, you know?"

"Well, I think it's awesome that you're teaching *The Bell Jar*. My God, that was one of our favorites," Tina boasted.

"Yeah. And for a progressive high school, would you believe they actually were concerned?"

"Jesus, you'd think it was the mid-60s."

"I know. I mean, what's so off-putting about a depressed young woman, when we're hearing about these young kids committing suicide?"

"I know."

"I had this one student... She was... She stood up one day in class. God, she reminded me of myself, Tina, you know? I mean, before college. Before you knew me. When I was so shy. She was the same way. And I was worried for her. I didn't know if she'd be able to break out of it," she continued, not even realizing that she had now stopped walking, clearly lost in her words. "She stood up one day and she gave her feedback on if Esther Greenwood was sick or just misunderstood. No one else in the class had really felt that she was normal. They all sort of held her at arm's length. But Tricia... That was her name; Tricia Wentworth. She got it. I mean, I felt she got it. At least she had a more nuanced understanding. She looked at that other layer that so many kids her age just can't see, but... this was someone who seemed to live beyond her years. At least I thought so. I mean, she sure didn't come from where *I* came from, Tina. She had wealthy parents. I saw them one day, when I took my in-laws out for brunch. She didn't look like them at all. I was certain that she was adopted. And then, I wondered if how she was was as a result of her birth parents, provided she ever knew them, or if it was a result of this rich, gorgeous couple who maybe...who maybe didn't understand her at all. Anyway,...that was a little victory. Feeling like I got through to her."

Tina took this in, "Is she no longer a student of yours?"

"What do you mean?"

"Well, you said '*was*' so, I assumed..."

"Oh, uh... Yeah, I only had her for a year," she recovered from her unintentional use of the past tense, especially as she was letting on that she was still living in Long Island and teaching full-time. At least Tina didn't seem suspicious, and only could appreciate how much teaching meant to Peggy. Writing would be a much more difficult subject to lie about, however, especially comparing her complete lack of output with the thousands of poems that Tina composed.

To the surprise of both of them, their conversation carried them on foot to Tina's building on West 73rd Street. Tina had an adorable apartment for a single woman, and it was more spacious than she let on. Peggy looked out of her living room window, eating up the view of downtown Manhattan. It made her dread all the more going back to Grace's house and only further emphasized how almost apocalyptically un-scenic Kelp Stream was. Out of the corner of Peggy's eye, she saw several published books of Tina's poems on her bookshelf. As Tina made them tea in her kitchen, Peggy pulled one out. It was a chapbook called *The Truth of This Life*. On the cover, it was noted "Winner of the Sparrow Prize". She smiled at this victory for Tina, just as quickly as she was jealous. It was a different type of jealousy though, since Tina was a peer. The other published books she observed on her shelf would only confirm that Tina's talents and drive went fairly unimpeded, regardless of being married or teaching full-time. Perhaps she had lulls, but the output was nevertheless considerable.

"Oh, God," Tina bashfully laughed, as she came out with cups of tea for them, "What a pretentious title, right?"

"What do you mean? I like it."

"*The Truth of This Life*? Like I knew what that even was then."

"When was this published?" Peggy looked to see the copyright date was from 2007, thirteen years ago.

"I was 27. I didn't know anything then. I just knew structure and tone. Hey, it was enough to win a thousand bucks and get my first chapbook published, but it's a little embarrassing now."

"Well, I'm proud of you. I mean, look at these."

"Peggy, you haven't even read them."

"Well, just the output. I mean... Having all these published isn't just blind luck."

"It's always a little bit of luck. You know that. How many great books got rejected time and time again, and how much shit gets through and becomes a best seller. *50 Shades of Gray*? I mean, are you kidding me?"

"I know, but this isn't that."

"Well, I certainly didn't make a mint with any of them, that's for sure. I mean, hey, it's poetry. You don't expect to get rich. Plus you can't adapt a poem into a film and have it directed by Rob Reiner or whoever."

"You're an artist, Tina. Why are you denouncing these?"

"I'm not denouncing them. I'm just saying, it's poetry. I won some contests, won some grants, got books published, and that's that."

She looked down at the book in her hand, feeling torn at Tina's flippancy. She wasn't sure what it stemmed from; was it Tina really being hard on herself for her younger creations or was she playing down what she was actually quite proud of in order to diminish Peggy's possible feelings of inadequacy.

"Well, I think you should be proud," as she placed the book back on the shelf and sat on the couch, where a cup of tea sat before her on the coffee table.

Tina looked at Peggy, picking up on her restrained frustration, "Peggy, I'm not saying I don't value your opinion."

"I didn't say that. I didn't even read them," she took a hostile sip, then gazed out the window.

Suddenly Tina felt regret, though she wasn't certain why. Perhaps they had covered so much ground in less than 3 hours that she didn't want to rush to any unpleasantness just as they were re-establishing their relationship.

"I'm sorry, Tina, I guess it's hard for me to hear you be blasé' about...what I think are nice achievements."

"Peggy, I'm not... I just... I guess, you know, I wrote them and got whatever I was going to get out of them, and now they sit there and that's it. They're sort of...old to me. And maybe,... I don't know. I wanted to be the next Anne Sexton. You know that."

"Well, you're you instead."

"You know what I mean."

"Oh, you mean you want to be dead soon."

"I'm not saying that. Hey, Plath died young too."

"Who says I wanted to be the next Plath?"

"Peggy, you know what I mean. We read them in college and we envied how...they were envied. I mean, they used to go to colleges and these respected venues and recite their work, and sign their books and... I mean, it's just not how it works anymore. And if it did, I guess, we'd have to be more depressed and willing to sacrifice years of our lives because an early death is pretty much the ultimate badge of respectability."

Peggy sort of understood this. Not everyone they admired as writers died early deaths, but many of them did. If not, they were drunks or addicts of some kind who peaked early. Tina had admitted bouts of depression, but nothing that she felt gave her much cache' that would make her name indelible. She did win a great many contests and grants, and had many poems published in small presses, but who would find these books who didn't already know her? What would resurrect interest in these obscure chapbooks unless she one day decided to go into a school with an AK-47 and embark on a massacre? It seems that that's what it took to obtain significant notoriety.

"I just think you've lost your perspective," Peggy retorted.

"Lost my...? What does that mean?" asked Tina, with a degree of offence.

"You've written. You've been published. You're still writing. You're teaching poetry at a college in New York City. You're...you're... I mean, that's what you wanted to be doing and you're doing it."

"Yeah, so?"

"Well, you act like it has no value now because you're not a heroin addict or dead. Jesus Christ, can't you just take some solace in the fact that you're doing exactly what you set out to do and you're alive and well enough to keep doing it?"

"Peggy, what's the matter with you?"

"What's the matter? Listen to yourself!"

Tina sat with this and looked at Peggy, unable to hide the fact that her accusatory tone was an overstep. Eggshells seemed to now be laid out on the floor and the tense momentum that was being created by Peggy was something that Tina wanted desperately to elude. In the old days, they would have had it out. Tina would not have ever been reduced to silence. Peggy questioned if this was maturity on Tina's part or the fact that she was desperately trying to not end this friendship just as it was beginning again. At the same time, Peggy was surprised to find herself revealing more in this moment than she had over lunch. She was embarrassed and, in her being so, could not help but at least incrementally unload:

"I'm sorry, Tina. I just... I admire you and...and I envy you. And that's not... It's not an easy thing to admit, okay?"

At this point, Tina was listening, but looking into her cup of tea, as though still stinging a bit from their earlier exchange.

"I mean, we always had a healthy sense of competition between us. But that was... I mean, things are different. I can't compete with what you've done because...I've done nothing."

She was gazing out the window again, accompanied only by Tina's silence. But before she would elaborate, she needed to get the biggest question out of the way:

"Do you know about what happened, Tina?"

"What do you mean?"

Peggy turned to her, "With Mike? Please, just be honest with me."

"Peg, I am. I don't know what you're talking about. What happened with Mike?"

"You really don't know?"

"Peggy, please, I'm lost here. Just tell me what you're talking–"

"Mike's in prison," she spewed abruptly.

"What?"

Now that it was out, she didn't feel the need to rush the details in an unfocused stream.

"Tina,...Mike has been in prison for over a month now. He'll serve 2 years. For insurance fraud. He was... I didn't know anything about it. He was basically falsely diagnosing people so that he could get more money from the insurance companies... It's all very unsettling, and I'm incredibly embarrassed by it."

"Jesus, Peggy, I'm... I had no -"

"Just let me get this out, Tina, because it's...not easy for me."

"Alright."

"We lost everything. I mean, overnight, practically. Our house, his car, furniture, art work... It was all seized. I lost my teaching job... I mean, everyone in that town knew. So many were his patients. There was nowhere to go. I lost friends. I lost...my life. Okay? I was in class one day, we were... we were discussing the fucking *Bell Jar*, and there was a knock on the door and...nothing has been the same since.   And... the thing is, for almost a decade and a half leading up to that, I was nothing but a wife and mother. I didn't work. I didn't write. I was a wife and mother. And, don't get me wrong, for the most part, I was... Well, I *thought* I was content. I was happy...enough. I knew that it couldn't be farther from where I came from. But I guess deep down I also knew it still wasn't success...on my terms. I didn't go to college to meet a husband, for Godsakes. I wanted *this*. I wanted what you have, and I guess I sacrificed it, but I was getting back to it. I mean, it was everything I could do to get out of the rut I was in, to start my career again. And I did. It had just begun again,...and then... My husband's in prison upstate, my kids are... I had to send them to live with their grandparents in Florida... And I'm...I'm living with my mother," she turned to Tina, between laughter and near tears.

Tina took this all in, clearly surprised on every level, "My God....," she uttered, without intending it to be audible. "Peggy, I'm..." Her unfinished sentence sat in the air for a while, as they looked at each other.

"It's just so funny that you would reach out to me when I was at the absolute nadir of my life. I mean, why the hell couldn't I hear from you 4 months ago?"

"Well, Peg,...it's not like this still wouldn't've happened. I mean, what's the difference about that?"

"The difference is that our friendship meant a lot and I didn't like that it ended any more than you did. But I didn't want to come back into your life as a homeless woman with no job and no prospects."

"Peg, it doesn't matter to me what your current standing is. You wanted to see me, I wanted to see you. Let's just focus on that."

"Well, it's not easy."

"Peggy -"

"I mean, I didn't want you *not* to be successful, but I also didn't want you to be successful and be modest about your success. Your poetry's been published, for Godsakes. Be proud. You're teaching poetry at a well-known college in New York City. You're writing and writing and writing, and I'm jealous of my 11 year- old daughter who gets to write poetry and children's books and short stories while I'm trying to keep them fed. And now they're not even with me because I can't have them living with my mother who, unbeknownst to them, tried to kill their own father. And if she succeeded, they wouldn't even be here. And I wouldn't have a husband who's in prison. And maybe I'd've been writing this whole time as well, and teaching and living in New York or Chicago or some nice, cultured city somewhere with a coupla' cats..."

She stopped herself, having been more raw in her self-expression than she ever thought she'd be, but it was hard to contain. She didn't have anyone to confide in since Carole, Larry's wife. In truth, in the whole of Peggy's life, there was no better person for her to bare her soul to than Tina. Therefore, it was of little surprise that, eventually, Peggy's regrets, shames and spurts of anger and resentment would come out like they did.

Now her biggest fear was if this would scare Tina away for good. Had she even been around such instability? Was she at the point in her life where she could take on such baggage by a person who inadvertently pushed her away after college?

There was an awkward silence, before Peggy finally sat back down on the couch, the tea having cooled significantly during all this.

"You should write about this."

She looked at Tina, surprised that this would be her first words after her spiraling monologue.

"What?"

"You should. Why not make it into something?"

"Into something? Into what?"

"Art."

"Art?!" Peggy couldn't remotely digest what Tina was referring to. It sounded like she was suggesting that she try to mold the shitball of her life into some sort of cathartic sculpture.

"Write about it. Why not?" Tina insisted. "You've needed some inspiration. Why not use this?"

"Tina, my God, I'm confiding in you. I'm just... I'm just trying to tell you what my life is."

"I know. And it sounds awful."

"Gee, thanks."

"Well, what do you want me to say? Would you rather I just agree that your life has taken a horribly tragic turn? I'm trying to give you some creative encouragement."

"Tina, I'm an adult, okay? I'm not one of your students. I'm not telling you all this for inspiration. I'm just telling you this...to tell you this."

Tina looked at Peggy, trying not to be insulted; "And is it helping?"

She now resented disclosing anything to Tina and wished that she simply let the afternoon be driven by Tina's stories and achievements. She laid herself bare for no other reason than wanting Tina to not have delusions about her life. If the friendship was going to truly resume, it seemed to Peggy that her brutal honesty would better serve this than her acting as if they were of similar standing in their careers.

She grabbed her purse and felt the best thing to do was to leave before anything else could escalate. These weren't the old days of arguing in their dorm about one or the other's feedback on a particular story or poem. Years had elapsed. They were older, different in more ways. Offensive words or insinuating tones didn't bounce off their skin anymore. A disagreement now, especially in their first time together in years, could definitively end this newly resumed friendship – which Peggy almost preferred at this point.

"Peggy, where are you – ?"

"Sorry, Tina, I realized I have to call my kids. They start at a new school on Monday, and I...I really need to check in. They're...they're really nervous and... Well, anyway. It was great to see you."

"Peggy, I wasn't trying to – "

"No, no, it's fine," she gave Tina a quick, rattled hug. "Thanks for lunch," then left.

As she rode the elevator down to the lobby, she finally shed a few tears. It wasn't always clear even to herself why she got emotional, but attributed this to the combination of recent life events with the fact that Tina seemed to be reducing her trauma to something diverting for public consumption. This suggestion, coming on the heels of her recent experience with *American Sleaze*, hit her in the worst possible way, even if Tina wasn't approaching this from a vapid commercial perspective.

Write a book about this shit?

She could not conceive of investing the time in transcribing the events that led her to where she was now. She then recalled the title of the story that Tina had mentioned; the one Peggy wrote in college that she was so impressed with: *Homeless but Happy.*

Talk about a pretentious title.

27

The ensuing days merged together in a formless blob of inactivity. A monotonous pattern had developed through her closed door; she woke up each morning by way of a howl from Little Pearl, followed by the cranky *"Alright, alright"* from Grace as she stomped into the bathroom. Little Pearl would then wait and whine by the opened bathroom door, as the more disturbing sound of Grace urinating soon followed. Eventually, she'd hear Grace stomp down the stairs before opening the sliding glass door to let Little Pearl out into the backyard. Grace would then proceed to stomp into the kitchen where the sounds of her making coffee, pouring Cinnamon Life cereal and making toast would remain unaltered. It astonished Peggy how much of a creature of habit her mother was, and she tried to recall if she was always like this. Of course, back then, she'd have heard the lighting of a cigarette by now, and that distinct exhalation and then, within minutes, a reverberating cough. But that much had changed. She had not seen nor heard her take so much as a puff from anything the entire time she was there – but she still couldn't fully believe it was not her making those calls; *and the caller was unquestionably a smoker.*

She usually kept herself in bed long enough to make sure Grace was out of the kitchen before going down to make her own bowl of flavored oatmeal, which she made a clear point to purchase herself. In fact, all the food she would eat in the house was of her own investment, just to safely avoid confrontations.

While she waited, she stared up at her ceiling; Sylvia's faded eyes looking down on her the same as all the previous sad mornings. Her car was still waiting at the shop, and she had no means by which to get it out, but knew it couldn't stay there in perpetuity. The one novelty of this day was that it was snowing for the first time in weeks. She sat up in bed and allowed herself to be transported by the descending flakes, thrust back to when she was a girl and was enamored with the snow, very much like her love of watching the sun-made stars that glistened on the ocean.

A text came into her phone, which was charging on the night table. It was from Tina, following up for about the third time since their lunch on Saturday; *"Peggy, please call me. I don't like how we left off. At least let me know that you're ok."*

While she was hardly in a position to be righteous, she still didn't feel compelled to allay Tina's concerns. She knew she'd respond sooner than later, but right now she felt she had a right to be irked. Writing about this tragedy just was not in her. *Of all the things I could write about, why would it have to be this?* she thought. *And how embarrassing.*

The train ride back from New York City that day also gave Peggy the opportunity of recalling the other things that bothered her as it related to Tina. She didn't appreciate the crack about not wanting kids or alluding that Peggy wasn't happy that she had them. *Yeah, she wasn't saying that, but there was an insinuation there.* And then there was all that mock modesty regarding her poetry. *Well, perhaps she just wasn't as fulfilled by them as she hoped she'd be, but still...* And then her only response to Peggy excavating her recent family history was a flippant *"You should write about this."*
Yeah, maybe she was trying to be encouraging and creatively supportive, but it just sounded like such a cheap response. I mean, not every horrible thing that happens is material, for Godsakes.

She felt she could at least make her sweat a little more. And if, by the time she did respond, Tina no longer cared,...so be it.

As usual, the TV wafted into the kitchen while Peggy prepared her breakfast and instant coffee. She would normally eat at the dining table or bring it upstairs, but something about the snow falling gave her a strange sort of courage to go into the living room and sit on the upright chair to the left of the couch where Grace sat. Initially, Peggy tried to be unassuming and simply placed her cup on the end table, mixed up her oatmeal and gazed apathetically at the morning news show where the meteorologist appeared far too enthused about the first snow the tri-state area had received since December.

Peggy didn't look at Grace. She felt it best to keep her focus on the television until she felt warmed enough to pivot her head in her mother's direction, which was unlikely.

"No *American Sleaze*?" Peggy asked.

There was a considerable silence, before she noticed Grace's head turn toward her, as if just having noticed that she was there, "Old one."

"I thought *all* the morning ones were old."

Another sizable silence, "That one I seen like six times already. Pisses me off anyway."

Grace slurped her coffee, and continued to gaze at the boisterous weatherman, then followed with "Big fuckin' deal. It's snowin'. Idiot."

Peggy was surprised to agree with her, feeling similarly nauseated by the façade of morning news personalities, but said nothing.

She continued to eat and occasionally look out the sliding glass door to see Little Pearl attempting to catch the snowflakes just before they touched the grass. It was a strangely pleasant diversion which she hoped would keep her outside for most of the day, though, of course, that was up to Grace. She preferred having Little Pearl in the house more often than not, but would usually keep her out back for a couple of hours at the start of the day before Little Pearl would beg to be readmitted and, of course, fed. Maybe her enthusiasm for the snow would at least tire her out and force her to take a longer nap than usual.

"She likes the snow, huh?"

Grace still gazed at the set, "What?"

"I said she seems to like the snow."

Grace apathetically turned, "Yeah. She's fascinated by anything that falls from the sky."

Peggy and Grace would watch Little Pearl jut her huge head out to slurp in as many flakes as she could. Peggy was surprised at how entertaining this was, and could barely take in that this was a moment she was sharing with her mother. Of course, it would only be a few seconds in before she would turn to Grace and see that her interest had already waned and was back to gazing at the imbecilic weatherman.

"How long've you had her?"

"Huh?"

"I said how long've you had Little Pearl?"

Under her breath, "I dunno. Few years now."

"Shelter?"

"Found 'er."

"Really? Like...where?"

"Side a' the road."

Peggy was suddenly intrigued enough to stop eating her oatmeal, "What, you were just driving along...?"

"Yep."

She continued to gaze at the set, as Peggy's curiosity grew, "So you were just driving down the road and saw her?"

Then Grace turned to Peggy, "Boy, you really know it all, don'tcha'?"

"I'm asking."

"You already seem to know the answer, so why bother?" as she turned back to the set.

It didn't take long for Grace to sour any potential for

prolonged discussion. In fairness, Peggy didn't come into the room expecting it. It seemed to accidentally evolve through Little Pearl's fascination with precipitation. Now she regretted her entrance.

She remained for a few moments before gathering her bowl and coffee cup and going into the kitchen. As she cleaned out the bowl and cup, she stared into the drain and took a deep breath, suddenly aware of the energy she expended in trying to simply converse.

She approached the foot of the stairs, before turning into the living room, "If I go out, do you need anything?"

"Like what?"

"Just...anything. From Mrs. Prager's?"

"You gettin' the car?"

"No, it's still in the shop. I just might walk that way."

"If I need somethin', I'll go."

Peggy was about to head up, but reluctantly stopped, "Um, look, if I need to go on an interview, could I borrow the car?"

"What?"

"Could I borrow your car?"

"Is that why you asked if I needed anything?"

"No, I just... Speaking of the car, I just thought I'd ask."

"Ask what?"

"In case I need to go on an interview and can't get a car service in time."

"You got an interview?"

"Not...no, not yet. I'm saying *if*."

"Maybe by then you'll have your car."

"Look, I can't get the car out until I pay for the repairs. I don't have the money. That's why I'm asking."

"Askin' for what?"

"Asking if I can use the car, if I need to."

"You can't take one a' them Ubers?"

"They don't run around here, okay? And the one taxi service you have is basically one guy and he can never pick up in less than an hour. I'd be better off riding on Little Pearl's back."

Grace sat with this, gazed back at the TV, "Why don't we just cross that bridge. We ain't even there yet. You got some place you need to be, n' if I'm not usin' it, we'll discuss it then."

Peggy wouldn't push. At least she put it out there that having the car to use would be helpful. She knew Grace hardly used it because she hardly went out, but that certainly didn't assure anything. Perhaps something would come along to render this need moot, but she still had no idea what that would be.

She went upstairs, then sat at the end of her bed and looked blankly at the falling snow.

A few hours later, Peggy woke from what had become her usual mid-afternoon nap. The house was silent, as Grace and Little Pearl were likely doing the same. She got up and looked out at the driveway to see Grace's car still there, and then gandered about at the few houses in her view, which all had accumulated white sheets of snow on the roofs. She was in such a deep state of depressed sleep that she had pretty much forgotten the events that led to her two hour hibernation, before coming upon something she had written that was sitting on her night table. She scooted over to read it, as if it were a note left by someone else:

White
that falls today
is not the same white
that once fell.

It was one line too many for a haiku, but it appeared to be a semblance of something that could be called a poem. Either that or it was a subconscious memory of a fortune cookie from the last time she had Chinese food. There was something about this that genuinely took her by surprise; if nothing else, it would be the first original writing she had done in years. And it wasn't a rough outline of a story she didn't know how to start. It wasn't a lame synopsis of an epic that she couldn't formulate the discipline to begin, let alone finish. It was, perhaps, just a simple way to dip her toe back into the pond; *a short, unassuming, innocent little poem.* She quickly wanted to compare this piece and reduce it somehow, but stopped herself. Instead, she momentarily killed the demons that would have thwarted her whenever she was itching to write something, and managed to just appreciate that this came out.

And it even made sense.

Now what?

"*Call from Hawking State Prison from...Michael Buhbone*": the machine pronouncing the last name with the usually incorrect shortened "u" sound. There was no specific holiday occasion for this call. It was the first week of February, and Mike's phone privileges had gotten a bit more flexible; perhaps through Larry's assistance, perhaps not. In any event, it would be the first time they would speak since the kids had been in Florida:

"How are you?" she asked.

"The same. I mean, it's not Riker's, but it's not the free world either."

She was restrained, trying to balance her emotions, as she hadn't heard his voice since their highly emotional visit a couple of weeks prior. But, of course, much had happened. She tried to suppress her suspicion about Mike's infidelity, but it had resurfaced when Mrs. Prager corroborated that Grace hadn't bought cigarettes in a while. The kids not being there would also give them time to address this, even if she was now forced to speak in hushed tones, with it being about 20 degrees outside.

"I can't speak too loudly, okay?"

"What?"

"I said I can't speak too loudly, Mike."

"Why can't you? It sounds like you're in a closet."

"I am. I'm in the closet of my closet-like bedroom."

"Why the hell are you in your closet?"

"Mike, do I have to explain everything? I'm living in my mother's house and I don't want her to hear our conversation."

"I was hoping you weren't there anymore."

"Where else can I go? I have no money to spend and the car's back in the shop."

"Jesus..."

"It konked out right after I dropped the kids off at the airport."

"I still can't believe you had to send them off."

"What can't you believe?"

"I mean, I know it wasn't practical as long as you're with...*her*, but why you're even there is boggling."

"She's letting me stay, so that's all I can ask. Our options had run dry and I wanted the kids going to a decent school."

"Jesus, Larry offered to give you money for an apartment and a few months rent. You could've -"

"Wait, when did he tell you this?"

"When I spoke to him last."

"He never offered me anything. That's completely untrue."

"Well, he says he did."

"Mike, I haven't spoken to Larry since I stayed with him and Carole."

"I know, but he says he's called."

"He hasn't called. He hasn't left messages. None of this is true, okay? So don't make this out to be like I'm refusing his offer. He's offered nothing to us."

"Well,...why you even left there is still a mystery to me."

"I really don't wana' get into this with the little time we have."

"But can't you see why that would be of concern to me, Peg? At least you would've been in a safe, welcoming environment."

"Mike – "

"But, no, you up'n left. And now you're speaking to me from the closet of your childhood bedroom and the kids are in another state. I mean, Jesus Christ – "

"Larry tried to jump me, Mike!"

"What?"

"One night when I was there, staying by myself in their carriage house, Larry came in and... Alright?"

"He what? Finish your sentence."

"Finish what? You want these details? He came in, he was a little tipsy, he sat on the couch with me, talking to me about how their marriage was strained, and the next thing I knew, he became an octopus."

Mike's indignant momentum was understandably halted by this revelation. It was obviously a complex thing for him to hear; his wife claiming that his trusted lawyer and close friend had crossed such a line. Every time they spoke now, it seemed as if Peggy needed to enlighten Mike. When she did, he could only relent. And for every enlightenment, Mike sounded smaller and more remote, even pummeled by what the outside world was inflicting on his family.

"And you know what his justification was?" she followed, now having the courage, to which Mike feebly responded, "What?"

She paused, then swallowed, "That you had a woman in Ohio."

As she expected, there was a silence on the other end. And while she was eager to hear how Mike would explain or deny such an accusation, there was something within her that already knew. She still had wanted to believe it was Grace that was making those disturbing calls, but the more that time elapsed and the more information she amassed, it appeared that it couldn't have been her. If anything, she was glad that she waited until now to broach this with Mike. At least now she had more information to justify this; not just Larry's words, but the other circumstantial evidence that had been mounting.

The biggest thing may have been that Grace just didn't seem like she could be that proactive in trying to disrupt Peggy's life. The anger and venom she had once exhibited appeared to have waned into disinterest. And with Peggy's sheepish return, it appeared that Grace was satisfied that her suspicion of Mike was warranted, and it was that justification that allowed Peggy to stay for a limited period of time.

"Honey,..."

"I knew it," she said, picking up on his apologetic tone...

"Honey, let me just – "

"Just what? Explain it?"

"Peggy, I'm not admitting to anything. You just hit me with this, so just let me – "

"Mike, please. Do us both a favor here, okay? I may've been naïve before all this, but I'm not now. If after all that you've put this family through, you can't even save time and admit to the obvious, then I don't know what else to say."

He didn't respond, and in his silence, it was obvious.

"What does she smoke?"

"Peg, listen – "

"What does she smoke?"

"I don't know what you... What does she...?"

"Those calls. The calls that were coming to the house for weeks that I couldn't trace. All this time, I thought it was my mother. I heard her sucking on a cigarette. I could only assume it was her, for some reason. Trying to make me crazy. And you went along. You knew who was calling. You probably picked up a few times, right?"

"Honey, – "

"Sure, you knew. It was like a fucking experiment to make me have a breakdown. What, was she threatening you? Big time dermatologist in town on conventions? She thought you were gonna' dump me and marry her or some such thing. Right?"

"That's not – "

"That's not what it was? Tell me who it was if it wasn't her, Mike? Tell me, you fucking imposter."

"I, Peggy, don't... Please, I just..."

"Yes?"

The silence returned, and she could almost see him on the other end, dejected in his orange suit; his wife knowingly betrayed, his lawyer and close friend betraying him, his kids out of reach... His weakened state could not combat Peggy's convictions, because they were accurate.

They remained silent on the phone, as the blissful unity they once shared all but faded out of sight...

28

By mid-February, she had managed some sporadic substitution work as an English teacher at Windham Willow High School in the neighboring town of Redmond. It paid little, but got her out of the house for a week. She filled in for a teacher who was out with the flu, since it was the heart of flu season, so at least Peggy was able to cash in on this annual malady. She hadn't taught English per se, but little was required of her, since she was only to follow the established lesson plan. It so happened that they were in the middle of reading *Ethan Frome*, which was by no means a favorite of hers, but the time passed quickly enough.

By the end of the week, the principal, Mr. Gaskill, approached her to let her know that the regular English teacher would be returning, thus ending her current stay at Windham Willow. If nothing else, her being in front of a class helped rekindle her enthusiasm for teaching, even if it was much less inviting than when she taught at Cold River. The school was drab and was much smaller by comparison. The kids were certainly not privileged, but the attention spans were the same.

On the drive home in Grace's car, Peggy could only ponder what was next. Yes, her name was out there as a substitute teacher now, but it was far too erratic. She simply needed greater stability, which seemed impossible now. Her car was still in the shop, and she was getting calls about it. She managed to come up with a variety of excuses for why she wasn't able to pick it up, just to assure they wouldn't try and sell it for scrap metal or some such thing.

One week of substitute teaching work at a public school was not going to put a dent into the balance for the repairs, and she wondered what else she could do to make a living, if teaching proved too unstable. She stopped in to pick up cigarettes and a few other items from *Ye Olde General Store*, especially as Mrs. Prager was always a welcoming sight, but was surprised to see a woman about Peggy's age behind the counter.

"That's it for t'day?"

"Yes, thanks."

"Okay, that'll be… Sorry, not used to this," she apologized as she voided the sale, then re-entered the prices in the register.

"No problem."

"Okay, that'll be $14.98."

As Peggy dipped into her wallet, "Mrs. Prager's off today?" she asked with a smile.

"Actually, it's not much of a day off."

"Oh. Is everything okay?"

"Well, she's in the hospital."

"Oh no. Is she alright?"

"Well, they say she's got pneumonia. Thought it was the flu, since it's the season, but… Anyway, that's where she is. My husband's with 'er."

"Are you her – ?"

"Daughter-in-law. Karen."

"Oh nice to meet you. I'm Peggy. We were just getting re-acquainted since I was away a while. When you see her, please give her my best."

"Thank you, Peggy. That's nice of you."

"I'll be praying for her, okay?"

"Oh, that's very sweet of you. Thank you."

She paid and left, her heart somewhat pulled by the pending mortality of Mrs. Prager. It even surprised her how connected she felt to her in that moment, to the extent that she would even allege to pray. Peggy hadn't managed to do that throughout all she had been through, most likely because she no longer could call herself a Catholic in any real sense. If anything, she seemed to have fallen into the apathetic category of believing in God by rote. Yet for one to say that they would pray appeared to be the most heartfelt way of expressing sympathy for the ill fortune of another. She did want to mean it and, if there *was* a God, she really did hope that He would be watching over Mrs. Prager.

Upon entering the house, she was as per usual greeted with the blaring TV from the living room, *"The spatter at the scene confirmed the blood was Pamela Henson's...!"* After putting some items in the fridge, she stepped into the living room, prompting Grace to instantly mute the sound, "Coulda' used the damn car today!"

"Well,...I thought you said you weren't going out today."

"Yeah, well, I needed somethin'. She's outa' treats."

"Do you want me to go back out and – ?"

"No, no, it's my damn car. I should be able to use it whenever I friggin' want, for Godsakes."

"I'm sorry, I asked you – "

"I don't know everything I may do on a given day. I gotta' know everything jus' so you can go wherever you want?"

"I went to school and came back. I wasn't joy riding. I'm done there anyway."

"Either way, you can figure somethin' else out from now on."

"I only used it for 2 days. I took a car service the other days and lost money."

"That ain't my problem."

"I'm not saying it is. I'm just saying that I'm trying to get on my feet – "

"n'that *also* ain't my problem. You're the one who went to college and got married to some fancy friggin' Goddamn zit doctor. You had it all set up for yourself. Now y'come back to the nest and expect me to pick up the slack for ya'."

"All I've asked is to have my old room for a few weeks. I've stayed out of your hair. I've bought all my own food – "

"That don't mean jack shit t'me, y'hear? You're here. You're taking up space in my house when I'm supposed to be enjoyin' my damn retirement, so don't act like you're doin' me a favor by gettin' your own oatmeal'n cigarettes. And that's another thing, you better not be smokin' up there!"

"I'm...I'm not," she lied.

"Had this place fumigated t'get the smoke out. Not gonna' have you bring it all back!"

Peggy bit down on her tongue as hard as she could without severing it just to keep herself from telling Grace off, before storming up the carpeted stairs.

She threw herself down on her bed with the same eerie similarity of her past. She even went so far as to shove a portion of her pillow in her mouth in order to primal scream into it. She then sat up and looked at the usually inactive Morgan Street, before turning to her old desk, which now held an opened spiral binder purchased at Mrs. Prager's shortly after managing to write her first poem in years. It was already opened to the last poem she wrote the previous night, which was unfinished:

Returning to your past
is a most unenviable task,

It was a rare attempt at rhyme, which was not necessarily her favorite type of poetry, nor her strong suit, but she tried to not judge her work and write solely as if there was no intention of it appearing before eyes other than her own. She stood up, walked back to the window only to return to her desk predictably uninspired. She then attempted to rest her aching back in the rigid wooden chair, then gazed up at the ceiling before closing her eyes. Suddenly she heard a loud smack from the sliding glass door opening downstairs to admit Little Pearl, whose excitable breaths indicated a recently accomplished, and no doubt gargantuan, bowel movement. This would soon be followed by Grace's instinctive *"Alright, alright,"* leading her to the kitchen to reward Little Pearl.

Peggy locked into these sounds all the more in this moment, having heard them so many times over days and nights, that it had become a most reliable syncopation. At this point, she'd hear Grace, having fed Little Pearl, tap the tiles with her plastic-bottomed pink slippers back to the living room. But after just a few steps, they stopped. By now, Peggy assessed that this would put her right at the entrance of the kitchen which, from downstairs, could view her bedroom door. She realized that Grace was likely standing there, peering at her door for an unusually lengthy moment.

Why did she stop? she thought.

She now felt an obligation to be still, to hide whatever limited activity was taking place in the confines of her bedroom, but her curiosity was getting the better of her, even as she was unsettled. She stepped slowly and quietly towards the door, still not having heard those taps on the floor from Grace's slippers, then gingerly kneeled down to peek under her closed door, remembering as a child that she'd at least be able to make out if someone was at the foot of the stairs.

Sure enough, she saw her silhouette, unusually still,... with the sounds of Little Pearl gobbling out of her bowl behind her. After a few more seconds, Grace stepped back into the living room, while the lump in Peggy's throat slowly faded.

She stood up, exhaled at how chilling this was, before venturing back to her desk. She needed a cigarette. She hoisted the window open, which wafted in the arctic air, and leaned out as she exhaled smoke to the cool wind and shivered, gazing at the dead trees. Within minutes, she found the last two lines for her short rhymed poem:

> *Returning to your past*
> *is a most unenviable task,*
> *especially when it yields*
> *no more than a darkened field.*

The disturbing turn of events of the last few minutes, at least for the moment, appeared to be distant in her mind compared to the slight satisfaction of finishing yet another short poem, and one that came from a certain moment; a moment that now could not be classified as just another unsettling fragment of her life, but as inspiration.

She felt good enough later that night to check in on the kids. By now, she was calling Nicky's direct cell phone to speak with both of them, all to avoid hearing Vic or Elaine's voice.

"How're you getting along at school?"

"s'alright," he mumbled, not unlike every call she had with him since he'd been there.

"Do you have homework tonight?"

"Yeah, I'm doin' it now, actually."

"What kind?"

"What kind?"

"Yes, Nicky. That's not a strange question. What subject?"

"English n' Pre-Algebra."

"Good. Alright. Well, is everything else okay? You sleepin' okay?"

"Yeah, fine. You?"

She was surprised that Nicky thought to ask, especially as disinterested as he sounded, "Um, well, thanks for asking. I'm ok. I did some teaching this week, so that was good and...

uh... Yeah, things are getting a little better. Still trying to find more steady work, but... I miss you." There was the shy, introverted silence that Peggy expected, "Nicky?"

"Yeah."

"I said I miss you. Don't you miss me?"

"Yeah. Luna's buggin' me. You wana' talk to her?"

"Of course, I do. Listen, it sounds like you're doing what you need to do in school, so just...keep at it. If you're unsure about something or feel...weird about something, just call me."

"What would I feel weird about?"

"Just...your new environment. Being there, being around new people. You know what I mean."

"Alright."

As usual, she resigned that the tone of her exchanges with Nicky would likely not improve for as long as they were down there, "Alright, why don't you put Luna on. Love you."

"Love you," he echoed.

Luna would quickly change the energy, "Hi, mommy!"

"Hey, honey. How are you?"

"Good. I got an A today."

"Yeah? In what?"

"It was a quiz in History."

"History? That's great."

"Yeah, it was the first quiz I took in the class."

"What did it cover?"

"Well, it was mainly the Monroe Doctrine, which we already studied back home anyway, so I knew a lot of it."

"Is that the one where no could invade the U.S. to colonize anymore?"

"Yeah, yeah. Europe or anyone else couldn't come into America and take any part for themselves."

"Right, right. Wow, good, honey."

"Yeah, and I'm writing another story."

"Oh, yeah? What's it about?"

"It's a sequel to *The Hyena Ballerina*."

"Oh, wow. I like that story. That's one of your best, honey."

"Yeah. I don't wana' give it away, but it's gonna' continue on where that story left off."

"Good, honey. Send it to me when you're done, okay? Or you can read it over the phone."

"Okay,"

"You know, I've started writing again too."

"Yeah? What?"

"Well,...nothing big. Just some poems," she modestly revealed, but with some pride.

"Have you talked to daddy?"

Peggy was a bit disappointed that Luna decided to ask this at that moment, especially as she even wanted to share one of her poems with Luna, "Well,...not since a couple of weeks ago, like I told you before, honey, but...he's doing okay. Your grandparents haven't spoken to him recently?"

"No. Not for a few weeks," she sulked.

Peggy knew that Mike had more flexibility now and could call Vic and Elaine too with a little more frequency, but it was odd that he hadn't contacted them in a while. Especially since she last spoke to Mike, a couple of weeks back. She realized that much of the life may have been sucked out of him by how their call ended, with her all but assuring him that a divorce was imminent. She even expected that he might try and use the kids for sympathy in order to keep Peggy from severing their marital ties, but even she couldn't think of that in the moment. It was just another distraction She was just content to not speak to him for a while, and didn't care how frequently he called Vic and Elaine, but still realized that it was important the kids at least hear his voice. Eventually, she would follow up with him, but it couldn't be now.

"Are you fuckin' kiddin' me?!" came from downstairs, as Peggy tried to focus on closing out the call with Luna. "Holy fuckin' Shit! Peggy, you might wana' see this!"

The worst possible feeling overcame Peggy, along with

the question of why her mother would suddenly be inviting her into the living room.

"Hold on, honey," as she cupped her phone, "I'M ON THE PHONE!" she yelled through the door."

"OH, I DON'T THINK YOU WANA' MISS THIS!"

It quickly hit Peggy what it could be, but she wanted desperately to be wrong about it.

"Honey, I'll... I'm sorry, let me let you go. I'll call you in a couple of days, okay? I love you."

"Alright, mom, I –"

Peggy cut off the call, and braced herself before descending down the stairs to the living room, out of which blared, "...a respected Long Island dermatologist, a husband, a father, a beacon of an elite community..." as she continued down the steps – oh, dear God, she thought. Did he kill himself?

"Ho-ly shit," Grace muttered, through a stunned grin which Peggy could see through the walls...

By the time Peggy touched down in the entrance to the living room, she looked at the screen to see a photo of Mike in his lab coat, smiling – the very photo used from the glowing write-up he received last year in Long Island Life, in which he was affectionately referred to as "One Man You Want Under Your Skin." Her jaw dropped wide enough for Little Pearl's enormous head to fit in. For the few incremental steps she was taking forward with substitute teaching and getting some mildly creative momentum back, this brand new episode of American Sleaze felt like God's foot stomping it all into dust.

She didn't remotely consider, after walking out of the studio almost a month ago, that the show would have any authorization to go forward with the episode. After all, Peggy was led to believe her interview segments would be "the driving force of the narrative," in Jane Madden's slithery words. So how could they manage to put this episode together?

Her unbridled apoplexy resurrected the high-pitch whistle sound in her head, which she feared would set off Little Pearl, assuming she could hear it. It overshadowed much of Len Getz's introductory monologue, and faded out just as her former best friend, Claire Resnick, appeared on the screen, "Jesus Christ...," Peggy said under her breath. It dawned on her very quickly that, with Peggy not contributing, they could simply nix the focus on their marriage and, instead, get mileage out of his former patients and colleagues. The episode would unfold like the bleakest possible version of *This is Your Life*;

"He told me that I had a mole that was cancerous. After he was arrested, I went to 3 other specialists who all agreed it wasn't."

Then came Monique, apparently benefitting from a professional make-up artist, *"I worked for him for 8 years and had no idea."*

Then came Peggy's former teaching colleague Cinda's husband, *"I had what used to look like Stalin hugging Art Garfunkel. It was a mole on my arm. And he said half of it was too dark, which was a sign of melanoma. But I've since learned that it didn't warrant being removed."*

Then, much to Peggy's further surprise, was the voluptuous Violet Summers, Monique's temp replacement whom Larry had all but eviscerated in court just months ago, now getting the last laugh, *"I was a dermatology student and I knew what these skin diseases looked like. And I addressed this with him."*

The whistle came back into Peggy's ears, as she dropped into the nearest chair, having tuned out everything around her. The faces of virtually their entire circle flashed before her on the TV as if she were dying; Judy, Gwen, Ray – *even the fucking mohel!* In addition to at least 7 or 8 other patients whom she had never seen before, including the last patient Mike would have before he was busted, Audrey Kovalt, who was about to have a mole on her behind lanced as federal agents barged in.

The few words she could make out through the piercing

whistle were unequivocally condemning; *"betrayed"*, *"crook"*, *"thief"*, *"grifter"*, *"repellant"*, *"audacious"*, *"shameful"*... She couldn't tell if her name was mentioned, and was praying the kids weren't, but she could hardly keep pace with how her senses were being so rapidly assaulted. It was a bad dream, and yet she was sitting upright with her eyes bulging out of her head as her heart palpitated.

And it would manage to get worse.

For a moment, the piercing whistle ceased long enough for her to hear the voice of Len Getz expel, *"We scheduled an interview with Peggy Bubone in order to have her shed light on her relationship with her husband and confirm if she knew of any of the improprieties that Dr. Bubone was engaging in prior to his arrest, even though she was never tried nor under any suspicion. But this is all that we managed."*

And then it came, the surveillance footage of Peggy running amok in the halls of *American Sleaze*'s studio offices, before finally being cornered like a panicked animal;
"GET ME OUT OF THIS (BLEEP)ING BUILDING NOW, DO YOU HEAR ME?!!!"

Of course, there was nothing of what led up to that unhinged moment; how Peggy fervently was opposed to exploiting herself and her family. Nothing close to respectability. All that would be aired was her brief, rage-filled display, which, of course, made her look like nothing short of Medea.

"Turn it off," she mumbled, as she closed her eyes and started to rub her temples...

"Unbelievable," Grace said, through her unwavering grin.

"Turn it off, please."

"s'my TV. You don't wana' watch, you can go – "

"No, I don't want this on. Change the channel or turn it off."

"Hell, no!"

Peggy stood angrily, "Are you getting some sort of pleasure from this? Do you really wana' watch this while I'm standing right here?"

"Then go upstairs, n'I'll watch it while you're *there*, okay?!"

"They will probably re-run this forever, and you can watch it ad nauseum when I'm not here. I'm asking that while I *am* here, you show me some respect and turn this off in my presence. That isn't asking – "

"Show *you* some respect!" this made Grace abruptly sit up, as Little Pearl lifted her sleeping head off her lap, "*You* came back. *You* came because you needed somethin' from me, and I didn't have to give you shit."

"It really isn't that big of you, you know?! I'm your daughter!"

"I don't know who the hell you are! I haven't known since you decided to kick me to the curb. See, it all comes back, don't it. You thought you could just cast me aside like old weeds, right?"

"That is not – "

"Well, look how it all turned out, missy. You get your life fucked over by him, and y'come crawlin' back to me. And then you think you can deny me the satisfaction a' seein' his comeuppance?"

"To you this is morbid fascination like everyone else who watches this crap!"

"So what if it is?!"

"IT'S NOT THAT WAY TO ME!" Little Pearl began to growl, but it wasn't yet heard by Peggy... "YOU ARE WATCHING MY FUCKING LIFE! AND I DIDN'T ASK FOR IT! AND I DIDN'T DESERVE IT! I HAD EVERY RIGHT TO NOT THINK MY HUSBAND WOULD DESTROY OUR FAMILY, BUT HE DID!"

Little Pearl began rising and growling more intensely at Peggy the more she raised her voice and inched closer to Grace...

"AND YOU KNOW AS WELL AS I DO THAT YOU HATED HIM ANYWAY!"

The growl was getting even louder...

"REGARDLESS OF WHAT HE'S BECOME, YOU WOULD'VE STILL TRIED TO FUCKING POISON HIM!"

Grace sharply rose as Little Pearl jumped off the couch towards Peggy, but Peggy's rage was without precedent, and without a second guess, she jutted her face out toward the approaching beast and regurgitated the most violently primal scream imaginable, "AAAAAAAAAAAAAAAAAAAAHHHH-HHHHHHHHHHHHHHHHHHHHHHHH!!!!" which, much to the surprise of Grace, would halt Little Pearl in her tracks,...before she would recede under the glass table.

At least for the moment, Peggy was a pack leader, and Little Pearl was hollered into submission.

But even her considerable anger could not overlook this turn of events, as she looked at the dog through the glass, then up at Grace, who looked down at the dog, before looking back up at Peggy, momentarily speechless.

They continued to stare at each other, before Peggy decided it was as good a time as any to exit back upstairs and make sure the kids didn't see the episode. As she stormed up, she could sense that Grace was still frozen in place, as was Little Pearl – a most pleasing immobility she had rendered on them both, as the closing music came on...and the credits rolled.

29

First thing the next morning, Peggy called Jane Madden:

"Read what you signed, Peggy," she spewed.

"I didn't authorize anything, Jane. If you didn't have me, you shouldn't've been able to do anything with my story."

"No, that's actually the opposite of true. Your release pertained to your own performance and not to the story. And you did sign that release which, I might add, you violated."

"I didn't violate shit, Jane! You can't take a person's life like that and just create your own story."

"Our story *was* the story."

"It was *your* story!"

"Peggy, listen to me. What we aired is all on record. Those were actual patients, actual doctors and actual local journalists who reported on this. They gave of their time to provide us everything you saw last night. Now this might not've been the story you expected us to tell, and perhaps it would have had more nuance had you elected to fulfill your agreement, but you didn't."

"Oh, didn't I? What about the surveillance footage you used? What the hell was that?!"

"Those were *our* surveillance cameras, and we had every right to use the footage if we thought it was pertinent to the story – "

"What are you calling pertinent? Making me out to look like Lady Macbeth?"

"Like who?"

"Jesus Christ…! She's the wife of *Macbeth*!"

"Peggy, please..."

"Please what? I'm lucky my kids didn't see this! You're a Goddamn thief!"

"Then sue me and see if you have a leg to stand on, Peggy. Everything we did is in writing. Just look at what you signed. Now I don't know what else to tell you. The episode has aired, and we can't turn back time. Nor will we remove it from syndication. This may have been something that you lived through, and I'm sorry about that, but it's our episode and that's that."

Peggy sat with this, stewing in her anger, though realizing the fruitlessness of speaking to a party that clearly was not going to do anything to benefit her, especially since the show had gotten all that it needed to make this one of the more memorable episodes of *American Sleaze*. The only consolation was that the kids had no idea, at least for now. And thank God they weren't visible in the episode.

"So that's that," she said defeatedly under her breath.

At this point, Jane was void of her defensive tone, and said something that, surprisingly, sounded almost sincere; "You wana' tell the story that *you* want to tell? Well, then I suggest you tell it. But you can't do it on TV for a year. Remember. That's also in writing."

Peggy remained, now speechless, as Jane seemed to be leaving it to her to end the call. Peggy tried to think of something, as she looked over at her opened spiral pad on her tiny desk, but realized it would all just be wasted words,...

"Okay, Peggy?" Jane asked, surprisingly delicate.

Peggy clicked off, not wanting to give Jane the satisfaction of a proper goodbye. As far as she was concerned, Jane was just another person she had hoped to never see again in her lifetime.

She sat back down on the bed and gazed out at the boring street as snow started to descend again. As always, she tried to see it with the same pleasure as she did as a young girl, but it was getting more difficult every time it happened now. It was harder to go to those memories embedded deep in her brain while more bad news of the present was piled atop it. She wasn't sure if Vic and Elaine caught last night's airing, since Vic had once even mentioned watching *American Sleaze*. If they did, she wondered if they would have reached out, given the tension now between them, but she also didn't particularly care if they saw it or even what they thought, as long as they didn't reveal anything to the kids.

A beep momentarily intervened with her trance, as she looked down at her phone to see that a voice mail message had been left. She didn't recognize the number, and could not conceive that it would be a school calling for another substitute job, especially after last night's debacle. *Not everyone watches this stuff, but many do,* she thought.

The world is large…until it's not.

As Peggy laid back on the bed, still in her nightgown, she heard the requisite *"Alright, alright"* from Grace as she slid the glass door open for Little Pearl to take her usual morning shit out back. Apparently her explosion at both of them last night was not enough to deter their normal routine. She'd hear Grace's tapping slippers make their way to the kitchen where she would proceed to make her usual breakfast; Cinnamon Life cereal, toast and instant coffee. She didn't know the kind of reception she would receive from Grace now. They had already existed on very few words until Peggy's television debut that evening. No words would actually be preferred now.

She had acted out with her mother as a teenager, but it was the first time she as an adult had asserted herself in such a way. It was unsettling. She didn't know if her mother would insist she leave or would just clam up and act as if nothing had ever happened, out of pride or some such thing. Or perhaps she would react another way. Even all these years later, she never put anything past her mother. When she was 16, she remembered coming home with her friend, Jodie Frick. It was the rare time Peggy brought a friend home after school, and to do nothing more than listen to music. At that age, it was not uncommon for musical taste to be a source of bonding between friends, and so Peggy was eager to initiate Jodie into the world of The Go-Gos and Blondie. This was the mid-90s, so these were groups considered prehistoric to kids of Peggy and Jodie's age, but Peggy always gravitated to older tastes; older music, older books, older films. It was part of why it was not as easy for her to assimilate in school, since she was often averse to current trends.

It also didn't help that she was not encouraged to bring friends home, for Grace hated feeling encumbered in any way. When she came home from working at the nursing home, it was usually all she could do to simply grunt, let alone converse. And this would be a particularly distressing day, as Grace would be defecated on by two nursing home residents. She saw a lot of grotesque things over the many years, but odds are probably good that, at that point, she hadn't had the honor of being christened by two dementia patients.

She remembered Grace coming home from work particularly angered and, on such occasions, would often relish the opportunity to slam pots onto the stove and shut the cabinets with a ferocity that would kick up the dust to the ceiling lights. Upon hearing the Go-Gos "Our Lips are Sealed" bleeding through Peggy's bedroom door while Peggy and Jodie euphorically sang to it, she remembered Grace yelling, "LOWER THAT SHIT, GODDAMNIT!"

It was clear to Peggy that she wouldn't have been as ferocious had she not heard another girl's voice. If she had any doubt, Grace would assure her. Peggy lowered the music, and this time, they were both too afraid to sing along. And yet, within minutes, even with the volume at half, there would be a harsh bang on the door from a hoisted frying pan that Grace managed to hurl from downstairs, "I SAID LOWER THAT SHIT, MARGARET!!!"

Those would also be the times where Grace would spew out Peggy's legal first name like acid. It would also be the last time she would have anyone over. That is, until she brought Mike years later. And to say that that didn't go well would be the understatement of the century.

Later that night, after Jodie had left, Peggy took the opportunity to admonish Grace for scaring off her new friend who, in all likelihood, would tell others of the monster that her mother was. Even then, she used words that Grace probably didn't even know the meaning of, but her strident hostility was more than enough to set Grace over the top. She remembered Grace rising, picking up a nearby aluminum bat she kept under the old couch, mainly because there were some break-ins around the neighborhood at that time, before charging at Peggy, "You think you can talk that way to me, you little bitch?!"

Peggy's indignance had quickly evaporated into fear, as she ran to the stairs, "I PAY FOR THE ROOF OVER YOUR HEAD! I PAY FOR YOUR FOOD! I GAVE YOU FUCKING LIFE, LITTLE GIRL, AND YOU WANA' SASS ME 'CAUSE I DIDN'T LET YOU PLAY WITH YOUR LITTLE FRIEND, AFTER I WAS SHIT'N PISSED ON ALL DAY BY UNGRATEFUL OL' CROWS, YOU FUCKIN' LITTLE BITCH!..."

As Peggy went for the steps, Grace hoisted the bat which landed right in front of her path and banged off the railing, instantly forcing Peggy to change her route, the only other one being out the front door, into the cold, icy December night. She kept running in her socks, while looking back to make sure that Grace wasn't still on her tail. Once she got far enough, she resigned that she simply needed to hide out, with her cold, wet feet. She thought of going to a friend's house who lived within a couple of blocks, but was embarrassed to show up in socks, and so she elected to bide time by the nearby electrical plant, shivering, until enough hours had elapsed when she thought it was safe to return home. She even remembered being in bed that night, with frostbitten feet, thinking that Grace would barge in, or try and suffocate her in her sleep. She had never tried to actually kill Peggy before, but now Peggy started to see that those possibilities were in the air, especially as she was getting older.

As per usual, Peggy would try and avoid Grace this morning. She'd shower while Grace watched her morning shows, and then finally gained the stamina to listen to her voicemail message back in her room and brace for what it would reveal. A somewhat affected, stammering male voice came on:

"Hello. This is for Mrs. Bu- I'm sorry, Mrs. Bubone. My name is Randall Kismin, and I'm with Bloom Publishing. I was actually interested in speaking with you to discuss the possibility of ... Well, of your experiences as it relates to... Well, I should say that I happened to be informed of your story, and thought it would be of interest to us, as we are trying to branch out a bit as a company. I'm sorry, I know this is a very crude message, but it'll be much easier to explain what we're proposing if we can speak directly. In any event, please do call me. My direct number is..."

The man sounded like Dick Cavett, the talk show host who Peggy had seen in re-runs. The voice was obviously intelligent, maybe too much so for Peggy. There was a strong sense that it was all this man could do to make this call, given that Bloom Publishing, upon her quick internet research, had predominately published romance novels and reprints of certain classics. She actually didn't see anything in their catalogue that would resemble crime books or anything remotely in the topical, mind-numbing genre. She honestly didn't know what to think, other than that this was, perhaps, a less soul-sucking opportunity for her to make some money, get her car out of the shop and get the hell out of this house.

The next day, Peggy found herself back on the train to New York City to meet with Randall Kismin, chief editor

and founder of Bloom. Their brief conversation the previous afternoon did little to shed much light on his or Bloom's
intent, as Kismin wanted the opportunity of meeting with
Peggy in person. What was covered was that he was "informed" of her story, but was clandestine on if the source was
the previous night's airing of *American Sleaze*. It struck Peggy
that a man of Kismin's seeming intellect would probably not
want to divulge that he personally watched such programming or that he would ever consider any subject presented on
the show to be worthy of their publishing it. Still, as with
every trip to New York City, whether it was to meet with Jane
Madden or Tina or, now, Randall Kismin, there was a similarly
disturbing twinge in her stomach. She felt vulnerable in every
encounter with someone new or, in Tina's case, someone she
hadn't seen in years.

With regards to Tina, Peggy had thought she would
finally respond back. She had admittedly put it off after their
get together in late January. Her affrontery at Tina's suggestion of using her recent life's events as creative inspiration
eventually developed into embarrassment. Now it had been
more than a couple of weeks, and, for all she knew, Tina
may've given up. Peggy thought she'd send her a text on
her way into the city and propose getting a bite, if Tina was
free, but she also had no idea what this meeting with Randall
Kismin would lead to. She feared, afterwards, that a further
sense of dejection would only put her in an increasingly fragile
state. For now, she left well enough alone and tried to focus
on having what seemed like the first in-person meeting with
someone that wouldn't end in disaster.

Again, she would be in midtown, as she entered the mar-
ble-walled lobby, before heading up to the 16th floor. It surprised her how small their offices were, especially considering that Bloom was a fairly known publisher. Randall came
out, looking not unlike how she thought he would look; thin,
white, with a brown suit and bookish bow-tie. It made it all
the more absurd that someone who looked like he slept on a

boxspring of Dickens novels would call her in to discuss her soiled life.

A few minutes into their meeting in his office, wherein Randall's nearly identical assistant, James, sat nearby taking notes, Randall would become more revealing as to the intent, "So our company, as you may or may not know, has been around for some time. Almost 50 years is it, James?"

James did a quick search on his phone to confirm this, "49, actually."

"Very good," he haughtily laughed. "So there you have it: 49. And, well, I don't know how much you know about what we've been known for putting out, heretofore. Our mission, per se."

"Well, I've researched a bit. So I'm familiar – "

"Very good. So you're aware that, heretofore, we've committed ourselves to more..., how can I say this, distinguished fare, if you will. This is not to...diminish why we're interested in yourself, of course. By that, I'm speaking in terms of genre."

"I...yes, I understand," she tepidly responded.

"Yes, and so, well, to put it bluntly, Mrs. Bubone, the economics of modern publishing has, in recent years, been steadily forcing our hand, if you will, to where we are now. Which is to offer more...universal subjects that may appeal to...shall we say, a greater facet of consumers. In short, we're trying to broaden our commercial appeal, if you will. And so our reaching out to you is as a result of finding your story, or, I should say, the story of your experience. That is to say, you appear to be the best source by which a story like yours can be told from, perhaps, a more objective perspective. I don't want to impose my assumption on what you feel, and your feelings towards your husband. But it struck us that the perspective of the actual, or alleged, felon, if you will, might be less interesting than someone who was/is, presumably, close to that... felon, if you will, and, thus, it may make for a more interesting narrative."

He concluded with a slight grin, finally yielding the floor to Peggy.

"So you want to turn this into a book, then."

He and James shared a guffaw, which Peggy awkwardly observed, "Yes, after all of my verbosity, you can certainly say that. And thank you for your indulgence."

"No, I appreciate you – "

"Now we have an excellent writer whom we feel can work with you and allow you great comfort. You can speak by phone, if that works best, or by Zoom or Skype or whatever means is convenient for you. But we are prepared to - "

"Wait a second. What do you mean, exactly? A writer?"

"Well, yes. A book needs to be written and we need to have writers to write them, of course," he said with playful haughtiness.

"No, I'm... I was under the impression that if you were interested in a book about this, that, of course, I would write it."

"Well,... I'm sorry that that wasn't clear, but – "

"No, no, no, please. I... This would have to be something that I would write. There's just no other way I would want to do this."

Randall looked over at James, as if bracing themselves for a display, before coming back to Peggy with a widened smile, "Mrs. Bubone, we contacted you as a subject. Not as a writer. You see, we don't know you as a writer. We don't know if you can write."

"Well, I *am* a writer," she spit out, with surprising force.

"You are?" he responded, incredulously.

"Well, ye... I mean,... My God, you contacted me as a subject, but you don't know anything about me. And you don't know anything about me because you wanted me to just give sordid details to a stranger so that you can make some cheap sales?"

"Mrs. Bubone, please, we don't want to make this contentious. We simply wanted to offer this opportunity."

"But who's opportunity?"

Randall looked again at James, both seeming to not expect to be thrown.

"This is my life, okay?"

"I understa – "

"No, you don't have a clue, Mr. Kismin. I have lived this!"

"Mrs. Bubone – "

"I won a scholarship to fucking Princeton, okay? Was that in that episode you saw of *American Sleaze*? Of course not. I majored in Literature. Was that? Of course not. I wrote stories and poetry. And then I taught while working as a secretary to help put my husband through dermatology school, and then I got pregnant. What timing, right? I got pregnant and he finished school in time to start a practice and, for the last 13 years, I was a wife and mother. I was the hostess of our family. And I thought I was happy. And I thought I had everything, but I didn't. I had sold myself, and deluded myself to think that I didn't. I had just gotten back into teaching, just got back to having a sense of myself as an individual, and with one knock on my door, my life changed. Everything was on its head. My kids and I have been homeless. Living out of hotels, motels, living with friends who I can't even call friends anymore... Now I'm living with my mother who I hadn't seen hide nor hair from in 17 years. A woman I despise, and yet there I am in my tiny bedroom, with my little rolltop desk, staring at the snow and writing poetry, and trying to avoid her for fear that she may actually kill me in my sleep, if I don't kill her first. Trying to keep stimulated, while my kids are in Florida with my in-laws who actually wana' blame me for all this. Then I get an offer to sell my life to that show, and I couldn't lower myself. Couldn't bring myself to be a talking head in my own life, and look at what they did. They say two words about me and then use surveillance of me having a meltdown, which is probably why you think I can't even put two words together, right?"

Much to her surprise, she was now on her feet, as Randall

and James gazed at her, speechless, even a tad fearful, as she continued, "Well, have *these* words been enough to tell you that no one can write this but me? Because, Mr. Kismin, I have news for you; no one WILL write this – but me."

Had this been an audition for the Drama department at Juilliard, she thought she may have had a shot, but as an inadvertent endorsement of herself as a writer, she felt otherwise. Still, there was some sort of catharsis in just getting it out. She felt strong compared to these two bowtie-wearing dorks, even if the decision lay with them. She almost didn't care what this resulted in. It all felt justified, like a healthy purging after a poisonous meal.

The silence hung for what seemed like eons, before Randall adjusted his tie, looked at James, then back at Peggy, "Mrs. Bubone, thank...thank you, for...that. Um, I wonder if you would allow James and I to speak a moment. There's some coffee and water outside, if you wouldn't mind waiting there for a few minutes."

His weak grin conveyed to Peggy that there would be little reason for her to return to the room once she left, but she did so anyway, and without a word.

She sat in the waiting area and watched the office manager across the floor typing into her computer, next to her was a coffee machine and a water cooler. Coffee was the last thing she needed, while her blood was still percolating from her display, but she'd have a cup of water to calm down. Upon looking over the front desk, she spotted a paperback book, *Indecent Offerings*. It was, ironically, the kind of crap crime book that Bloom hadn't thus far dared to publish. Peggy could always tell the legitimacy of a book by the shininess of its cover. Bad romance or crime novels often appeared to have bright red, gold or silver covers, just to stick out. Whereas you'd actually need to search for anything that was good. If nothing else, it made her realize that the audience was out there for this type of book and so, even though it belied Bloom's mission to publish such work, she understood why they would feel the need to concede and yield to the greater masses. But, if given the chance, hers would be better, she thought. The ambition would at least be greater. She would strive for real depth and not mere sensationalism.

"Mrs. Bubone?" summoned James. Peggy looked at him, as he smiled, then lifted his hand towards Randall's office, "Please come in."

She was nervous again. *Rejection never gets easier*, she thought, and she now felt it would have been best if she just kept walking out the door and into the street,...but she felt a greater force leading her back into the office.

"Well, Mrs. Bubone," Randall began, "James and I have spoken," he looked at James, then back at Peggy, "and...I think this can work."

She sat with this, not knowing exactly what he was referring to, "*What* can work?"

Randall suddenly smiled, as did James, "Well, in so many words,...we're actually willing to let you write this."

A different sort of deafness came to her ears. Not the usual whistle that accompanied trauma that she had grown so accustomed to. This was like a sudden but pleasant death, like a volume knob was turned off but she could still see. With the lack of sound, it somehow felt like the speed of the world stopped and, for the first time, there was a semblance of light bleeding through a dark tunnel she had been within for months.

She opened her mouth, not expecting to be heard, "I'm... Well, that's... O...okay..."

Randall looked at James again, then back at Peggy, then awkwardly resumed, "So...normally what we do, in such instances of acquiring a new writer, is to request an outline of what they see as the arc of the book. But, since you pretty much gave us that already with your...rather intensely galvanizing speech," again looking at James, then back at Peggy, "I think we have what we need, for the moment."

In that moment, Peggy realized that what she managed

to expel was not merely a defense of herself as being a capable writer or venting about all that she had undergone; it was, in fact, the book that she didn't even know she wanted to write. Actually, she still wasn't sure, but she realized that what she told them was not solely about victimization, nor was it even about Mike. It was *her* story. And that seemed to be what they were interested in, except even *they* didn't know it until she enlightened them.

For the first time, Peggy's unhinged emotions appeared to be of benefit to her. Now there was suddenly a chance for some sort of vindication.

About two hours later, Peggy stepped out onto the sidewalk with a feeling of nervous exhilaration. She had actually signed a deal with Bloom that morning, and would receive an advance of $15,000 over three installments; $5,000 upon signing, then $5,000 for delivering a completed manuscript (within one year) and then another $5,000 when it was actually published. This meant that this would be all the money she would receive until the book sold over the advance total. Thereafter, she would receive royalties. Despite the fact that they had once owned paintings and sculptures valued at so much more as a result of Mike's unbridled spending, being offered $15,000, especially considering how impoverished she had been living, was more than acceptable to Peggy. More so because it was not $15,000 for her to sell her soul; it was $15,000 for her to write, for her to tell *her* story with a significant amount of creative freedom. In other words, it didn't need to be salacious. It didn't need to be the surface aspects of her recent experience.

Perhaps they'll even give it a respectable cover, as opposed to the bright red or gold or silver ones that screamed for the attention of the inane.

But she knew she was getting ahead of herself. She wanted to just be in this moment of feeling respected. She didn't want to feel like she fooled them or bullied two waif thin men into a deal. They could've just as easily called security. *But they didn't.* Somehow, they were sold on this. Now she had to write it. And as she knew from experiences of the past, beginnings were daunting. So daunting that they often led to the death of past stories she thought she wanted to tell.

She felt this moment was too good to spoil by rushing back to Kelp Stream. And she couldn't think of anyone better to share this with than Tina, especially while she was in the city.

She called Tina, assuming she'd get her voicemail but, to her surprise, she picked up, having a shortened day at Hunter College. It had been about 3 weeks since they had lunch, and since they'd even spoken, but Peggy was pleased to feel that Tina was pleased to hear from her. Within a matter of a couple of hours, she was experiencing true joy; a book deal with money on the way, and an old, dear friend whom she could share this with.

Since Tina was already at home, Peggy had little issue with taking a cab up to her place, and, since it was almost lunch time, even brought bagels and cookies from *Zabar's*; certainly not exorbitant accoutrements for a celebration, but serviceable.

"Do you believe it?" as she excitably took a bite from her cinnamon raisin bagel.

"That's wonderful, Peg," Tina still taking it in.

"I mean, Tina, I went there not knowing what was gonna' happen. I mean, anytime I took the train in, I felt like I was preparing to give away pieces of myself."

"That's unbelievable."

"It is. I mean, you don't know. Between seeing that awful episode, staying with my mother... It was... I didn't know what else could happen."

"Well, I guess *this* did, huh?" Tina asked rhetorically, with a smile.

"Right? I mean, God, how nice to get some *good* news for a change," she took another bite, her emotions still getting the better of her, but at least they were positive ones for a change...

"It's wonderful. I'm so happy for you."

"Thanks, Tina. I appreciate that."

Peggy gorged, as Tina observed her supplementing her sudden euphoria with carbs...

"So...what now?"

"Well, they're going to directly deposit the first install-ment in a few days, so I'll finally be able to get my car out of the shop. My God, it's been sitting there for weeks."

"Sure. Good idea."

"You're not eating. Eat, Tina. Please."

"Oh, I will, thanks," Tina didn't appear to have much of an appetite for the pumpernickel bagel with butter in front of her, and seemed to be filling up on Peggy's enthusiasm. "So... how much are you getting?"

Peggy sipped her coffee, "The advance?"

"You don't have to tell me. Just curious."

"No, I'll tell you."

"You don't have to, Peg – "

"You asked. I'll tell you. I'm getting fifteen."

Peggy resumed eating, smiling, but not wanting to let that figure sit in the air so as to give Tina the impression that she was gloating. Still, Tina looked surprised.

"Thousand?"

"Yeah."

"That's... Gee, Peg."

"Well, not all at once. It's over three installments, but - ."

"Still, that's..."

At this point, Peggy could not help but pick up on the fact that Tina now needed to lean back in her chair to absorb this.

"Are you okay?" Peggy asked.

"Yeah, I'm... They gave you a $15,000 advance?"

Peggy was almost afraid to confirm this. She resisted her tendency of the past, particularly when she would be among her old, fair weather friends, Judy, Gwen and Claire, of speaking too proudly about her teaching, especially since they never seemed to really appreciate her stories anyway. It was barely a three month window she had then to speak about any career, and felt compelled to boast. But being significantly humbled had made her wary of giving off the slightest hint of superiority to Tina. It was clear in Tina's reaction that she may have won some grants and contests, but this appeared to be a different level of acknowledgement.

"I'm sorry, Peggy, that's just... I mean, it's wonderful for you. I mean, considering how you left here, I know...you needed a boost. I certainly wanted to help, but...you didn't seem to want to hear from me."

"Well, I... It wasn't so much you, Tina. It was me, I guess."

"I mean, did you forget that I actually suggested that you write about this?"

Peggy placed her bagel down on her plate, her appetite gradually waning, "I... No, I didn't, Tina."

"I just think it's funny, right? You get insulted that I mention it. Then ostensibly blow me off, then call me out of the blue to tell me you scored this big deal."

"Tina, I was planning to call you anyway, regardless of what happened today."

"I mean, I've been writing my whole life, Peggy."

"Yes, I know – "

"My whole life, awards, ribbons, publications, and it's all been barely enough to pay 6 months rent for an apartment in Chicago, let alone New York. You have a kanipshin fit on TV, and get a book deal."

"Tina, listen, I'm sorry, okay? I'm sorry I brought up the

money. You asked. And it's not like I'm getting it all at once. They – "

"It's not just that, Peggy."

"Then what is it?"

"It's a real publishing house. I mean, they won't just put out the book. They promote it. It's all about money to them. Why do you think they even contacted you? You think they're looking for great literature? No, you know better than me that they want you to write some sordid shit that's an easy sell – and it probably will. And I'm thrilled that it will, Peggy. For you, I'm thrilled."

"*This* is thrilled?"

"I am. I am genuinely thrilled for you. But I'm also aghast at how people fall ass-backwards into fame in this business."

"What are you talking about? You think I fell ass backwards into fame? I was thrust into infamy, Tina."

"Right, 'cause you married a felon."

In an instant, this was starting to sound like a far more literate exchange with her mother. Whereas Grace was filled with resentment and bitterness, Tina now appeared overcome with jealousy.

"Tina,...look,...I was planning to contact you, and I'm sorry I waited so long. Maybe I just needed to be on better footing before I could see you again. I mean, it was very hard to come here and see that you've been doing what you always wanted to do. I haven't had that. But...I shouldn't be made to feel bad for having some good fortune, okay? I shouldn't be made to feel like a reality TV star. You know I can write. You knew it then. You just don't know it now, because...I haven't written. I mean, I started writing some poetry and... But this is different. And, yeah, I'm scared. I'm scared to death, okay? I don't know how the hell I'm gonna' begin this. I don't know if I can. I'm just trying to savor this moment and...I really did want to share it with you."

Tina stood throughout, looking at the carpet, not quite

sure how to respond. Peggy waited for a movement or a word, but it was becoming awkward, to the point where she realized she should leave. She grabbed her purse and coat, stopped to look at Tina again, who remained still,...and then went to the door.

"Peggy, I wish you the best with it, okay?"

She turned around to see Tina still in place, with her back to her. It felt like it was all she could summon to send Peggy off with a hollow well wish and, for the moment, Peggy couldn't really expect more from her. But she also didn't have the energy to indulge her. She couldn't feel guilty anymore.

She just needed to write this book.

30

She got a taxi from the train station and had the driver stop off at Mrs. Prager's store. She didn't really need anything, but felt she needed to see her before arriving home. The positivity that had been suddenly brimming within Peggy was fading as a result of her deflating lunch with Tina. She immediately approached the counter but didn't see anybody. Instantly, she started to get an unsettling feeling.

"Uh... Anybody...? Mrs. Prager?!"

Peggy waited and looked around. There were no customers and no sounds of anyone approaching. She looked through the few aisles, just to make sure no one was there.

She then heard a young man's voice, "Yes? Can I help you?!"

She jutted her head out of the aisle to find a teenaged boy behind the counter.

"Uh, yeah, hi."

"Sorry. I was out back. Can I help you?"

Apparently, he'd been smoking, judging by the pack in the pocket of his flannel shirt.

"That's okay. I... I'm... I actually just stopped by to see how Mrs. Prager was."

"Oh. Sorry. She died," he said.

"Oh. No, that's... Oh my God..." Peggy wasn't as prepared as she had hoped to hear such news, before she delicately asked, "Are...are you her grandson?"

"No, I'm a friend of her granddaughter. They needed to make arrangements'n stuff, so I'm just sorta' helpin' out, for the time being."

"I see."

She looked at him, then took in the store around her. It was clear that the young man was trying to be respectful, and assumed Peggy was an old friend of sorts, but he seemed ill-equipped to provide a bedside manner. She came back to him, now as if in a trance, "Was she...? When did this happen?"

"A coupla' nights ago. She went into a coma and then died pretty quickly, they said. At least she wasn't in pain, y'know?"

She looked at him, "Do you know that?"

"Know...?"

"Know if she wasn't in pain?"

"Uh, no, but...I mean, it was quick. She didn't, y'know, she wasn't suffering."

Peggy knew she was asking him more than he was naturally able to provide. It almost felt like she was talking to Nicky in three years. He looked at her now, leery of where else Peggy would go with her emotional questioning of Mrs. Prager's last days. She looked back around the store, with unexpected nostalgia for her past, "I... I used to come in here as a girl. Up until I was around your age, I guess. Her and her husband were such nice people. I'd... I'd been away for a long time, and just came back. And it was...it was so nice to see her."

She continued gazing across the store at nothing in particular, as the young man looked at her. Then under her breath, "7-Up and Bubble Yum." She smiled, though by now she had shed some tears. The young man handed her a few nearby napkins, which she blew her nose with. She touched the counter, "Thank you," then slowly left,...unsure if she could return.

Snow had started to fall again as she arrived home. She

was solemn as she closed the door, feeling guilty of even thinking about the most positive aspect of this day. Between her exchange with Tina and the news regarding Mrs. Prager, the good news felt increasingly remote. As usual, she heard the TV blaring instantly upon her entrance. It was late afternoon, and Grace was watching Trial TV reruns of the 1995 OJ Simpson trial; "*Officer Fuhrman, have you ever used a racial epithet?*" blared during a cross examination. She looked into the living room and saw Grace in her usual position, with Little Pearl beside her, oblivious to the falling snow in the back yard.

There had still been no words exchanged between them since two nights ago, when Peggy howled at both her mother and Little Pearl, which only made the tension in the house that much more palpable. Still, she felt that it was worth breaking the silence to tell her the news:

"Mrs. Prager passed away."

Grace sat there, not hearing Peggy due to the volume.

"I said Mrs. Prager – "

Grace suddenly muted the television, then looked over at Peggy, intensely, "What?"

She repeated, only slightly louder, "I said Mrs. Prager passed away."

Grace turned back to the set, looked at it a moment, then softly, "When?"

"The kid at the store said a couple of days ago. She was... in a coma and then she..."

Grace was never one to react in a typical fashion to death. She had lived with death as a nurse for much of her adult life, and perhaps was best suited for it because of her emotional detachment. She had gone into that store for decades and probably never said more than a few words to Mrs. Prager; something which even Mrs. Prager couldn't help but note to Peggy upon their reuniting. She watched Grace sit with this, unsure if she was actually pondering anything.

"Well,...she was a nice lady," Peggy followed.

Grace kept the television on mute and continued staring at it. Peggy still couldn't decipher if Grace was just waiting for her to exit or if she was in silent mourning; perhaps even ruing a relationship that could have become something more over 40-plus years than the mere exchange of product and money. As she continued to watch Grace, she tried to recall a time where she had seen her mother exhibit even *this* much in the way of possible reflection. It certainly was not when Peggy's grandmother passed, Grace's own mother. Theirs was a relationship that swung from tolerance to unbridled contention almost at will. There were many patches of them not speaking over the years, but somehow they were more often tethered by a sort of toxic adhesive.

She then remembered when they had to put her childhood pooch Wojo to sleep, whose kidneys were failing him. On the drive home from the vet, Peggy, then 17, was all but a waterfall of tears, while Grace stared ahead. At first, Peggy wondered how Grace could say nothing, when she knew how much Grace adored Wojo. But then, she noticed an odd glistening in her mother's right tear duct. It was odd because no such emittance had appeared there before, at least to Peggy's eyes. Upon a second glance over at Grace just moments later, it was gone. She then questioned if it was ever there, but wanted to believe that it was. If it was, this would be the closest her mother would ever come to a display of grief.

"Anything else?" Grace now asked, softly but gruffly, as she continued to gaze at the silent television.

Peggy was deflated by this response, even as she expected it. She was about to walk up the stairs to her room, but then stopped, "Uh, yeah. I'm... I have a work opportunity and...I'm going to get a little advance so, once I do, I'm gonna' get the car out and look for a place. So...I just wanted to let you know. Okay?"

Her mother remained, gazing at the muted TV. Again, Peggy was unsure what was going on inside her head; *is she just waiting for me to finish and leave or...?* And, in truth, Peggy would not have enough to keep an apartment after the payment for the car. She would still need to look for teaching work. Of course, the quicker she could complete a manuscript would speed up the time to receive her next installment, but she could barely envision starting it let alone finishing it at this point. The only logical thing for her, given her desperation to be out of the house, was to get the car and stay at a cheap motel somewhere out of town. At least she would be some sort of a distance away, and have a semblance of pride returned to her after it being on respite for so long.

The moment continued to sit, as Little Pearl raised her head, having caught sight of the snow that was now falling as if dumped from the sky by giant buckets.

"It's snowing. You may want to let her out," as she exited up the stairs. After a couple of minutes behind the closed door of her room, she was at least happy to hear the slap of the sliding glass door. She then looked out the window and extended herself to see the portion of the backyard where Little Pearl was gleefully jumping to eat the falling snow.

The next morning, Peggy woke up to the most massive blizzard she could ever recall experiencing. It was so white and windy outside, that it looked as if the neighborhood had all but been erased overnight. The snow accumulation was already almost 3 feet and steadily growing, and the primal screaming gusts led her to believe that this was not going to end anytime soon. It was only about 7:30, which meant Grace was asleep. Knowing this, Peggy headed down the steps and into the living room. The light that normally would come into the house at this time was noticeably blocked by the mounting snow.

She checked the weather forecast on her phone, which was now buzzing with alerts. A text came in, *"This is a message from the National Weather Center. A severe nor'easter is making its way up from the Atlantic through the southern New Jersey Area.*

The governor has declared this a state of emergency and is ordering all residents in the following counties, with the exception of law enforcement and emergency workers, to remain inside..." It now looked as though, even with the money soon being directly deposited into her account, she was not going anywhere for the next few days.

She sat on the end of her bed, the gusts in a constant stream along with the ferocious clangs of street signs being hoisted like javelins. There was the distant sound of a struggling car, its wheels spinning ad nauseum. There was shoveling as well, though at this point, it was like trying to cure a leaking battleship with a band-aid. While much of her life in the last few months could be said to have been a bit more than unpredictable, she hadn't foreseen being literally trapped in her childhood home. The plan was that, once she obtained some money, she would get the car, move to a motel and then, ideally, begin her book. It didn't seem possible that she could write it, let alone begin, in this room – *in this house.* Little haikus and poems were one thing, but this environment could not be remotely ideal for a much lengthier work.

I mean, there's just no way.

She laid back down, gazed up at Sylvia's eyes and, before she knew it, it was 9am by the sound of Grace and Little Pearl; the whining, the tinkling, then the clomping foot steps down the stairs. Soon after, "Holy fuckin' shit!" from Grace would change the trajectory of the morning routine. Peggy had no idea what the plan of action would be as far as how Little Pearl was going to relieve herself, considering the house was now within walls of snow, but it wasn't her concern.

She sat at her rolltop desk and glanced at her spiral notebook. She figured that, when she would begin, she would try to do as she had done back in college; start with longhand and then type it up. However, that seemed to make this all the more daunting. Again, little poems were easy to jot down. A book needed momentum. She wondered what would happen if her mind and creativity couldn't keep up with her handwriting. Perhaps she would just type and save herself the trouble of transcribing.

The contract with Bloom stipulated that they should have a manuscript in 12 months for review, if not sooner. And while Peggy understood what a complete book's length of this genre should be, it frightened her to look up a mountain of unwritten pages; *what if I can't do this? Oh, dear God, I can't do this!*

The doubt was creeping in, certainly not eased by being snowbound in her tiny room with howling winds and metal garbage cans flying into the street. By early afternoon, her anxiety had become overwhelming. She felt as if she were living out an Edgar Allan Poe short story, the way that ambient sounds would start to rattle the protagonists, particularly in *The Tell-Tale Heart.* The winds continued, the snow was falling horizontally, the TV blasted from downstairs, the dog kept barking at the gale force winds which had begun to sound like coyote wails.

She looked at her phone for the distraction of a message, but there was nothing. No texts from Tina, no one in Florida checking in. Admittedly, the kids were in school and likely had no idea of the inclement weather ransacking the north east. Vic and Elaine may or may not have heard or saw a national weather report, but she didn't want nor expect to hear from them anyway. She gazed out the window and realized that if she wanted to smoke, she would need to lean out of her window and, thus, risk being decapitated by a flying stop sign.

The hours of the day went by with Peggy rotating between gawking at the blank page on her computer and lying in bed, practically clenching her body for just a few opening sentences. She had roughly scrawled what she remembered telling Randall and James at Bloom, in the hopes that her inadvertent pitch would give her the focus she needed to begin. *What is this book ultimately going to be about?* Yes, it would be her perspective, how her life was affected by the actions of her husband. That was the most obvious. But it also would be about how she managed to return to her childhood home.

And, maybe, why she left to begin with. And how all her efforts to become everything her mother wasn't ultimately led her to something else – something she never really strived to be, but became anyway. Was there something in Mike that was just a safer route? Was he the missing father figure, as psychologists have so often written about?

Sitting with all of these questions did little to give her focus and, by contrast, served to make her feel like she did when she went to the *American Sleaze* studios. She had even started to forget the fact that she now had a publishing company that was waiting on her to write something. That sort of attention and sense of respect, to the extent that they were actually going to pay her, now seemed to be anti-climactic. And what would it all mean anyway if she couldn't come up with anything? *They could sue for their money back. And what if I still can't get full-time teaching work? Oh, my God...*

"JESUS H CHRIST!" came from downstairs in the late afternoon, "GODFUCKINDAMNIT...!"

Peggy would normally not care to know what the source of Grace's current ire was, but with the weather being what it was, she felt obligated to go down and make sure that a cyclone hadn't blown through the living room. And, in truth, she now felt she needed the distraction.

"What happened?" as she stood at the foot of the stairs, while Grace sat on the couch with Little Pearl,

"Cable's out."

"That's it?"

"Yeah, that's it. I pay for this shit, for Godsakes."

"Well, I mean, it's a blizzard, so – "

"Yeah, yeah, I know it's a damn blizzard," as she slammed down the remote on the coffee table. "The one damn thing," as she rose and approached the kitchen, whisking past Peggy. "The one damn thing. I work for over 40 goddamn years to have this time, and now they're gonna' have me stare out the window."

In her fashion from when Peggy was a child, Grace took

her frustration out on the nearest pot, filling it with water for coffee before slamming it onto the stove and, as a result, forcing half the water to spill out, "Goddamnit!"

Peggy didn't quite know how to respond, as Grace was never one to be consoled. And it seemed that, next to Little Pearl dying, the worst thing that could happen to her was to not have access to her daily shows, even if many were likely reruns she'd seen a dozen times. She by now understood that the opportunity of her mother sitting on her ass for much a day watching television was the equivalent of living a life she had been deprived of by having to work a job she seemed to have had nothing but contempt for. Therefore, there would be little that she could do other than stay out of the way, as she had been.

At the same time, there was something in this moment, as she watched her mother grunt and curse under her breath while waiting for her water to boil, that made Peggy realize what else her book should be; in essence, *who the fuck is this woman that I came out of?*

Two days went by in which Peggy managed to write not a word. There was easy justification; the winds had continued, as did the snow's horizontal descent, wi-fi would be intermittent, as was electricity. The cable was still out, but that was more a loss for Grace. The plumbing was the one thing that, blessedly, continued unimpeded.

"Ah, shit!" Grace barked from the small area of the backyard patio that wasn't a wall of snow. Peggy came down to find Grace hunched over, still grasping a snow shovel, while Little Pearl innocently watched her wince.

"Are you okay?" Peggy feebly asked.

"Yeah, I'm fine," she barely grunted, as she attempted another motion to pick up some snow. "Ah, fuck!"

"What are you doing?"

"I'm tryin' to give her space to take a damn shit so she doesn't go in the house."

Grace had been creating small areas for her out back, but they were quickly covered by the ongoing blizzard. There was no way to keep up with the pace of the snow, so the house was all but encased at this point, except for a very small patch under the patio awning, which still had about 2 feet of snow. This made Grace have to stand inside the house in order to have a semblance of traction.

Peggy watched this pathetic site of her hunched-over mother with her squealing dog helplessly watching on, obviously needing to go and trying to avoid going on the rug.

She wasn't quite sure what she could offer here, but eventually hiccupped, "Why don't you lie down and let me do it?"

This offer of such manual labor surprised her more than it did Grace, since Peggy probably hadn't picked up a snow shovel since she was 15, during the famous blizzard of '95.

Grace did not seem to acknowledge this offer, instead attempting to foolishly try again, only to drop the shovel altogether, which eventually compelled Peggy to approach her.

"Nah, I'm good," Grace dismissed her while sticking her arm out, still unable to move from her bent position. This made her resemble the positional center of a football team about to hike the ball to the quarterback.

"How are you good? You can't even stand."

"I'm fine."

"Look, just lie down on the couch and I'll shovel for her, okay? This is ridiculous."

She surprised herself further with her insistence, which seemed to be enough to send Grace to limp to the couch, tepidly aided by Peggy, who managed to guide her while barely touching her. It dawned on her in that moment that this was the first physical contact they had had since her return, and even in her bare grazing of her mother's back, she could feel her age. She wasn't nearly as toned as she was. Certainly the few years of retirement atrophy had something to do with it. She remembered that her mother always appeared to be in decent shape, despite occasional work injuries. One couldn't say she was necessarily tone, but was husky and strong. She certainly needed to be to maneuver and sometimes even lift patients. But Peggy now sensed her weakness. Yet there was no sentimentality in her reaction, even internally. If anything, it eased the possibility of Grace being a physical threat to her.

She picked up the shovel and attempted to dig into the white snow wall on the patio. The first motion was akin to her trying to bench press 100 pounds, which she hadn't done since college. She even felt a slight twinge in her own back, "Shit!" which Grace happened to observe.

"See?"

"See what?"

"It ain't easy."

"I didn't say it was."

Of course, Peggy understood that her mother was quick to denounce her assistance. Her pride no doubt still damaged from Peggy's outburst a few nights ago. But Peggy wasn't about to relent. She knew she could very well be snowbound for who knew how long, and wanted to at least have the satisfaction of displaying to her mother that her years as an affluent Long Island wife and mother did not completely sap her physical strength.

After nearly an hour, she managed to make a sizable dent in the snow, which was big enough for Little Pearl to enter and take her requisite dumps. Since it was still under the awning, Peggy had hoped it wouldn't be filled up with snow by day's end. Little Pearl was now jogging in a small circle in the living room, desperately holding in her business, as she apparently had been trained well enough to know what was forbidden.

She stepped inside and allowed a clear passageway for Little Pearl to go out and indulge in her new arctic bathroom. Little Pearl looked oddly up at Peggy, as if surprised herself at the accomplishment.

"Go. It's for you," she insisted.

Little Pearl was not quick to walk by Peggy, as it appeared, in the days since Peggy's explosion, that Little Pearl had become wary of her; even afraid. She decided to place the shovel against the nearby wall and step further away. After nearly a minute of this, Little Pearl finally walked outside, ventured directly into the newly dug-out area amidst the mass of snow, and relieved herself.

This moment pleased Peggy in a strange way, but perhaps it would have pleased her more had her mother still been on the couch to see it. However, at some point during Peggy's excavation, Grace managed to drag herself upstairs. Peggy waited for Little Pearl to finish, then let her back in and led her to the kitchen where she would feed her, as per the tradition she had been overhearing through the door for weeks now. Little Pearl now seemed fine to trust Peggy with anything that made her life, in essence, a dog's life. *I guess the way to a pit bull's heart is through her stomach and bowels*, she thought. Of course, Peggy had had pets before, but indeed Little Pearl was something else. Their initial, nearly fatal meeting may have felt remote, but she still was not quick to forget it. Also Little Pearl felt very much like an appendage of Grace's, and, like her mother, Peggy felt she could turn on a dime.

She went back upstairs. Her instinct was to go right to her room, but thought she should check on Grace, considering the level of pain she seemed to be in. She knocked on the door, which was slightly ajar, before peeking her head into to see Grace strewn out on the bed atop the covers, still fully dressed and sound asleep, with an open bottle of pain killers on her night table. She looked at the bottle to make sure it wasn't empty, for fear that she may have overdosed, but it was at least a half-full bottle. Who knew how long she had these and how long she had needed them. In any event, she was satisfied to let her sleep through the day and into the evening, and made sure to leave the door ajar for when Little Pearl came back up.

She went into her room, closed the door and, again, looked out at the unyielding storm. Along with the still bellowing gusts was the nearby sound of a plow truck, seeming to have arrived about two days too late. She almost appreciated the momentary diversion of shoveling out back, as it at least got the blood flowing a bit. With even such minimal stimulation, she hoped it would lead to some creative inspiration, but nothing seemed to take hold as she stared at her blank computer screen. She then checked her bank account and saw, to her near fright, that the advance from Bloom had been deposited. Her heart began to beat rapidly, as if already late for a deadline, even with the snow halting life in much of the north east.

She wanted to simply write more than fear not writing.

31

The scratches on her door woke her up the next morning, which was already unusual. Peggy looked at her phone to find that it was 10:15am. By now, she would have already heard the sounds of Grace stomping to the bathroom, then down the stairs to let out and then feed Little Pearl, but that didn't happen on this day. She opened the door to find Little Pearl squealing to be let out, "What the...?"

Before she went downstairs, she peaked into Grace's bedroom to find that she was still asleep. She knew she was alive by her buzzsaw snoring. Rather than wake her, she opted to bring the eager Little Pearl downstairs. However, to her dismay, the area she had dug for Little Pearl had been filled overnight, which meant she'd need to try and dig another area which would give the dog enough room to excrete.

"What a way to begin a day," she mumbled to herself. As was similar to yesterday, Peggy shoveled as Little Pearl rotated in a small circle in the living room, desperately containing herself. After a grueling half hour, she managed a small nook by which Little Pearl could go.

"Peggy! PEGGY!" Grace yelled from upstairs. Upon her entrance into the room, she was struck by Grace struggling to sit up in her bed.

"Are you okay?"

"Can y'let the dog out?"

"I already did. I had to dig her another hole. It didn't stop snowing all night."

"Alright. I'll be up to feed 'er in a bit."

"Can you get up?"

"I'll get up. Don't worry."

"How long have you had back problems?"

"Longer than you care to know."

"Well, I'm asking."

"I had 'em since I was working. Had 'em for most a' my life, but it acts up and, when it does, I can't move too well. I'll be fine. Jus' need to get some hot water on my back."

"Look, I'll feed her, okay? You don't need to go down for that."

Grace took a moment, as though she wanted to argue, but realized it made sense. The pain was likely much greater than she would willingly let on, "s'fine. Give her fresh water, two cans a' wet and top off her Kibbles'n Bits. Everything's in the cabinet under the sink."

"Okay," as she started to leave...

"Any cable?"

"I haven't checked. I just got up myself."

Grace tried to reach for the remote on her night table, but had difficulty, "Shit...," before Peggy handed it to her. She immediately aimed the remote at her small bedroom television on her dresser, "Goddamnit!"

"Well, it's a pretty bad storm."

"I'm payin' for this shit."

"Mom, I'm sure the cable company will credit you."

"You work for 'em?"

"That's just common business practice. They're not going to charge you for this. It's a natural disaster."

"I'll believe it when I see it," Grace grunted, her indignance no less subsided at this. The importance she gave to the television continued to baffle Peggy.

"Maybe reading a book?"

"What?" she looked at Peggy as if she just spoke in tongues.

"A book. Do you have a book you've been reading? Maybe now's a good time to finish it."

"I don't' wana' read a book. Why dontcha' feed 'er now. Poor thing's usually already eaten by now. It's, what, 10:30?"

"Well, as I said, I just got up, okay? And I spent the last half hour shoveling a space for her to shit."

"Sorry if it put you out."

"I'm not saying it... I'm going to feed her now, okay? Do you want me to bring you anything up?"

"No, I'll be down."

"What do you mean you'll be down? Why am I going down to feed her if you're planning to go down anyway?"

"Because it's gonna' take me some time. Now don't make me explain everything. I don't have the damn energy."

"I really think you should stay in bed while you're feeling like this. I can bring you up your cereal."

"I can do it jus' fine."

She wanted to contest her mother again, but thought better. *Why am I caring?*

She also wondered if her mother had ever read anything other than owner's manuals. How could Peggy have such a love for literature and come from someone who was practically allergic to it? Now she tried to recall if she *ever* noticed Grace sitting with a book. When she went back into the vault of her adolescent memory, the only image she could resurrect was Grace with a dangling cigarette, dropping ashes into a *TV Guide*.

She fed Little Pearl, ravenous as always, but a bit more expressive with her appreciation now, as her cold snout tapped against Peggy's calf. The thumping from upstairs indicated that Grace was out of bed and slowly making her way to the bathroom. Peggy approached the foot of the stairs and carefully watched her mother make her way down the hall, "Do you need...any help?"

"s'fine!" she barked.

"I'll make you breakfast and bring it up, okay? I really think you – "

The bathroom door slammed shut. She knew this was

an intended reply, since Grace never closed the door, in case Little Pearl wanted to visit. Now she pondered whether she should go through the trouble or just make her own breakfast and head up to her room.

She elected to prepare Grace's breakfast, and carefully brought up the bowl of Cinnamon Life cereal, buttered toast and coffee, along with milk and sugar over the course of several trips, since there wasn't a serving tray in the house. Grace was in the bathroom throughout, as the shower water continued spraying.

Peggy then managed to make her own breakfast before heading into her room.

About a half hour later, "What the hell is this?!" came through the door.

She went into Grace's room where she stood in her bathrobe, still red and moistened from just exiting the shower, "What?" Peggy asked.

"How long's this been here?"

"Well, I didn't know how long you'd be, so – "

"I didn't even tell you t'make me anything. Now it's been sittin' here for God knows how long."

"I didn't know how long you'd be."

"And that's why I didn't want you to make me anything. My back's out, for Godsakes. Y'think I need to concern myself with runnin' to my room so that the toast doesn't get cold? It's like rubber, n'I'm almost outa' bread as it is. A damn waste."

She looked at her mother, and the similar feelings of anger and resentment started to resurface. She wanted credit for the attempt, at least, even if her mother never technically asked nor agreed to this. But the fact was that her back would have gone out even if Peggy wasn't there, and *then* what position would she be in? *The dog would be shitting all over the house and starving– and she'd be starving as well.*

But she chose to say nothing, and went to her room. Again, she stuck her face in her pillow and primal screamed into it, not unlike when she was a teenager. And the snow was keeping her from moving on. She now had money in the bank, means by which she could at least get her car and go to a crappy motel to start writing her book while looking for teaching work, but the world as she knew it was at a standstill. The only thing not was her mind and fingers. And then something clicked.

She then started typing:

Chapter 1 – Mrs. Prager died earlier this week. I never thought she would play much of a significant role in my life, other than the woman who sold me 7-Up and Bubble Yum as a kid. Yet somehow, when I returned to Kelp Stream, she would end up being the only presence that made me feel at all like I was missed. I never really felt like I was returning home in any sort of storybook, Wizard of Oz-like way. It was more as if I were sucked into my past like a merciless vacuum and amidst the kaleidoscope memories that I had preferred to forget was this kind woman who simply remembered me as a nice girl. She knew nothing of my adult life. Only what I chose to tell her or lie about, as we reacquainted. She told me her husband died a few years earlier. She had kids, grandkids. Now she was dead. As I write this, I'm still wondering why I can't seem to get over it. It feels like all the good that there was in this oppressive town has died with her, and left me alone with the yellowed photo of Sylvia Plath on my childhood ceiling; her eyes still there looking down at my twin bed like an eccentric aunt. Even she must be saying "Why haven't you killed yourself, like I did?"

I had everything once. That is to say that I thought I did. Now it all feels like a ruse intended to lead me back here, at least for a time. Perhaps to see Mrs. Prager before she left the earth.

Or, perhaps, to see my mother before she does.

She managed to get through a semblance of what appeared to be a chapter, writing until fatigued enough with her own past experience to sleep. The chapter ended with her most cherished experience in her classroom, Tricia Wentworth's response to *The Bell Jar* and defense of Esther Greenwood. This all led up to the infamous knock which changed her life, which she felt was a good note to end on.

She woke up to Grace's bark the next morning, "Peggy! PEGGY!!!"

She eagerly got up and loathingly entered her mother's room to find her hunched and on her knees at the side of her bed.

"Jesus..." she went to her. "What happened?"

"I tried t'get the hell up, that's what happened."

She awkwardly managed to get Grace back onto the bed, as Little Pearl watched on, more concerned at the moment with her own agenda.

"What do you want me to get you?"

"Let 'er out. I jus' need to get to the shower."

"I really think you should stay in bed."

"I'll be fine."

"You couldn't be farther from fine."

"I'm fine."

"Look, I'll take care of the dog, but you really need to stay in bed. We're snowbound, okay? If you fall and break your neck, there's no way an ambulance can get here."

"I'm takin' a damn shower!"

"Fine, then wait until I get back up and I'll help you! Alright?!" Peggy was increasingly aggressive in speaking with her mother, which actually was the best way to communicate to her. She didn't respond to mere suggestion. She needed to practically be forced to do something, and there would be no one on earth who could get away with this other than Peggy, yet even Peggy was surprised that her mother would yield to her demands in any way. It made her aware all the more of her mother's mortality. This realization had already spilled into the opening of her book – seeing her mother again before she left the earth. No doubt that what would come out of this experience would fuel all the more the content of it – what she came from, who her mother was, what from her mother had stuck to her throughout, and what was she still trying to shed. It almost seemed as if her instinct to help her mother was more out of the need for material than anything else. In truth, she didn't feel her mother had earned her help.

She opened the sliding glass door and was at least pleased to see the nook she had created for Little Pearl was still preserved, thanks in large part to the snowfall having finally ceased by yesterday evening.

She then went into the kitchen to change her water and feed her, before she headed upstairs to tend to her mother, sitting on the side of the bed, wincing...

"If you want to take a shower, I'll help you, okay?"

Grace said nothing, but remained bent and grimacing...

"Okay?" Peggy repeated, unsure if she should make any assertive motions, as Grace remained, cursing her misfortune under her breath.

After an awkward few moments, Grace jutted out her arm like a punch. This made Peggy feel uncertain if Grace wanted her help or her to go away. The gesture appeared to be an intentional merging of the two. She reached behind her mother and, with feeble assistance from Grace, hoisted her up before they both slowly made their way to the bathroom. By this point, Little Pearl could now be heard gobbling in the kitchen. Each step they took together seemed to take minutes.

"I got a shower chair in the garage."

"What's it doing in the garage?"

"I usually don't need it."

"Well, at least have it close to the bathroom. Why did you put it in - ?"

"Jus' get the damn chair. I gotta' explain everything I do to you? *I never need it!*"

Of course, it made little sense as to why Grace would have experienced enough pain in the past to get the chair in the first place, only to store it downstairs in the garage where it couldn't have been less useful to her. Obviously, these were questions that were futile, and perhaps Peggy understood why anyway; keeping the shower chair at bay would also, in essence, keep the ravages of aging equally so.

She closed the sliding glass door, then went into the freezing garage to extract the shower chair and brought it upstairs, while Grace waited atop the closed toilet in her bathrobe, still cursing her pain under her breath. Peggy placed it in the shower, with some effort, then took the initiative to rinse it off with the portable shower head.

"Okay. Are you able to – ?"

'Yes," Grace barked, with utter loathing.

She left and went downstairs, leaving her mother to disrobe and bathe. At the foot of the stairs was Little Pearl gazing up at Peggy as she descended.

"Hello," she said, somewhat formally, as if to a co-worker she knew at a distance, especially as she wasn't sure what Little Pearl's intent was. She walked past her to the kitchen and began to prepare her oatmeal and coffee, not even motioning to make Grace's, as a result of yesterday. Little Pearl simply watched her, occasionally wagging her tail. She looked at the dog, still distrusting of her, but not afraid anymore. It even seemed as if Little Pearl was playing nice so that Peggy wouldn't bite.

She ate her breakfast in the dining room, still hearing the water spray from the shower upstairs. Little Pearl had since gone up to wait outside the bathroom door. As she cleaned out her bowl in the sink, she heard the swipe of the shower curtain opening, before turning off the sink to hear if her mother was able to make her way out without capsizing. Soon her horse-hoof steps made their way into her bedroom, as Peggy observed her ankles from the kitchen entrance.

She peaked her head into Grace's room, "Any better?" she asked, as Grace sat on the side of the bed in her bathrobe.

"Yeah, m'fine."

Peggy resisted further inquiries, as she was always cautious of being dismissed. Just as she closed the door in her room, she heard "Goddamnit!" which prompted her to rush back in...

"What?"

"Cable's still out!"

She sighed at this, stunned that Grace not having her inane programs seemed worse for her than the chronic pain she was enduring. She exited again and went into her room.

She assumed that the hot shower was enough for Grace to make her way down to the kitchen to feed herself. Again, she wasn't quick to offer help to her mother, especially since "please" or "thank you" weren't exactly a part of her vocabulary, but she somehow knew she'd be required to assist her more. While there was some dread with that thought, there was also the potential for material. With no cable and her mother's disinterest in anything else, eventually some sort of conversation would have to take place, she felt.

But is that even possible?

She looked at her computer screen, optimistic for the words she would soon add to last night's, but was stuck. Something about the knock on the classroom door from the Cold River High School principal telling her of Mike's arrest was not a place she wanted to go just yet, and yet it felt as if her story could go nowhere else. It also felt too soon to reenact the life-altering experience from barely over three months ago, even though she knew that exactly what occurred then was the very reason she had this opportunity now.

She continued gazing at the screen, in between rising, staring out the window at the buried neighborhood, lying on her bed and gawking at Sylvia on the ceiling. Before she knew it, it was early afternoon and she had managed not a word.

A crash came from the kitchen, "Goddamnit!!!"

Peggy headed halfway down the stairs before she saw Grace bracing herself against the counter, a broken glass on the floor in front of her.

"Are you okay?"

"Yeah, jus' slipped…"

"Watch your step. I'll clean it up. Where's your dust-pan?"

"Under the sink," as Grace started to walk out of the kitchen into the living room, at a snail's pace.

Peggy swept up the broken glass, as "Fuckin' shit!" came from the living room. She rushed in to see Grace with the remote needlessly pointed at the television.

"You already knew the cable was out!"

"That was this morning. I was hopin' they finally fixed it."

She couldn't respond anymore to Grace's frustration over the cable, "You want something to eat?"

She took a moment before tossing the remote onto the couch, then begrudgingly, "Yeah, Cinnamon Life and a piece' toast n'coffee, if y'don't mind."

"That's breakfast."

"That's right."

"You didn't have breakfast? It's almost three."

"No, I didn't."

"Well, why not? You could've just asked me."

Grace sat there, apparently loath to answer, and still angered at her pain and the cable outage. Peggy decided to not press further and went about making her mother's breakfast at three in the afternoon.

She brought her cereal, buttered toast and coffee and placed them before Grace on the table. Little Pearl lay near the sliding glass door, with the white light of the afternoon snow beaming down on her.

After she cleaned up in the kitchen, she decided it made more sense to sit with Grace then head back upstairs and be uninspired until summoned with another expletive. She had a cup of coffee herself, perhaps more of a ruse to justify sitting in the recliner near her mother than anything.

She sipped, as Grace alternated slowly between biting her toast and scooping her cereal. There were only sips and crunches for several minutes before a word was uttered:

"So why does she hate strangers so much?"

Grace took this in, oddly, "What?"

"You said when I first got here that she hated strangers."

Grace took another moment, not quite sure what would spawn such a question unrelated to anything, before finally indulging, "She just does. Whoever had 'er before me musta' trained her that way, if ya' wana' call it that." She sipped her coffee, "Delivery people, inspectors, whatever. Any surprise visitors, forget about it. Had to repair the window in the dining room like 5 times now. If she's in the house and someone she don't know jus' shows up, she'll try'n fly right through the damn thing," she bit her toast. "Also can't have 'er around other dogs. She sees another dog, she'll kill it. Think she was a dog fighter."

"A what?"

"She was probably trained to destroy other dogs. They bet on 'em. Fuckin' assholes. They should all be castrated."

"Who?"

"The ones who breed fight dogs. They don't care about the damn dog. They care about money. Scumbags is what they are."

She continued to chew, as Peggy looked at Little Pearl so sweetly lying in the sun. It was hard for her in that moment to think that this dog was probably so traumatized that it now had irreparably fatal instincts. And yet Grace found her in the street. She actually saved her. This dog undoubtedly loved Grace more than anyone in her life. She knew what Grace had done for her, and no doubt would die for her. If there was any hole in Grace's life, Little Pearl appeared to fill it aptly. But then again, Peggy wondered if it was more that Grace should have just been a dog owner from the beginning and not a mother. For all this dog's deficiencies, Peggy envied her. She envied the simplicity of her life and the love she must have felt.

Somehow, this helped trigger what she would write

later that night:

Much to my surprise, I can now see through the haze of recent events to the moment he said his first words to me in the Princeton dining hall, as he held a tray of meat loaf and asparagus spears; "Do you mind if I sit here?" I remember the feeling, which was unquestionably new. His liquid blue eyes looked at me with adoration, which had apparently been budding from weeks of observing me from afar. A reading I gave of a short story I can no longer recall at the campus coffee house would be the impetus; the dawn of his fascination with me, as he put it. How wonderful to be adored when one has never been, I thought. Once we got a few sentences in to our first conversation, he was beyond his years; assured, confident, intelligent, warm. As if he knew the world would be his. Yet now I ask myself why his knowledge of this mattered more to me than the plans I had for myself.

Is this what an absent father does to you?

Of course, I didn't forgo my dreams then and there. It took time. By the time we moved in together, I was already teaching and working in an office, while Mike was in dermatology school. It still didn't feel like a compromise. Things felt more-or-less in bloom, as I suppose beginnings often do. Over the coming months, however, my writing output did begin to wane and rejections from work I had been sending out were no longer in short supply. Perhaps then the reality of the outside world began to leave me unsettled. But in Mike, there would be stability.

Soon he would be a successful doctor, and I would be the entrance by which our two children would come into the world.

In a blink of an eye, we would be the family I never had.

And then the years passed…

32

____

"Peggy! PEGGY!!!" seeped through Peggy's door the next morning. She entered Grace's room to, again, find her wincing but sitting up...

"What is it?"

"Can't friggin' budge."

"Have you been taking your pain killers?"

"All they do is knock me out, so I try'n take 'em before I go to bed."

"Then you're in pain throughout the day."

"I know what I'm doin'."

"Well, you shouldn't be moving."

"I can't jus' sit here, for Godsakes. I need to get to the shower."

"It didn't do much for you yesterday. You still needed me to bring you upstairs from the couch."

"It'd be worse if I didn't get that hot water on my back. Now I jus' need you t'help get me into the bathroom."

"Alright, but I think you should stay up here today, okay?"

"I'll do what I want."

"No, you *won't* do what you want!"

"Look, you don't own me jus' 'cause I'm askin' for help to the bathroom, so jus' get that thought outa' -"

"I'm not saying any such thing. I'm saying that if you want to go downstairs, you're more than likely going to need me to bring you up. And it's not gonna' do either us much good if we *both* pull our backs out. And there's still 5 feet of snow outside, so there's no way for an ambulance to get to us until it starts to melt, and by then we could both be dead. Now just listen to me here, okay?! I'll bring you to the bathroom to shower and then you come back here and stay in bed. I'll bring up your meals."

Grace remained silent, which was as close to appeasing as Peggy could expect.

"Alright? Let's go." She reached out her arm to her mother, who eyed it with contempt before conceding. As was now the standard, she attempted to hide the embarrassment of seeming at all enfeebled by cursing under her breath, to which Peggy could only listen. Her imagination attempted to distort Grace's epithetic murmurings to the sounds of the ocean from when she used to pick up seashells along the shoreline and watch the stars on the water made by the sun. It at least made transporting her mother a bit more tolerable.

While Grace was now sitting in her shower chair under a hot stream, Peggy went downstairs to let out the anxious Little Pearl, who was coming increasingly to view Peggy as the bearer of good fortune since Grace had been laid up. The bathroom nook she had made for Little Pearl still remained, since no new snow had fallen. She would even shovel out Little Pearl's poop nuggets and toss snowflakes on the frozen pee so as to keep it somewhat sterile for her.

She prepared the dog's food, as per usual, and prepared her own breakfast in the hopes of gaining some creative fertility so she could add to the two pages she had managed to write last night. Grace would soon after stomp slowly out of the shower, a tad more mobile as a result, but not confident by any means. In fact, it was getting harder for her to act like she was improving. After Peggy ate, she went upstairs to check on her.

"Goddamnit!"

Peggy rushed in, only to find Grace with the remote, cursing at the blank screen – yet again.

"Is this *Groundhog Day*?"

"What?" Grace crabbily barked.

"The movie where the same thing happ..." it wasn't worth Peggy's explanation. "Do you want breakfast?"

Grace remained, staring bitterly at the dresser just below her now useless television. Often such silences would symbolize a dread. The thought of living such a simple, no-frills life and yet needing assistance was the nadir for Grace. But Peggy was never going to fill in the blanks for her. If Grace wanted something, she needed to ask for it. At least then, if she wanted to bitch about stuff, Peggy had a leg to stand on other than her instincts. There was also something strangely pleasurable for her in being needed by her mother, just as it was bizarre that she would just manage to be at home when her mother was experiencing such debilitation. At least it was now less embarrassing for her to be there; she was no longer the needy, fallen daughter who came back with her tail between her legs. She was taking care of her aging mother.

This seemed so admirably normal.

About twenty minutes later, Grace was sitting upright in her bed with a nearby TV table, atop which sat all of her requisite breakfast items: Cinnamon Life, buttered toast and coffee. Peggy thought of sitting in the nearby chair which overlooked the backyard and the back of a neighbor's house, but coyly remained by the door with her own coffee in hand. Again, she didn't want to seem as if she was actively seeking Grace's company, but was more there out of necessity. As long as that ruse could be kept up, she felt in a better position in case of a sudden ornery display.

From across the room, she looked out the window at the white world, as Grace alternated between crunching bites of toast, sips of coffee and slurps of cereal. Peggy recalled memories of playing in the backyard as a young girl and peek-ing through that same old wooden fence at the family that lived in the nearby house. They had a pool, which was gone now, but she remembered her envy with every splash. Her only option for swimming was a 45 minute trip to the shore, which she always enjoyed. On rare occasions, Grace would take her, but she hated the sun and became increasingly sensitive to it. This left Peggy to ride the local bus which she'd sometimes do with a friend, but more often alone, sitting among senior citizens and some disparate types who likely had their licenses suspended. A few times she went with boyfriends. Despite her shyness, she managed two in middle school and two in high school. Only one of which she made the mistake of bringing home.

This occurred a few months before the incident with her friend Jodie. For some reason, Peggy thought Grace would like Greg Potts. He came over after school, a sophomore like her, as they were studying for an Earth Science test together. He was good-looking enough, and had a modicum of intelligence for a jock. His parents were nice and so Peggy felt that it might be a good time for Greg to meet her mother, as if that would somehow balance things out. Grace would come home and, as with Jodie, sensed another presence. It was clear almost instantly that having a boy over was not a good thing. It was never discussed, at that point. Never prohibited in words. Of course, Grace would have another awful day at the nursing home, and even had a few drinks at the local bar on the way home. She then proceeded to make her first impression to Greg by slamming a skillet on the stove and then violently chopping a potato (a fresh vegetable seeming to only exist for acts of aggression), while screaming about the injustices of the world; eyeing him intensely as he nervously held an embarrassed Peggy's hand by the front door. He would stop returning Peggy's calls by the next week.

At that point, Peggy had assumed that, while she was living at home, she would just avoid bringing boys over, which was why she was even surprised at her mother's reaction when she invited Jodie over later that winter. In hindsight, it seemed like an unwritten agreement that Peggy would have little social life that Grace would have knowledge of. She was simply to be content with solely her mother and her mood swings while being forced to indulge the occasional boyfriend of *hers*. These would often be men who Peggy avoided, unless they happened to be around for a holiday, as was the infamous case with Clyde from when Peggy was 11, who managed to get arrested on Christmas day for swinging at a female cop. *What on earth could she see in these men?*

As she looked at her mother now, she realized that Grace would only be satisfied with Peggy as a loner, not unlike her. And yet she didn't seem to object to Peggy being creative and, even on occasion, would listen to her essays, poems and short stories, if sober and in the right frame of mind, which was becoming increasingly rare as Peggy got older. She often couldn't grasp them, and thought she used "too many 10 dollar words" which ultimately sapped Peggy's enthusiasm to read more to her. She eventually would recite her work exclusively in class for her teachers or to her smarter friends. But she really never felt her work was appreciated until she got into Princeton.   Like Tina recalled, Peggy's work never sat unseen for long. She was often published in Princeton's student magazine as well as small outside publications, and soon became the belle of the ball when reading in class or at coffee houses on campus, instilling both inspiration and envy among her peers. It was sheer will and drive that got her to such a place, as if she were defiantly swimming against a Philistinian undertow. But it wasn't just defiance. It was liberation. Through books, she began to see the light of other cultures, other worlds. And through them, she saw the ability to live another type of life. In college, it was as if the gates of opportunity had opened wide for her. She could do no wrong, and *did* no wrong. That is, perhaps, until she met Mike in the dining hall.

For the moment, all this took a back seat to her curiosity regarding her mother's recent relationship, as she observed Grace slurping her coffee.

"Who's Joe?" she asked, a suppressed curiosity that came out like a gastric slippage.

"What?" Grace responded, while continuing to eat.

"Joe. You had a Joe living here at some point?"

"Who told you? That Mrs. Prager?"

"No," Peggy was at first stunned by such a reply. "How would *she* know?"

"That's what I'm asking you."

"Well, it's not like *you'd* tell her. You barely said two words to her."

"What the hell's your point?" as she stopped eating.

"I heard his name on your answering machine when I first tried to call you. And then I called a few days later and it was gone."

Grace went back to eating, "He was here for a time. I threw 'im out."

"Was he...?"

"What?"

"I'm just assuming you were...seeing each other, right?"

Grace's eyes rolled up, as she sipped her coffee, "Briefly."

"Briefly? How briefly? He was living here," Peggy found herself a bit more brazen with her questioning.

"We went back a bit'n reconnected. He called me up. Was in a bad place. Got evicted, owed money. I took him in under conditions."

"Conditions?"

"Look, what the hell's in this for you?"

"Nothing. I'm just asking. I can't make conversation?"

"What kinda' conversation is this?"

"I can ask you a question. I can ask who the medicine in the cabinet belongs to."

"It's his, okay?"

"Yes, I figured it was. Why would he leave it?"

"'cause he's an idiot, that's why."

"Doesn't he need it?"

"It's jus' thyroid medicine, for Godsakes. Not chemo drugs," Grace gazed at Peggy, clearly wanting that response to suffice. She went back to her breakfast, occasionally peering out of her window. Peggy alternated between looking out herself and then at her mother, occasionally sipping her coffee...

"Just seems strange."

"What does?!" Grace bellowed.

"That he'd leave his medicine. Has he called you?"

"I kicked 'em the hell outa' here, okay? Believe me, after what he pulled, the last thing he'd wana' do is reconnect with me or try'n come back here for his meds."

"What did he *pull*?"

"What is this?"

"What?"

"Why are you so curious about this alluvasudden? You been here for over a month, *now* you bring this up?"

"I had other concerns."

"So now you got nothin' to concern yourself with?"

Peggy thought to respond, but for some reason was pulled to remain silent and, perhaps, see if Grace would volunteer something. There was a considerable moment that went by, as Grace went back to finishing her toast and cereal,...

"I think you've been around long enough to know that sometimes the folks that gravitate to us aren't necessarily ones we should keep around. I think you know more than well what I'm talkin' about," she gazed at Peggy, with a hint of that prideful grin from when she saw Mike's episode on *American Sleaze*.

There was something about Grace's sudden neediness that had softened Peggy's long-established feelings towards her mother. But in this moment, she hated her again.

The next two days went by without notable incident, but it *was* becoming like *Groundhog Day* to Peggy. She'd continue to wake-up to Grace's barks, escort her to the shower, open the sliding glass door for Little Pearl, feed her, as Grace would curse at the cable outage, then Peggy would make her and her mother breakfast. Lunch and dinner time would more or less follow the same pattern. The upshot was that Peggy found herself using the dormant hours in between to write. Somehow having the distraction of tending to Grace, along with the distant memories that were being increasingly triggered in her presence, was making her prose come out more fluidly.

She made an internal vow to herself that she would not overanalyze what she was writing. It was more important that something was coming out and, while it was, it was keeping the demons at bay that, in the past, would have inhibited her.

At lunch time, she made them grilled cheese and more coffee. Now Peggy was sitting across the room from Grace's bed with her own TV tray. They ate in silence for a while, but soon Peggy would pick up where she left off a couple of days ago when asking about the infamous "Joe". At least now she had some confirmation as to who he was and, not surprisingly, was affirmed that his character was questionable at best. It still struck her as odd that he would so recently leave and yet not call. Perhaps they indeed had a falling out of emphatic proportions, which would not be the first time for Grace. She remembered her coming at Clyde with a knife while Peggy, now 11, watched from upstairs, almost certain her mother would stab him. From what she overheard, Clyde may have been coming on to another woman at the bar they met at which, obviously, was the last straw for Grace. Being cuckolded was one thing, but being so while also providing a roof over his head was something else:

"You ain't gonna' do shit to me," he dizzily bragged.

"Try me, you fuckin' loser pieca' shit."

"You ain't gonna' – "

"TRY ME! You live here with not a dime to your name, while I'm cleanin' shit'n piss and dealin' with nutty ol' coots all day!"

"Hey, that's your choice, honeybun. Your fuckin' choice

- !"

"YEAH, N'IF I WASN'T, WHERE WOULD YOU BE? WOULD THAT BITCH TAKE YOU IN?   SHE PROB'LY WOULDN'T EVEN LET YOU USE THE BATHROOM IN HER HOUSE, BUT YOU'LL TAKE MY MONEY'N BUY HER DRINKS, WHILE I'M BUSTIN' MY ASS!"

Clyde's intoxication lulled him into calling Grace's bluff. His inebriated bravado may have also been the only thing he had to cling to, but it was clear that this was not going to be one of their loud arguments that would just end with him passed out on the couch. It seemed ever so close to being the end of him, at least from where Peggy stood. It was one of the first times she remembered thinking her mother was capable of being more than angry. Her rage appeared capable of manifesting itself into something else - the worst possible thing.

"Mommy, please don't...!" she remembered crying out, prompting Grace's head to sharply turn upstairs.

"PEGGY, GET IN YOUR ROOM!"

"Please don't – "

"GET IN YOUR ROOM, MARGARET!"

She remembered running into her room, slamming the door fearfully and simply praying over Grace's screams at Clyde. Somehow she forgot what happened after that. She only remembered willing herself to sleep and, by the time she woke the next day, Clyde was gone, as were most of his few be-longings,...and there was no mention of him ever again.

Finally, with about two bites of her grilled cheese left, Peggy broke the silence, "Do you know where my father is?"

As with previous conversation openers, Grace's first re-sponse sounded like a disbelief in the question, particularly this one, "What?"

Of course, by now Peggy expected this, and was already prepared to ask again, albeit a bit slower, "Do you know where my father is?"

Grace bit into her grilled cheese, sipped her coffee,

"Who the hell knows."

"You really don't know?"

"Why the hell would I? He left when you were 4, for Godsakes. Y'think we're pen pals?"

"I just... I never knew what happened."

"You knew what happened."

"I was 4. I barely knew my name at that age."

"I told you later what happened. You know."

"He left."

"That's right."

"He left and...what, you never knew what happened once he walked out the door?"

"Pretty much," she sipped and looked out her window.

Peggy took this in, knowing she was not going to let the thread of this conversation become frayed and done until she had a semblance of satisfaction. Once the snow melted, she was leaving and was not intending to return, so there was now an urgency to be more informed about the man who was half of the pair that made her possible.

"Don't you think that's strange?"

"*He* was," as she chewed, a bit more aggressively now.

"I just... I mean, I just find it so odd that him and these other men – "

Before she could finish, Grace abruptly turned her eyes to her, seeming to know what she was suggesting. For the moment, this froze Peggy's tongue, before she managed to work through her trepidations...

"Don't you see why I would want to know more?"

Grace slurped her coffee harshly, then turned back to the window, "No, I don't."

"I'm gonna be 40 years old in June and I still don't have a clue as to who my father was. I don't have a photo of him, anything. And I'd like to know something before it's too late."

"Too late for what?"

"What do you mean too late for what? We don't have any other familial ties. I'd have to register through one of those ancestry DNA sites to find out anything."

"So do that."

"Why should I when you're right here."

"Look, he left and that was it."

"Did you ever actually get divorced?"

"What kinda' question is that?"

"It just strikes me that it'd be hard to go through a divorce if the husband couldn't be traced."

"I didn't say he couldn't be traced."

"You said he left."

"He did. The divorce was already in process before he left, I jus' never told you, okay?"

"So you got divorced."

"Yes! For Godsakes, enougha' this. Y'make me a grilled cheese, so now you get to cross examine me?"

"I'm not cross examining you. I'm asking questions about my roots."

"*I'm* your damn roots!"

The stillness hung in the air for a while as their eyes locked. Peggy again saw the two roads in her mind that she could go down, and was getting to a point where she wanted to match her mother's ferocity, but knew that that would only obstruct her goal here.

"I had a father," she said, softly.

Grace seemed to calm a bit, before turning to the window. She then spoke as if unpacking words long stored in an attic somewhere, "It was a man who was in my life for little more than 2 years, who impregnated me, but who never wanted to be a father to you or anyone else."

"Why?"

"Whata' y'mean why? It wasn't intended."

"It...? You mean *I*? I wasn't – ?"

"Yes."

Peggy couldn't say she was particularly surprised by this, but it was nevertheless painful to hear.

"It's jus' as well he split. Believe me. You think I was

such a terrible mother? If he were around, you might not even
be here."

"What does that mean?"

"He was abusive, okay?"

"Physically?"

"Yes, physically! Physically, verbally! He wasn't always
that way, until I got pregnant n' when you came into the world,
that's how he was. He resented you. He didn't wana' be encumbered by anything, n' thought I was a fool for havin' ya'. I
was the one that knew you'd be better off without a father
than with him, n' that was it."

Peggy sat with this a moment, "*What* was it?"

"What the hell d' you mean *what*? We filed for divorce' n
he left. Once we got the signature, I never heard from 'im
again."

"I don't understand. Were you not getting alimony?
Child support?"

"He didn't have shit. He was on' n off disability as it was.
Couldn't hold down a job for more than two months at a time.
I jus' wanted him the hell outa' our lives."

"And you never – ?"

"Enougha' this, y' hear me?! All I want is to watch some
Goddamn TV'n I can't even have that. Instead, I get you takin'
advantage a' my pain by asking me these things."

"I have every right to ask these questions."

"Do you?"

"Yes, I do."

"You left me for dead, as far as you were concerned."

"Will you stop saying that! You know why – "

"You had your man n' your family, and you cut me off!
That was your choice! You came back here because you were
desperate. You're lucky I was still here. I coulda' been dead.
And then where would ya' be?"

"Where the hell would *you* be if *I* wasn't here, you...?!"
Peggy stopped herself. She had never managed to call her
mother an actual profanity, but it was clearly dangling from

the tip of her tongue in this moment. She took a deep breath, as Grace looked at her, clearly wishing that she could lunge from the bed...

"I can't help what I came from, mom,...but I had every right to leave here. I would've loved to have you watch me become smarter and more confident, and actually appreciate it. I tried to share my accomplishments with you, especially when I was in college, but you just dismissed everything – "

"We're done."

"*This* is what you wanted. You never wanted me to leave this fucking house!"

"Bullshit!"

"I was supposed to be exactly like you or else you were threatened!"

"I'm done. Take this plate," as she angrily moved the TV tray and attempted to lay back in bed...

"I'm not your maid! I'm not gonna' just take your plate and end this conversation."

"Then converse with yourself. I'm done talkin'."

As she stood, she watched Grace struggle to align herself properly in her bed, not knowing what else she could say, though wanting to say so much. Grace then angrily picked up the remote, which she had just tried a few hours earlier...

Peggy yelled, "You know that the cable is out – !"

A blast of sound came from the television, followed by the opening credits of an *American Sleaze* rerun...

"It's about fuckin' time!" Grace exulted, between relief and anger.

Peggy lunged onto the bed, grabbed the remote from Grace's hands, shut the TV off, "We're not done."

"Give me that Goddamn – "

"WE'RE NOT DONE!!!!"

They were now locked in nothing short of a death stare. Peggy still didn't know how soon she'd be able to move out, between being able to get the car and finding a motel, but she couldn't slow the pace of her need to know things. Yes, it was all possible material,...but it was also a sense of completeness she was after.

She remained with the remote in her now sweaty, trembling grip, "I want to talk with you, and it doesn't have to be nasty. I just... I just want to know..."

"What?! What the hell are you saying?!"

"I...I want to know – "

"WHAT?!!!"

Peggy desperately tried to calm herself and not allow her emotions to overpower her mother's anger, because she was so angry herself. It was getting to a point where she didn't know her own limitations, having her mother within range, constrained by her aging body. She kept clenching the remote as if it were a knife, waiting for the echo of Grace's bellow to leave the room before she resumed her questioning...

"Why did you think I brought Mike back here to meet you?"

"I'm done," as Grace folded her arms and gazed back out the window.

"You thought I wanted to rub it in your face, I bet. But that...that wasn't what it was," she felt tears coming, as she shook. "It actually mattered to me to have your blessings, you know that? And yet I don't know why on earth I imagined that you'd give them. You never did before – for anything. You never wanted me with anybody. And that's why you put that drug in his coffee when he was here. That sedative from your job. You knew how much it would take. Maybe because you did it before. Except I wasn't there before, was I."

Her mother looked at her; a gaze that was unquestionably paralyzing. It was the ultimate insinuation, and Peggy could not believe she made it within such proximity of her mother. At the height of the still silence, Little Pearl approached the doorway, but Peggy shut the door before she could come in, distrusting of her or the distraction she would cause. Grace looked at the door, then back at Peggy. She motioned up to open the door, but was instantly pulled back by the pain, "AH!" she yelped. Her painkillers were within a few feet of her on the night table, and she was about to crawl across the bed to them, before Peggy stepped over and grabbed them. She then walked back in front of the foot of the bed, now with both the sweat-laden remote and the vile of Vicodin in her hands, like inanimate hostages.

She continued to stare at her mother, attempting with all her ocular strength to leer her into some sort of admittance.

Finally, after managing to sit up with her back against the headboard, as though pinned against it, she spoke slowly and intensely, "And so where do you think I put 'em all? Your father, Joe, Clyde...You think they're all in the backyard, where you had your little garden?

They left. Either on their own, or because I tossed 'em out. Your father left because I wouldn't abort you or put you up for adoption. In one way or another, I chose you over every Goddamn man in my life until you left, little girl, and that's the truth. I didn't have a father either, y'know? Did I think *my* mother killed 'im? No. I knew he just left, 'cause at the end of the day, most men will. Yours did too, didn't he. In his own way," she said this with a subtle grin tinged with pride in her alleged prophecy. She then took a moment, as her grin faded before Peggy's eyes, "Didn't it ever cross your mind after all these years that maybe I was jus' tryin' to spare you? Spare what you're feeling now?"

She absorbed these words from her mother as she had never absorbed anything she had said before. She felt immobile; frozen by what she concluded was as honest and forthright an answer as she could ever imagine receiving from her mother, while also being deeply disturbed. If her mother died tomorrow, she felt she knew enough of what her roots, in fact, were. They were no better than she had always concluded, but there was clarity now.

She tossed the remote onto her bed, placed the pills nearby and left without a word.

Among the 24 pages she would compose into the wee hours of the next morning would be the following:

I think many of us ponder what we come from, what makes us who we are. For many years, I looked at my upbringing as something I needed to combat to alter my fate, like a lion that was continually attacking me, with myself being initially equipped with a mere butter knife and saucer which eventually developed into a sword and shield. I wanted nothing less than to be my mother. For years, I saw the weight of the world on her face when she came home from a career that many would find admirable, but was one that she detested. It still makes me wonder why she chose the healthcare profession. Did she think it would balance out her immense flaws as an individual? Was it just better than working for the electric company or any administrative job? I think, like most things in life, she just gravitated. Perhaps she once had aspirations kept to herself without sharing them with the world for fear of seeming weak or delusional. She's now coasted through a life perfectly content with what she now has, for as long as the cable works.

But when it doesn't, the holes show. I took advantage of those opportunities, as she is now a woman of 67, to ask questions that had been with me for years. Mainly, why did she have a nearly homicidal need to keep me close, despite never really saying or showing that she loved me. She would say that she was trying to spare me the inevitable; "Most men leave," she'd tell me, as her husband had left her, just as her mother's left her. She said this as a justification – believing that I too fell prey to this, which brought me back to her. This return to Grace, if you will.

Though I didn't say it then, I'll say now that there's a difference. Mike never left me. He wanted me enough to lie to the doctors when my mother tried to poison him. He wanted me enough for him to say that it was simply an accident. He wanted me enough so long as we both agreed that my mother would be gone from our lives forever. He never left me.

He was taken away by his own misdeeds but, having his druthers, he'll hope that when his sentence ends, I will be there, waiting for him.

But I won't be.

     This last line that she would write at about 3:30 the following morning would affirm her decision to divorce Mike. It was just one more layer she would soon be ready to shed. She'd allow him visitation, even though a convicted felon would not have many legs to stand on, but she was certain that the offspring they had created would be all that would keep them tied in any way for the rest of their lives. She wanted the kids to know their father, and know him as much after his sentence as before; he would from here on out serve as a cautionary tale. He probably would move out of state and try and obtain a medical license elsewhere. He would certainly remarry, perhaps even that woman in Ohio. He was smart enough to get back on his feet, even if he lived his remaining years by much more modest means than he had gotten used to.

     She also discovered, in the last passage that she would write that morning, a title: *The Return to Grace. A nice double-meaning*, she thought. Perhaps Bloom Publishing would say it sounded too much like a Christian-faith book, but it did have relevance and gave her book the focus she wanted, since it was now clearly about the view of the family tragedy from the perspective of her childhood home. From that vantage point, it was easier to see everything as opposed to simply being overwhelmed. Knowing her mother in the present helped to affirm what kept her away – what she was afraid of becoming.

     It was all so clear now.

❖ ❖ ❖

33

The next two days managed the same ritual, except now there were no words between them. It appeared silently agreed upon that Peggy would be there for Grace, as she had been the previous few days. Peggy had her phone alarm set so that she could transport Grace to the shower on schedule, then go downstairs to open the sliding door for Little Pearl; her bathroom nook was becoming wider as a result of the melting snow. She'd then feed Pearl and prepare Grace's breakfast, which she'd bring upstairs.

She sat with her in her room, but would simply stare out the window as if visiting a stranger in a hospital, sipping her coffee. She'd then take Grace's plates and empty coffee cup, wash them and then do some writing in her room. There was never any curiosity on Grace's part as to what Peggy was doing or what job gave her the advance she had vaguely mentioned. Having the cable back was the ultimate pacifier, of course. It made it all the more unnecessary for them to speak, and there was really nothing else that Peggy wanted to hear, nor anything she wanted to say. Occasionally it would strike her as surreal that she was in this position of taking care of her, and more so that Grace offered no resistance. It had simply become a habitual dance of tedium; two people resigned to the same daily choreography without much affection for each other.

In these two days, Peggy would amass over 125 pages, which she felt was about halfway to where she wanted to be as far as length. Being transported by the life she had experienced, which she was remaking into literature, was miraculously making the current life she was living tolerable and necessary. Again, she needed a distraction, and being snowed in obviously limited her, so it was just as well that her mother would end up incapacitated. And, again, it was material. Nothing was for naught.

As dusk fell, she looked out her window, having just cleaned Grace's dinner plates. The streets were now close to drivable, and many roofs were continuing to stream icy water courtesy of the week's first visit from the sun. She knew tomorrow morning, after feeding Grace, that she would get a taxi to take her to the shop to finally retrieve her car. She had also found a decent looking motel in Cherrybrook, about a 40-minute drive north, which from the website looked respectable enough, given the nightly rate. But while she had initially planned to leave literal skid marks at the door once she got the car back, her conscience had started to intercede, and she now resigned that she would likely stay with Grace until she appeared able enough to care for herself. Perhaps it was the peaceful silence between them that made this seem amenable. Perhaps it was the fact that it was inspiring more than inhibiting her writing. It also didn't make sense to rush to a motel, since the remains from the first installment of the advance would not last long, unless she managed to get some regular teaching work soon. Yet, despite these constraints, she couldn't help looking at apartments in Brooklyn. Her ultimate goal was to have a stable residence by the time the kids finished school, and she loved the thought of them being close to the city, if not in it. It was a good place to begin again.

She wrote some more and, before she knew it, saw that it was already 1:30 in the morning. She took a prideful back stretch, still hearing the volume of Grace's TV bleeding into her room. She went in and saw her asleep, snoring almost louder than the television, which was now showing a rerun of the local news with the same annoying weatherman now disappointed that the devastating nor'easter had made its way back out to sea.

"Idiot," Peggy murmured under her breath, as she turned the set off, which slightly jolted the sleeping Grace. She went to turn off the lamp on the night table, but first took a moment to look at her mother's face – long and leathery. It was only when she was unconscious that she seemed approachable, and she regretted that there weren't moments in her life when she felt approaching her mother would be reciprocated. Maybe they existed somewhere in the deepest realm of her memory. Perhaps one would come to her before submitting her book to the editors. Perhaps not.

She turned off the light and heard Grace turn in her blankets, now fully committing to a night's sleep. Peggy remained standing there a moment, looking outside at the snow illuminating the night sky, then back down at her mother. She wasn't quite sure why she was taking such time to depart. Her feet felt unusually heavy, like something was keeping her there. She didn't resist. She stayed looking at her mother, then back out at the night sky. Little Pearl soon came in, apparently still used to being downstairs this late, but was ready to join Grace. She stopped to look at Peggy, almost like a shift nurse coming in to take over, before Peggy left the room.

They were in that barren landscape again. Grace looked at her this time with a most unusual expression - one of almost peace. In turn, Peggy looked at her mother without words and could only watch as Grace coasted away. She couldn't see her legs, but it looked as if she was being supported by an invisible force. She didn't motion for her, only watched. Eventually, her mother started to squeal as she faded. It became frightening for Peggy to see her mother be pulled into the distance while only being able to emanate such bizarre sounds. At that point, Peggy stuck her hand out and appeared to try and will her mother to say words, an effort which became more desperate as the squealing built to a piercing crescendo...

She woke suddenly, her first sight were the eyes of Sylvia Plath on her ceiling, but the squealing continued outside her door. Peggy looked at her phone and saw that it was 7:55am, and was struck by the abnormality. It sounded like Little Pearl, but it was more than an hour before she would normally be let out. She rose, opened the door and followed Little Pearl's squeals to the bottom of the stairs, where Grace lay.

"What the...?" She quickly made her way down the steps, where Little Pearl continued in a distressed circle around Grace, "Mom? Can you...?" She realized it was fruitless to ask, before she urgently motioned to feel her mother's pulse. Of course, unlike in movies, she couldn't really tell if blood was still flowing in her. She thought she may have felt something, but then realized that it was her own shaking hand, "Mom, can you hear me?"

Grace remained still, as Little Pearl looked at Peggy, still in motion, occasionally rubbing her enormous head against Grace's side. Under her breath, Peggy mumbled, "Why didn't you...?" which faded in its importance now.

It took the paramedics about a half hour to arrive, given the icy roads. Once there, it didn't take them long to note that she had probably been dead for at least a couple of hours. This meant, in all likelihood, that Grace got up at around 6am, thinking she could manage the stairs she hadn't walked down by herself in several days, and lost her footing. The ambulance took her to the hospital, while Peggy remained at the house. As the sliding wheels of the ambulance faded down Morgan Street, Peggy stood at the entry way to the living room, while Little Pearl cried at the front door. Peggy took in the house as she had never before. The few things that were new were upstaged by all that had always been there; the walls, the sliding door, the ceiling lights, the carpeting... The way the light came in through the backyard.

She looked back at Little Pearl who remained at the door, and it was only when she did that Peggy began to feel overwhelming sadness. Through the eyes of this animal, she felt the loss of her mother more so than through her own. No doubt that Little Pearl had been the rose in her mother's life the last few years, as Grace had been for her. Even Peggy was grateful to Pearl for just being there to love Grace in the only way that was probably possible. Between the two, there was that unspoken understanding; Grace saved Pearl and would feed and care for her until she could no longer, as Pearl would, in turn, protect and love Grace until *she* could no longer.

Their connection appeared so strong that Peggy even wondered if Little Pearl dreamt of Grace, as she did. It seemed more appropriate that that would be the case. Little Pearl truly loved her, yet Peggy could not say the same.

In the end, she could only say that she was her daughter.

The next few days were particularly active. She would finally get her car back and even made arrangements with the auto shop to buy Grace's car, which helped offset the cost of the repairs. She would pick up her mother's ashes from the funeral home in Baldwin; the same place that cremated her grandmother. Little Pearl was her co-pilot throughout, with the distraction of being out of the house proving a healthy diversion for both of them. The most surreal moment for Peggy was when she had the box of Grace's ashes in the backseat, which prompted Little Pearl to nestle next to it just as if they were on the couch watching television.

Later that day she would contact a local real estate firm to put the house up for sale. The market wasn't ideal, but the agent felt a sale would come through once the weather warmed up a bit. She decided it was wise to stay until such time, as it also made sense to finish her book there. Plus the money from the sale of the house would allow her more flexibility in finding a new home. Having her druthers, the house would be sold by the late spring and she would be moved in advance of the kids finishing school.

When she arrived home that afternoon with Pearl and Grace's ashes, she saw a rather frumpy man in his early 60s waiting outside, attempting to peer through the dining room window. A tremoring gurgle began to surge within Little Pearl, "It's ok," Peggy assured, as she warily exited the car and closed the door.

"You wouldn't be here about the house, would you?" she asked with an ironic smile.

"The what?"

"I just posted a listing for it."

"A listing? No, I'm... Where is she?" he asked, genuinely confused.

"I'm sorry, who are you?"

"I'm Joe. Who are *you*?"

"Oh," she took this in. "Hi, Joe. I'm her daughter."

"Her daughter?"

"Yeah."

He too took a moment to digest this, "Wow, she told me she barely had one."

Aside from what little undesirable information she had on him, such candor did not endear this stranger to Peggy, as Pearl's growls within the car were getting more pronounced.

"Well, she had one. She had some pretty nice words to say about you as well, Joe," she replied, with a sudden lack of restraint.

His face read *touché'*, "Yeah, well... Is she around?"

"She's in the backseat. Wana' see her?"

"What?" He squinted incredulously at the back seat, but only saw the intense gaze from Little Pearl. "All's I see is that dog. That thing almost took my leg off, y'know."

"Really. Why would she try and do that?"

"Because she's psychotic, that's why. I kept tellin' her she needed to put her down. That thing's gonna kill somebody."

Peggy looked at Joe, and was surprised at the developing contempt she had towards him. He went from being a name on a pill vial in the cabinet to someone who she now felt was more than just a ne'er-do-well schlub. The fact that Pearl was reacting how she was towards him fueled her suspicion. Grace had said as much that he was broke, owed money, was likely cheating on her, and she was stupid enough to take such an imbecile in. But Pearl's reaction led her to believe he may have actually been physical with her, especially since he wasn't a stranger. He was a tall, pudgy, unimpressive man who was likely kicked out of wherever he was now staying.

Peggy responded to his recommendation for Pearl's demise, "Well, she's not your dog, is she."

Joe looked at her, sensing her desire for him to not be there, but nevertheless persistent regarding Grace's whereabouts, "Look, I jus' need to talk to her. Is she inside?"

"No, I told you she's in the car."

"What, is she ducking? I can't see her," as he remained several feet from the car, vividly aware of Pearl's penetrating gaze.

"No, she's there. I'll get her for you, okay?" Peggy walked to the car, went to the back window where Pearl was primed for an attack. She looked at her through the glass, "No!", Pearl barely lowered her growl, "NO, PEARL! SIT! SIT!" she pointed through the glass, her eyes now locked into Pearl's, before Pearl gradually laid down on the seat. Peggy opened the front door and reached in the back to get the box with Grace's ashes, then closed the door and pulled the urn out before presenting it to Joe.

He could barely manage, "What the...?"

"She died two days ago. Fell down the stairs. We had her cremated. Got anything you wana' say?"

He looked at her, then at the urn, "Shit, I..."

"Here she is. This is as quiet as she'll ever be. Why don't you seize the day, buddy?"

Joe looked at the urn, then back at Peggy, "You're kidding. This isn't her."

She then abruptly displayed the box which donned a label with Grace's name on it. He absorbed this, stunned, "Jesus Christ..."

"Well, He probably doesn't want much to do with her, to be honest. Can I do anything else for you, Joe?"

Joe was taken aback by Peggy's tone, as he looked at the urn, then at her, "Well, I just...wanted to see her."

"Why?"

"Why? She was... We're friends. We've known each other a long time."

"She kicked you out, didn't she?"

He weakly grinned, half-acting as if he was reluctant to speak ill of the newly dead, "I'm sure you knew your mother enough to know how she was."

"Were you coming back for your meds or because you needed a place to stay?"

"I...what kind of a thing is – ?"

"No?"

"I have a place, okay? I was jus' comin' by to see her."

"Really? Just coming by? You don't need anything from her?"

"Alright, that's enough. Your mother'n I knew each other for over 10 years."

"Yeah, and in all that time, did you ever help her out or was she only there for you?"

"I helped her, okay?"

"How did you help her, Joe? I know the kind of men she gravitated to. I knew it when I was a kid. My own father was like you. How are *you* different?"

"Look, how many friends you think your mother had? How many friends do you think she managed to have for over 10 years? Where the hell were *you*?"

She took a moment, almost not wanting to dignify his words with a response, but nevertheless - "As far away from her as I could get. As far away from her and the drunk assholes she used to bring home as I could get, okay? This woman was a fucking bitch and a mother from hell, but any man who would need to rely on her and use her so they could keep on living like they're 17 is even worse than that, in my opinion."

"You don't know what the hell you're talking about," he tepidly defended...

"Get off of my property."

"This isn't yours."

"It *is* mine, NOW GET THE HELL OFF!"

Her hostility towards Joe was now in direct sync with Pearl's resurged rage, as she again eyed Joe through the back-door window, the exhales from her nostrils managing to fog the glass...

Joe looked at the dog, then back at Peggy. In this moment, their faces seemed hardly distinguishable, "You know, I see where you get it. Like mother like daughter. You're both fuckin' nuts."

He walked to his rusted car, a Nova that probably had 30,000 miles on it when Peggy was born, took a last look at them both, and sputtered off. How interesting, she wondered, that just a few days ago she nearly accused Grace of possibly killing him, and yet she felt so close to doing it herself. *Like mother like daughter?*

She stood on the front lawn and watched him drive off. As his car turned out of sight, she realized just why she reacted as she did. Joe would come to represent them all; the men in her mother's life who barely acknowledged her. But, more than any, Joe would serve as the stand-in for her father who left, whom she couldn't recall. In admonishing this stranger, it was the closest thing she would have to telling her father what she felt about him.

Weeks went by, with Peggy taking care of Little Pearl and writing almost exclusively. Her only other deviation was calling the kids along with an occasional exchange with the realtor. The kids sounded well-enough, but there was satisfaction in being able to tell them that they would be coming back up in June and have a new home. She was still eyeing Brooklyn, just over the bridge from the city, but now was thinking about living in the city itself. It'd be more expensive, but she craved being as close as she could to culture, and wanted that for the kids. The East Village was looking like a possibility, and she knew it was still an area largely unscathed by tourism; near off-Broadway theatres, museums, galleries, used book shops and nice little cafes and restaurants, a stone's throw from midtown, and a good proximity to the other boroughs. She could get to LaGuardia Airport in about an hour, as well. This was certainly an appealing option for them.

Pearl would spend most of her time close to Peggy, lying on her bed as she typed. In between writing bursts, Peggy would come over and sit with her and they would gaze out the window. Occasionally Pearl would emanate a frustrated gurgle at a passing flock of geese or sparrows building a nest on the tree branches that hung nearby, but by and large she seemed to want peace and quiet as much as Peggy did.

By evening is when she started to feel most inspired; something about the darkness that unveiled things she was unable to reveal in the light of day. She had thus far structured her book as going back and forth in time; between the beginnings of her relationship with Mike, to the events leading up to his arrest, back to her childhood and then the near present. She still wasn't sure exactly how present she wanted her book to be. Did she want to depict the exact place in her life she would be at when she typed "The End"? Or could it end in the past – even the distant past?

Later that evening, with Pearl's head asleep on her foot, she would write the final passage:

It has only been a month since my mother died. I'll remember it for the rest of my life, the image of her strewn out and lifeless. And it baffles me that it happened as it did. She had been a nurse for others most of her life, loathing more than loving the opportunity to provide such care, without question. And so there I was, unknowingly in her last days, in her role of caregiver, while she played the patient. Words would not have permitted it to happen, only silence. And, in fact, we said not a word to each other for those last days.

I think most parents have kids so that they'll have someone to take care of them when they become debilitated. That seems to be more of the goal than their kids actually becoming successful. And yet, my mother seemed content to have neither – desiring not my success nor my return to care for her.

It was all she could probably do to lower that harsh and abrasive wall to take my arm. In the end, it was likely her desperate need to not want to take it that led to her fall. She could've called my name. She had a voice that could break glass and stab you with the shards, but...she didn't want help, I suppose. Perhaps she tried to wake me and I was too busy dreaming about her death to hear her, but I doubt it. As I write this now, I'm certain that she would sooner die at her own hands than the hands of someone else, perhaps even God's.

I guess we are alike, and in ways that I would never want to admit. I too have anger in me – rage even. I've had resentment at Mike, my in-laws, former friends, at times even my own children... I've hated my mother, and won't suddenly love her in death.

But I must admit that something got me through all this. Something made me resist madness. Something made me unwilling to die by another's hands.

Something made me endure whatever the hell all of this has been... and not be beaten.

It would be the closest thing to a complement she could give her mother.

◆ ◆ ◆

By June, Peggy had sold her mother's home and moved to a 3-bedroom apartment in the East Village. It was a ground floor apartment, and they even had a private courtyard. The kids had been back for a couple of weeks and were just getting used to another new environment, but at least they were there with a sense that this was where they would be until they both finished high school. It was home. They also were getting used to Little Pearl, and her to them, with Luna and Nicky now at a point where they could pet her without hesitation.

Initially, Peggy worried that Pearl preferred the life she lived her best years in, with a solitary person taking care of her. But Pearl's respect and love for Peggy seemed to broaden her outlook. At least to Peggy, it was as if Pearl had adopted her own openness for change, to begin anew. Their connection would be closer than any animal she would own and love in her life. It was as if their pasts were merged through osmosis and tethered them.

Later that month they would drive out to the Jersey shore where Peggy rented them a summer home for a couple of weeks. It would be the first pleasurable excursion they would have as a family in about a year. Of course, Mike would not be there. He would remain upstate for another year and a half, and, until then, Peggy would bring the kids up to visit him – but it would only be for them. The divorce papers were filed, which was almost as profound for her as Bloom's approval of her final manuscript, which would be called, *The Return to Grace*. They would begin marketing it in the fall, with a book tour lined up.

"When can I read it?" Luna pleaded, as she and Peggy sat on the beach, watching Nicky toss a frisbee to Little Pearl.

"I'll let you read it in a couple of years, honey."

"Why so long?"

"Because you're only 11 and I want you to at least be Nicky's age before you read it."

"Is Nicky allowed to read it?"

She grinned, "He hasn't asked. And I actually think he can wait a couple of years too."

"Why?"

"Because there's a lot of stuff in there that's very personal."

"Am I in it?"

She smiled, "Yes, you're in it."

"I wana' read it."

"You will, honey. Just not right now. This is mommy's 40th birthday, you know. We should be celebrating."

"We *are* celebrating."

She could not help but laugh at Luna's unaltered precociousness. She knew she would only get smarter with age and had little trepidation for what she could accomplish. She wasn't as assured with Nicky, but he was still young enough to learn. Being away had humbled him. To her surprise, he didn't come back from Vic and Elaine's with a chip on his shoulder, but appeared to know that the 5 months in Florida was merely a way station. He wanted a home again, his own room. He wanted to make new friends and keep them. And she wanted that for him.

Luna eventually inserted herself in Nicky and Pearl's frisbee toss, and Peggy watched on. The sun was strong, but a cool breeze blew in. Eventually, her gaze turned to the unoccupied water and the stars atop it which glistened from the sun.

The brief gust made her tighten her new sun hat, and then she thought of the photo from Carole's gallery, when they were staying with her and Larry. The image came to her as she was living it now; the woman in the sun hat, gazing out at the ocean. She remembered her wish then - to be a clean slate untainted by life,...*if only for a moment.*

◆ ◆ ◆

Daniel Damiano is an Award-winning Playwright, Screenwriter, Poet and Novelist based in Brooklyn, NY. His plays have been performed throughout many areas of the U.S. as well as London, England and Sydney and Melbourne, Australia. His acclaimed play *Day of the Dog* was recently published by Broadway Play Publishing. Other noted theatrical works include *The Wild Boar* (2019 Woodward/Newman Drama Award, 2019 Janet & Bruce Bunch Award), *Harmony Park* ("4 Stars" - Detroit Free Press) and his acclaimed solo play, *American Tranquility* ("5 Stars" - DC Theatre Scene). He was also a Finalist for the 2012 Arts & Letters Prize for Drama and the 2013 Pushcart Prize for Poetry. His poetry book, *104 Days of the Pandemic*, will be released later in 2021. *The Woman in the Sun Hat* is his debut novel.

Made in the USA
Middletown, DE
18 March 2021